TELL ME WHEN I'M DEAD

PRAISE FOR TELL ME WHEN I'M DEAD

"The zombie genre has exploded in recent years, and unfortunately, so many similar stories have begun to run together, making it less of a desirable avenue for both writers and readers. However, there is still hope for this genre niche in the form of *Tell Me When I'm Dead* by Steven Ramirez. The first book in a trilogy, this slow-burning thriller does far more than simply promote an everyman into a zombie-killing hero, introducing readers to a uniquely compelling protagonist."

— SELF-PUBLISHING REVIEW

"As Dave's life slowly starts to unravel, and the body count continues to grow higher through the help of an unknown virus, he is left with a gruesome choice: either wallow in his sorrows or stay alive. In this thrilling novel, Ramirez details an antihero's struggles for family and love, and to find beauty in a world ruled by the dead."

— READERS' FAVORITE

"The sense of pace in *Tell Me When I'm Dead* is impressive, Ramirez building the suspense and stakes with skill, and ensuring that you care about the characters at the heart of events. As a lead character, Dave is layered, with a compelling backstory and an admirably drawn humanity. He's not your run-of-the-mill horror hero, and his decisions are believable yet at times unexpected, keeping the reader on their toes and ensuring that this isn't a predictable tale in the slightest. Chilling, pulse racing, and hugely compelling, Ramirez has brought something new to a popular genre."

— THE BOOKBAG

BOOKS BY STEVEN RAMIREZ

HELLBORN SERIES

Tell Me When I'm Dead

Dead Is All You Get

Even The Dead Will Bleed

HARD TO KILL SERIES

Brandon's Last Words

Faithless

SARAH GREENE MYSTERIES

The Girl in the Mirror

House of the Shrieking Woman

The Blood She Wore

OTHER BOOKS

Chainsaw Honeymoon

Come As You Are: A Short Novel and Nine Stories

Come As You Are: A Novella

Glass Highway
Los Angeles, CA
stevenramirez.com

Publisher's Note: This is a work of fiction. Names, characters, places, and incidents are a product of the author's imagination. Any opinions expressed belong to the characters and should not be confused with those of the author. Locales and public names are sometimes used for atmospheric purposes. Any resemblance to actual people, living or dead, or businesses, companies, events, institutions, or locales is coincidental.

Tell Me When I'm Dead / Hellborn Series Book 1 / Steven Ramirez. 3rd ed.

Paperback: 978-1-949108-14-9
EPUB: 978-1-949108-15-6
Kindle: 978-1-949108-16-3
Library of Congress Control Number: 2023900367

Edited by Shannon A. Thompson
Cover design by Damonza

For Richard Matheson. You are legend.

TELL ME WHEN I'M DEAD

HELLBORN SERIES BOOK 1

STEVEN RAMIREZ

glass highway

AUTHOR'S NOTE

I first published *Tell Me When I'm Dead* in 2013. While writing it, I thought the tale of an ordinary man caught up in a science-gone-wrong nightmare would be a standalone work. Something entertaining along the lines of George A. Romero's *Night of the Living Dead* (1968). I love that movie—the simplicity of the plot, the documentary, matter-of-fact telling. And the humor.

Richard Matheson's masterful 1954 novel, *I Am Legend*, was another significant influence. Unlike Romero's ghouls, these hostiles were vampires. Later, the book would become the basis for three movies—*The Last Man on Earth* (1964), *The Omega Man* (1971), and *I Am Legend* (2007). I wouldn't be surprised if some studio has another one in development.

In my story, Dave Pulaski is a twenty-something recovering alcoholic. But, unlike the protagonists in *Night of the Living Dead* and *I Am Legend*, he's a bona fide antihero. He has a violent temper, and though he loves his wife, Holly, he lacks as a husband. In other words, he's real. When a plague decimates the Northern California town of Tres Marias, his instinct is to run.

After finishing, I realized Dave's journey was far from over. There were many unanswered questions about the virus's origin. I had introduced Black Dragon Security, the Red Militia, and a mysterious bioscience lab located deep in the forest—too much material to ignore. So, I wrote two sequels.

And now, to celebrate ten years of conspiracy and mayhem, I've rewritten all three novels. They still take place in 2013, but I've clarified plot points, added dialogue, and eliminated prose I felt didn't move the story forward. As a writer, you constantly evolve. What I create now I was not capable of ten years ago. *Tell Me When I'm Dead* and the subsequent books represent my best writing so far. I hope you enjoy the result.

Glendora, California
April 1, 2023

"Oh, Robert," she said then, "it's so unfair. So unfair. Why are we still alive? Why aren't we all dead? It would be better if we were all dead."

— RICHARD MATHESON, *I AM LEGEND*

TELL ME WHEN I'M DEAD

PART ONE

IN THE SHIT

CHAPTER
ONE

NOT ALL DRAGGERS want to eat your flesh. Some just want to play. That's what I was thinking as I sat frozen in the corner of a cold storage area. My body halfway to dead, and my breath stuttering like a concertina with a leak. You remember those, right? Wheezy little wanna-be accordions that make music for drunks? Never mind.

The pounding on the steel door was deafening. And the wailing of the flesh-eaters tore at my brain like a jagged shard of glass. It was only a matter of time before they got in. If I was lucky, I might take out one or two, though I had no weapon. But in the end, they'd finish me.

I couldn't get my mind clear. At one point, I thought I heard semiautomatic gunfire and the sound of people shouting. Had a horde gotten in? And wasn't anyone defending the exits? Maybe my captors were passed out drunk.

It would've been better for me had I done the same—drinking myself stupid before they tore me to pieces with animal claws and razor teeth. The filmy gray eyes unseeing as they grinned with delight. Numb from the cold, I probably wouldn't even feel it.

In my delirium, I prayed that Holly and Griffin had made it to the Arkon building under Warnick's protection. No way for me to check—my phone was busted. I hadn't slept in days, and I was hurt. Bad. Surrounded by enormous aluminum tanks of ice-cold beer waiting to be tapped. Nice touch, God. Back atcha.

Through the constant pounding, I wondered if my friend Jim was outside with the others. Trying to force his way in so he could eviscerate me. It wasn't my fault he turned. Like they say on the news, there were other forces at work. Sciencey things that were better left to Mary Shelley or H. P. Lovecraft.

I once saw a horde tear a guy to pieces. Big as he was, he was no match for them. In seconds, they had him on the ground as they ripped open his belly. Exposed the soft, pulsating organs. They cored the dude like an apple—bottom to top. His head was the last to die. I remember his eyes, frozen in terror at seeing his own hollowed-out remains as he shuddered into stillness.

But it was the screaming. I'd never heard a man cry out like that before. Was I capable of making that sound? I stared at the door, wondering if it would hold. There was no way for me to barricade it from the inside. Besides, I was too weak. I wished I had a gun.

It was the nailheads who had left me in here. They planned to kill me, according to the one they called Ulie. It didn't matter that I'd agreed to join their insane movement. Maybe the draggers would find me instead. *You 'member that guy Dave Pulaski? Whatever happened to 'im? Oh yeah, he's dead.*

The horde hadn't made it past the door yet. Craving one last beer, I thought about Black Dragon and the Red Militia. Both had proven to be fake remedies in these delirious times.

The security guards were overwhelmed. And the militia? They started out as a movement to save people. But soon, their mission devolved into chaos and violence. At the behest of their insane leader, they fought Black Dragon. They went after civilians and, eventually, themselves. When that wasn't enough, they drank.

Ormand Ferry—a man with a dream. A new order that disintegrated into a long, debauched night of madness here in this godforsaken beer factory. Even he couldn't stop it. I didn't know which was worse—the draggers or Ferry. Either way, I would be dead and forgotten.

It was so cold in here as I sat thinking about these past weeks. About Holly, Jim, and Missy. Everything went wrong after that night—that damned, lost night. And what about me? I was a good person—I am. Used to be. I didn't even know anymore. But it was after that star-crossed night when it all went sideways. And hell came looking for the good people of Tres Marias.

That was when our lives changed forever.

CHAPTER
TWO

I REMEMBER JULY 5TH, when Jim got shitfaced and showed up at our house. It was after ten when I answered the door, and I was tired. He must have fallen because his lip was bleeding, and he had a chipped tooth.

"Got any beer?" he said.

"You know I don't."

"Communist."

Tres Marias was one of those sleepy Northern California towns you pass on your way to something better. There was nothing to do except get drunk. And since high school, that's pretty much what Jim and I did. Before all that, I played hockey. And when I wasn't on the ice, I devoured books like a glutton.

Somewhere along the line, I decided beer was better. There was no reason for it other than it tasted good and got me high. What followed was no college and no high-paying job far away from the stinkhole I called home. Instead of a bright future, I looked forward to low wages and getting lit. Then, I met Holly.

I don't know why she spent two minutes on me. As we

lay in bed for the first time, she said *I can't wait for you to become the man I know is inside you.* With all that pressure, any other dude would have walked—run, probably. I chose to stay.

At Holly's urging, I attended AA meetings and took online college classes. Jim kept going the way he was. Though he was my friend, it got harder and harder to see him because I saw myself—my old self—when I was with him. And I didn't like it.

Holly padded downstairs and stood behind me with her arms folded. I knew she was mad. After I stopped drinking, she told me how much she disapproved of Jim. She was afraid he'd get me started again. But I knew better—I had changed my ways for good.

"What do you want, Jim?" she said. It was the same tone she used when I forgot to take out the trash.

Holly was a knockout of a girl with a high school educa-tion. Smarter than most people I knew. Her all-time favorite movie was *The Notebook.* Though she was a head shorter than me, she could be scary. Her blonde hair hanging over her shoulders, and those clear green eyes that could see into your soul.

Jim opened his mouth to speak and vomited something black on the star jasmine my wife had planted the week before.

"Oh, for— Get him out of here. Puh-leeez."

"I'll drive him home," I said.

Jim lived at the edge of town near the national forest, in the house his father had built. Like me, both his parents were dead. He used to have a dog named Perro, but the animal went missing a few weeks back. He'd followed Jim on one of his drunken nighttime hikes along the 299 when an eighteen-wheeler almost flattened them.

I always thought that big rig was meant for Jim and the dog had sacrificed himself. When my friend recovered, Perro was missing. Once I read a story about another dog that saved his owner's life in a house fire and later died from smoke inhalation. Those kinds of stories brought out the romantic in me.

We glided along the dark highway with no other cars in sight.

"What happened?" I said.

"What do you mean?"

"Why did you go on a bender?"

"Thinking about the old days, I guess."

Jim Stanley and I used to be best friends, as close as any two brothers. We went to high school together. Got summer jobs together. Celebrated twenty-one by heading up to the Point and drinking enough beer and vodka to bring down a moose. We passed out up there, too. It was December, and when we awoke, it was in the twenties. I ended up in the hospital suffering from hypothermia.

We liked pretending we were badasses, though we never did any real harm. After the birthday incident, my mom—sick as she was—did her best to keep me in line. And whenever Jim came over to hang out and eat—which was all the time—she went to work on him, too. But when it came to advice, my friend had a tin ear.

"Dude, I keep telling you," I said. "Those days are gone." Smelling the beer and puke on his breath, I was glad we were no longer hanging out. I didn't know how I had made it to twenty-four. Holly had everything to do with it, I suppose.

I met her working at Staples, where I managed the copy center. Two years younger than me, she was the new cashier and seemed to have her eye on me from day one. I don't think a week had gone by when she invited me to dinner at her mom's in Mt. Shasta. Afterwards, we returned to her little apartment.

She was all over me in bed. Before anything happened, though, she laid it on the line. I would have to stop drinking—that was the deal. No sobriety, no Holly. I saw the determination in her eyes. It was like she was on a mission from God. That made me hotter for her, and I signed on.

After we got married, Jim came around less and less. I would see him downtown every so often on my lunch break. For the most part, though, he was out of my life. But that all changed the night he showed up at our door.

"Why don't we hang out anymore?" he said like a hurt child.

"Don't do this."

"What?"

"Lay the guilts on me. I'm married now. I have responsibilities."

"What you've got is a steady piece of—"

"She's my wife, asshole." I looked over to see if he was crying and found him trying to pull his lower lip over his nose.

"So? What about a boys' night out once in a while?"

"Next, you'll be wanting a sleepover."

"Shit, let's do it."

"Why don't you grow up?" I said.

The resulting silence carried us for another mile or so. Jim started singing the chorus from Adele's "Someone Like You." I don't know what made me angrier—him knowing the song always brought tears to Holly's eyes or what he might be insinuating about us. I smacked him on the ear. When I turned back, there was an animal in the road—Jim's dog. I swerved to avoid him.

After that, I don't know what happened, but I couldn't get on top of the situation. Next, we were going over the embankment, heading for the trees. Neither of us made a sound. And it was at this moment I regretted never having fixed the passenger airbag. Vaguely, I heard Jim's voice.

"I need to tell you something," he said.

Suddenly, there was a hundred-year-old pine in front of us. We hit it hard. My airbag stopped me from getting killed. Unfortunately, it didn't go so well for Jim—he wasn't wearing his seat belt. I can still hear the sound his head made going through the windshield.

Soon, my eyes closed against my will.

CHAPTER
THREE

WHEN I WOKE UP, I was alone. Beads of safety glass lay everywhere. I stared at a large hole in the windshield, dripping with fresh blood. Bits of torn flesh hung from the jagged edges. The passenger door was open. A little ways off, raccoons waited in the glare of the headlights, their eyes shiny with anticipation. They'd be all over that windshield as soon as I got out.

It was hard to move—I was jammed in pretty good against the steering wheel. Feeling intense pain from the neck down, I inched sideways. Forcing the driver's-side door open, I fell on dry pine needles. The only sounds were a hooting owl and the wind whistling through the trees.

"Jim!" I said. "Come on, man, this isn't funny."

It took me a half-hour to get up the embankment. Each time, I would get a good start. But with all the pain in my neck, back, and legs, I kept slipping on those damn pine needles and ending up at the bottom. Cursing, I kept at it, but I was forced to rest after each try.

At last, I reached the top and lay on my side till I could catch my breath. I didn't see Jim anywhere. He might be lying out there somewhere in the darkness, bleeding to death. I needed to get to him before a wild animal did.

"Jim, where are you?"

I was in the middle of nowhere, surrounded by trees. Choking back a stab of pain, I dug into my jeans pocket for my phone. I'd forgotten it at home, and it was a long walk to town. I took one last look at my car as the raccoons pawed at the windshield. Stupidly, I hoped they wouldn't hurt themselves on the bloody glass.

After only a few yards, I spotted Perro again. The canine stared at me in the yellow moonlight. He had always been a friendly dog. But now, he seemed threatening. His head was low, and his body expanded and contracted like a bellows.

Though it was dark, the animal's eyes glowed red. Snapping and snarling, he came after me. I tried running, but I couldn't move very fast. And because of the intense pain, it was impossible to turn my head to see if he was gaining on me.

In seconds, blue-white headlights bore down on me from behind. A horn blasted, followed by a meaty thud and a grisly yelp. Out of breath, I stopped and turned around. A white van with a logo I didn't recognize was in the middle of the road with the engine idling.

The blinding headlight beams illuminated the dog's body, which had been thrown several feet. A car door opened, and the dark shape of a man climbed out. He approached the softly panting animal and knelt.

"Careful," I said. "I think he's rabid."

"You okay?"

I limped towards him. "I could use a ride. Did you see anyone else on the road?"

"Like who?"

"My friend. We were in a car accident, and I need to find him."

"I didn't see anybody."

I was next to the stranger now. The dog howled, and we backed off. The man ran to the rear of the van. But when he returned carrying a catchpole, Perro had limped off down the embankment and into the woods.

"Shit," he said.

"Are you animal control?"

The stranger looked at me like I was an idiot. "I'll give you a lift."

"Thanks." I read the side of the van as I climbed in. ROBBIN-SEAR INDUSTRIES, OLD ORCHARD ROAD, TRES MARIAS, CA. The name and address meant nothing to me.

The good Samaritan was in his forties and dressed like an academic—sport coat and jeans. He was pale, with curly black hair and black frame glasses. A thin scar drifted from his upper lip to his nostril. I thought maybe he had been born with a cleft palate. He volunteered his name—Bob Creasy.

We didn't talk. Distracted, he continually checked the rearview mirror. I must have looked scary because even though he tried to be helpful, he insisted on driving me to the police station instead of my house.

"Were you bit?" he said.

"I told you I was in a car accident."

"And you're positive you didn't get bit?"

A noise in the back of the van startled me. It sounded like growling.

"What was that?"

"Lots of injured animals on the road tonight."

We pulled up in front of the police station. Keeping up the good Samaritan act, he came around and helped me out of the van.

"Take care, buddy," he said.

Though Holly never said anything, I knew she was mad. We stopped at the emergency room, even though I had insisted I was fine. The X-rays came back showing there was spinal damage at C3 and C4. They made me wear a cervical collar. Told me I was lucky I wasn't paralyzed.

While we waited, a man with a goiter walked in, asking for a tetanus shot. Some kid in the park bit him. The patient insisted that something was wrong with the boy. *It was his eyes—like he wasn't right.*

On the way home, Holly and I talked about what had happened.

"Were you drinking?" she said.

That was her go-to question whenever I screwed up. I was in too much pain to argue.

"How long is it going to take before you trust me?"

"Let's see. You stopped going to your AA meetings three months ago."

"It was two months. And anyway, I don't need those people telling me once an alcoholic, always an alcoholic. I'm fine on my own."

"Why did you lose control of the car?"

"Jeez. I swerved to avoid a dog, okay? Smell my breath."

"Never mind. I was worried, that's all."

Holly acted all hard on the outside, but inside she was a marshmallow. I knew I was supposed to be the man, but I was pissed off and let her stew in it. I closed my eyes and let myself drift.

The ER doctor had prescribed Vicodin for the pain, but I asked for Motrin instead. When we got home, I was so sore I couldn't make it up the stairs. My wife had gotten past her anger and made me a bed on the sofa in the TV room.

"I need to find Jim," I said.

"The cops are out looking for him. And besides, you need to rest."

I let her help me lie down. Soon, I was out.

In my dream, I woke up in daylight. Jim was standing there with a dark red gash ringing his neck like a lei. I tried screaming, but when I opened my mouth, black blood gushed out—gallons of it running down the sofa. The dark pool formed a lake on the oval area rug, seeping into the grooves in the hardwood floor. Shiny parasitic creatures that looked like kidney worms writhed and convulsed in the blood. Had I coughed them up, too?

Someone touched me, and I opened my eyes. It was dark. Holly stood next to me in the Giants jersey I had bought her the previous summer. She looked so good—I wasn't mad anymore. I took her hand.

"You were moaning so loud," she said. "I could hear you upstairs."

"Bad dream. What do you think happened to Jim?"

"I don't know. But he can't be too messed up if he walked away from the accident. He's prob'ly at his house, sleeping it off."

"Maybe you're right," I said. "He was pretty damn drunk."

CHAPTER
FOUR

I WAS in too much pain to go to work and decided to take a sick day. Though I felt terrible about not looking for my friend, I was a mess and wouldn't be of much use. Having filed a missing person report, I figured the cops would locate Jim eventually.

The police had impounded what was left of my car as evidence. They insisted it was the standard procedure when someone went missing. Later, a Detective Van Gundy called to say he had taken a ride out to Jim's house but didn't find anyone.

I felt stupid wearing the cervical collar when I returned to work, but Holly had insisted. And anyway, I owed her big for looking after me. Off and on throughout the day, I got headaches from the pressure on my jaw. There was an upside, though. My wife tied my shoes for me, which, even in my compromised state, got me aroused.

At lunch, I took a walk outside, thinking I might see Jim. Everything appeared normal. Cars came and went. Mothers pushed children in strollers. And some girl dressed as the Statue of Liberty hawked burners on the sidewalk. A couple stewbums hung out under an elm tree, their short dogs tucked inside wrinkled brown paper bags. Some things never change.

Tres Marias had always been a strange little backwater town. But over the next few days, the place I called home got even weirder. The local news reported that people had begun behaving erratically. Later, I saw one for myself at the pizza joint next to Staples.

A delivery guy left the shop and, with short, halting steps, made his way to the parking lot. I tried greeting him as he passed me. His eyes were glazed over like he was on drugs—he didn't know what planet he was on.

The morning sports guy dubbed the condition "the jimmies." Pretty soon, everybody was using the term. *Two for one night. Bring a friend—even if he's got the jimmies.* Everyone thought it was funny till people began defecating in the street.

Later, I saw that guy from the emergency room—the one with the goiter. Like the pizza dude, his gait was off, and he seemed unaware of his surroundings. Kids on skateboards followed him, imitating his walk. They laughed cruelly and called him a tard. If that had been me, I would've kicked their middle-school asses into next week. Instead, Goiter Man ignored them as he lurched down the sidewalk.

A crowd had assembled in front of City Hall, which in true Tres Marias fashion, had originally been a saloon. The town had converted it into an office building in the early nineteen hundreds. Now, our seat of government stood proudly next to Dunkin' Donuts.

A man dressed in a crisp brown suit with a red pocket square stood on the steps with a bullhorn. Ormand Ferry, self-appointed leader of a nonprofit organization known as the Red Militia. In his spare time, he sold shoes. His beefy lieutenants, also wearing suits, formed a defensive line in front of him.

One of them I recognized—Travis Golightly, owner of the Beehive. That was the bar Jim and I used to hang out at in the old days. Travis was a well-known bully and racist who did not look good in a tie. We never paid any attention to his ravings, though. And anyway, the beer was cheap.

While Red Militia members collected donations and handed out pamphlets, Ferry spoke passionately of *the blood of our countrymen* and *the Apocalypse*. Some in the crowd laughed, but I found his manner disturbing.

He was slender and tan, with blond hair cut short like a Marine. He wore round glasses that glinted whenever he moved his head. And he wasn't stupid. He made every effort to sound reasonable. Mostly, he talked about the charitable work his organization was doing. Feeding families in need and giving the homeless a place to sleep.

I recalled reading something about Satan once. When he appeared, it wouldn't be as a demon but as an ordinary-looking fellow with a convincing message of peace. As I moved past the crowd, a volunteer handed me a pamphlet. On the cover, a hand-drawn black wolf with bright red eyes slavered over a much smaller cowering family. At the top, there was a single word in large red print—PREPARE.

After two weeks, the cervical collar came off. A new set of X-rays showed that my vertebrae were fine. I hadn't seen Jim, and the cops no longer seemed interested in finding him. Everyone thought he had wandered into the forest and died. A search party turned up nothing.

When I was well enough, I decided to look for myself. I never did find him. Meanwhile, people's pets went missing.

Then a hunter found a deer that had been gored. It was barely breathing when the outdoorsman put it down.

The latest news was all anybody wanted to talk about at Staples. People coming down with the jimmies and ritualistic animal mutilations.

"It's nothing," Fred Lumpkin said. "Prob'ly rabid bats or something."

Fred was our store manager. Chubby and likable, he had a weakness for Baby Ruths and Diet Dr Pepper. He never got angry and was always good for an advance if someone found themselves a little short. Our boss was the kind of person who always saw the bright side, even when the evidence pointed to End of Days. I imagined him losing his shit one day and chopping everyone up with the fireman's axe we kept in the back. Or, maybe he was genuinely kind.

One night, in the middle of all this strangeness, Holly announced that she was going off the pill. My mind was a blank, and I became anxious. But once she explained—reasonably—how badly she wanted to start a family, I began to warm to the idea. Hell, we were young. And wasn't this how it was supposed to be for married couples?

"Are you sure?" I said.

She punched me in the arm. "Well, come on. I wanna hear what you think."

"I don't know. I'm scared, I guess?"

"That's okay. So am I."

I took her hand. "I never thought about me as a dad. Are you sure?"

She was laughing now. "You literally asked me that already."

For the first time in our relationship, Holly trusted me. She believed that I had gotten control of my addiction and would make a suitable father. Maybe I was the man she'd hoped for—or at least within spitting distance.

"Let's do this," I said and kissed her.

Looking back, that was the happiest time of my life. I was sober, and I had a beautiful wife who loved me. Though my Camry had been totaled in the wreck, I was now the proud owner of a new Dodge truck. And I had a steady paycheck, which I figured would carry us if Holly decided to stop working. I was on top of the world.

But you know happiness is always temporary, right?

CHAPTER
FIVE

THE TEXT MESSAGE glowed as I awoke to the sound of a garbage truck outside. Let me just say I don't like trouble. Better to avoid it—always. But sometimes trouble shows up and takes a shit on your welcome mat.

> When can i see u?

Panic plowed into me like the van that hit Jim's dog. Holly might've seen the message. Vaguely, I recalled hearing my phone chirp. Looking over, I realized I was alone.

After dressing in a hurry, I jammed the phone into my jeans and headed for the stairs. My wife was sitting on the floor in the spare bedroom. She had on her work clothes. Blue light streamed in, illuminating her hair as she gazed out the window. She looked like a blonde angel.

"What're you doing?" I said.

"Daydreaming. Once I'm pregnant, we're going shopping for baby furniture. I already know what I want."

I kissed her head. "I need to shower."

"It's your day off. What's the hurry?"

"I want to get an early start. That leaky toilet isn't going to fix itself. And there's the dodgy lock on the sliding glass door, and—"

"Aren't you excited?"

Wearing a stupid grin, I tried to think. What was there to be excited about?

"You know, about a baby?"

"Oh yeah," I said. "I can't wait."

I kept my phone with me in the bathroom. After a quick shower, I grabbed coffee and a bowl of cereal. Holly turned on the morning news. The top story was about a local woman who had gone missing. She was last seen days ago, going for a run.

The way Holly was acting, I thought maybe she suspected something. Then again, if she had seen the text, I'd be dead.

"We know her, right?" I said.

"She's our neighbor."

"Wow, I hope they find her." I cleared the table.

"Dave, is anything wrong?"

The way she was looking at me made me nervous. "I'm making a mental list of everything I want to get done today."

"Don't overdo it. You're still recovering."

"Okay, Mom."

I rinsed off the dishes and loaded them in the dishwasher. She pulled out her phone and snapped a pic. What now? Was she collecting evidence for the divorce?

"There," she said, showing me the photo. "The perfect husband."

She slung her purse over her shoulder and headed for the door. Before she was gone, I opened the refrigerator and grabbed her lunch. When I handed it to her, she pulled me in and kissed me.

"I really wanna play hooky today," she said. "Am I a bad person?"

"New baby furniture, remember? Mucho dinero." I kissed her. "Have fun at work."

"Right. I hear we're getting in a pallet of red Swingline staplers."

"Say hi to Fred."

I waited for her to drive off before checking my phone. So far, no other texts. I reread the words. *When can I see you?* I was about to delete the message when another one appeared.

R u there? I want to see u.

A part of me thought that if I ignored the problem, it would go away. It was how I used to deal with my drinking. I know—real mature, right? But this was different. If I didn't respond, the situation would escalate. Swallowing my bile, I replied.

Now is good.

CHAPTER
SIX

THERE WAS a Starbucks up the 5 in Redding. A lot of tourists stopped there on their way to Shasta Lake. We had decided to meet there to avoid seeing anyone we knew. Sipping tea out of a blue mug, she reacted to something on her phone. I took a seat across from her.

With her shiny dark-brown hair pulled back, warm brown eyes, and full lips, she looked luscious. She wore a white V-neck T-shirt cut way low and denim shorts that showed off her tanned legs. I smelled the perfume I had bought her at Sephora. Everything about her was hungry for my company. Maybe if things had been different, I might have—

"Hey," she said.

"Why did you text me?"

"Do you want a coffee or—"

"I want to know what we're doing here."

I was somewhere between angry and turned on. It had been two months since Missy Soldado and I last saw each other. That was before the craziness in Tres Marias had started. Towards the end, I was going to her house two or three times a week.

After quitting AA, I struggled to stay sober and needed a distraction. That's what I told myself anyway. The truth was I had seen through my own bullshit and wanted to end the affair. But first, I needed as much of Missy as I could get before I shut her out of my life for good.

I had planned to go to her house one last time and break it off clean. Naturally, we ended up in bed. It was the best sex I ever had with her in the six weeks we were together. Afterwards, I slunk away. I hadn't seen or spoken to her since.

"Why did you text me?" I said.

"I had to see you again. I've been thinking a lot about us. I drove by Staples the other day and saw you talking to Holly. I almost walked in."

"You need to let this go."

"I know," she said. "But I can't."

"I never lied to you about my situation."

"People split up all the time."

"I'm not doing that."

"Let me guess. You feel some kind of obligation to her. What was she, your high school sweetheart?"

"Lower your voice," I said. "I love her."

"You loved me once. And you can't be in love with two women, Dave."

"You're right. Try to understand. Holly and I have been together for three years. We're planning to start a family." I thought about walking out.

She stirred her tea. "I don't believe you. You don't have the cojones to get out of a dead relationship."

At the register, a family of four was ordering the works. In the corner, a businessman with a laptop and earbuds was on a conference call. At another table, some sincere-looking guy pitched life insurance to a middle-aged woman. Across from us, baby-faced bible students argued about Corinthians and

25

Saint Paul's views on marriage. I would have given my soul to be any one of those people.

"What did you see in me?" I said. "I'm an alcoholic. Was it because I'm married? You can have any guy you want."

"I don't want somebody else."

Though she sounded vulnerable, I didn't fall for it. "Don't contact me anymore—I mean it."

She drummed her fingers on the table, the long shiny red nails clicking. Looking up, she gave me a dark smile.

"I'll do what I have to," she said.

Getting up, I slammed my chair down next to her, giving her a scare. People stared. Did I mention I have a temper?

"What do you mean?"

Her eyes were shiny and defiant. "It means I love you, and I'm not giving up on us."

I hated her and wanted out. This wasn't fair. Why couldn't she understand that what happened, happened? Time to move on. Did this stupid girl actually believe she could talk me into leaving Holly?

"Listen carefully, Missy," I said. "I'm only going to say this once. There is no us. There's you with your life and me with mine."

"I have no life! Okay?" All eyes were on us again, and she lowered her voice. "Not without you."

I noticed a barista talking to the manager. It was obvious what would come next. I had seen it a thousand times at the Beehive. First, they would ask us to leave. If we refused, they'd call the cops.

Faking a laugh, she touched my face. "You're so funny."

I snatched her wrist and placed her arm on the table. When I released it, I saw the reddish depression my fingers had left on her skin. Without another word, I walked out, nearly colliding with a toddler who had wandered away from his heavily tattooed mother.

"Watch it, asshole," she said.

I needed to think. Wandering the aisles at Home Depot always seemed to calm me. It must have been the orange aprons. On the way over there, I thought about Missy. We met when I started going to the gym. It was innocent at first. We would acknowledge each other on the treadmills and carry on with our workouts.

After about a week, I stopped watching television with my earbuds and talked to her the whole time. I learned that she was a medical coder who worked out of her house. Though I found her attractive, I never thought about doing anything. In my mind, we were passing the time.

One night, she told me someone tried to break into her house. She was scared and begged me to follow her home. I remember asking if she had a boyfriend she could call. *I'm not in a relationship right now.* I asked about her family. *They don't live in the area.* Like an idiot, I agreed to help her out.

There were no streetlights where Missy lived, and I could see why coming home at night would make her nervous. I stayed in my truck, watching as she parked in her driveway. She walked to the front door and, giving me a cute wave, went inside. No intruder. No danger. I assumed that was the end of it.

The next time, she said she wanted to thank me for helping her out and offered to buy me a drink. When I told her about my history, she suggested Starbucks. In hindsight, I knew what I was doing. I fooled myself into thinking that nothing would happen. But I wanted it to—more than anything.

Outside in the Starbucks parking lot, I walked her to her car. Grabbing my face, she kissed me. I should've pulled away, but I didn't. When she pressed her firm, supple body against mine, I was gone. After that, I didn't need to be talked into following her home.

So, here's the irony. It had been Holly's idea for me to exercise. Part of her master plan to keep me off the sauce. Not that I'm blaming her for what happened—that was on me.

Maybe Missy was bluffing. After all, the girl was twenty and emotional. In time, she would get over me. *I sound like a dick.* On my way home, my phone vibrated. Incredulous, I stared at the text message.

This isn't over, tty soon.

Looking up, I slammed on my brakes at a red light where people were crossing. What if the bitch confronted Holly? I knew my wife. There would be no negotiation—she'd leave me cold. I couldn't allow that to happen. Sure, I messed up, but I fixed it. I was supposed to be happy—supposed to make Holly happy.

Something would have to be done.

CHAPTER
SEVEN

I SPENT the afternoon organizing the basement. The whole time, I worried Missy would show up at the house. Later, when I walked into the kitchen, I found Holly still in her work clothes, chopping onions. The TV was on. I gave her a hug.

"How was work?" I said.

She nodded at the TV. "They haven't found our neighbor yet."

We watched footage of police and community volunteers combing the forest with search and rescue dogs. I thought of my friend out there somewhere. By now, he was probably rotting in the pine needles.

I rubbed her shoulders. "You must be tired."

"Just my feet. What have you been up to?"

"The toilet upstairs doesn't leak anymore. The sliding glass door locks now. And the basement is almost livable. Hey, maybe we can rent it out."

"Wait a sec. I want to call my mother and gloat."

"Also, I drove around the neighborhood putting up more flyers of Jim."

I kissed her neck and turned her around. Her eyes were watery from the onions. I kissed each of them.

"Let me buy you dinner," I said.

Her body tensed. "What did you do?"

"Why would you ask that?"

"You didn't get a speeding ticket?"

"Can't a guy take his wife out to dinner without it being—"

"Okay, sorr-eee. Clam down."

Holly had a charming habit of scrambling certain words at inappropriate times. My very own Mrs. Malaprop. She had picked up the habit from her late father, a career salesman. He'd used the technique to break the ice with new clients.

She scooped the onions into a plastic container and put away her apron. As I watched her, a feeling of raw desire came over me. Reaching around, I cupped her perfect breasts.

Playfully, she slapped my hands away. "I thought we were going out."

"We will, I promise. But I need to take care of something first."

I spun her around and pulled her close. Laughing, she seemed to enjoy the attention.

"Mr. Pulaski, why is there a road flare in your pants?"

I was beyond hot. Scooping her up, I carried her upstairs as she fake-screamed and pretended to pound my chest. I was a caveman—I didn't recognize myself. It was like I was meeting her for the first time. And I adored everything I saw.

"I thought we agreed, no animals in the house," she said.

I let out a feral growl. As we reached the top of the stairs, the doorbell rang. I grabbed her butt.

"Let's pretend we're not home."

"With both cars in the driveway?"

Setting her down, I sighed theatrically and limped all the way to the front door. I was going to kill whoever had cock-blocked me.

It was Detective Van Gundy. I had forgotten how large he was. He was around six-eight, with dark wavy hair, a worried brow, and smelling of cigarettes.

"Can I come in for a minute, Mr. Pulaski?"

This guy was a humorless bag of police procedure. And his being here made me nervous as we walked into the living room. Sitting on the floral sofa, he pushed his tree-trunk legs out in front of him. His shoes were easily sixteens.

"Play any basketball?" I said.

He pointed at his chest. "Heart murmur."

The detective rose as Holly walked in wearing a loose-fitting summer dress. She had put on fresh makeup and looked gorgeous.

"What's going on?" she said.

"I'm assuming Detective Van Gundy is here to give us an update on Jim."

"Oh?"

I sat opposite the policeman as my wife leaned against the arm of the leather chair. I could smell her perfume. We found each other's hands.

"That's not why I'm here," he said. "We're investigating several animal mutilations in the area near where your friend lives."

Holly side-eyed me. "I read about that in the paper. You don't think Jim had anything to do with it?"

"We're considering the possibility. Would you describe Mr. Stanley as a violent person?"

"No," I said. "He drinks, though. But he never harmed anyone, even when he was hammered."

"How long have you known him?"

"Since high school."

"And you, Mrs. Pulaski?"

"Three or four years? Detective, you're not asking these questions because of some missing pets."

The cop looked at his Frankenstein shoes as if seeing them for the first time. "This morning, a jogger found a body in the woods."

"Was it that missing woman? We saw the news report."

"We don't know. There wasn't much left." He got up to leave. "I hope I didn't ruin your evening."

"It's fine," Holly said. "I agree with my husband. I don't think Jim could've done that."

Van Gundy nodded. "Let me know if you hear from him."

"We will," I said and took his card.

He was halfway out the door when he stopped. "I have to ask. Are you sure he hasn't tried contacting you? It's not uncommon for well-meaning people to protect their friends."

"I get it, but we haven't seen him."

After the detective left, I put my arms around Holly and kissed her nose. I could always tell when she was upset.

"That body... It's our neighbor—I know it is. Whoever did it is wandering around Tres Marias."

"Let's forget about it for now. I want us to have a good time."

"I'm not sure I feel like it."

"Honey, it's got nothing to do with us. Come on."

"Fine. Let me get my purse."

I took Holly to our favorite Mexican restaurant, La Adelita. They had the best carne asada in the area.

"That detective thought we were lying," she said. "Don't you think?"

We drank iced tea, but what I wanted was a beer. And it didn't help that there were people around us celebrating with oversize margaritas rimmed with salt.

"What?"

"Are you even listening to me?"

"He's a cop. It's his job to be skeptical."

"Would you tell me the truth if you had seen Jim?"

"Why would I lie about that?"

"Forget I brought it up," she said.

A power outage had taken out the streetlights as we made our way home. Feeling better, Holly decided to massage my thigh while I drove.

"I hope this is going somewhere," I said.

"We'll see when we get home."

Up ahead, I spotted a dark figure on the side of the road, tottering towards us. I slowed and went around. As my headlight beams shone on him, he looked at us. His eyes were as vacant as an empty promise. Holding his head, he let out a horrifying shriek. I hit the gas.

The sight of that weirdo put a damper on the foreplay. I kept thinking about how the virus was spreading. First, it was the jimmies. And now, apparently, the symptoms were getting worse. What if Holly or I got sick? Was there even a cure?

At home in familiar surroundings, we couldn't wait to get into bed. It was like when we were first dating. I smelled her hair and let myself get lost in it. Though I was ready to go off like a Roman candle, I took my time. Instead of straight sex, we made love. Afterwards, I held her.

"We're good together, aren't we?" I said.

"Like fleas and parrots."

I kissed her perfect fingers, her wedding ring. Holly was everything I wanted. And I would do anything to protect her —anything. I kissed her lips.

"I love you so much."

"You butter," she said and pushed me onto my back.

CHAPTER
EIGHT

WE READ the headline in the morning newspaper—*Man Finds Body of Missing Jogger*. A local hunter discovered her in the woods. The body had been eviscerated. Dental records confirmed that the remains were those of the missing woman.

Her name was Sarah Champion. She was a writer in her forties who enjoyed running in the forest. Holly and I had seen her many times on our way to work. She left behind a husband and two young sons. The hapless hunter was not considered a suspect.

With the news of our neighbor's slaying, a feeling of uneasiness took over our lives. Fear of the woods, fear of the night, and fear of other people. I considered purchasing a gun. When I mentioned this to Holly, she begged me not to. She hated guns and believed I would be borrowing trouble—a term her mother always used.

Driving to work, I didn't see any of the flyers I had put up. Hundreds of new posters blanketed the telephone poles and streetlights. Instead of missing pets, all featured grainy photos of men, women, and children. The town was beginning to look like a war zone.

Everyone at Staples talked about Sarah's murder. Some were convinced the hunter had killed Sarah himself and gone to the cops to toy with them. Those numbnuts watched too much cable television.

"Had to be a drifter," Fred said. He was incapable of believing anyone in Tres Marias would commit such an atrocity. "A psycho from across the border."

I gave him a knowing smile. "And by *border*, you mean Oregon?"

"Or farther north even. Remember the Green River Killer?"

"How do you explain the animal mutilations?"

That was Zach, the wise-ass kid who spent all his time in the alley smoking dope when he was supposed to be stocking inventory.

Fred regarded the pothead like a patient teacher. "Maybe there's a rabid bear or—"

"I'll bet someone with the jimmies did it."

Our manager had had enough. "Why don't you unpack those fax machines like I told you."

"I'm tellin' ya, man," he said.

Zach was the only employee the boss ordered around. The rest of us knew our jobs and did them without being asked. I often wondered why Fred didn't fire him. I suppose it was because he considered himself a good judge of character and couldn't admit he had made a hiring mistake.

At Subway, Holly and I tried keeping the conversation light. But we always returned to the disturbing events that consumed our lives. For me, it wasn't only the murder and the missing townspeople. I kept seeing Missy everywhere, and I was terrified she would confront me in front of my wife.

"Don't you like your sandwich?" Holly said.

"Not that hungry, I guess."

"I like the way you held me this morning."

I happened to glance out the window. Missy stood across the way from us, looking defiant with her arms folded over her chest. From her expression, I could tell she was thinking about walking over. But before she could make a move, I marched outside. She disappeared inside a dress shop. When I rejoined Holly, she looked at me with her mouth open.

"Some kids were trying to break into a car," I said.

"Should we call the police?"

"It's fine. They ran when they saw me."

She seemed to buy my explanation. But how many more stories would I have to come up with each time Missy showed her damn face? All it would take was for her to catch Holly one time when I wasn't around, like on my day off. Then my wife would know what a lying sack her husband was.

She reached for my hand. "When did you decide to become a hero?"

"I'm no hero," I said and bit into my sandwich.

CHAPTER
NINE

WORRYING about Missy had exhausted me. When we got home in the late afternoon, I fell asleep on the sofa in the den. Holly had insisted on running to the grocery store even though I promised to go later. The house was quiet. After a few minutes, I opened my eyes. Jim stood there, watching me with flat eyes.

Awkwardly, I climbed over the sofa and hid. Why was I so scared? This was Jim. Taking a breath, I stood and found that I was alone. I convinced myself that it was a dream. Then I saw the dirty footprints on the carpet.

If there was ever a time that demanded a drink, this was it. Fighting the urge, I went into the kitchen and made a pot of strong black coffee. Minutes later, I was still shaking and didn't notice when Holly walked in with the groceries.

"I hope you don't expect me to clean up that mess," she said.

She must have noticed my hands as I struggled to bring the coffee to my lips. Taking the cup from me, she set it on the counter and waited for me to explain.

"I saw Jim," I said.

"Wait, are you serious?"

"He was standing next to me when I woke up. Then it was like he was never there."

"Are you sure it wasn't—"

"A dream? Dreams don't leave muddy footprints."

"How could he get in, though?"

"Maybe you left the front door unlocked when you went out."

"What if he's in here now?" she said and took my hand.

Neither of us had ever considered Jim a threat. As a precaution, Holly remained in the kitchen clutching a carving knife. After locking all the doors, I searched the house. There were no other footprints, and I was beginning to doubt my friend had ever been there. I returned to the den. Except for the footprints, the room looked the same. Yet, there was something...

"Holly, can you come in here a sec?" I said.

"What is it?"

"There's something different about this room."

"I don't see—" She reached up to a shelf on the wall near the TV. "Hey, look at this."

The area was dusty. I ran my finger over a spot that was dust free. "Didn't there used to be a picture here?"

"Of you and Jim."

"I remember. We were showing off the one fish we caught at Shasta Lake. Wow, that was before you and I were married."

Jim might have thought of that as a fun time. But I remembered it as tense and awkward. It was our last trip together. He spent the whole time drunk, and it was hard for me not to join in. The only thing keeping me sober was the thought of my future with Holly. A tourist happened by and snapped the pic. After that, I refused to hang out with my friend anymore.

"It was a great trip," I said.

Over dinner, we tried taking our minds off the ghostly visitation and made plans for an imaginary baby girl named Jade. We had her graduating from Berkeley and starting a post-graduate program at Stanford. Eventually, we returned to the subject of Jim.

"Maybe he had temporary amnesia," I said. "And found his way out of the woods."

"Jim knows those woods. He would've made it home in no time. How did he look?"

"Like he was hurt bad. I'm going to take a ride out there."

"Tonight? Dave, no—let the police handle it."

"He's my friend. I need to see if he made it home."

Holly began cleaning up. "What if he's not normal?"

"Jim was never normal."

"You know what I mean. What if he's—"

"Dangerous? You think he killed Sarah Champion? I'll hit him with a shovel and call 911. It'll be fine."

My casual attitude didn't make Holly feel any better, but it eased the tension a little. If only she knew how scared I was. Grabbing my keys and my phone, I headed out.

"Make sure you're not being followed," she said.

Good point. The last thing I needed was that dour detective on my ass. I walked to my truck without looking back. The moon was big and bright through the trees. Though it was summer, the air was crisp and smelled of pine.

When I was younger, I used to want to get away from this place. Relocate to San Francisco or LA. After meeting Holly, I began seeing the beauty around me—the trees, the fresh air, the quiet—and I understood why my parents had settled here.

Checking the rearview mirror, I made sure no one was tailing me. A colony of bats swooped out of the forest into the night. You can never tell whether they're scared or out on a joyride. A lot of times, they carry disease—primarily rabies. I wondered if that might be what caused the jimmies.

I heard the unmistakable sound of a screech owl somewhere in the darkness, followed by a distant shriek. After pulling over, I rolled down the window and listened. There was only the wind. I thought about that guy Holly and I had come across after our night out.

Mountain lion, I told myself and got back on the road.

CHAPTER
TEN

THE HOUSE WAS dark when I arrived. I grabbed a flashlight from the glove compartment and got out to investigate. Immediately, I stepped on something soft—it made a crunching sound. I pointed the flashlight at the ground and discovered an orange house cat that looked like it had been gored with a screwdriver.

Backing away from the rotting carcass, I wiped my shoe on some crabgrass. I directed the flashlight beam all around the front yard. There were dead animals everywhere—hundreds of them. Most were dogs and cats. The tags on their collars glinted like jewels. I didn't see Perro and decided to try the house. The remains of a raccoon lay in pieces on the porch.

I caught myself thinking this was like one of those horror movies where the audience is screaming *Get out of there now!* No one in their right mind would be stupid enough to enter the house in real life. Yet here I was. Despite the danger, I had to find out what happened to my friend.

Jim never locked his doors because he didn't own anything worth stealing. Having become familiar with the sparse furniture and lack of refinement, I tended to agree. Hoping I wouldn't get jumped, I swung open the door and walked in.

When I flicked on the lights, I expected the walls to be smeared with the words *Helter Skelter* in blood. What I saw shocked me all the same.

A tall sculpture stood in the middle of the living room. It was made of green longneck beer bottles held together by chicken wire. And there was a hole in the center. A rope anchored to the ceiling held the artwork in place. Had Jim built this before the accident?

Moving closer, I stepped on an orange tail that must have belonged to the dead cat outside. I remained in the living room awhile, admiring Jim's creation. Memories of all those nights we drank ourselves stupid flooded into my brain like those errant bats. I lost count of how many times I woke up in the morning on Jim's floor, covered in sick.

Picturing myself at eighteen, I wondered to the depths of my soul what I thought I was accomplishing with that life. We had spent so much time here, talking about everything under the sun. Yet now, I couldn't remember a single conversation.

Much as I had done at home, I carefully checked the house, calling out Jim's name. After ten minutes of searching, I ended up in the avocado green kitchen. The used aluminum table and chairs looked like they came from a condemned diner. Jim had sold off his parents' furniture long ago for beer money.

The refrigerator was one of those old round-cornered Frigidaire jobs that might have looked good in the 1950s. Opening it, I found what I expected—beer. With the stress of these past few weeks, I craved that wicked drink the way a baby thirsts for his mother's milk.

All those shiny bottles dusted with condensation were waiting for someone to twist off the tops. To try to quench a thirst that could never be satisfied. Catching myself starting to spiral, I slammed the refrigerator door shut and choked on a scream at the person standing in front of me.

It was Jim.

CHAPTER
ELEVEN

HE WATCHED me with birdlike curiosity. His clothes were a mess, caked with mud and dried blood. His sandy hair was matted with dirt. His eyes were like two wafers of slate, gray and lifeless. And his eyelids were rimmed with red. Whitish goo oozed from the tear ducts.

The gash ringing his neck was dark and ragged. The skin was gray, and the fingernails were a blackish purple. He looked dead. I didn't know whether it was the bad fluorescent lighting or the fact that I was tired. But there was no indication that he was breathing.

Ignoring my panic, I sank into a chair. "Been watching me long?"

He acted like he hadn't heard me. Instead, he tried to form words, but nothing came out. I got up again as he came closer. Why in hell hadn't I brought the shovel?

"Jim, what're you..."

He brushed past me and continued to the refrigerator. The pungent smell of excrement brought up my gorge. He grabbed a beer and tried twisting the top off. His fingers were stiff—the tips doughy—and he couldn't manage it. This was the worst I had ever seen him.

Taking the bottle, I opened it for him. He stared at it like he didn't know what it was for. Then, he drank. As bad off as he was, I envied him. I kept thinking about all those other frosty beers. Why shouldn't I join him for one last round?

The sound he made was indescribable, like dirty runoff down a storm drain. He didn't even swallow. Instead, he let gravity pull the beer down into his gut. I half-expected liquid to come squirting out of the gash in his neck.

My friend could finish a beer faster than anyone I knew. We used to have contests, and I always lost. It was the same now. Soon, the bottle was empty. He always used to belch afterwards. Now, he gawped at me stupidly.

"Where have you been all this time?"

Instead of answering, he gave me a broken smile. I decided to keep talking, more to calm myself than get information.

"We had the whole town out looking for you. I even made flyers. I think you might need a doctor. Can I have a look?"

He smelled of rotting meat, and I had to fight to keep from letting go a spray of vomit. His dull eyes followed my hands as I examined his neck. I didn't notice any fresh blood. Using my finger, I felt the roughness of the tear.

Eventually, I reached the left side. There was a large flap of mortified skin, dry and crispy at the edges. It lay loose over the shiny, dark red muscle. As I lifted it, something fell on the floor that sounded like a pebble.

It was a glass bead from my car's windshield. Jim looked at it and groaned. Suddenly, the flap moved on its own. I thought my mind was playing tricks. When I looked again, a fat kidney worm dripping with gore raised its bald, blind head and glowered.

Screaming, I fell backwards against the gas range. Still holding the skin flap, I pulled my friend with me. His head slammed into the range hood, making a dull, squishy noise. Enraged, he bared his teeth, which were covered in bits of entrails and fur. I tried getting away, but I was pinned. As he hovered over me, I tried defusing the situation.

"It was an accident," I said.

He tried grabbing my legs, and I kicked him away, but he wouldn't stop. I caught him in the nose with my boot and heard the crunch of bone and cartilage. He managed to get ahold of one leg. I wished I had listened to Holly and not come.

"You need a doctor. Let me drive you to the hospital."

He backed off. I expected blood to gush from his nose, but there was nothing—not a drop. Though it was bent to one side, it didn't seem to bother him. He craned his neck around to the sound of stretching tendons and cracking bones. I scrambled to my feet and scooted to the door.

"I'm calling for an ambulance."

When I turned around, Jim was standing in front of a cupboard. He opened the door and reached inside. I fumbled for my phone to dial 911 and didn't notice that he was facing me. Before I could punch in the numbers, he showed me what he was holding. It was the framed photo of us at Shasta Lake, now bloodstained and filthy.

He stared with cold, crazy eyes that seemed to look through me. Out of my mind with fear, I ran. Outside, I tripped over the dead animals in the yard. Cursing, I climbed into my truck and hit the gas.

After a mile or so, I felt better and tried to make sense of everything. I recalled the missing pets and the mutilated deer. And now, the dead woman. I considered the fact that Jim could no longer speak and thought about all those towns-people with the jimmies.

No one had any idea how this sickness could spread so quickly. I was scared because I had touched his wound. I thought about calling 911 for my friend. But he would only disappear into the forest again. When a text came through, I assumed it was Holly.

> I'm outside ur house. Where's ur truck?
> Should i knock?

I was filthy and scared, and I needed medical attention. Didn't I have enough on my plate? I told myself I was a good person and didn't deserve this. But I couldn't ignore Missy. I had to do something. And what about Jim? He'd have to wait. I decided to go to her house and texted her.

She was waiting at the door, barefoot, legs shaved, dressed in tight cotton shorts and a soft V-neck T-shirt with no bra. I was like a trained dog. She played me with a bad hand, and I fell for it every time.

"I'm so glad you came," she said.

I wanted to smack her, but I knew if I resorted to violence, she would go straight to Holly. Dammit, she smelled good.

"You need to stop," I said.

"It's like I told you. I'm fighting for us." My anger seethed as she threw her arms around my neck and kissed me, her warm, luscious body molding itself to mine.

"Ew, what's that smell?"

She turned her head and, taking a deep breath, rubbed against me. I was getting aroused. And I was sure she felt it, too, as she worked my crotch. Pulling her arms away, I stag-gered back.

"I know you want me," she said. "Don't even bother pretending."

"I'm not leaving Holly."

"Is that what you came here to tell me?" She pulled her T-shirt up, revealing her firm breasts.

I tried not to look at them. She grabbed my hand to make me touch them. Instead, I pulled down her shirt. Furious, she raked her nails across my face. Turning away, I held my stinging cheek. I could already feel the wet, sticky blood.

She watched me as I got in my truck, her arms folded across her chest and her lips wearing a smirk.

"Say hi to Holly for me," she said.

CHAPTER
TWELVE

WITH EVERYTHING GOING ON, you would think I'd want to be truthful about what happened at Jim's house. But after speaking with Van Gundy, I realized my friend was the prime suspect in Sarah Champion's murder. And the fact that he was unable to talk meant there was no way he could defend himself. How would he account for his whereabouts on the day in question? Also, there was the possibility that he did kill the woman. God help me, I was beginning to believe it was true.

"Did you find him?" Holly said when I got home.

"I checked his house. Nothing."

"How did you get so dirty? And what happened to your face? It looks like—"

"It was dark—I fell."

When she tried kissing me, I motioned for her to stay back. "I need a shower. There were a lot of dead animals."

"Animals?"

"I'm pretty sure he's been eating them."

"Oh, that poor man."

"Guess his luck finally ran out," I said.

. . .

The next morning, I went to see the doctor. It was Holly's day off. To avoid suspicion, I booked a lunchtime appointment. The waiting area was packed. They escorted me to an examination room, where I had to wait another fifteen minutes. After a quick knock, the door opened.

"Hey, Isaac," I said.

"I don't have time for social visits. There are a lot of actual sick patients."

Dr. Isaac Fallow was a medical examiner with an internal medicine practice in town. A genial man, he was somewhere in his early sixties. He was our family physician and had known me since I was a baby.

He motioned for me to take a seat on the examination table. After sticking a digital thermometer in my mouth, he checked my blood pressure and took my pulse. I could tell he thought I was faking.

"I'm worried about all these people running around with the jimmies," I said.

"So am I." He checked my eyes, ears, and throat. "Stop moving." He listened to my heart and lungs. "You're fine. See you next year. Want a sucker?"

"The other day, one of those sick people came into the store. I think I might have gotten infected."

"We don't know if the virus spreads via respiratory droplets. In the cases I've treated, the patient was either bit or somehow exposed to an infected person's blood."

"I think I might have handled something that had their saliva on it."

"I see." He scrubbed his hands in the sink. "Did you wash right away?"

"I used hand sanitizer."

"Soap and hot water are still the best. I don't think you have anything to worry about. Next time, wear gloves."

"Thanks. Any idea what we're dealing with?"

"It could be a coronavirus, maybe from a bat. We just don't know yet."

"It changes people's moods, and not for the better."

My friend was halfway out the door. "I've noticed that, too. In some cases, there's a rage factor."

"Any advice?"

"Don't piss anyone off," he said.

CHAPTER
THIRTEEN

OKAY, so here was the Missy problem in a nutshell. Did I tell Holly everything and hope she would forgive me? Or was it better to convince the bitch to stop before my wife learned the truth? As I explained, I like to avoid trouble. If I can lie my way out of a situation, I will—every damn time. It's the alcoholic in me. Still...

All this must sound pretty stupid coming from a twenty-something who had spent six years of his life getting drunk—not giving a rat's fart about marriage or family. Shit, who knows? Maybe I did grow up a little. Because now, all I wanted was to protect what I had. But confronting Missy again would just piss her off, and she'd blow it all up. That left me with one choice—I had to confess. Next to quitting drinking, it would be the hardest thing I ever did.

It was getting dark. Outside, a hot wind rattled the windows. Somewhere, a siren wailed. Holly sat across from me at the kitchen table. It was hard to read her expression. It looked somewhere between disbelief and sorrow.

"Say something," I said.

"Why?"

Hers was a hurt that would never heal—not in a lifetime of good deeds. I could become a missionary and spend the rest of my miserable, groveling existence in some faraway, war-torn country. But it wouldn't move the needle. Nothing would ever take away the pain I saw in her eyes.

"I don't know what made me get mixed up with her." Shit, I'd played the victim card.

"Where... Where did you meet her?" Her voice was small and distant, like she'd already left the room.

"The gym. It started out as talking. They were conversations to pass the time."

"I can totally see how that could lead to sex."

"She asked me to follow her home. Said she was scared of a break-in."

"So you were being noble. Did she invite you inside? Did you look under her bed? Role-play?"

"I left. But after that one time, I don't know what happened. It's all mixed up in my head. I'm not making excuses—I let myself get sucked in."

"All those nights you were gone. You said you were with Jim. And here I thought you'd started drinking again. What a relief."

"I broke it off. That night after I went to find Jim, I drove to her house and told her. I never wanted you to know. She got it in her head that we were meant to be together. Said she wouldn't stop till we were."

"And what did you say?"

"I told her to forget it. There's something else. She might be crazy."

"Perfect."

A faraway shriek cut through the tension like a bone saw. The room felt cold. I had no idea what was going through my wife's mind, but I was scared we might be over.

She set aside her tea and looked at me. "What're you gonna do now?"

"Tell her you already know—that I don't care what she does. I'm hoping she'll come to her senses and leave us alone."

"You said she was crazy."

"Crazy, confused..."

"Are we in any danger?"

"No. Maybe." I tried reaching for her hand. "I don't know what else to do."

"Do whatever you want," she said. "I can't be around you right now."

She put her cup in the sink and walked out. Despite the pain in my gut, I felt the worst was over. Life would be rocky for a while, sure. But I could see Holly forgiving me at some point. I had gone to her with the truth. And it was this—I wanted her and not Missy.

Often, we lie to ourselves to get through the next five minutes.

CHAPTER
FOURTEEN

THE NEXT DAY WAS SATURDAY. I ended up sleeping on the couch in the den. Holly had gone out early. After showering and dressing, I called Missy and told her I wanted to meet. The excitement in her voice said it all—I'd reconsidered. I wished I could avoid going, but ghosting her wasn't an option.

When I arrived, she was on the porch, ready for action. I had already been through hell with Holly. Now it was Missy's turn. There's nothing worse than delivering bad news to a woman. I hoped I wouldn't get good at it.

"Want to come inside?" she said.

"Let's take a walk."

Her rented house stood at the edge of the forest. Though it was only after nine, the air felt hot and sticky. Behind her place, we found a trail that led into the woods.

"I told Holly," I said.

A young deer cut across our path. Squirrels chased each other in the pine needles. All seemed normal. Another summer day.

"Now you know I was serious when I said this is over."

She stopped and took my hand. "But it's not over."

"Holly knows. There's nothing you can do to us."

"I never wanted to *do* anything to you. We belong together —can't you see that?"

"If I led you to believe—"

"This isn't some game. You don't get to use me and go back to your perfect life."

"I don't love you."

Those words stopped her cold. Letting go, she backed away as if I had slapped her. Something moved behind her. It was Jim, staggering out of the trees.

What was left of his clothes clung to his bony, putrefying frame. Most of his hair had fallen out, and his eyes were scaled over. The flesh around his neck had slid away, exposing dry, dark red muscle and a gray esophagus.

"Missy!"

"What? You want to apologize now?"

"Run!"

But she turned too late. Jim let out a shriek and grabbed her, his vise-like jaws snapping at her face. Screaming, she tried to get away. Total, paralyzing fight or flight blinded me. I managed to grab her and, elbowing my friend in the face, freed her. Together, we ran.

Why is it that when you're out of your head, you lose all sense of direction? Instead of going to Missy's house, where we'd be safe, we headed deeper into the forest. I knew it was wrong, yet I couldn't stop. For a sec, I was too messed up to notice I was alone and turned around. Missy had fallen, and Jim came for her like an enraged animal.

"Get up!"

Her attacker grabbed her foot. She began kicking him with the other one. I didn't wait for her. Up ahead, I found a ranger station built out of flagstone and rough-sawn beams.

Standing under a canopy of pine trees, it had a slanted roof and a door. I pounded on it.

"Help! Somebody help!"

No one answered. I noticed a cord of wood—and an axe. I banged on the door till my hand went numb.

"Is anybody in there?"

Missy was somewhere far away. When I tried the handle, the door swung open. I locked myself in. My mouth tasted like metal—adrenaline. I couldn't think—couldn't reason.

"Dave!"

Missy was close now, but Jim was there, too. He was no longer my friend but a beast. If I opened the door, I could die. Now I knew what he had done to those animals. And I realized he was the one who had torn Sarah Champion to pieces in the forest.

"Dave, please!"

She beat her fists on the door, begging me to let her in. My hands were shaking, and no matter how much I wanted to save her, I couldn't move. Outside, she scraped the door with her fingernails, calling my name over and over. Gritting my teeth, I pressed my head against the rough wood and closed my eyes, wishing it would just be over.

The sounds of tearing and screaming startled me like something out of hell. There was a dull crack, followed by a groan. Minutes went by, and I couldn't move. I listened to the sound of my heart hammering in my chest and my ears. I wiped my eyes on my sleeve and cracked the door.

Jim's body lay sprawled on the ground, his head cleaved in two. His arms and legs twitched for a beat and stopped. A dark stream of black blood leaked from his brain and pooled in the dirt.

The greasy axe lay next to him. Bloody footprints led away into the forest. A shiny red fingernail was lodged in the door.

A lunatic's laugh welled inside me. Somehow, she had managed to overpower her already-dead attacker and kill him again with the axe. After a performance like that, she would stop at nothing to get to me—and Holly. I needed to turn the situation around. Steeling myself, I ran to Missy's house to confront her. The door was unlocked, and I went inside.

"Hello?" I said in a strangled voice.

I checked everywhere, but the house was empty. When I returned to my truck, I expected her to lurch out of the forest at any second. Before I could get behind the wheel, I retched.

On the road, I checked my phone. One new voicemail. It was Holly wondering where I was. I called her back, trying like hell to sound normal.

"Where've you been?" she said.

"I went to see Missy."

A long silence. "Will you be home soon?"

"On my way."

Nothing mattered now—I was screwed. Missy would report me to the police. Was it against the law to ignore someone in trouble? My imagination took over. I saw myself in the interview room with the cops as they accused me of planning Missy's death. I had the perfect motive, too.

Holly and I had no money for an attorney. I'd end up with some lame-ass public defender with bad breath. Justice would be swift, and they would convict me. On her own, Holly would hate me forever while I rotted in state prison.

I nearly ran off the road when the text message came through on my phone.

You shouldn't have done that, dave.

CHAPTER
FIFTEEN

HOLLY WAS WAITING for me when I walked in.

"They found Jim," she said. "Come into the kitchen. You smell like death."

Swallowing a mad giggle, I grabbed a chair and rubbed my eyes. I felt like I was in a drainage pipe. Holly was at the other end, waving. When I looked up, there were two cups of tea on the table. The way I was shaking, I didn't think I could pick mine up without spilling it.

"Someone murdered him outside a ranger station."

I burned my tongue on the tea.

"Detective Van Gundy called. A neighbor reported hearing screams. And you know the cop—he won't say any more. They want you to go down there and identify the body."

"Me? Don't they have dental records?" Jim hated the dentist.

She looked away as if she had heard something. "What happened over there?"

"I ended it," I said.

In my mind, I saw Jim's head split open like a rotting melon and leaking black blood. It was all clear to me. I would have to let this play out. This wasn't my life anymore. I was a spectator who'd won front-row seats to a shitshow.

I stood to get more tea and heard my own voice. *I ended it.* I pictured Missy bringing down the axe, a look of sheer, vile hatred in her eyes. The image made me dizzy. And now she was coming for Holly and me—I could feel it. My legs gave out, and I slumped against the counter.

"You need to get it together," she said, helping me up. "It's over."

But it wasn't over. I pushed my cup away. Holly turned on the local news. I could barely focus as we watched footage of the front of Missy's house. There was yellow barricade tape everywhere and cops pushing people out of the way. Evie Champagne, a local reporter, jammed her microphone into Van Gundy's face.

"Detective?" she said. "Can you confirm this is the home of Melyssa Soldado?"

"Not confirming or denying. We have to notify the family—"

"Where is Ms. Soldado?"

"We found the house empty. A team of officers is out looking for her. We suspect the deceased assaulted her."

"And the unsub? Who is he?"

Van Gundy hesitated. "A John Doe."

"Excuse me," she said. "But isn't the man you found Jim Stanley? Isn't he, in fact, the missing accident victim you've been searching for?"

"You're unbelievable." He pushed his way off camera. "No more questions."

Evie faced the camera. "There you have it. Police neither confirming nor denying the identities of the attacker and his victim, who is, as of this moment, missing. This is Evie Champagne. Back to you, Felix."

I switched off the TV and took my wife's hands in mine. My legs felt like cooked spaghetti. A searing pain shot through my head. My neck hurt, and I felt woozy. Pulling away, she stared at me with a horrified expression.

"You were there," she said.

"I need to tell you what happened." It was impossible to block out the sound of Missy's desperate screaming in my head.

"I don't think I can take another one of your confessions."

I went to the sink for no reason. The faucet was dripping, and I made a mental note to repair it. I wished I could throw up and get it over with.

"I was at the ranger station," I said.

"I asked you to stop."

"Dammit, you need to hear this."

"What did you do?" She was next to me now.

"It's what I didn't do. I didn't help her."

"Missy was there?"

"We were in the woods near her house. I'd gone there to tell her we were through. Then Jim showed up. But it wasn't him anymore. He was like an animal full of rage. I tried getting Missy out of there, but she fell. I ran away and hid."

"Wait, you didn't go back for her?" she said.

"I was too scared."

"But he was killed with an axe. That was you, right? That's self-defense."

"It wasn't me. I didn't do anything."

"Are you saying you left her there with a crazed killer?"

She began walking in circles like she was playing her version of the events in her head. Then she hurled her teacup at me. It glanced off my forearm and shattered on the floor.

"You let her die?" she said.

"I don't care about her. I care about us. Why aren't you happy about us?"

"Because what you did was evil."

"But she didn't die. She— She got away."

"It doesn't matter. Admit it—you wanted her dead."

"I wanted her out of our lives."

As I moved towards her, she backed away. Was she scared of me now?

"Missy killed him," I said. "Split his head open with an axe." I didn't notice that she had taken a seat at the table. "Holly?"

"Shut up, Dave. I need to think."

She sat there with her hands folded and looked straight ahead. I wanted a drink bad. I imagined going to Jim's house and emptying his refrigerator one bottle at a time. How long could I survive on beer and dead animals? Instead, I refilled my cup. The tea had cooled and tasted like pond water.

Incredulous, she shook her head. "And to think I was going to forgive you for what you did. It was a lapse, I know. And I'm pretty sure you wouldn't do it again."

I sat next to her. "Never, I swear."

"But to stand by when someone is being attacked. What were you thinking? What if it had been me?"

"But it wasn't."

I needed something to do and got a broom and a dustpan from the hall closet. Holly's face was expressionless as I swept up the broken cup and threw the pieces into the trash. The tea set had been a wedding present from her mother. When I'd finished, I sat down again.

"Is she dangerous?" Holly said.

"What do you mean?" I was so tired—I wanted to sleep and forget.

"I mean, genius, whadda you think she'll do?"

"Come after me, probably. She's nothing but a vindictive little—"

"Great. Well, we can't stay here—we have to leave."

"We?"

"You're not off the hook." She buried her face in her hands. "You stupid, stupid bastard."

"What about our jobs?"

She stared at me like I was an imbecile. "We have to get out of here. At least until the police find that woman, and we can—I don't know—get a restraining order."

Holly had always been smarter than me. More practical. More focused. Especially when it came to solving tough problems. And she was right—we needed to leave town.

"There's something else," I said.

"You started drinking again."

She wanted to hurt me, and this was the best she could do. I let it slide.

"It's about Jim. He... When I saw him, I don't think he was alive."

"Was that before or after the axe to the head?"

"Before. It was like he was decomposing. He wasn't even breathing."

"That's crazy, it's the jimmies."

"Maybe." I pictured the kidney worm in my friend's neck. And the black blood leaching into the ground. No, he was sure-as-shit dead when I saw him. "Are you leaving me?"

She didn't answer for a long time.

"Holly?"

She got up and went to the door. When she looked at me again, I could see the disgust in her eyes.

"You're a real prick," she said. "You know that, right?"

CHAPTER
SIXTEEN

IN THE MOVIES, morgues are always creepy. But when I arrived, the waiting area was clean and pleasant—comfortable chairs and colorful artificial plants. I glanced at the magazines on the side tables. No *Morticians Monthly*, just *Us Weekly*, *People*, and *Better Homes & Gardens*.

Van Gundy greeted me as I walked in. I didn't want to see Jim—or what was left of him. Would they bring out the body? Leer at me with anticipation as they raised the sheet? I thought of the photo of us at Shasta Lake. That was how I wanted to remember my friend. Happy. Alive.

"What am I doing here?" I said.

"It's a formality." He led me into the viewing room.

I expected someone to roll in the body on a stainless-steel table. Instead, a morgue attendant placed a set of photos face-down on a table. Van Gundy took a seat across from me and waited. I told myself that whatever I was about to see wasn't Jim anymore. Then, I flipped over the pictures.

At least they had done him a favor by stapling the two halves of his head together. But no amount of mortuary makeup would fix his face. I looked at the cop, reminding myself I was nowhere near the crime scene.

"Why is his head like that?" I said.

"We think Ms. Soldado split it with an axe. We found the murder weapon lying nearby."

I couldn't believe Missy was capable of that kind of violence. The same could be said about my cowardice. They had done a good job of cleaning up the body. Other than the staples and the reddish seam running down the middle of his face and neck, Jim looked the same.

"For the record, can you identify the deceased?"

"It's my friend, Jim Stanley."

I tried picturing him alive. Turning away, I threw up in my mouth. The vomit burned as I swallowed it. There was a loud banging coming from a different room. Another attendant ran in, his face drained of color.

"One of them is alive!"

The attendants hurried off, leaving the detective and me alone with the photos.

"How often do you hear that in a morgue?" I said.

Van Gundy had more questions, so we continued our conversation in the hospital lobby. How long would it take before he connected me to Jim's death? I was pretty sure Missy hadn't contacted the police. What was she waiting for?

"Do you know if Mr. Stanley knew his attacker?" the cop said.

"What?" I was a million miles away.

"Ms. Soldado. Was Mr. Stanley acquainted with her?"

"How should I know?" I got to my feet. "I don't feel well."

He followed me to the exit. "I have some more questions, but they can wait."

"What about the woman?"

"We're obtaining a search warrant for her cell phone records. That should tell us something."

"Right." A profound dread ate at my guts. "See you."

The detective called to me as I walked away. "It seems Mr. Stanley had no next of kin. Are you handling the burial arrangements? The hospital told me to ask."

"I'll take care of it," I said.

Heading to my truck, I couldn't shake the feeling Van Gundy was watching me. Like he knew what really happened and was waiting for me to slip up. Even if it was all in my head, it was a matter of time till they learned the truth. Missy's phone records would show all the calls and texts to my number. Might as well get my affairs in order.

A naked woman with gray skin and bloodshot eyes staggered in front of my truck. She looked like a mean drunk. Her abdomen was slit open, and white plastic tubing protruded from the incision. Her hands sliced at the air as she bared her pin-like teeth. I'd assumed she was a patient who escaped the operating table—until I saw the toe tag.

I slammed on the brakes as the morgue attendants and an orderly grabbed her. Shrieking, she sank her teeth into the orderly's face. He screamed as she ripped away his ear and part of his cheek. The attendants stumbled back, terrified.

The fear that had gripped me in the forest came rushing back like a runaway train. Desperate to leave, I couldn't move. A crowd had gathered behind my truck. The woman was in front of me. Her arms windmilling, she gibbered and drooled. Her flat eyes, cold and dead, focused on me through the windshield. It was the same look Jim had given Missy before he attacked her.

Van Gundy appeared, his gun drawn. He pushed the

wounded orderly away and waved the others back. His face was filled with fear as he aimed at her.

"Lie down on the ground. Now!"

Enraged, the woman came at him. He shot her twice in the chest, leaving two holes the size of quarters—no blood. When she kept coming, he fired at her face.

The bullet pierced her forehead and exited the back, leaving a crater. The fragments shattered the windshield of a nearby vehicle, setting off the alarm. The woman dropped to her knees, her tongue lolling in her bloody mouth like a red eel. Falling on the pavement, she hugged the ground in a death spasm.

I got out and joined the cop. All around us, people stared. The orderly's face was covered in gore. The attendants helped him into the emergency room. Trembling with adrenalin, Van Gundy holstered his weapon and turned to me with haunted eyes.

"Eighth one this week," he said.

PART TWO

MAYHEM

CHAPTER
SEVENTEEN

I SAT IN MY TRUCK, ignoring the commotion in the hospital parking lot. The cops had ordered me to move, and I ended up across the street. My phone vibrated—it was Holly. Her heaving voice came at me loud and close over the truck's speakers.

"Missy was here," she said.

It took me a sec to comprehend what I'd heard. Frantic, I glanced out the window to see if Van Gundy was in the area. He was near the emergency room entrance, talking to a beat cop.

"Are you okay?"

"I don't know. I think she was trying to break into the house. Dave, I'm shaking."

"How do you know it was her?"

"Because her picture was on television."

"Right. Hang on."

Steeling myself, I pulled into traffic. The police had cordoned off the area where the crazy dead patient lay. As I drove past, Van Gundy watched me with a curious expression. Stupidly, I waved.

"Dave?" I had forgotten my wife was there.

"I'm coming home. Are you somewhere safe?"

"The basement. I don't know if she found a way in—I'm scared to check."

Her breath came out in short, choppy bursts. There was a tremolo in her voice, and I imagined her frightened eyes. I tried to concentrate. The cops in Tres Marias were notorious. I needed to make sure not to speed.

"I called 911," she said. "But they kept me on hold forever. They said on the news there's trouble everywhere. What's happening?"

"I don't know, babe."

I was happy no cops were available to respond. How do you explain a strange woman attacking your wife for no reason? The rest of the way, I tried comforting Holly. I told her how much I loved her. Though heartfelt, the words sounded tinny, like music through dime-store speakers. Everywhere, sirens blared. It was as if Tres Marias had gone mad. I thought of Jim and that surgery-gone-wrong piece of work at the hospital. What if more of these freaks—what else could you call them—went on a rampage and overran the town?

"I'm in front of the house," I said and disconnected.

I found a tire iron in the back of my truck and ran to the front door. There were scratches on the casing and the door itself. It looked like someone had tried to claw their way in. I grabbed the door handle. Locked.

Holding the tire iron like a weapon, I inched past the front windows and made my way to the back gate. It was open part-way. The hinges squealed as I pushed on it and entered the backyard. The glass door leading to the den was intact. I tried it—also locked. Using my key, I let myself in the front door.

I trotted down to the basement, calling Holly's name.

Scraping noises were followed by the sound of the door unlocking. When I walked in, my wife was clutching a baseball bat. Though it was summer, the room felt cold. One bare incandescent light hung from the ceiling. Its glow cast harsh shadows, making the atmosphere even more unnerving.

All that was down here were the washer and dryer, the water heater, an old sofa, and boxes of my books and other stuff. Holly had blocked the door and covered the narrow windows with newspaper. I moved past the barricade and went to her. Dropping the bat, she fell into my arms.

"I was so scared," she said.

I kissed her head and held her. As we stood in an embrace, I heard scratching noises by the windows. Holly started to scream, and I covered her mouth.

"Go upstairs," I said. "It's okay—everything's locked."

When I handed her the bat, there was an odd look on her face. It was as if she saw me as a stranger and not her husband. I waited as she climbed the stairs. Clutching the tire iron, I went to the hopper windows and listened. Nothing. Taking a breath, I reached up and pulled back the newspaper.

Missy glared at me, her unblinking eyes gray and filmy. Her mouth was bloody from a recent kill. An ear-piercing shriek assaulted my ears, and I fell backwards onto the floor. When I recovered, she was gone.

As I recalled the events at the ranger station, one thought played in my head. I was wrong—she hadn't gotten away unscathed. Somehow, she had managed to kill Jim, but not before he infected her. I imagined her somewhere in the forest, bled out and dead. And then suddenly, turning—into what I didn't know.

And now, she was coming for us.

CHAPTER
EIGHTEEN

HOLLY SAT at the kitchen table while I made us tea. The bat lay at her feet. I decided not to tell her what I saw in the basement.

"I saw her through the front windows," she said. "It was like she had the jimmies, only worse. And her skin color—it was awful."

I'm no scientist, but we were way past the jimmies. The woman at the hospital, for instance. What if she was infected at the time of the operation? There would have been no way to tell from the blood tests. And if she'd died on the operating table from a Lap-Band procedure gone wrong? *One of them is alive!*

I handed my wife a cup. "Did she say anything?"

"She tried to. It was like she couldn't form the words."

I thought about how Jim had attempted to communicate with me when I went to his house. "Was she injured?"

"I don't— Wait. Her arm was torn open, but there wasn't any blood."

I sat next to her and took her hand. She let me hold it

until she used both hands to drink her tea. I pretended it was nothing.

"You were right," I said. "We need to get out of here."

"I shouldn't have called 911—I didn't think. Now they'll find out about you and that devil woman."

"This is all my fault. Did you ask your mom if we can stay with her?"

She was suddenly distant. But it was her face that said it all. She hated me. Cheating on her was one thing, but Missy tried to kill her. I had brought this evil down on both of us— me. The person she'd bet everything on. As she pursed her lips, I prepared myself.

"I've decided to drive to Mt. Shasta alone," she said. "I'll call Fred to let him know."

"Okay." Nothing else I said would stop her.

Our tea untouched, we remained that way. Galaxies apart. I listened to the ticking of the singing-bird clock I'd bought her for our first anniversary. Any minute, birdsong would startle us. I had to do something, if only as a penance.

"I'll follow you to your mom's to make sure you're safe."

"You don't—"

"I want to."

"You should find someplace to stay," she said. "For your own safety."

I touched her warm hand, but she withdrew it. Would I ever see her again? I wanted Holly more than anything. And I would do anything to protect her—from Missy or anyone else who tried to harm her. But it was what I had done that put my wife in danger in the first place. Climbing into Missy's bed that first time had lost me everything and left behind a one-way ticket to hell.

What's that saying—*bad things happen to good people*? It's not true. It's bad people doing bad things to themselves and others. Or people who are more stupid than bad. Me, I was somewhere in the middle.

I didn't think I was bad, just stupid. What scared me was the belief that bad people can become good if they want to, but stupid people can't become smart. They continue living out their pathetic lives, hurting others along the way till they're killed, or they die.

"I need to pack," she said and left the room.

CHAPTER
NINETEEN

IT WAS an hour to Holly's mom's house. As I got on the freeway, a blue-and-white highway patrol helicopter hovered over an industrial section of town. More trouble. I stayed behind Holly's Prius all the way to Mt. Shasta. She had tried again to leave by herself, but I refused to let her.

After her dad died, her mom sold their home in Tres Marias and bought a cabin not far from the lake. They called them cabins, but in reality, they were townhomes in a community called Shasta Heights. Thirty had been completed before the builder declared bankruptcy. Holly's mom got hers at a bank auction, paying cash.

Seeing the lake shimmering through the trees reminded me of the last time I was here with Jim. It was warm, and there were a lot of boats pulling people on water skis. No one had any idea what was happening in Tres Marias, and that was a good thing. It meant the virus hadn't spread beyond our community.

Holly didn't tell her mother what I had done. Instead, she explained that waves of random violence had made the town unsafe, and I felt she would be better off up here. Her mom bought it. She was a plainspoken woman who'd worked hard all her life and took everything at face value.

"Nice to see you, Dave," she said.

She had never liked me all that much because of the drinking. But as I walked in carrying my wife's bags, I could see she was making an effort. Sometimes, it was hard to understand her because most of her teeth were missing. Holly told me once that whenever a tooth fell out, her mother would toss it into a mason jar with her daughter's baby teeth.

"Good to see you, too, Irene."

Knowing my wife didn't want me around, I planned to go straight home. But she informed me that, for appearance's sake, I had better hang around till morning. Later, I could make up an excuse about having to work.

"I didn't bring a change of clothes," I said.

"After Mom goes to bed, you can sleep in the living room."

There's no better way for a wife to punish a husband than to make him sleep away from her. Most men are incapable of handling rejection, and I was no exception. I tried looking on the bright side. At least we were under the same roof.

"What's this I hear about gangs and violence?" Irene said at dinner.

Holly rolled her eyes. "Mom, that's not what I—"

I patted my wife's hand. "It's not like that. It's these random incidents. No one seems to know why people are acting out."

"According to Evie Champagne, Tres Marias has gotten awfully strange. That used to be such a nice little town. Seems like nothing is nice anymore."

Holly began clearing the table. "You shouldn't believe what you hear on TV."

"I like Evie Champagne," Irene said. "She seems honest."

Like any typical family, we played Scrabble. Around nine,

Holly's mom went to bed. My wife and I stayed up watching *Mrs. Doubtfire*. Neither of us wanted to talk about what lay ahead. We sat at opposite ends of the sofa, pretending to laugh at Robin Williams in a wig.

After the movie ended, I tried talking to her. "I love you, Holly, and I'm—"

"Don't," she said.

She opened the French doors leading to a small backyard. The forest lay beyond that. Hoping we could discuss things, I joined her. She didn't object. There was a full moon. A cool breeze blew in from the lake, bringing the smell of pine and lilac. Great-horned owls hooted in the trees. Standing beside her, I fought the urge to take her hand.

"I wish..." she said. "I wish you'd never told me. Why couldn't you have kept it as your dirty little secret? We could've raised our children and grown old together. And I would die believing you'd been faithful to me. That's the life I wanted."

"Babe, I—"

"But I can't have that life now because you killed it. I gave up so much for you. And I thought that if I loved you enough, you would change—I was so stupid. All this time, I thought it was the drinking that was the problem. I never realized it was something deeper."

"I don't want to lose you."

"You can go to hell."

Seeing what was coming, I let it happen. She slapped me as hard as she could. My face stinging, I listened to her crying as she went up the stairs. Though it had turned cold, I remained outside, trying to think of a way to fix this—to redeem myself. I needed forgiveness. A piercing shriek shredded the blackness of the night. Shivering, I went inside and tried to sleep, but a voice chided me. *Sleep is for babies and old people. And the dead.*

I left early, having gotten little rest. All night, I waited for a call from the police saying I needed to tell them where I was that day because they had tied me to Jim's death. As I got ready to leave, Holly came to the front door and put something I recognized in my hand. It was the gold crucifix she had received on her First Communion and still wore. I'm not religious—eight years of Catholic school had seen to that. But she believed in the power of prayer. Was she trying to save me?

"I'm going to hell, remember?" I said.

"I want you to take it. For protection."

"In case something bad happens?"

"You might wanna start praying, too. And go to Confession."

"I'll text you when I get back," I said, but she was already on the stairs.

Irene was in the kitchen, cleaning up the breakfast dishes. She looked at me in the strangest way, like she knew. It made sense. I was the husband who was unworthy of her little girl. And she was right.

On the way back, shrill sirens forced me to pull over. Police cars, an ambulance, and a fire truck sped towards the lake. Neighbors came out of their houses to see what was happening. I assumed there had been a boating accident.

"Why else would they be in such a hurry?" I said.

CHAPTER
TWENTY

I DIDN'T HAVE to be at work till ten, and I dreaded returning to an empty house. So I decided to get off the 5 and take the scenic route through the forest. There would be plenty of time to shower and change clothes. I thought I saw Jim stumbling along the backroad with Perro trotting behind. Wishful thinking.

Up ahead, an old bridge spanned a dry riverbed. The day was already warm, and I rolled down my window. Below, some guy was running over the rocks and weeds. Dressed in hiking shorts and a straw hat, he looked scared. When I saw the camera bouncing off his chest, I guessed he was a tourist who had managed to enrage a mama bear. I pulled over to get a better look. It was hard to tell his age as he wheezed with each step. When he saw me, he tripped and did a faceplant, screaming and swearing.

A group of around eight or ten men and women charged after him. Their arms were outstretched like he'd stolen their wallets. Though they moved fast, their bodies didn't look right. Twitching and snarling, their eyes unfocused, they shrieked like deranged birds. It was the most awful sound I'd ever heard—the same sound Missy had made. And they were getting closer.

"Hey, get up!" I said.

The man looked at me, then at his pursuers. Adrenaline must have kicked in because, like a torsion spring, he shot to his feet and took off again, blood streaming down his face.

Though my brain told me to get out of there, I wanted to help him. Driving to the end of the bridge, I got out and waited. The tourist made it to the riverbank. He tried scrambling up the side but kept slipping on the dry grass and loose gravel. Behind him, the mob gained on him. I pointed at a beaten path through the weeds.

He stumbled down a ways and started climbing. I thought he might have a shot. But one of those crazies was on him now—a woman in her fifties. She had short gray hair, swollen ankles, and JCPenney summer clothes. And a raw, vicious mouth.

Talking gibberish, she grabbed his foot and tried pulling him back. He screamed. I maneuvered halfway down and reached out to take his wrist, but I was too late. The others dragged him back like lions bringing down a wildebeest. After that, the real horror began.

In a blood fever, they tore at his eyes and tongue—anything soft. It astonished me the way they moved as one. Like razors, their fingers ripped through his clothes to get to the swollen, hairy abdomen. And the whole time, the tourist kept looking at me, his expression a wordless question—*Why?*

I stood frozen on the dirt path, unable to comprehend what was happening. When his intestines spilled out, I ran to my truck and shot down the road like a cannonball, narrowly avoiding a boulder.

My hands shaking from the adrenaline, I made a U-turn and headed over the bridge towards the freeway. By now, the mob had dispersed, and there was no sign of the tourist.

As I left the forest, someone blasted their horn. A white Lexus SUV was coming straight at me. Thinking fast, I swerved. The vehicle missed me by inches and ran into a tree. Stunned but unhurt, I stopped.

I ran to see if I could help. Peering through the window, I found an older man sitting behind the spent airbag, semiconscious. Blood streamed from his forehead. It was my friend, Isaac Fallow.

"Hey," I said. "Can you move?"

After several tries, I got his door open. I unfastened his seat belt and walked him to my truck.

"My medical kit," he said.

Returning to the Lexus, I opened the liftgate and found a large black plastic tub among old newspapers, file folders, and crushed diet soda cans. A chorus of shrieks came out of the forest as I placed the container in the truck bed.

"Dave, hurry!"

The mob was behind us, maybe fifty feet away. I climbed into the truck and took off. Someone lurched into the road in front of me. It was the tourist. He was gored from neck to groin, organs and intestines dangling off him like meat ornaments. Too terrified to think, I ran him down.

"What have I done?"

I hit the brakes and checked the rearview mirror. The victim sat up as if nothing had happened. Though his legs were crushed, he kept crawling. Isaac turned around to look. The mob was almost on us.

"Drive." My friend's voice was calm.

My thoughts were all jumbled. I had forgotten how Van

Gundy put down that woman patient at the hospital. Was I doing it again—leaving someone to die?

"Maybe we should try to—"

"Just drive," Isaac said. "He's already dead."

CHAPTER
TWENTY-ONE

IN THE EMERGENCY ROOM, I texted Holly to let her know I was back. I didn't mention what happened in the forest. It took her forever to respond. And when she did, she one-worded me with a *K*.

There was no way I would make it to work on time, so I called Fred. I told him I wasn't feeling well and promised to come in later. Except for the accident, I hadn't taken a sick day since I started there. He knew it, too, and didn't challenge me.

An hour later, Isaac walked out, wearing a white adhesive bandage on his forehead. Besides a few bruised ribs and a sore neck, he was fine. I drove him to the Tip Top Café for coffee. Two doors down from the Beehive, this place had become a refuge since I quit drinking. Though the proximity created a temptation the AA people would disapprove of, it gave me comfort, knowing I could be so close to that den of pain without allowing myself to set foot inside.

The Tip Top was old-school, and tourists loved it. It opened in the early sixties, before the British Invasion. The booths were made of shiny red vinyl. The menus were trifold and laminated. It was a great place to get a burger and a shake. A soda fountain featured banana splits and fresh cherry pie. Each booth had a jukebox, and for a quarter, you could listen to Elvis singing "Can't Help Falling in Love."

For a time, Isaac and I stared at the world through the plate-glass window. Outside, life went on. A mother walked past, holding a child by the hand and laughing. A postal worker delivered mail to a shop owner. A teenage boy kissed his girlfriend as she leaned against a streetlight. No one had the jimmies.

"What were you doing in the forest?" I said.

He spoke into his coffee cup. "Research. Trying to prove this isn't happening."

"What is happening?"

"I don't know, but it's bad." He had that same haunted look as Van Gundy at the hospital.

"What did you mean when you said the guy I hit was already dead?"

He set down his cup and folded his hands like he was giving a consultation. "I'm of the opinion that what you hit was no longer a person."

I told him about the Lap-Band patient at the hospital—how she had attacked the staff. And what the cop did to stop her. My friend didn't seem surprised.

"And Jim Stanley?" I said.

Isaac had performed the autopsy, and what he discovered was troubling. Van Gundy had told him about other similar cases. And that's when my friend came up with an explanation. People who got infected died, but they didn't stay dead. Something—an unknown factor—revived them. And when they came back, they were no longer the same.

He pushed away his cup and wept into his hands. I didn't know what to do. Isaac had always been strong and wise. I decided it was better not to say anything. A clueless server walked over with a coffee pot in each hand.

"Anyone need a refill?"

I tilted my head towards my friend. She left and said something to one of the other servers. Wiping his eyes with a napkin, Isaac gave me an apologetic smile.

"About the accident," he said. "I must've panicked."

"Don't worry about it. I want to get back to what we were discussing. How is it possible that dead people are—"

"It's not possible—that's the point."

"Okay, but say it is. The jimmies was only the first phase. You treated those patients, right? Did anyone improve?"

"No way to tell. They never returned for a follow-up. They might've recovered, or—"

"They died and came back as something inhuman."

"And now we're talking about a new variant. I called the CDC over a week ago. They were supposed to send someone out to investigate."

I got up and left cash on the table. "I'll drive you home."

A man in a cheap suit stared at us as we walked out. He looked feverish, and he was drooling. Isaac ignored him.

It was a short ride to my friend's house. Two police cars were parked on the street. A man and woman and their teenage daughter waited at the curb, looking helpless. I pulled into the driveway, and we walked over.

"Kate, what happened?" Isaac said.

The woman looked at us with red-rimmed eyes. "Someone attacked Patty's husband in their backyard. We're waiting for the ambulance."

Another woman, who I assumed was Patty, joined us. "Dr. Fallow, thank goodness. They won't let me see my husband."

"Give me a minute." He grabbed his medical bag from my truck.

"This mob attacked him for no reason," Patty said when he returned. "I can't understand it. All he was doing was watering the lawn."

A police officer was making notes when Isaac walked up to him. "Hey, Dr. Fallow."

"Did you see who did it?"

"Naw, they're long gone. We got a couple of officers combing the neighborhood."

"I'd like to see the patient. Dave, you might want to stay here." I gave him a look, and he rolled his eyes. "Fine."

We made our way around the side of the house and entered the backyard through a redwood gate. A second cop checked all the doors and windows. We found the victim sitting in the middle of the yard. His wife went to him and, crouching, took his hand.

Other than the bites on his arms, the guy didn't look too bad. A German shepherd sat next to him, panting. Isaac put on latex gloves and, kneeling, examined the patient.

"How are you feeling, Sal?"

"Shaken up, I guess." He patted his dog's head. "If ol' Atticus hadn't come to my rescue, I don't know what would've happened."

"These are some nasty bites."

After cleaning and bandaging the wounds, my friend gave the patient a tetanus shot.

"Who are you?" the first cop said to me.

"Dave Pulaski. Friend of Isaac's."

"Oh?"

I didn't like the tool's attitude. When the ambulance arrived, Sal protested, saying he was fine. But Isaac insisted he go in for blood tests. Patty climbed into the back with her husband. For some reason, Officer Dickhead had a hard-on for me and followed me to the street.

"I need you to show me some identification," he said.

Side-eying my friend, I handed over my driver's license. Another cop examined my truck's front bumper and waved his partner over.

"Hey, Norm. Check this out."

"In a minute."

I felt sick as Officer Norm ran my information through the computer. After a short time, he returned. His expression was hostile.

"There's a wanted notice on you," he said. "I have to take you in."

Isaac answered before I could. "What for?"

"A detective wants to ask him some questions, is all."

My friend took me aside. "Don't tell them anything without an attorney present. Give me your keys. I need to go to the hospital. I'll meet you at the police station as soon as I can."

After thanking him, I got into the back of the cruiser and stared at my feet. The people on the sidewalk looked at me like I was a criminal. I had never been arrested, not even in my darkest drinking days. And let me tell you, it's not a pleasant feeling. There's a sense of unreality to it—like you're dreaming it was someone else's screwup.

The two officers stared at my front bumper. Joining them, Isaac said something and pointed. Though I couldn't hear, I could only imagine what the cops were saying about the blood. Then, they laughed. My friend walked past the cruiser and gave me a thumbs-up on the sly.

A coward and a murderer, I thought, as the officers climbed into the front seat. Holly already hated me. Now she'd for sure be scared of me, too. Could this day get any worse?

"That was some raccoon," Officer Norm said. "He must've been huge."

I couldn't believe Isaac had lied to them. "Yeah, I think he was on steroids."

"You may want to hose that off so you don't get pulled over again," the other cop said.

"Thanks, I will."

As we turned onto the main road, the dispatcher announced that a violent mob had overrun a convenience store. So far, two employees were dead.

"All units respond," she said.

Officer Norm looked at his partner. "What do we do? We're supposed to take this guy to the station."

"The store's on the way. Let's check it out."

The dispatcher's voice droned on with more details. Whatever was going on over there, it sounded hellish. I thought I heard her use the word *mayhem*.

The nameless cop looked at his partner. "You ever think about quitting?"

"Every damn day," Officer Norm said.

CHAPTER
TWENTY-TWO

WE ARRIVED at a wood structure with peeling green paint and faded cartoon advertisements for dancing slushies and hotdogs. Twenty or more police cruisers surrounded the convenience store, their light bars flashing. Dozens of cops with weapons crouched behind car doors. Overhead, the blades of a highway patrol helicopter raised clouds of debris. On the roof, store employees waved their arms, begging to be rescued. But from what? Then, I heard it—that awful sound I came to know as a death shriek.

Officer Norm let out a whistle. "Holy mother of hell."

An ABC7 Eyewitness News van was parked along the road. The reporter Evie Champagne forced her way through the police barricade, microphone in hand. Fearlessly, she covered the scene up close as her pudgy, bearded cameraman shot over-the-shoulder video. A cop—I think he was the police captain—blocked their path.

"I thought I made it clear to you people," he said. "Go home and let us do our jobs."

"We have a right to be here."

Without another word, he grabbed the camera and threatened to drop it on the ground.

"Hey!" Evie's sidekick said.

Another cop popped the cameraman in the head with his baton as Evie delivered an impressive string of obscenities. Cursing, her partner cradled his bleeding head.

The police dragged Evie and her cameraman to the news van. Flinging the side door open, they forced them inside—Tres Marias cops in all their glory. Instead of protecting people, they were more interested in preventing the story from making the evening news.

One stood guard to make sure the reporter and her companion didn't leave the van. After the captain left, I noticed Evie recording a video on her phone through the window. I had to give it to her, the woman had cojones.

The other cops remained behind their vehicle doors. Their weapons were pointed at... I didn't know what they were. Though they resembled people, they weren't right. Like those crazies in the forest, they climbed over one another, trying to reach something on the ground. I strained to see—it was someone's arm.

As the police watched with disgust, the freaks ripped a body to shreds and ate it with a hellish hunger, like carnivores at a pig roast. Eyes, ears, fingers, belly—anything they could grab. No one knew what to do. When the police captain waved at us, Officer Norm switched off the engine and looked at me in the rearview mirror.

"You stay here," he said.

"Wait, don't leave me!"

Drawing their weapons, he and his partner got out and joined the others as the unsated horde turned their attention to the cops.

"Halt!"

With lifeless eyes, they advanced. I wanted to run, but there was no way for me to escape. A gunshot startled me, and I pressed my face against the glass.

A man with a bad hairpiece turned sideways, a gaping hole in his chest. Shaking it off, he kept coming. Someone gave a new order, and a volley of gunfire riddled him. But it hardly made any difference. As bullets rained down on the horde, a round struck a woman in the head. She went down hard and didn't get up.

"Aim for the head!"

One by one, the flesh-eaters hit the ground, their faces blown to shit by the deafening gunfire from shotguns and .44 Magnums. What was happening was unreal. Incredibly, the horde was growing as cops got bit trying to reload. Lying on the ground, moaning and delirious, they stopped breathing. And then, they reanimated.

Afraid for my life, I called out. But no one heard me. A sudden crash sent beads of glass everywhere. As I turned, what used to be a convenience store employee reached for me through the shattered side window, his teeth dripping with gore. I moved as far away as I could.

Pushing against the door, I tried kicking the freak's arms away. But he managed to grab a foot and, with a powerful grip, began pulling me towards him. I screamed for help, and still, no one came. Then, as my leg passed through the window, my attacker's head exploded. A second later, Officer Norm peered through the opening, gripping his .44. Trembling, I drew my leg back inside.

"You okay?" the cop said.

All was quiet. The pungent smell of blood and gunpowder hung in the air. Every member of the horde was dead, including the infected cops. The helicopter was gone, and so was the news van.

Clinging to each other, the store employees on the roof stared at the carnage below. Many prayed. A police officer picked up a comrade's severed head and puked. The dispatcher had called it right. This was mayhem.

As I lay in the backseat, knowing I could have died, I wished I could talk to Isaac. Those who got bit were turning faster now. How long before everyone was infected?

"Thanks for saving my life," I said to Officer Norm.

CHAPTER
TWENTY-THREE

OFFICER NORM BROUGHT me to an interview room where Detective Van Gundy was already waiting. A dark green file folder lay on the desk. After closing the door, he signaled me to take a seat.

"Can I offer you something to drink?" he said.

I couldn't feel my legs. Doubling over, I vomited on the floor. The cop stepped over the sick and flung open the door.

"Can I get a mop and bucket in here?" He helped me up. "Let's find another room."

In a nondescript office, I sat in a metal-and-vinyl chair, holding a cup of tepid water. Van Gundy sat behind a desk, flipping through the papers inside the folder. Something was on his mind, and it wasn't me.

"I want to apologize for what happened," he said. "Those officers should've never put you in danger. With everything going on, not everyone is thinking right. What happened out there?"

I was about to answer when Isaac entered without knocking.

Irritated, the cop looked up. "Can I help you? Oh, Dr. Fallow. What can I do for you?"

"I came to see if I could be of assistance."

"Um, sure." Resigned, Van Gundy waited as my friend took a seat next to me.

"I was about to tell Mr. Pulaski that we recovered Ms. Soldado's phone in the woods and—"

"I knew her, okay?" I said.

Isaac frowned. "Son, you should really get yourself a lawyer."

"Don't you get it? It doesn't matter. None of it matters now."

The cop found the page he was looking for. "Her last text was to you. Want to explain why you didn't tell me the truth before?"

"Hang on a minute," my friend said. "Dave, I strongly advise you to—"

"Because I was cheating on my wife with Melyssa Soldado, okay? I didn't want anyone else to know."

"I see." Van Gundy made a note. "And your friend? How does he fit into all this?"

I gave him as much of the truth as I was going to. The detective would have to work for the rest.

"I don't know," I said. "He might've been jealous."

"Jealous." The cop side-eyed Isaac. "Her last text to you was..." He referred to the page he was holding. *You shouldn't have done that, Dave.* What shouldn't you have done?"

"No idea. Have you located her?"

"Someone saw a woman fitting her description wandering in the forest near where Ms. Soldado lives. They also reported that she was badly injured. We don't have any other leads at this time."

"So, are we done?"

He looked at the file again. We both knew he didn't have shit—at least, nothing he could charge me with. And adultery wasn't a crime in California. If he was hoping for a confession, he could forget it. I was saving that for the priest.

"For now," he said. "Don't leave town. I know that sounds cheesy, but seriously. I might have more questions later."

"I'm not going anywhere. I have to go to work."

As we left the office, Van Gundy said, "Mr. Pulaski? I understand your wife is not currently living with you."

"How did you— Never mind. I told her about Missy. She doesn't want to see me anymore."

"That's too bad. I'd like to interview her, though."

I tried not to react as he slid over a pen and paper.

"If you could jot down her address and a number where I can reach her."

The cop read what I had written. "She might forgive you. In time."

"You're probably right," I said.

I wanted to get home and shower, but Isaac insisted we discuss my situation. So we headed over to the Tip Top for coffee and pie. After placing our orders, I told him what happened at the convenience store. Like Van Gundy, he was horrified that the cops had deliberately put me in danger.

"They're turning faster," I said.

"Which means we're no longer dealing with the jimmies. How long before..."

"Minutes...seconds—I don't know."

"Until we can isolate the virus and study it, there's not much we can do."

"But there must be something—"

"In the meantime, you need an attorney." He wiped the olallieberry juice from his chin.

"Why?"

"Son, in addition to bringing babies into the world, I've been investigating homicides for going on thirty years. Looking at the medical evidence. Trying to guess at the killer's state of mind. Now, I'm not saying you murdered anyone. But what I see is a man with a big secret."

Listlessly, I stirred my coffee. "I'm not a bad person."

"Course not. But sometimes, we make mistakes, and other people end up paying the price."

"Missy is dead," I said.

"An eyewitness said she was injured. How can you be sure?"

"Because I was there, trying to talk sense into her. Jim came out of nowhere, and he wasn't right."

"You mean he was like those people on the bridge?"

"I'd seen him days earlier. He was, I don't know, out of it but not violent. When I touched him, he was ice cold. Smelled like something rotten. And he wasn't breathing. When he attacked us, he was like a rabid animal. Missy killed him, but not before he chewed her arm to shreds."

"And infected her. What were you doing this whole time?"

I couldn't look him in the eye. Instead, I gazed out the window, hoping for a distraction.

"You ran?" he said. "That's your secret?"

The truth hadn't set me free—I felt numb. "I should've helped her."

"Why didn't you explain all that to the detective?"

"Because I didn't want it getting out that...I'm a coward."

"You're human. And anyway, the truth always comes out eventually."

The last time we were here, it was Isaac who had lost it.

Now it was my turn. I tried choking back the guilt, but it was no use. Desperate to gain control, I dug a fork into my palm under the table. The sudden jolt of pain cleared my head.

"You okay?" Isaac said. "Look, I don't pretend to know what's happening in Tres Marias."

"I thought you said it was a virus."

"Sure. But the way it behaves doesn't make sense. Normally, pathogens don't turn their hosts into cannibals."

My phone vibrated—it was Holly. "I got a call from Detective Van Gundy."

"I need to take this," I said to Isaac and walked outside. Then to my wife, "I was going to call you. Did you speak to him?"

"I didn't know who it was, so I let it go to voicemail. He's going to ask me about what happened with Missy. What do I say?"

"The same thing I told him. I had an affair and admitted it to you."

"What about going to see her? They could call me as a witness in court."

"They can't make you testify against your husband. Anyway, he's fishing."

"I hate you for making me lie."

"Then tell him everything—I don't give a shit anymore."

After disconnecting, I found Isaac picking the seeds out of his teeth with a flat toothpick. "Everything okay?"

"Couldn't be better," I said.

CHAPTER
TWENTY-FOUR

WHILE DRIVING ISAAC HOME, I expected to see police cars and infected people, but the street was quiet. I followed him into his home office and found the walls covered with maps and sticky notes. His bag and medical kit lay on the floor next to piles of medical books and scientific journals.

"What's all this?" I said.

"I've been trying to put it all together to learn how the outbreak started." He walked over to a map. "The best I can figure, it began in the forest. Somewhere around here."

"How do you know?"

"I'm basing my theory on all the deaths in the area—both animal and human. Take a look at this spot." The place he'd circled in red looked familiar. It was near where Jim and I had crashed.

He pointed at a different spot. "Here's where that hunter found Sarah Champion. None of my patients had gone anywhere near the forest. All claimed they were bit by a stranger on the street or a family member."

"What if the first people to be infected had been in the forest, though?"

"The real question is what was the source of the infection?"

"Bats? Or some other animal?" I thought of Jim's dog coming after me the night of the accident. But somehow, this didn't feel like rabies. "When you performed the autopsy on Jim, were there any bite marks?"

"Not that I recall. Of course, the corpse was in pretty bad shape. Hang on."

Opening a file cabinet, Isaac pulled out a thick manila folder. He arranged a dozen or so photos on the floor. As he pored over the pictures with a magnifying glass, it hit me. When I drove Jim home, I noticed what might have been a bite mark on his hand.

I flipped through a few photos. "Do you have a closeup of his left hand?"

He searched through them. When he found the one he wanted, he started to pass it to me. But before I could take it, he peered at it through the magnifying glass.

"I'll be damned. How did I miss this? Guess I could blame these glasses or a lack of sleep."

He handed me the magnifying glass, and I squinted at the spot where he was pointing. There it was—a partially-healed bite mark.

"It doesn't look like a human did this," I said.

"It's definitely an animal—maybe a dog."

I thought about the night of the accident. Seeing Perro on the road, vicious and rabid. And the guy in the van who gave me a ride. I wondered why he kept asking if I'd gotten bit. When I told my friend, he returned to the map.

"Jim's dog may very well have had rabies and bit him," he

said. "But that doesn't explain what we're seeing now. The symptoms are different."

He indicated the red arrows he had drawn, radiating from a single point to beyond Tres Marias. It was anyone's guess how far the disease—if that's what you wanted to call it—had spread. I worried it might reach Mt. Shasta.

"What's happening with the CDC?" I said.

"I tried them again. They won't even take my calls."

"What happens when the police can no longer contain the situation?"

"You may have seen the highway patrol out in full force. I assume they'll send in the National Guard if the governor declares a state of emergency. There's a rumor that's about to happen."

"What are you going to do?"

"I'm driving up to San Francisco tonight to meet with an immunologist friend of mine." His phone rang, and he answered it. "Isaac Fallow. When? I'll be right there."

He disconnected and looked at me like his favorite aunt had died. "I need a ride to the hospital."

"I'd like to, but I should really—"

"I'm not asking," he said.

CHAPTER
TWENTY-FIVE

A POLICE CRUISER was parked outside the hospital when we arrived. Isaac and I went up to the office of the administrator. Dr. Vale was around my friend's age. With her was Isaac's neighbor Patty, who looked like she had been crying. I wondered where her husband was.

"Isaac, thank you for coming," the administrator said. "Who's this?"

"Dave Pulaski. He's with me. Where's the patient?"

She glanced at Patty. "I'm afraid we had to lock him up for everyone's safety."

"Tell me what happened after the ambulance brought him."

"He seemed fine. We drew blood, and an ER doctor examined him. I had to step away, so I'm not sure what happened after that. Patty?"

Sal's wife gave us a self-conscious smile. "He said he felt tired and wanted to rest. I went to get a cup of coffee, and when I returned, there were all kinds of people in there."

"The doctor had called a code," the administrator said. "It

happened so fast. One minute, he was conscious. And then..."

Isaac took her arm. "Eileen, listen to me—this is very important. Did Sal bite anyone?"

"The doctor and two orderlies."

"Find them and isolate them."

"They've already gone home."

"Give the police their addresses and ask them to bring them back on my orders."

"But they haven't done anything."

Let's hope they don't," he said.

I remained with Dr. Vale and Patty at the end of the hallway leading to the operating rooms. Isaac and two police officers approached a janitor's closet. One cop waved Patty over and gave her an instruction. Nervous, she pressed her hand against the door.

"Sal? It's me, honey—your wife."

An ungodly moan escaped the closet, followed by an ear-piercing screech. Backing away, Patty almost fell over. The sounds of inhuman tearing and wailing turned my blood cold. Gasping, the administrator held onto my arm.

Isaac signaled Patty to get out of the way and positioned a cop on either side of him. Saying nothing, he pointed at their holsters, and they drew their weapons. His hand trembling, my friend turned the key and, with a labored breath, flung open the door.

The neighbor who had been attacked only a few hours earlier stared at us. His left arm hung limply, gnawed to the bone. His face was livid, and the gray, unfeeling eyes were dull and cloudy. His lips stretching into a grimace, he reared.

Patty screamed as her husband lunged at the men. Everyone scattered. A cop tried aiming his weapon, but Sal was too quick. Before anyone could stop him, he was on the officer, biting off his fingers and goring his face. The victim's ululating voice drowned in a gurgle of choking blood.

Losing all sense of reality, Patty tried going to her husband. Isaac and I restrained her as best we could.

"Shoot him!" my friend said to the other cop.

Patty pummeled my chest. "No!"

The officer squeezed off a couple rounds, striking the attacker in the back. Unaffected, Patty's husband turned around. An eyestalk hung from his teeth.

"Go for the head!" I said.

Patty continued to fight us. "You're not killing him!"

The cop fired three times. Chunks of bloody brain matter splattered the beige wall. Shuddering, Sal dropped to his knees and collapsed on the floor. Crumpling in a heap, Patty tried crawling to her dead husband. It took three of us to hold her.

Her voice was a whimper now. "Sal. Dear God, what is happening?"

Isaac examined the injured police officer. As he lay there bleeding out, he mumbled like a frightened child. My friend turned to Dr. Vale, who looked at him, uncomprehending.

"We need to isolate him," he said. "Eileen, now!"

It was dark when we left the hospital—too late to pick up Isaac's rental car at Enterprise. Instead, I drove him home. He grabbed his bag from the backseat and came around to the driver's side.

"I appreciate the ride," he said.

"Any time. I wish I could've done more to help."

"I want you to listen to me. Get away from here while you still can. Join your wife."

"She's done with me. Besides, Van Gundy ordered me not to leave the area."

"The cops are going to have their hands full. Trust me and do as I say."

"Don't you understand? I can't see her anymore. Shit. What am I going to do?"

"Go be with Holly."

I wiped my eyes. "I'd better stay here and figure something out."

"They might arrest you. I suppose you could tell them the truth and hope for the best."

"It was stupid."

"Stupid doesn't begin to describe it," he said. "Look at it this way. If you had saved the girl, you'd be a hero. Next time, all right? Take care of yourself."

After Isaac left me, I remained in the driveway with the motor running. He was a good friend—the best. I was confident he wouldn't say anything to Van Gundy. But if I was arrested and the case went to trial, they would call him in to testify. I'd bet my left nut Isaac had never lied to a jury in his life. I wondered if Holly ever told the detective the truth. If she had, I was screwed. Unless all hell broke loose—not something I wished for.

Still, an outbreak would be just the thing to get me out of my troubles.

CHAPTER
TWENTY-SIX

I HATED HOLLY. All I wanted was to make everything better so things could return to the way they were. Kind of hard when you're a cheating, cowardly piece of crap. And let's not forget the recently dead feasting on the living. But how was that my fault? I wasn't conflicted or anything.

Though it was late, the streets were filled with people moving numbly down sidewalks like over-medicated mental patients. The jimmies? No, worse. Blue-and-red lights flashed as overworked police officers randomly stopped the moody drifters. Beaming flashlights in their faces, the cops tried to get these unaware ghosts to answer their questions. And when they did, I realized they weren't infected. Maybe they had witnessed something gruesome. A parent mauled. A child torn to pieces. There were hundreds of them, and all with that same vacant look.

I pulled into my driveway and noticed the front door was ajar. I was positive I'd locked it before driving to Mt. Shasta. Panicked, I walked around to the truck bed. The tire iron was missing—I had left it in the basement. I picked up a four-way lug wrench. Better than nothing. Pushing open the door, I flicked on the lights and peered inside. My gut told me to run.

There was blood everywhere—the walls and furniture were smeared with it. And the smell. It was the stench of meat rot and excrement. Cold-sweating, I sucked down my bile and scanned the room, looking for any kind of movement. I thought I heard something and pivoted. The neighborhood was deserted—not even a stray dog.

Passing through the living room, I made my way to the stairs, turning on more lights as I went. There were animal carcasses everywhere—dogs, cats, and raccoons. All had been gored. A heart-stopping banshee scream broke the stillness. Turning, I found Missy standing between me and the front door.

Her complexion was gray, her dark hair matted with twigs and crawling insects. Her fingers were long and pointy, with bone jutting through the torn fingertips. She smelled like a charnel house, even from where I was standing. With her black tongue flicking, she narrowed her flat eyes at me and gave me a hideous grin. I thought I would pass out.

I didn't know what to do—she had me. When I tried hitting her with the lug wrench, she caught it and, with a wrestler's strength, tore it from my hands and flung it at the window, shattering the glass. I bolted past her and tripped on a dead dog ripped in half. She reached out to grab me. Scrambling away, I got to my feet. As I tried again for the door, she did something extraordinary.

Like a superhuman broad jumper, she leaped, landing on my back. I didn't know how to get her off. Her reeking body generated no warmth. Terrified of getting bit, I spun around as she clung to me. I managed to stumble into the kitchen, certain she'd sink her fangs into my neck at any second. In desperation, I drove us backwards to the sink, where I heard a crack. Her grip loosened, allowing me to free myself. I stood in the doorway, gulping air. She tried straightening up, but something was wrong. With a hard twist, she fell into a sitting position.

Unalive and unbreathing, she stared at me with doll's eyes. She opened her mouth wide and let out a death shriek that sent me reeling in terror. I wanted to scream with her. Instead, I bolted out the front door and climbed into my truck.

A police cruiser screeched to a stop, blocking the driveway. Van Gundy's beige sedan pulled up behind it. The detective and the officer approached the driver's door and, with weapons drawn, yanked it open. I couldn't speak. My teeth were chattering, and I was breathing so hard I thought my lungs would explode.

"What happened?" Van Gundy said.

I pointed at the front door. "Inside... Missy..."

Drawing their weapons, the men entered the house. I expected to hear the death shriek again, but the only sound was the chatter on the police radio. As I tried to calm down, I could smell Missy's vile scent on me. There's this old Donovan song, "Catch the Wind." My mother used to sing it to me when I was little. As I mouthed the words, my breathing returned to normal.

Time passed to the rhythm of my stuttering heart. After long minutes, Van Gundy and the beat cop appeared at the front door. I climbed out and walked towards them on shaky legs. I had hoped to hear gunshots as they put Missy out of her misery. No such luck.

"She's not in the house," the beat cop said. "Must've gone out the back."

"I'm so glad you guys showed up."

Van Gundy put away his gun. "A neighbor called 911. I

was on my way home. When I heard it was your house, I came over. Did she bite you?"

"Tried to."

"Did a pretty good job of redecorating, though."

"She's one of them now," I said.

The beat cop gave me a crooked smile. *"Them?"*

"The undead—whatever you want to call them." I couldn't believe this idiot. Was he new in town? "There were maggots in her eyes. I'm telling you, she's dead."

The beat cop drove off, probably to have a good laugh with his buddies over beers. Van Gundy accompanied me while I threw some clothes in a bag. There was no way I was ever staying here again. What if Holly was on her way home? Angry as I was at her, I didn't want her to see this. I texted her, warning her to keep away from the house.

"Don't worry," the detective said. "We'll find her."

"Thanks again." I was pretty sure he was talking out of his ass.

"Why did she come after you?"

"I don't know."

"Still with the lies?"

I decided to tell him—hell with it. "She hates me because I wouldn't leave my wife."

"Makes sense, although hate doesn't seem to cover it."

As Van Gundy drove away, I thought about how to describe Missy's feelings towards me. He was right—*hate* didn't cut it. Backing out of my driveway, I took a last look at the place where Holly and I had been happy once. Knowing I would never return, I imagined setting the house on fire.

Better to burn it to the ground, along with my past.

CHAPTER
TWENTY-SEVEN

I HADN'T SLEPT in more than a day. There were plenty of cheap rooms at the Pine Nut Motel, located near the railroad tracks in a crappy part of town. After what happened at the house, I was amazed I wasn't guzzling beer by the barrel. So I had to laugh when I saw the 7-Eleven next door, with enough alcohol to help me forget my troubles for a good, long while.

After a shower and a change of clothes, I collapsed on top of the coverlet and closed my eyes. Soon, vivid images of Missy plagued me till I fell into a dreamless sleep.

When I awoke, it was late afternoon. I called Fred at Staples. He wasn't too pleased that I never showed up. I made up some excuse, promising to get over there right away and work till closing. That seemed to mollify him.

"This isn't like you, Dave." There was genuine concern in his voice. "Everything okay? How's Holly? Really hated losing her."

"Me, too," I said.

Fred was the kind of guy who took failure personally. He thought everything that didn't come out right in his or anyone else's life reflected poorly on him. For example, he tried to convince a new employee to stop smoking. Through sheer nagging, he got the guy to cut down to a pack a day. But when it came time to quit, the ungrateful little shit told Fred to go screw himself and walked out on the job.

My manager was devastated. Over and over, he would analyze the confrontation, pleading with the rest of us to tell him what he'd done wrong. Had he gone too far? Was he insensitive to an employee's needs? I think, deep down, all Fred Lumpkin wanted in life was to be liked.

Stacey, a pretty cashier, advised him not to worry. She had two years of community college under her belt. And in her learned twenty-year-old's opinion, the guy was an asshat who didn't know what was good for him. Fred seemed to accept this explanation, but I doubt it made him feel any better.

Starving, I stopped off at La Adelita for a couple soft pork tacos. It was almost six when I got to Staples. Part of the front door was smashed. The glass had been cleaned up, and plywood covered the hole. Fred greeted me as I walked in.

"What happened?" I said.

"Some weirdo. Went through the glass like it wasn't even there."

"Anyone else hurt?"

He waved his bandaged hand at me. "I called 911. The ambulance took the poor guy away. He was pretty wound up, I gotta tell you. You better get over to your station. Copiers are acting up again, and we have print jobs up the yin-yang."

"What about you?"

"Oh, I cut my hand on the stupid glass. Paramedic gave me a tetanus shot and fixed me right up."

Typical Fred—downplaying the incident so as not to worry the rest of us. What a martyr. But what if the perpetrator was sick and his blood had spilled onto the glass? That would mean Fred might be infected. All we knew was that if someone got bit, the virus would infect them through their blood. Fred had cut his hand.

"Are you sure you're okay?" I said.

"I'm fine—a little tired. Guess I lost more blood than I thought."

He walked stiffly over to a cash register. Shit, did this guy have the jimmies already? Instead of dwelling on the situation, I decided to get to work. Twenty minutes later, my manager announced he was going to the break room to lie down, saying he felt funny.

"It's kind of like a fever," he said. "And there's this buzzing in my ears."

He limped to the restroom at the back of the store. I had to pee anyway and followed him in. I watched him walk into a stall and vomit.

"Shit!" His voice sounded an octave higher.

I swung out the door to see. Woozy, he straightened up and wiped his mouth. Whatever he upchucked, the water in the toilet bowl was black. It reminded me of what Jim had puked up when he came to my house that first night.

"You need a doctor," I said.

"Naw. Going to lie down awhile. I'll be fine. Let me know if you need me."

An hour later, Stacey came running into the copy center, scared shitless.

"There's something wrong with Fred! H-he's not breathing!"

"Keep your voice down." I looked to see if any customers had heard.

In the break room, our manager lay motionless on the

brown Naugahyde sofa. His skin looked gray under the fluorescent lights. I found a pair of the plastic gloves we used to change the toner in the laser printers. Afraid to get too close, I checked his eyes and listened for breathing.

"Call 911," I said.

Stacey pulled out her phone and dialed. Suddenly, Fred sat up straight and blinked like we weren't even there.

"Fred? You okay, buddy? You gave us a scare."

As the cashier waited on hold for the 911 operator, he moved his mouth unnaturally. It was like he'd awakened to find that he had these things called jaws. When he tried in vain to say something, I knew we were losing him.

"We're calling the paramedics. You're going to be—"

He took a weak, angry swipe at my head, and I jumped back. His gaze settled on the girl.

"Stacey, get out of here."

But she was frozen, unable to comprehend what was happening. I grabbed her by the shoulders and made her look at me.

"You need to leave," I said.

Snapping out of it, she ran. After another feeble attempt to claw me, my manager stopped and looked around. The brightness of the ceiling lights seemed to bother him. Frustrated at his inability to communicate, he ground his teeth. I could hear bone scraping against bone. A tooth broke, and he spat out the bloody pieces.

The urge to run away was overpowering. The only thing keeping me going was the thought that I might be able to help Stacey and the others. I scanned the room, looking for a weapon. Coffee maker, water cooler, five-gallon plastic water bottles. And a push broom.

The broom wasn't much. But it might make the difference between life and eternal darkness.

CHAPTER
TWENTY-EIGHT

THE BROOM HANDLE felt light as I gripped it with both hands. The thing that was no longer Fred watched me as if I were an actor in a play. He seemed unaware of any threat. Outside, Stacey screamed. Then someone grabbed me from behind. I tried getting away, but they had a firm lock on my head. My attacker wasn't breathing. When I saw the hand—bone sticking out through ripped fingertips—I knew it was Missy.

I dropped to my knees and rolled to one side. She looked at me the way a cat watches a mouse. How had she gotten into the store without anyone noticing? On my feet now, I held the broom handle in front of me like a lightsaber. What happened next was incomprehensible.

Missy called to Fred using short, piercing chirps. When his ears pricked, she directed her dead eyes at me. Fred came at me like a linebacker in sudden death. Using my makeshift weapon, I pushed him back. Outside, a siren blared. Two paramedics rushed in with Stacey.

"Watch out—they're infected!" I said.

Too late. Missy swiped a razor-like claw at a paramedic's

face, ripping it half off. Wailing, he fell back with blood gushing everywhere. Stupidly, the other one tried grabbing the attacker. That's when she and Fred went after him. With the cool efficiency of dire wolves, they went to work, starting with his throat.

"What's happening!" Stacey said.

I had to get us out of that room. As I moved past, Missy latched onto my leg and sank her teeth into my shoe. But the bite didn't penetrate the leather. I kicked her in the face and grabbed Stacey. We ran.

When I shouted for everyone in the store to get out, the customers didn't know what to think. Panicked, they tried plowing through the inner exit door. A woman cried out as the others crushed her against the glass.

"Dammit, one at a time!" I said.

Missy and Fred stood in the doorway, their faces and arms slick with fresh blood. I glanced back as customers continued to exit. Taking Stacey's hand, I dragged her towards the doors. Missy tore across the room to block our escape, and Fred was behind us.

We ran to the manager's office in the front, thinking I could lock us in till more help arrived. The door was locked. I searched for the right key on my belt as Stacey whimpered behind me. At last, I found it. But before I could get the door open, Missy leaped a good ten or twelve feet over the checkout stations and brought Stacey down like a frightened gazelle. I hit her attacker in the back of the head so hard that the broom handle snapped in two.

I kept beating Missy as she feasted on Stacey's eyes and tongue. When she hit an artery, a jet of hot blood squirted onto the front windows like an automatic sprinkler. Excited, she washed her face in it as her disciple joined in.

Repulsed, I ran to the exit. Fred grabbed me, screeching in

my ear as we tumbled outside. On my feet again, I drove the jagged end of the broom handle through his gaping mouth till it lodged in the back of his neck.

It was dark, and the parking lot lights cast everything in a sickly orange glow. A frightened cop watched as Fred wandered in circles, trying to dislodge the stick. Then Missy appeared, hungry for my blood. The officer drew his gun and emptied it at her. The rounds that struck her in the arms and chest had no effect.

"The head!" I said. "Shoot her in the head!"

Out of ammo, he tried reloading as Missy straightened up and continued towards us. She was three feet away when a police cruiser screeched to a stop. Hissing, she fled around the side of the building. Officer Norm and his partner took off after her.

I sat on the curb, covered in Stacey's blood. Unsure if I'd gotten bit, I wished I could pass out. The first cop looked at me, stunned.

"I-I don't understand. How could she—"

"Can't you see what they are?" I said. "They're all dead."

Fred staggered forward, lowing like a cow that had fallen into a pit. Side-eyeing me, the officer pointed his weapon.

"For the last time, shoot him in the head!"

I'd had enough. Disgusted, I ripped the gun from his trembling hands and mag-dumped my manager. God help me, but it felt good.

A bullet tore through Fred's left eye, and he dropped. Twitching uncontrollably, his body stood propped at an unnatural angle on the broom handle.

Officer Norm and his partner jogged over, their weapons drawn. I laid mine on the ground and raised my hands. The scared cop retrieved his gun and pointed it at me, his voice like Barney Fife.

"You're under arrest!"

"Knock it off," Officer Norm said and pushed away the gun.

It was late as I sat on the curb, mourning Fred. How could I have shot him? *But it wasn't Fred.* No, it was something vicious that only resembled my manager—a monstrosity hell-bent on ending my life.

When I was a kid, my dad liked taking me to the shooting range. It was something he had gotten into after he stopped drinking. Purging his demons, I guess. Though I had a talent for it, I'd never killed anything—not even a deer. I recalled those Sunday afternoons with fondness. Me shooting, and my proud father encouraging me to keep doing better. After he passed, I never again picked up a gun.

I felt nauseous as I replayed the scene in my head. Grabbing the policeman's gun and blasting a baseball-size hole in Fred Lumpkin's face. What made it worse was the realization that no one was going to do shit about it. Certainly not Officer Norm. It was self-defense, pure and simple.

As more ambulances arrived to deal with the carnage, I imagined Missy lurking around the corner. I wasn't sure whether all those bodies would rise again, but I guessed we would know soon. Fred was gone. Stacey was gone. And I was alive.

The paramedics had checked me out—no bites. After the last ambulance had left, Detective Van Gundy came over and sat next to me. I hadn't realized he was there. He looked at me with sympathy.

"How're you holding up?" he said. "The guys told me what happened. Under the circumstances, you did what you had to."

"Those bodies they took away? They need to destroy the brains."

"I'll let them know." He lit a cigarette and took a deep drag. "I quit years ago."

"I should be getting drunk."

"I might as well tell you. This sickness is spreading faster than we can control it. We're getting reports of the infected being spotted as far north as Mt. Shasta."

"I have to get out of here." Grabbing my keys, I started to walk away.

"You can't leave town."

Balling my fists, I glared at him. "Are you going to shoot me?"

He tossed the butt. "It's not that. Security forces are en route. Soon, they'll block all the main roads into town."

"I have to try."

"I know." He extended his hand, and we shook. "Good luck, Dave."

I wished him the same and headed for my truck, afraid of what I would find in Mt. Shasta.

CHAPTER
TWENTY-NINE

WHAT WOULD I say to Holly when I saw her? Beg her for forgiveness? Try to convince her I was a changed man? No matter what she thought of me, I had to find her—had to protect her mother and her from what was coming. Though I was anxious to get on the road, it was after midnight when I arrived at the motel. I was exhausted and didn't want to risk nodding off behind the wheel. So I decided to catch a few hours' sleep.

As I lay in bed, visions of Stacey dying chased away any good dreams. Her bright blood shooting from her neck. Her pitiful cries for help. And that infernal shrieking in my ears as the freaks feasted on her. In that moment, I vowed to kill Missy but had to settle for Fred. And the way this was playing out, there would be a lot more killing. People like to talk about survival. What they mean is taking out the other guy first.

In the morning, I trudged over to the office, bleary-eyed. Except for me, the place was deserted. The motel manager was an Indian national named Ram Chakravarthy. He had a Duchenne smile as big as the moon and an accent thick as honey.

"I'm checking out," I said.

He looked up from his laptop. "Minimum stay is two nights. I must charge you for tonight. Help yourself to complimentary coffee."

I didn't have time to argue, so I paid. Sitting in my truck, I sipped coffee from a styrofoam cup. I made several attempts to call Holly. Each time, it went to voicemail. I texted her and waited. No response. After several more tries, I gave up.

Looking for breakfast, I made my way through the deserted streets of Tres Marias. When I reached downtown, the scene was surreal. Armed security guards wearing black-and-tan uniforms assembled on street corners. Black military-style vehicles were parked everywhere. Not a citizen in sight.

Inside a mini-mart, two security guards were getting coffee. They eyed me suspiciously as I walked past them to the refrigeration units. I thought about buying a beer—one drink to take the edge off. For most people, this might seem reasonable. How bad could one beer be? Conveniently, I had forgotten that one turned into six into a case. Into oblivion. It was the original slippery slope, and no drunk had ever mastered it. Instead, I bought a six-pack of Mountain Dew, a package of little chocolate donuts, and some jerky. I hoped the roadblocks hadn't gone up yet. To be safe, I took the backroads.

Driving to Mt. Shasta, I thought about the security personnel I had seen earlier. Why hadn't the governor called in the National Guard? And what about my job? Now that Fred was gone and with the potential for more violence, I decided it was better to avoid the store altogether. Soon, the money would run out—at least I had my credit cards. I wondered how long currency would be of any value if the outbreak spread to other states. Or was I getting ahead of myself? In the forest, a death shriek sent a flock of birds tearing out of the trees. I closed my window and concentrated on getting through the woods. By the time I reached Shasta Lake, it was almost lunchtime.

Earlier, I had left Holly a voicemail to let her know I was coming. When I got to the house, her car was gone, but her mother's was still there. Wary, I climbed the gray wood steps to the front door. It was unlocked. I jogged around the side to where Irene kept the firewood. Taking the axe, I slipped into the house. My skin pricked with anticipation. Though everything appeared normal, I knew they weren't. For instance, there were dirty dishes in the sink. Holly's mom hated a mess. Whatever the reason, they must have left in a hurry. I tried calling my wife again.

Outside, two strangers appeared from the darkness of the surrounding trees. Standing on the porch, I watched how they moved, looking for any sign of the jimmies. I raised the axe to my chest and waited for them to identify themselves.

"It's okay," the older man said.

He was in his forties. Bald and slight, with a mustache and wire-rimmed glasses. He carried a pump-action shotgun and walked with a slight limp. His companion was maybe eighteen or nineteen—with reddish hair and freckles and carrying a hunting knife. Both looked nervous as they approached the house. The first man took a tentative step forward.

"I'm Ben Marino, and this is my son, Aaron."

I lowered the axe and shook hands. "Dave Pulaski."

Aaron peered behind me at the house. "You live here?"

"It's my mother-in-law's place. My wife was staying with her, but they're gone now."

Ben gazed out at the lake. "You know what's going on, right?"

"Pretty much," I said. "Want to come inside?"

I scrounged up canned chili and coffee. Ben and his son seemed grateful for the hospitality. Afterwards, we sat in the living room. Though I was committed to finding Holly, I had no idea where to begin. Maybe these guys could help.

"Aaron and I were camping," Ben said. "You know, a little father-son time. We were out on the lake today fishing..." When he choked up, his son touched his knee.

I gave him a minute. "What did you see out there?"

"I can't explain it—it's too unbelievable."

"There was this other boat," Aaron said. "A little ways from the shore. Couple of guys just drinking and fishing— well, mostly drinking. We were maybe fifty yards away. One peed off the side and fell into the water. It was funny at first. Neither had on life jackets. And the guy who went in couldn't swim."

Ben picked up the story. "We see him go under, right? His friend is too drunk to help, so Aaron and I row as fast as we can. We're almost there when the second guy decides to rescue his buddy. He dives down—the water couldn't have been more than fifteen, twenty feet deep. We waited for several minutes."

"They drowned?" I said.

"That's what we thought." Ben circled the room like the devil was after him.

Aaron looked at his father. "I was about to dive in myself, but Dad stopped me. We'd brought along this high-powered flashlight in case we were out after dark. At first, there were just fish. Then we saw them."

Ben stopped in front of me and spoke haltingly. "Those

men were being held down by people. At the bottom of the lake. And they were…"

"They were eating them," Aaron said. "We couldn't believe what we were seeing when, all of a sudden, something bobbed to the surface."

"It was a torso." Ben grimaced as if he had tasted the waterlogged flesh. "Completely hollowed out."

I tried imagining dead people down there. They could have fallen into the water and, unable to swim, sank to the bottom like rocks. Without the need to breathe, they remained down there. Hungry. Waiting.

"Got anything to drink?" Ben said.

I went through the kitchen cabinets and found an unopened bottle of Johnnie Walker Double Black. It surprised me that Irene had kept it around. Her husband was a heavy drinker and died from esophageal cancer when Holly was fourteen. It's funny what people hold on to out of sentiment. She also kept a chipped "Gone Fishing" mug containing a half-smoked cigar, toothpicks, and a pack of matches from the Titties Galore Bar in Redding. That's where her husband used to entertain customers. I brought the booze with two glasses and placed them on the coffee table.

Ben reached for the bottle. "Aren't you having any?"

"Little too intense for me." I noticed Aaron didn't take a glass. "What else can I get you? I think we have Coke."

"Thanks, I'm good."

His hands unsteady, Ben unscrewed the cap, tearing the seal, and poured out two fingers. He drank it greedily and poured more into his coffee. Watching him, my lips went dry. When the faint odor of smoky scotch hit me, I returned to the kitchen to get more coffee. In the living room, Ben was deep in thought. His son had lain back, his eyes closed, the hunting knife lying next to him on the sofa cushion.

"You always bring a shotgun to fish?" I said to the kid's father.

"My dad owned guns. I never liked them, but I keep this one around for protection. What in God's name is going on?"

"I don't know, but the virus has spread all over Tres Marias."

"Is that where you're from?" Aaron said, sitting up.

"Just came from there. I'm looking for my wife. What about you, Ben?"

He poured another drink. "Wife's gone."

"You messed up too, huh?"

His ears turning red, he laughed a little and side-eyed his son. "Probably."

Ben laid the shotgun on his lap and slid his fingers along the barrel. "We should stick together. Who knows how many of those things are out there."

"Sounds good," I said. "I'm not one of those hero types."

CHAPTER
THIRTY

WE DECIDED to remain at the house in case Holly and her mother showed up. It wasn't like my wife not to return a call or a text, even if she was mad at me. To keep myself from going crazy, I spent the afternoon watching the news with Ben and his son. Evie Champagne gave a blow-by-blow with the information she had gathered firsthand. When she didn't have the facts, she offered reasoned speculation. The station intercut the reporter with footage of uniformed security guards descending on Tres Marias and blocking off major roads.

"Felix, this is extraordinary," Evie said. "A private military outfit called Black Dragon Security has been given full authority to lock down everything within the city limits. We know very little about this company, which is headquartered in Pittsburgh. When I contacted the mayor's office earlier, I was given a one-sentence statement. *Until further notice, Black Dragon is in charge.*"

The camera panned around her. Every military-style vehicle had a black-and-red logo with the image of a dragon. Security guards wore the same symbol on their uniforms. The reporter didn't say what the rest of the state was doing about the situation. And we had no idea how many other towns were at risk.

Around six, I asked the guys if they wanted to eat. There wasn't a lot of food. None of us were hungry anyway, so we decided to skip it. I checked all the doors and windows and made sure the lights were on outside. We had the shotgun with plenty of shells, the hunting knife, and my axe for protection.

I found some extra blankets in a closet. The other guys camped in the living room, and I took the guest bedroom. We left the TV on with the sound muted in case there was any breaking news. The night was long and dark. I imagined what was out there, lurking among the trees. Unable to sleep, I lay in bed looking at photos on my phone. There must have been a couple hundred—shots of Holly and me mostly. The places we went. The food we enjoyed. And those quiet, candid moments I loved. It all seemed a lifetime away.

I was never much for domestic crap, but I got up early to fix breakfast. When Ben and Aaron walked into the kitchen, I remembered something Holly had told me—*the perfect husband*.

"Smells good," Aaron said as he and his dad sat at the table.

"Cheese omelets. There's no bread, but we have coffee and a little milk."

As Ben dug in, bits of egg got caught in his beard. "This is fantastic."

We didn't talk much. After cleaning up, we went into the living room to watch the news. An annoying weather girl gave us a bubbly account of the scorching days ahead. After that, there was a slew of commercials.

When the top story came on, I turned up the sound. Footage of LMTVs—light medium tactical vehicles—and Humvees rolled through the streets. It was like a military parade, only no one was cheering. Evie interviewed a Black Dragon Security supervisor. He explained that there had been a viral outbreak, and their mission was to keep it from spreading. I was surprised at how young the Latino was—late twenties, maybe. Good-looking and fit.

"Are we talking about a novel coronavirus?" she said.

"I'm not a scientist."

"Can you describe the symptoms?"

"Sure. High fever, dizziness, loss of speech." *And an unexplainable hunger for human flesh.*

Evie redirected. "Can you tell me why your organization is here and not the National Guard?"

"You'll have to take that up with the mayor."

"Are you permitted to use deadly force?"

"We're here to maintain order, ma'am."

"But you have guns and live ammunition."

"We are authorized to do whatever it takes, within reason, to protect the citizens of this town."

"Thank you, Mr. Chavez. This is Evie Champagne reporting. Back to you, Felix."

I hurled the remote at the sofa. "He's lying."

"Of course, he's lying," Ben said. "What did you want him to say? Oh, and folks, all these dead people are wandering around, so stay safe out there, hear?"

"I need to find my wife. Where's your car?"

"Our motorhome is parked a little ways from here." Wincing, he got up.

"You okay?"

"Titanium hip. I won't be entering any marathons."

"Let's hope there's no reason to run," I said.

We saw them in the distance through the trees. Dressed like tourists, they were lost souls wandering through the forest, unaware of any real purpose. Word must have gotten out about the danger because we didn't see anyone else as we made our way along the lake in my truck.

Maybe this was why Holly and her mother had left in such a hurry. There was no sign of violence in the house—and, more importantly, no blood. How could two people survive out here, given one was elderly? On the other hand, Holly was resourceful. She would find a way to keep her mother safe.

Near the camp where Ben and his son were staying, we spotted a young girl in the road. She had on shorts and a bloody T-shirt with the words *L'il Princess*. One shoe was missing. She couldn't have been more than ten. I slowed down. Unaware of us, she drifted from one side to the other. The flies buzzing around her head didn't seem to bother her.

"Let's see if we can help her," Aaron said.

But I knew the truth—she was infected. She was like those hellish freaks at the bottom of the lake. Waiting. Hungry. Though I was opposed to it, I pulled over. Before getting out, I advised Ben to bring the shotgun.

"Hello?" Aaron said as he approached the little girl.

She continued to waver. Her arm was torn open, exposing tendon and bone. Blowflies swarmed around the open wound. My instinct was to run her down with my truck. Stopping, she looked at us with flat eyes, trying to form the words that would never come. There were so many questions in her expression. *Where's my family? Why did this happen to me?*

"Look, she sees us. I don't think we're too late."

When I reached for Ben's shotgun, he seemed to understand. I walked up to his son and took his arm.

"Get out of the way," I said. "She's dead."

"No, look. She's in shock. We can help her."

"She's gone, Aaron."

"Please don't do this—I'm begging you."

He tried taking the weapon away from me. When I shoved him back, he fell to the ground. The girl whipped her arms and mewled like a sick animal. As he stood, she tried to get ahold of his arm. Even now, he didn't get it.

"No, please! We could take her to a hospital."

She was getting closer, and Aaron wouldn't let up. I drove the butt of the shotgun into his gut. As he doubled over, Ben grabbed his son and yanked him out of the way.

Hating myself for what I was about to do, I pumped the shotgun once. For an instant, I saw the young girl she used to be. Her soft blonde locks falling gently around her sweet face, her trembling lips. Her hurt green eyes boring into mine, begging to know why I was doing this. I must have been feverish because now they were Holly's eyes. Snapping out of it, I pointed the weapon at her.

"God forgive me," I said and squeezed the trigger.

The blast sent her to heaven. Her head half blown off, she shook like a mechanical doll whose works had exploded and lay still in the road. Aaron buried his head against his father's shoulder. When I turned to face them, Ben glared at me with the kind of hatred reserved for mass murderers.

"I told you," I said. "She was already dead."

CHAPTER
THIRTY-ONE

WE FOUND Ben's motorhome intact. In the surrounding area, there were human tracks in the pine needles. We figured a horde must have come through and, detecting no life inside the vehicle, kept moving. Aaron wasn't talking to me. Ben pulled out three beers from the little refrigerator. He handed one to his son and tried giving me one. After a beat, I waved it away and sat at the table.

"Got anything else?" I said.

He returned with a Red Bull. "You don't drink?"

"Used to back in the day."

"I figured. Good for you."

His son took a sip of his beer and made a face. Pushing it aside, he got himself a Diet Coke. I could tell he wanted to say something to me.

"About earlier," he said at last. "I can't get used to this."

I leaned over and squeezed his arm. "I didn't mean to hurt you. Are you okay?"

He massaged his abdomen. "A little sore is all."

I took a swig of my drink. "You did what anybody would've done. You're a good person."

"How do you know, though? That they're dead?"

"Instinct, I guess."

"And if you're wrong?" Ben said.

"There's no time for right or wrong."

He scoffed. "That kind of thinking leads to anarchy."

I tried not to let him get me riled. "That sounds great on paper. Okay, I know it sucks. But if you get bit, you become one of them. And I will do whatever it takes to keep that from happening to me. Or you."

"That poor little girl," Aaron said.

"After you're infected, it's only a short time till you turn into a freak. At first, it was days, then hours. Who knows how long it takes now."

"Is that what you call them?" Ben said. *"Freaks?"*

"You got a better word? It's like this—you die. You stop breathing, you smell like hell, and you look really, really bad. All you want to do is feed on the living. Come on, you saw it yourself on the lake."

Aaron looked at his hands. "And the girl?"

"She would've gored you in seconds."

"We need to get out of this forest," Ben said.

There was a sudden pounding like a stampede in a Hollywood Western. We rushed to the front and peered out the windshield. Hundreds of terrified animals came at us—deer, raccoons, and squirrels. We braced ourselves. The motorhome shook as an eight-point buck skidded and crashed into the vehicle. Righting itself, it continued past and disappeared with the rest. But what came next was worse. A horde poured out of the forest into the clearing.

"I need to get to my truck," I said and grabbed my axe.

His hands shaking, Ben started the vehicle. "What if I circle and drive you next to it?"

"You need to hit as many as you can on the way."

"Can't we wait for them to—"

"To run past? What if they decide to attack? Ben, you have to take them out. Can you do that?"

"Okay. Dammit."

"What do I do?" Aaron said.

He reminded me of my younger self. How would I have dealt with something like this at his age?

"I want you to take the shotgun while your dad drives."

There was no way he could handle an axe—I wasn't sure I could. As Ben pulled forward, the horde milled hungrily around the vehicle. Shit, they could smell us. I kept my eye on the door.

"Run them over!"

Finding his nerve, Aaron's dad hit the gas. He swung around sharply, catching men, women, and teenagers. They groaned as the motorhome rolled over them, crushing arms and legs. A front wheel found a woman's head and popped it like a balloon filled with dark, infectious blood. Now more of them came into the clearing, livid and shrieking. The noise was unbearable. As they attacked us from the sides, Ben turned into them hard, dragging them under the wheels.

One got stuck in the right front wheel well, and we came to a halt with the tire spinning. If they managed to get the door open, we were finished. I dug around in my pocket for my keys.

"We're close to my truck," I said. "Aaron, get over here. Anything gets near me, you shoot. On three. One... two...three!"

I flung open the door and started out. A man in a bloody Dodgers jersey came at me from the side. I brought down the axe and whacked off his arm in mid-grab. Ignoring the inconvenience, he reached for me with the other one. Regrouping, I tried swinging the axe again and dropped my keys. Shoving the freak away, I bent down to retrieve them when an explosion ripped the air above me. When I came up, my attacker no longer had a face. Teetering, he fell backwards.

Seeing my chance, I chopped away at the body stuck in the wheel well and dragged out what was left. Then I jumped into my truck. There was nothing left for me here—I needed to return to Tres Marias. I didn't know where Holly and her mother were, so I decided to contact Black Dragon. Maybe the security guards had picked them up.

We made our way out of the clearing and onto the road. Across from us, there was a grassy field. In the distance, I saw something disturbing and signaled Ben to pull over. Standing outside my truck, I shielded my eyes from the sun and peered at the lone figure wandering directionless. With dawning recognition, I fell to my knees.

It was Holly's mother.

PART THREE

HELL'S WAITING ROOM

CHAPTER
THIRTY-TWO

WEARING HER FAVORITE HOUSECOAT—A turquoise number with little yellow ducks—Irene lurched forward. She was drenched in blood. Lugging my axe, I sprinted across the field. As I got closer, I recognized the gray skin, the metallic eyes. Intense fear grabbed me by the throat as I imagined my wife wandering somewhere out there, too.

Wiping away the tears, I scanned the field. The only living beings were crows, too afraid to approach. Ben and Aaron caught up with me, and we remained a good twenty yards from Holly's mother. From out of nowhere came a whoop.

A man dressed in silver bounded out of the woods, the sun glinting off him. He wore a helmet with a black visor and carried a long catchpole—the kind they use on zoo animals. There was a childlike joy in the way he gamboled as he pursued his dark prey. I was convinced he would wind up dead.

Ben raised his shotgun. I grabbed the barrel and pushed it down as the man in silver slipped the noose over Irene's head and cinched it. He brought her down like a cowboy in a calf-roping contest.

"This guy is nuts," Ben said.

Holly's mother lay face down on the ground as the silver man removed his protective gloves and secured her hands with plastic ties. Next, he wound red duct tape around her head at the mouth to keep her from biting. My curiosity got the better of me, and I marched up to him.

"What are you doing?" I said.

"Capturing a specimen." His voice was familiar. "Look out!"

A man and woman came at us. They were naked and around Aaron's age. Ben aimed his shotgun and tried to fire, but he had forgotten to release the safety. I pushed him aside and swung my axe with both hands. The blow took the man's head most of the way off. He spun in circles, trying to right himself. I kicked him to the ground and swung again, splitting his skull. Then I went after the other one.

She had attached herself to the silver man's back, tearing at him in frustration. Incredibly, he remained unharmed. And that's when I realized he was wearing a shark suit.

"A little help?" he said.

I didn't want to swing the axe for fear of hitting the crazy dude. And Ben didn't have a clear shot.

"Any time, fellas."

I flipped the axe around and drove the handle into the woman's skull, which caved in like a rotten cantaloupe. Grabbing the limp creature by the hair, I pulled her away. The man in silver got to his feet and stretched as if nothing had happened. Ben and Aaron stared at me. When I looked down, I saw that I was covered in black blood.

Irene struggled on the ground, hog-tied and grunting through the duct tape like a sow. The silver dude pulled off his helmet to get some fresh air.

"Mr. Landry?" I said.

"Dave Pulaski. How the devil are you?"

Aaron came closer, pointing. "Wait, you know this guy?"

"My high school science teacher."

Landry wiped the sweat off his face. "Glad you fellas are here. My truck broke down, and I could sure use a lift."

"Unbelievable," I said.

Now in his sixties, Irwin Landry looked fit. He had a lean body, a white shock of hair, a hawk nose, and steely blue eyes —just as I remembered him. He had retired from teaching at the end of the last school year and bought a real cabin in Mt. Shasta. There, he proceeded to go insane from boredom. When the outbreak hit, he found his purpose again.

We parked our vehicles in front of my old teacher's house. There was a chain-link enclosure in the yard. And next to that, a pit slathered in black, greasy ash. Behind that stood a row of red five-gallon gasoline cans. Eight freaks milled around inside the enclosure. The teacher had removed the duct tape and plastic ties, allowing them to wander freely. Some looked like they'd turned only recently. A ninth one lay on the ground, emaciated.

"Everything dies," Landry said. "Even these monstrosities." His tone was grim and reminded me of all the cold, hard facts of science he had taught us.

"Ever since this business started, I've been studying them. And I can say with confidence they're no longer human."

A cat sidled up to the teacher. She had a sizable rip in the skin of her back, which was crusted over with dried blood. He pushed her away with his boot.

"What happened to the cat?" I said.

"That's Hawking. She got bit by one of them. Lucky to get away."

"Aren't you worried about her?"

He considered the animal. "That's the interesting part. This happened weeks ago. So far, she hasn't exhibited any symptoms. To her, it's nothing more than a wound. No worse than any animal bite. And it's healing."

Ben crouched, his hands on his thighs. "She doesn't appear to be rabid."

"She may have been vaccinated. She had a collar when I found her."

"You remember Jim Stanley?" I said.

"Sure I do."

"He's dead. Anyway, I'm pretty sure his rabid dog bit him before he turned."

"It's too bad about your friend, but I'm not sure there's a link. Rabies is pretty common in these parts."

The cat sidled up to me, purring. Without thinking, I bent down to pet her.

"Careful," Landry said. "She could still be a carrier. It's why I never let her get too close."

Ben pointed at the enclosure. "Why do you study them?"

"Because I have a curious mind. I want to see if I can learn something that might help put a stop to whatever this is."

I scoffed. "And for that, you had to remove their restraints? You always were a little off, Irwin."

"I like to think of myself as open to possibilities."

"I did enjoy your class the best, though."

"Really? I always thought Ms. Ireland was your favorite." Then to my new friends, "English teacher. Pretty formidable in the chest department."

"Uh-huh," Aaron said, grinning at me.

Landry punched me in the arm—something I did not miss. "How've you been?"

"Not good. My wife and I are separated."

"That's rough. I wish I had some advice I could give you."

When the captives rushed the fence, we jumped back—all except the teacher. The cat bared her teeth and took off hissing. Shrieking in frustration, they tried in vain to latch onto us. Landry walked over to my truck bed, where Irene lay mewling.

"Dave, help me get her into the cage. You two better go inside."

Ben started for the house with his son. "What's the hurry?"

"They're agitated," he said. "And once they get going, the sound is sure to bring others."

CHAPTER
THIRTY-THREE

OVER A DINNER of ham-and-cheese sandwiches and root beer, Landry explained what he was up to. He didn't own a television set, which irritated me. I wanted to check in with Evie Champagne for the latest on the outbreak. But my friend did have a generator and a phone he used to provide internet access to his laptop.

"It's not clear what's causing the dead to return to life," the teacher said. "But we do know three things for certain. First, we're in the midst of a community-level outbreak."

Aaron raised his hand. "What does that mean?"

"Human-to-human transmission. The virus had to have jumped from animal to human initially. Though, I don't think the culprit is rabies."

"Why not?" I said.

"Because rabies has been around since the Egyptians. And though it's transmittable by infected animals, it's never been known to do what we're seeing now. Second, the virus doesn't appear to be airborne. In the early days, many victims reported getting bit—that means blood. And third, decomposition doesn't cease. Eventually, the infected rot away, as you've observed."

"But not before doing a lot of damage," Ben said.

"Right. And to Dave's point, very similar to rabies in that regard."

I recalled Evie Champagne's interview with Black Dragon. "A reporter brought up the possibility of a novel coronavirus. What about that?"

"Possible. But at this stage, we don't have enough information."

"Why do they want to eat us?" Aaron said.

"Ah, yes." Landry's eyes twinkled the way they used to in science class, and I knew we were in for one of his famous lectures.

"Clearly, they get no sustenance from the flesh," he said. "They could be acting out of instinct. All life forms have fundamental needs. Maslow talks about a hierarchy. Dave, you remember this."

I didn't have the slightest clue and gave him a shit-eating grin. "Good ol' Maslow."

"For now, you can disregard the rest of the hierarchy. All that's important is the physiological needs. Air, food, water, sex, sleep, homeostasis, and excretion. From what I've observed, they don't need water, sex, or even sleep."

"And they don't need air." I side-eyed Ben and Aaron. "Trust me."

"Interesting. And they don't excrete, as far as I can tell. They eat and eat, and nothing comes out."

"Where does it all go?" Aaron said.

"There doesn't appear to be any kind of digestion. Though I haven't observed it myself, my guess is they fill up and can no longer feed. But that doesn't stop them from trying."

I nudged Aaron. "Like Thanksgiving."

"Maybe they explode," Ben said, totally serious.

That made me laugh. "I'd pay good money to see that."

Aaron raised his hand again. "What's homeo..."

"Homeostasis. The ability of an organism to regulate or stabilize itself. Like body temperature and so forth. From what I've observed, these unfortunates are always cold, so I don't think they're doing that very well either."

"That leaves hunger," Ben said.

The teacher pounded the table. "Right. And they are laser-focused on it."

"What else have you discovered?"

"Because most of the higher brain functions appear nonexistent, they can no longer speak. And I'm assuming they can't reason either."

"They can communicate with each other," I said. "I've seen them do it."

Ben seemed to be enjoying our conversation. "What about their other senses? Sight, hearing, and smell?"

Landry knitted his brow. "We know they can see. Not well, but they seem to get around okay. They can hear, too, because noises attract them. As for smell, I don't know."

"We were attacked by a horde earlier," I said. "I'm pretty sure they could smell us inside the motorhome."

Aaron shook his head in disbelief. "I don't understand. Aren't they clinically dead?"

The teacher gave him a knowing smile. "That's the million-dollar question, isn't it? They don't appear to have any of the normal life signs. No pulse, no breath. Yet somehow, they're alive."

"But how?"

"There are documented cases of yogis who can put themselves into a state of samadhi. They consciously lower their respiration and heart rate to almost undetectable levels. A brain in this state leverages some unique ability of the body we are unaware of. It allows them to operate in this minimalist fashion."

"But to what end?" I said.

Landry took a swallow of root beer and set down the can. "Survival."

We decided to stay with the teacher overnight. In the morning, we would discuss whether it made sense for everyone to stick together. Landry was an incurable scrounger. Previously, he had collected sleeping bags and stored them in case of an emergency.

Exhausted, Ben, Aaron, and I spread them out around the cold fireplace. As I lay there waiting for an uncertain morning, I couldn't stop thinking about Holly. Was she dead—or worse, like Irene? There was no sign of her in that field, and my fervent prayer was that she had escaped and was somewhere safe.

The teacher claimed he hadn't seen anyone in the area fitting her description. That's another need Maslow should have listed in his famous pyramid. It was something the undead were no longer burdened with—hope.

In the morning, over hard-boiled eggs and coffee, we sat around the table discussing our thoughts. There was no reason for Ben and his son to stick around. They could return home to Sacramento. On the other hand, it made sense for me to stick with Landry.

"I have to find Holly," I said. "If that means returning to Tres Marias alone, I'll do it. I don't expect any of you to follow."

The teacher shook his head. "Let's look at the facts. We're surrounded by the walking dead. I've spotted more and more

145

over the last few days. We're not sure if these Black Dragon people have the situation under control. If we're lucky, they've established a perimeter to contain the outbreak."

"No one gets in or out," Ben said.

Landry looked at me. "A person could take their chances out there alone, but I would advise against it."

Ben laid a hand on my shoulder. "I have to agree. It's too dangerous for one man."

"Okay," I said. "Anyway, I was kind of hoping Irwin would join me."

Landry drained his coffee cup. "My dance card is pretty open."

When Ben looked at his son, they seemed to be in agreement. "Aaron and I don't have to be anywhere. We'd like to help if we can."

"Guys, I'd be lying if I said I wasn't relieved. Thank you."

The teacher began clearing the table. "If we're going on the road, we'd better get some supplies together."

The three of us finished cleaning up while Landry went off to gather the stuff we'd need.

"Why Tres Marias?" Ben said to me.

"Because I haven't been able to reach Holly, and she had no idea I was coming up here. She probably thinks I'm still in town. I realize it's a long shot."

The teacher walked in, carrying a box of food and a first-aid kit. "There's more back there. By the way, cell service has gotten a lot worse, so we need to stick together."

"I think we have another problem," Aaron said. "Don't we need more weapons?"

I stopped what I was doing. "Shit, you're right. We won't last five minutes out there without some serious firepower."

"I think I can help you there," Landry said and let out a mad giggle.

CHAPTER
THIRTY-FOUR

LANDRY DIDN'T SAY much as I navigated the narrow dirt road. We were headed deep into the forest to I didn't know where—the teacher wouldn't say. Ben and Aaron followed us in the motorhome.

"I don't see what all the secrecy is about," I said. "Can't you tell me—"

"Humor me."

We arrived at a clearing defined by hundreds of rocks arranged in a circle. The ground looked clean—like it had been swept. In the center, an enormous concrete birdbath loomed darkly. In it stood Diana, holding her bow and arrow, with a dead stag at her feet.

"Communing with nature now, are we?" I said.

"Look harder."

The surrounding trees were dense. It took me a sec to realize there was a house in front of us, camouflaged in paint. And depending on how you looked at it, you'd swear you saw nothing but shadows.

"No way."

The front door squeaked open, and an old man appeared.

He was rail thin, with a white ponytail down his back and a Rip van Winkle beard. He wore khaki cargo pants, a bright Hawaiian shirt, and flip-flops. Except for the AR-15 slung over his shoulder, I would have taken him for a sixties-era surfer.

Landry hugged the stranger like they were long-lost brothers. "Boys? I'd like to introduce you to my dear friend, Guthrie Manson."

"Why don't we all go inside," the old man said. "I believe Caramel put the tea on."

The living room resembled something inspired by Tim Burton on a Thomas Kincaid bender. The handcrafted furniture sat askew—not a single piece was symmetrical. There were small tables and occasional chairs with five legs.

The angular sofas were covered in colorful cushions made from bits of paisley, velvet, satin, and, in one case, an American flag. The rugs looked expensive. In addition to lace over the windows, heavy blackout curtains were pinned back with stainless steel chains. But it was the ceiling that got my attention.

Potted plants intermingled with countless little Mexican calaveras dressed as mariachis, circus performers, and politicians in top hats. The room glowed courtesy of the light coming from hidden skylights.

As we headed to the kitchen, a woman appeared in the doorway. She was around the same age as Guthrie, with long, white hair that reached her tailbone. She had on a loose-fitting blue muslin skirt that lingered above the floor and a filmy blouse with no bra. These two must have been the first hippies.

"This is Caramel," the old man said, giddy as a teenager. "Honey, meet the guys."

We exchanged greetings and sat at the large kitchen table

made from unfinished pine. I couldn't take my eyes off Guthrie's beard and tried picturing him eating soup.

"I appreciate you helping us out," Landry said as the old woman set out tea and cookies.

"Thanks, darlin'." The old man squeezed his wife's hand and playfully spanked her on the butt as she went to stir a pot.

"So, Dave," he said. "Irwin tells me you need to find your wife over in Tres Marias."

"I'm hoping that's where she is. This tea smells interesting."

Caramel joined us at the table. "It's jasmine."

Our host's expression turned grim. "These are some bad times, boys. Seems like you can't go for a walk anymore."

"Can I ask what you folks do out here?" Ben said. It was a question I had been dying to ask.

"We grow pot."

My friend almost did a spit take and side-eyed his son.

"Purely for our own consumption, of course. And a few close friends. I can hook you up—just say the word."

"Is that why the house is camouflaged?" Aaron said, chewing on an oatmeal raisin cookie.

"We're pretty much done with people. Present company excepted, most folks are no damn good. Right, honey?"

"What if someone tries to break in and..."

Two nearly identical men who looked as if they'd stepped out of a *Spartacus* episode came in through the back door. Each had an AR-15 and a sidearm.

Guthrie couldn't have been more proud. "These are our sons, Jerry and Frank. Named after the two greatest musicians who ever lived."

Looking like a doll next to the giants, their mother hugged them. "Are you boys hungry?"

Our host swallowed the last of his tea and stood. "Okay, let's get you what you came for."

We left the table and followed him to the back of the house. We had to make our way past a pack of meowing cats.

"Jerry and Frank?" I said to the teacher.

"Jerry Garcia and Frank Zappa. Try to keep up."

I glanced out a narrow window and saw Caramel watering a fruit tree in the backyard. She puffed a joint the size of a Cuban cigar as Jerry or Frank patrolled the perimeter. The old man pulled out a set of keys and unlocked a steel door that stood inside a heavy steel doorframe.

We found ourselves in a thirty-by-thirty-foot room filled with hydroponic equipment. Hundreds of marijuana plants were suspended all around under bright lights. But that wasn't the amazing part. All along the walls hung weapons. I spotted rifles, shotguns, AK-47s, AR-15s, and other deadly hardware.

"Are you kidding me?" I said to Guthrie.

"When it all goes down, we'll be ready."

Aaron picked up a worn Uzi. "Is this stuff legal?"

Everyone stared at him. Red-faced, he set down the weapon.

"I have to warn you," Landry said, picking up a rifle. "And they never mention this in the movies. These guns are heavy, even without ammo. My advice is to choose wisely."

Examining a weapon tailor made for Arnold Schwarzenegger, I smirked at our host. "Seriously?"

"MGL six-shot grenade launcher. Bought that one off an ex-cop in Arizona." He tried handing it to me. "Unfortunately, it only came with one crate of grenades. I plan to make those last."

Poring over the other weapons, I found a strange-looking long gun.

"That's a Kel-Tec KSG twelve-gauge shotgun. Better known as a bullpup."

"It's so short." When I hefted it, it felt light enough, and I decided to take it.

Outside, the twins helped us load the truck and motorhome with weapons and ammo. As we got ready to leave, Landry embraced Guthrie and his wife.

"Sure you can't stay for dinner?" the old man said.

"Wish we could. Can't thank you both enough."

"Happy to help. Strange times, my friend."

"And they're getting stranger every day."

I walked over to shake hands. "Do the flesh-eaters bother you way out here?"

"Not really. I suppose the cannabis keeps 'em away."

The teacher gave us a devilish smile. "Time for some target practice."

"How do you know them?" I said as we headed out of the forest.

"Guthrie and I go way back. We met in high school."

"You guys were high school friends?"

"When we turned eighteen, I went off to college, and he headed to Vietnam."

"Drafted?"

"He enlisted. But when he got back, he was a different person—angry and self-destructive. I hardly recognized him. Eventually, we lost touch. I thought maybe he was dead. Then, years later, he showed up at my door, that sweet, happy guy you met."

"What changed him?"

"Caramel. I believe she saved him."

"Wow. Where did they meet?"

"At a McGovern rally." He brushed away a tear.

I had hit a nerve and didn't say anything else.

CHAPTER
THIRTY-FIVE

WE GRABBED our weapons and waited next to the vehicles. Though I was comfortable with my axe, I felt safer with the bullpup. Landry surprised us by choosing an AR-15. Aaron picked a handgun, and Ben stuck with his Remington.

I didn't know what kind of target practice the teacher had in mind and figured bottles and cans perched on a fence. Walking up to the enclosure, he thought otherwise. My stomach roiled at the thought of gunning down my mother-in-law.

"Wait," Ben said. "We're just going to shoot them?"

Landry reached for the shotgun and, making sure it was loaded, handed it back. "We've been over this. They're not human."

"But there are laws, dammit."

"I appreciate your position, Ben. But if we're going to survive, we have to kill them on sight without hesitation. And we need to be quick because the gunfire will attract others."

His neck flushed, Ben turned to his son. "Are you good with this?"

Aaron side-eyed me. "I don't... It's like Mr. Landry said. We need to defend ourselves."

"This is bullshit—I won't do it."

Ben fell back, keeping the shotgun pointed down at his side. Rolling his eyes, the teacher turned to Aaron and me. Judging by his expression, he wasn't about to tolerate any more dissent.

"Go for the head," he said. "It's the only way to stop them."

Aaron's father remained under a tree, defiant. "This isn't right."

Landry gave him a venomous look. "You've said your piece. The rest of us have work to do."

I could tell Aaron was starting to lose his nerve and patted his arm. "We need to train."

"Each of us has to be capable of doing this," the teacher said. "Either to save ourselves or someone else. This is not a movie or a video game—it's real life. There won't be time to think. You must respond quickly, which means being observant. We don't want innocent people getting shot. Remember. Observe, assess, and act. No hesitation. No remorse."

Aaron looked at his dad, who refused to meet his gaze.

Landry pointed at the enclosure. "There are eight in there, plus that one on the ground. Shouldn't be too difficult for the three of us to complete the job."

"What if they bite us?" Aaron said.

"Rule number one, don't get bit."

The teacher unlocked the gate and swung it open. Sensing freedom, the captives headed for the opening as he fell back and raised his weapon.

"Pick your target and fire."

I turned to Aaron. "I can't do Irene."

"I got her," he said. "You take that ugly sonofabitch next to her."

We began shooting, trying to strike them in the head before they got too close. Unused to the bullpup, I backed away as they picked up speed. Aaron aimed carefully and fired at Irene through her open, toothless mouth. Collapsing, she fell on her face. A sharp pain tore through me as if I had been shot.

In a few seconds, seven were down. Aaron aimed at what looked like a burly truck driver. He managed to wing it before shooting it through the neck, but it kept coming. The hostile was practically on him when he realized he was out of ammo.

"Oh shit, oh shit—what do I do?"

A blast tore through the side of the truck driver's head. It went down like a load of cement. We turned around to find Ben lowering his shotgun. Landry nodded grimly.

"Rule number two," the teacher said, pulling a handgun from his belt. "Always have another weapon."

Ben slipped an arm around his son. "And somebody watching your back."

Landry looked at each of us. "I think we're ready."

He walked into the enclosure and delivered a headshot to the lone captive lying lethargically on the ground.

"We need to burn these bodies," he said and went to get the gasoline.

We loaded up our vehicles with supplies. The plan was to head out before noon. The cat ran up to the teacher as he got into my truck. I didn't want the animal anywhere near me.

"What about the cat?" I said.

"She was a stray when I found her. And she knows how to take care of herself. Probably better than any of us."

Relieved, I fired up the engine, and we hit the road. I wasn't sure if I would ever see Holly again. We were in hell, and all I cared about was finding her alive. The thought that she might have gotten bit filled me with dread, and I put it out of my mind. Instead, I pictured her face—her eyes. That desperate image was the only thing that kept me going.

My friend glanced at what lay on the backseat. "You kept the axe."

"Guns can jam," I said. "That's my backup weapon."

CHAPTER
THIRTY-SIX

I SHOULDN'T HAVE TAKEN the freeway. As we neared Tres Marias, the traffic worsened till, eventually, we couldn't move. All around us, angry drivers leaned on their horns. When a fat biker tried using the right shoulder to pass, a guy in a Mercedes cut him off, causing the bike to skid out of control. Enraged, the biker punched the driver through his open window.

"And so it begins," Landry said.

I climbed into the truck bed to get a better look. The lines of vehicles spanned over a mile. Ben rolled down his window as I approached the motorhome.

"Looks like they're diverting the traffic," I said. "All I can see are flashing lights and CHP cruisers."

He thrummed his fingers on the steering wheel. "We should've taken that last exit."

When I returned to my truck, the teacher was thoughtful. "They've quarantined the town. Not sure we can get back in."

"We're getting in," I said.

We sat there for thirty minutes. While we waited, I tried reaching Holly, but there was no cell reception. Oblivious,

Landry read a science fiction novel. Finally, traffic began to move, but the right lanes were blocked to prevent anyone from exiting. If I could get past the barriers, I'd take the off-ramp and talk to someone in charge.

As we inched our way forward, a deafening noise shook the truck. It was a helicopter with the Black Dragon logo hovering over us. From what I could make out, the security guards aboard it were armed. Ascending, it turned and headed towards the town.

The teacher looked up from his book. "They might've set up an evac center. Maybe your wife is there."

The off-ramp was coned off, but there weren't any cops or security guards. Checking my mirrors, I eased up to a narrow opening and accelerated. Orange cones flew everywhere as I drove down the off-ramp with the motorhome on my tail. When we reached the end, we ran straight into a military-style checkpoint.

Several Humvees were parked there, surrounded by Black Dragon personnel carrying AR-15s. There was no doubt these guys were on high alert. When Landry and I got out, we were greeted by nervous men and women pointing guns at us.

"Whoa," I said. "We're just trying to get some information."

The guard in charge wasn't in the mood for chitchat. He gave the others a nod, and they lowered their weapons.

"You need to get back on the freeway, sir."

I lowered my hands. "I'm trying to find my wife. Is there an evacuation center I can check?"

He eyeballed us and looked past us at the motorhome idling alongside the truck.

I followed his gaze. "They're with us."

"Let me see your IDs. What's your wife's name?"

"Holly Mitchell Pulaski."

He gave our driver's licenses a cursory look and handed them back. "We're using the high school. But I can't let you through. Only authorized personnel."

I was about to tear this idiot a new one when the teacher took my arm. Pulling free, I gawped at him.

"Let's go," he said. "Man's just doing his job." He smiled at the guard. "Can you direct us to the freeway?"

The guard pointed at a service road that would take us to another onramp. Landry signaled Ben and Aaron. I climbed into my truck and slammed the door.

"What part of quarantine do you not understand?" the teacher said. "These people have shoot-to-kill orders."

It took me a minute to calm down. He was right. "So where does that leave us?"

"Take a breath and remember what I taught you."

I had to think for a sec. "*When things don't work out the way you want, get creative.* Shit."

With Ben following, I pulled around the checkpoint and got back on the freeway heading north. We continued for five miles. I spotted an exit that looked clear and took it.

"There's an old fire road that leads directly to town," I said. "If I can pick it up, we might have a shot."

"Now you're using your noodle."

When Jim and I used to go out drinking, we would end up on unfamiliar back roads, using the Force to get home. Landry and I did that now, feeling our way by gut instinct. Incredibly, it worked.

After waiting for Ben to catch up, I turned into an entrance that was barely noticeable from the main road. Jim and I used to hang out on this road, drinking and chasing down deer. About a hundred feet in, we reached a gate that was chained shut.

I examined the heavy iron lock. "We could shoot it off."

"That's bound to attract attention," the teacher said. "Get your axe."

The fire road was dusty and full of ruts from the last rains. I had to be careful not to drive too fast, or I might bust an axle. It was maybe ten miles to town via the meandering road. Though we didn't see any security guards, we passed random dead people—out-of-shape tourists who wandered like addicts looking for fresh meat.

When we entered downtown Tres Marias, I was sure we would be stopped again. But Black Dragon was preoccupied with keeping order as merchants closed their stores for good. Some civilians wore face masks, perhaps in the vain hope that they'd be protected from the virus.

There was one merchant I recognized—a toy shop owner. She finished taping a hand-painted sign to her window. It read SEE YOU ON THE OTHER SIDE. At the bottom, she had drawn a smiley face. Graffiti covered many of the buildings. One message read ATTENTION TOURISTS: HAVE YOU CONSIDERED TIJUANA?

Up ahead, guards trained their AR-15s on something in an alley. A gang of freaks staggered into the sunlight, covered in blood from a fresh kill. Someone gave a command, and they fired, aiming for the midsection. When that didn't work, they went for the head.

At the next intersection, another group of guards patrolled the sidewalk. As the light turned red, a drunk stumbled out of the Beehive. This was a long light, I remembered. As we waited, I watched the guy weaving badly and got a horrible feeling.

"Halt!" a guard said.

The drunk ignored them and kept going. When they drew

a bead on him, my stomach went into my throat. *No, don't.* Then someone gave the order.

The hapless idiot went down in a hail of bullets, and that's when I knew. If the people in charge couldn't tell the difference between a drunk and the infected, we were doomed. The light changed, and I hit the gas. As we cruised past, Landry shook his head.

"Poor sonofabitch," he said.

CHAPTER
THIRTY-SEVEN

A CHAIN-LINK FENCE with razor wire surrounded my old high school. Armed security guards manned a newly erected guard shack. On the roof, more guards scanned the perimeter for any sign of trouble. A guard wearing body armor left his post and approached the driver's window.

"I'm a resident," I said. "Dave Pulaski."

"What do you want?"

I didn't like his attitude. "I'm looking for my wife."

"I'm gonna need to see your ID." Then to Landry, "You, too."

"Got it right here, sir."

The guard pointed at the motorhome. "They with you?"

He signaled another guard to deal with Ben and Aaron. We waited while our IDs were processed using a magstripe reader on a laptop. I hoped the cops hadn't issued a warrant for my arrest. There would be no way for me to escape—not with all these guns.

The sentry handed back the licenses and waved us through. "Not sure how much parking's left inside."

We circled for ten minutes. I almost hit a kid on a skateboard. It was strange seeing someone taking the situation so lightly. For him, it was just another day at the skate park. With long, blond hair, he couldn't have been more than thirteen, dressed in jeans and a black Hurley T-shirt. He lingered for a beat in front of me with a peculiar look in his eyes. Giving me the finger, he skated off.

I realized what we were doing was ridiculous. Nobody was planning to leave. We gave up and parked on the street along the fence. We left our guns locked in our vehicles on the teacher's advice. Which turned out to be smart because they checked us for weapons as we entered the building.

The gym smelled like feet. Sleeping bags lay everywhere, along with cots for the elderly. There were families with small children, couples, and no pets.

It was hard to think with all the talking and babies squalling. In a corner, two men got into a fistfight over some food. The guards tased them both. An announcement came over the PA system.

"Attention. Anyone creating a disturbance will be escorted off the premises. Have a nice day."

Landry scanned the room. "This is unfortunate."

Ben had been talking to his son and turned around. "What do you mean?"

"They can't protect these people. Look at all the kids. And the old folks. It'll be a bloodbath."

I looked at where he was pointing—a line of people waiting for the restrooms. "I guess positive thinking was never your style."

"I'm facing facts. What's the plan?"

Though I knew it was hopeless, I tried texting my wife, but I didn't have any bars. "I'm going to see if I can find Holly."

"I'll talk to the authorities," the teacher said. "Ben, you and Aaron, come with me."

I started at one end of the gym and went down every aisle. It was hard to walk in some places since people's stuff was spread out everywhere. A woman screamed at me because I almost stepped on her kid. Everyone was on edge.

The last time I was in this gym was for my high school graduation. My dad had passed away the year before. Sick as she was, my mom had made it to the ceremony. Though it was no big deal to me, I remembered how proud she was. She had never completed high school. Right before she died, I promised her I would go to college. Another commitment washed away in a river of beer and regret.

There were lots of people I recognized from the town. All had the same hollow expression, as if their spirits had departed. My parents' neighbor, Mrs. Hough, touched my arm as I walked past. Her hair was white. The last time I'd seen her, she was dyeing it. In her early seventies now, she looked older and frailer.

"Dave?" she said.

"Mrs. Hough. Are you okay?"

"Not really. They rushed me down here, and I forgot my medication. It's at the house, and I can't go back for it."

She was a chatterbox, and I wanted to find Holly. The old woman used to come over and look after my mom during those last weeks and months. She brought her soup and magazines and helped with the bathing. I decided to take a seat on the floor and visit.

"They won't tell us what's going on. They keep saying there's been some kind of, of contagion. I don't even know what that means. They're not the police. Who are these people?"

I patted her arm. "What's the medication for?"

"Diabetes, blood pressure, arthritis... Don't ever get old."

"Tell you what. I can take a run over there."

"Oh, would you? My son sent word that he was coming to get me. I told him not to leave school, but he insisted."

"Right now, I have to find someone. But I promise I'll go to your house in a little while, okay? Think you can hold out?"

She dug through her purse. "Here are my house keys."

"Why don't you try resting?" I fluffed her pillow and helped her lie down.

"God bless you, Dave," she said and closed her eyes. "You're a saint."

It took me a few minutes to cover the rest of the floor, and I couldn't find Holly anywhere. I didn't think she would return to the house. Why hadn't she called or texted? There was the obvious answer, but I didn't want to think about it.

"No luck?" Landry said when I rejoined the group. "They're telling everyone it's an endemic outbreak."

"I heard. What exactly does that mean?"

"It means there's a virus that's prevalent in this area, and it's spreading from person to person." He shook his head. "Pretty much what I guessed. We can't stay here."

That got Ben's attention. "Why not? Look at all this protection."

The teacher signaled us to follow him outside, away from everyone. Several guards were taking a smoke break. He spoke in a low, deliberate voice.

"You've seen what the undead are capable of," he said. "Once they discover there's a building full of fresh meat, they'll attack without mercy. If you think these guys can stop them, think again. I don't care how well trained they are. This place is hell's waiting room."

Ben wasn't buying it. "These security guards are professionals. They have weapons."

"Keep your voice down." Landry watched the guards, who were smoking and laughing. "And if it were only a few, I would agree. But they travel in hordes. All they have to do is bite a guard, and he turns into one of them. We can't risk it."

"How many do you think there are out there?" Aaron said.

The teacher stared at the fence. "Could be in the thousands by now."

Defeated, Ben looked at his son. "Where are we supposed to go?"

"Shit, I forgot," I said. "I promised a neighbor I'd get her medication. It's no big deal. I can do it on my own."

"Take Aaron with you," Landry said.

Ben grabbed his son's arm. "Absolutely not. I'll go."

Though Aaron was green, I didn't have a lot of faith in his father. He was an even worse survivalist than me. And his artificial hip made him a liability.

"Dad, it's fine. I can do this."

"Son, are you sure?"

"I'll be okay, I promise."

"I love you. Be careful."

"We'll remain in the motorhome until you return," the teacher said.

As the four of us headed out, a security guard stopped us. "You need to go back inside."

"A neighbor of mine is in there," I said. "We're going to her house to get her medication."

"We're not supposed to let you people come and go at will."

"I get that, but she needs her meds. She has diabetes."

"What's her name?"

"Eleanor Hough."

He signaled a second guard, who used his laptop to look her up. When her information popped up, the guy gave his partner a thumbs-up.

"Okay, make it fast," the first guard said. "But be back before sunset, or we can't guarantee your protection. They seem to prefer the darkness."

"Thanks. Hey, what's going on with the cell service?"

He side-eyed his friend. "Last I heard, we were looking into it."

"What does that mean?"

"It means we're looking into it." Before I could respond, both of them walked away.

"What do you think's happening with the phones?" Aaron said when we were in the truck.

"Shit's breaking down. Next, it'll be the power."

"You sound like Mr. Landry."

"Don't even joke about a thing like that," I said.

CHAPTER
THIRTY-EIGHT

MRS. HOUGH LIVED on a cul-de-sac across the street from the house where I grew up. As we drove in, I could see how easy it would be to get trapped, with only one way out.

"Which house?" Aaron said.

"See those pinwheel petunias?"

"Cute."

"Is that a sarcastic cute?"

"No... Yeah, sarcastic."

The street was deserted. There used to be a flock of wild parrots that hung out in the maple trees, squawking their heads off. No birds sang now. Before going in, we grabbed weapons and scanned all the houses, looking for movement of any kind.

Holding his dad's Remington, Aaron watched for intruders while I let myself in the front door. Mrs. Hough was a widow, and her house smelled old. Inside, I saw dated furniture and lots of family photos. There was a framed picture in the center of the sofa table. I recognized her son. He was in his thirties now, surrounded by a wife and two small children.

In the master bathroom, I opened the medicine cabinet

and found nothing but toothpaste, mouthwash, and various lotions. Next, I went into the kitchen. Prescription drugs were lined up neatly on a beige tile counter. On the side, there was a grocery list written on a yellow notepad, a ballpoint pen from some real estate agent, and a stack of store coupons.

I found a plastic grocery bag and tossed in all the medication. On the way to the foyer, I heard a growl. Scanning the room, I backed up to the front door, which was partially open. Nervous, I peered outside and got Aaron's attention.

"I could use your help," I said.

He came in, gripping his weapon. I set down the plastic bag and raised my handgun. We waited. A persistent scratching came from the hall closet.

Aaron gave me a nervous look. "We should leave."

"If there's something in there, I'd rather deal with it now."

Bracing myself, I swung open the door, and a small animal leaped out at us. It was a white-and-gray Shih Tzu, baring its teeth at us. He was cute, with his bugged-out eyes and impressive underbite. Relieved, I lowered my weapon. With his head cocked, he stared at us. I didn't recall Mrs. Hough ever having a dog. He must have been a recent addition.

Aaron inched closer. "Come here, boy. You scared?"

"What if he's rabid?"

He gave the dog a pat, and the animal rolled onto his back. "How could you forget your dog?"

I opened the plastic bag and rummaged through the medications. One was Aricept. The poor woman had dementia. They didn't allow pets at the evac center, but why would you lock the animal in a closet? While I waited by the door, Aaron ran into the kitchen and found food and a bowl.

"What're you doing?" I said.

"We can't leave him here. He'll starve."

"Don't we have enough to worry about?" When I saw how he fawned over the animal, I relented. "Hey, why not?"

Cradling the dog, Aaron headed to the front door. A livid hand reached for him. It was an undead mailman in blue shorts. Its ear had been torn off, and the head was covered in crusty blood. Before he could react, it dragged him onto the lawn. The dog escaped and ran around in circles, barking. Dropping everything, I followed. The attacker tried to bite Aaron in the face, but he blocked it with the shotgun.

"Help me!"

I put my gun barrel in the attacker's ear and fired, praying the bullet would miss my partner. The blood spray left a star pattern on the asphalt. The mailman went limp as Aaron skittered away, waving his arms like he was in the middle of a bee swarm. The sound of the gunshot sent the dog running.

I examined myself for wounds. "Did you get bit?"

"I don't think so." Breathing hard, he patted all around his head. "What about the Shih Tzu?"

Movement in the distance caught my eye. A horde had entered the cul-de-sac, attracted by the gunfire. I handed Aaron his weapon.

"Don't move," I said.

Advancing, they scanned the street like predators. Luckily, they hadn't seen us. Halfway up, they stopped and listened. All was quiet except for Aaron, who was panting. The one in front let out an echoing death shriek, and the horde came for us.

I pointed my weapon at them. "Take out as many as you can."

"I don't know if—"

"Dude, don't die out here."

I kneecapped the lead attacker. Spinning once, it kept coming, dragging its bad leg after it. Taking a breath, I aimed for the head. It went down. Copying me, Aaron did the same with three others.

"Get to the truck," I said.

Aaron jumped into the passenger seat. Before I could get inside, something grabbed me. Now more claws were on me. I tried aiming my handgun, but it was no use. I was about to die in the stupid street because I had tried to help an old woman. Which proved for all eternity that no good deed goes unpunished.

As my attackers snapped and grappled with me, I got off a couple rounds, killing several. Across the street, a man in his fifties watched us. He had on sweatpants and a bloodstained undershirt. His face and hands were splattered with fresh blood.

"Do something!" I said.

A hand reached for me—it was Aaron. He pulled me out of the way and blasted away at the marauders till nothing moved. The guy was boss.

When it was over, we stood in the middle of the street, taking in the carnage. Somewhere, the little dog yipped. The man watching us stuck a handgun under his chin, his vacant eyes never leaving ours.

Then, he squeezed the trigger.

CHAPTER
THIRTY-NINE

THE SOUNDS of gunfire and screaming swelled as Aaron and I neared the evac center. I headed for the main entrance and stopped suddenly in the middle of the street.

Someone had failed to lock the doors. And now a horde surrounded the gym. Shrieking, they climbed over one another to get inside. As Landry had predicted, the security guards were overwhelmed. Those who were on the roof shot the attackers one after another. But it was too late.

Soon, security forces and civilians alike would join the ranks of the undead. Already, mangled guards were rising like broken puppets and following the others into the gym. The people inside didn't stand a dead drunk's chance.

The motorhome was nowhere in sight. My guess—Ben and the teacher had fled the violence. I pulled forward to make a U-turn when their vehicle barreled towards us. Ben pulled up next to me and rolled down his window.

"We barely made it out," he said. "Are you guys okay? Aaron?"

"We're good, Dad."

I was grateful he hadn't mentioned the cul-de-sac. "Where to now?"

Landry leaned over. "We need supplies pronto."

On the road, we passed ten or twelve Humvees and LMTVs heading for the evac center. I wished them luck. Black Dragon had gathered enough victims in one place to feed an undead army. My phone vibrated, startling me. Text messages began flooding in. Frantic, I read the last one.

Where r u?

It was from Holly. I turned onto a side street and called her.

"It's me," I said, my hand shaking.

"Are you in Tres Marias?"

"Near the high school."

"I'm at St. Monica's."

"Are you safe? Never mind—don't move. I'm on my way."

Aaron called his dad to tell him what happened as I broke the speed limit to reach the church. I attended St. Monica Catholic School for eight years. Before the outbreak, Holly went to Mass every Sunday. And each time she invited me, I came up with some lame-ass excuse not to go.

The street was deserted. A Humvee whizzed past, followed by more Black Dragon vehicles. Men with handguns and long guns stood guard outside the church. It was like a scene from *The Godfather*. I was about to walk in when Aaron pointed out my blood-stained shirt. After changing, I went inside.

St. Monica's was built in 1900. The church had survived numerous earthquakes and was recently renovated. The outside was granite with tall stained-glass windows. The inside was filled with cherrywood. A crucifix imported from Italy hung behind the marble altar.

People were scattered in the pews throughout. Many held their children close as they prayed the Rosary. An elderly priest made his way among the crowd, providing solace where he could. Not all my memories of this place were terrible. I attended two funerals here—first for my father, then my mother. And this was where Holly and I were married.

I spotted my wife near the front, praying. Seeing me, she joined me in the aisle, and I held her.

"I'm so sorry," I said. "For everything."

"My mom..."

"I know."

"You saw her?" When I didn't answer, she went on. "We were walking by the lake when one of those dead people attacked us."

"Did you get bit?"

"Mom did. I tried to protect her, but it happened so fast. She begged me to leave her, and I... I ran all the way to the house. God, I should've stayed."

"You did the right thing. You couldn't have saved her."

Seeing us, the priest walked over. "Can I help?"

"She lost her mother," I said.

He took her hands. "My dear child. We must continue to pray and ask for God's mercy."

I pictured Aaron shooting my mother-in-law, and I snapped. "That's it? We're supposed to pray, and then everything gets all better? Innocent people are dying out there."

Holly grabbed my arm. "Dave, please. He's trying to help."

Everyone was staring at me. Reddening, I lowered my head. But my rage still burned.

"You have every right to be angry, son," he said. "But use your anger to help others."

After making the Sign of the Cross over us, he left. My wife and I sat in the nearest pew. We kept our voices low.

"I kept trying to contact you," I said. "Something's wrong with the cell service."

"I know—I must've texted you, like, fifty times."

"You didn't go to our house, did you?"

"I came straight here right before they blocked the freeway exits. What are we going to do?"

"We have to leave."

"And go where?"

"I'm with some other people now. We're going to get supplies and see what happens."

"What about the high school? Maybe we can—"

"That's not an option now. It's been breached."

A woman behind us had overheard. Frantic, she took my arm. "I have relatives staying there. We were going to join them later."

"Maybe I was mistaken," I said.

I helped Holly with her stuff, and we headed out. Near the narthex, I spotted Detective Van Gundy sitting alone in a pew. His hands lay in his lap like dead birds. I waved, but he didn't look up. We continued to where the others were waiting.

"Holly, you remember Irwin Landry from high school?"

"Sure."

"And this is Ben Marino and his son, Aaron."

Ben squeezed her hand. "So glad we found you. Dave was going out of his mind."

On the way out, I crossed myself with holy water. Outside, the people guarding the church were still in place. Holly got in the truck with me, and the others went with Ben.

"What about my car?" she said.

"Leave it. I'm not letting you out of my sight."

She stared out the window at the church as I started the

engine. Before I could put the truck in drive, Van Gundy jogged over. I got out and came around to meet him.

"I wasn't being rude," he said. "One of them attacked my wife and son. I got home and... I found them in the backyard, barely breathing."

Holly had joined us and laid her hand on the policeman's arm.

"I called 911. While I waited, they must've died. They..." Leaning against my open door, he wept. "I had to shoot them."

He wandered away in a stupor. I wished I could have done something for the detective. Instead, I climbed into the truck and waited for Holly to get in. We sat there, sullen and silent. The woman I had spoken to earlier hurried out with her husband. When she saw me, she looked away and kept walking.

"Did you notice Van Gundy's hand?" Holly said. "I think he got bit."

This was our world now. We witnessed things no human should ever see. Made choices no sane person should ever have to. It all came down to survival. And our odds were worse than bad.

"I love you," I said.

My wife looked at me with a cool detachment. It was like meeting someone on the street you recognized but had no connection to. I didn't care—I was determined to protect her. It might be the last good deed I would ever do. Would God even notice?

More people made their way into the church. Driving off, I said a silent prayer that they would do better than those poor bastards at the gym—the ones who, by now, were lost to the world.

And very, very hungry.

CHAPTER
FORTY

WHEN WE ARRIVED at the Royal Ranch Market, the place was in shambles. The parking lot was littered with over-turned baskets, trash, and cars with slashed tires. And the building was covered in fresh graffiti. Looters had busted out the windows, and as police sirens wailed in the distance, they ran off with whatever they could carry.

Holly startled as I grabbed my bullpup from the backseat and joined the others. Landry, Ben, and Aaron stood next to the motorhome, their hands on their weapons. We watched with grim stoicism as giddy thieves scampered past. I raised my gun when one slowed to check out the motorhome.

"Keep moving, asshole," I said.

As more looters rushed past, my wife gripped my arm. "I don't understand why we have all these guns."

"We have to protect ourselves," the teacher said.

I scanned the area, hoping Black Dragon was somewhere close. But there was no sign of them or the cops.

"What do we do?" Holly said to me.

"We get what we need and leave."

"Shouldn't I have a gun, too?"

"Not unless you know how to use it," Landry said too quickly.

My wife glared at him. Taking her hand, I got in front of her. "Stay close. Ben and Aaron will guard our vehicles."

Inside, a group of laughing men in ball caps brushed past us, their arms loaded with small electronics and bargain-bin DVDs. They made me sick. I knew the people who owned this store and could only imagine what they were going through. Seeing everything they had worked so hard for destroyed by a bunch of freeloading lowlifes.

Near the manager's office, checkers and cart pushers observed the madness, their expressions hollow. A greasy-looking scumbag wearing a hoodie and carrying a toaster oven ran by me. I tripped him. Hurtling forward, he did a faceplant on the linoleum and slid into an end cap filled with gift cards.

In a rage, he confronted me. "That funny to you?"

Holly grabbed my arm. "Dave, no..."

I pushed the bullpup's barrel into his oily nose, and he pissed himself. "Get out."

Cursing, the loser left the toaster oven and ran.

"I was about to do that myself," the teacher said. "Let's get moving."

We grabbed shopping carts and collected piles of food, water, flashlights, and batteries. There was a little pharmacy at the rear of the store. Landry let himself in and returned with the medical supplies he thought we might need—antibiotics, bandages, and painkillers.

When we were done, our carts were piled high. Most of the stuff we would load into the motorhome. The rest could go into the truck bed in case we got separated. I approached the frightened store employees and gave them my best smile.

"Can someone ring us up?" I said.

A checker—a Latina around my age—led me to a check stand. The teacher kept watch as I pulled out my credit card. Two cart pushers came over and bagged our stuff under my wife's direction.

After putting away the supplies, Aaron, Holly, and I returned to help the employees secure the store. Ben and Landry guarded our cargo while we boarded up the broken windows with plywood we'd found in the back.

We finished around twilight. I remembered what the security guard had said about the flesh-eaters preferring the darkness and swept my eyes across the parking lot, where the lights had just come on.

I turned to my wife. "It's time we left Tres Marias."

Ben pointed at a Black Dragon helicopter zipping across the sky. "Not sure that's going to be possible."

"Then we make a run for it," I said.

We headed for the northbound freeway on-ramp. Ben's motorhome took the lead since it was larger and could break through the barriers. Other drivers with the same idea sped past us, cutting in front. The old me would've gotten into it with them, but there was no time for that. Instead, I focused on getting out.

Near the freeway, we encountered bright lights and Black Dragon vehicles. Above us, a helicopter moved into position, shining a spotlight on an SUV speeding towards the on-ramp. A voice boomed over the chopper's PA system, ordering the renegades to stop. Everyone braked.

The guards opened fire on the vehicle, aiming for the tires. The SUV spun out and crashed into a barrier. Guards double-timed it and surrounded the disabled car as the stunned driver—a middle-aged man—crawled out, followed by a woman. They ordered the couple to lie on the ground. A female guard removed their crying children from the backseat.

Another driver made a dangerous U-turn and shot past us. I decided to get out of there, too, and signaled Ben. When we were far enough away from the roadblock, we pulled over. I tried taking Holly's hand, but she refused me.

"Time for plan B?" Aaron said.

The teacher shushed him and listened. It was the sound of distant gunfire. "We need to hunker down. This is going to be a long fight."

Ben headed for the motorhome. "I vote we return to the grocery store."

"Hold on. Too hard to secure. We need a place with cooking facilities and showers."

I took a moment to think. The answer was obvious. "The Pine Nut Motel. Each room has a hot plate and a refrigerator."

My wife nodded. "The motel sounds good. Ben?"

Before he could answer, a death shriek sounded through trees that looked like sentinels in the darkness. Holly slipped her hand into mine.

"We'd better get moving," Landry said.

CHAPTER
FORTY-ONE

IF THERE WAS one thing I learned from Ram Chakravarthy, everything comes at a price. No pissing and moaning—take it or leave it. On the plus side, he ran a clean operation. There were always fresh towels and sheets. And I had yet to spot a speck of mold or a cockroach.

"Hi, Ram," I said. "We need three rooms next to each other. Preferably on the second floor."

Tapping a key repeatedly, the motel manager didn't look up from his laptop. "Bloody internet is down again. I charge you ten dollars extra per night."

Ben pushed past us. "Now wait a second."

Ignoring him, I turned to Ram, "That's fine."

Making a face, Ben got out his wallet. "Do you take Visa?"

"There is a bank charge, which I must pass on to you."

"Right." Checking his anger, Ben handed over his card.

After settling in, we stood on our respective balconies and gazed at the town in the distance. All seemed quiet, though the tree line made it hard to see much. I thought I spotted smoke rising from somewhere near the downtown area. I imagined looters and weirdos turning Tres Marias into a perverted block party, and I cursed them.

We agreed not to make any decisions till we had gotten some sleep. Each of us had food we could prepare in our rooms. The plan was to rise early and reconvene. Holly and I had canned goods, but we'd also purchased cheese, lunch meat, and bread. As she fixed sandwiches, I switched on the TV and clicked around till I found the local news.

Evie Champagne was at ground zero, her mouth and nose wrapped in a silk scarf. The air looked orange and toxic. I couldn't help wondering if the quarantine had prevented the cameraman and her from leaving the area. And no other reporters were covering the outbreak.

"Felix, I'm standing outside a vacant lot. As you can see, Black Dragon has dug a makeshift pit. And now, it's filled with burning bodies. The smell is overwhelming. I've asked officials to confirm the numbers. Either they won't say or don't know. It looks to be in the hundreds from where I'm standing."

"Evie, are these civilians?" Felix said from the newsroom.

"Unknown."

"Has Black Dragon given any indication whether they have the situation under control?"

"I've asked several people, and the answer is always the same. They're focused on securing the area and will provide an official update later."

Looking for a place to eat, I settled for the bed while my wife brought paper plates and water bottles. Sitting beside me, she remained focused on the TV as the names and faces of the dead and missing scrolled past on a news ticker. We hadn't discussed sleeping arrangements. I glanced at an over-stuffed chair, wondering whether there were any extra blankets.

"...reporters were not allowed into the area. The mobile phone video you're seeing was taken earlier this evening."

On the screen, there were shaky images of looters scattering across a parking lot as vehicles burned. The ground was covered in broken glass. As Black Dragon security guards moved in, they fired live rounds over the heads of the mob.

"There are unconfirmed reports about looters being shot on sight. We will update you as we learn more."

The news anchor reported that the epidemic was spreading. In faraway communities, there were isolated reports of attacks. Some attributed them to mass hysteria, others to the end of days.

"There are also reports of survivalists clashing with Black Dragon security personnel," he said. "We're being told that a group calling itself the Red Militia has attacked security guards and stolen their weapons. Their motives are unclear."

Holly switched off the TV and looked at me with a profound hurt in her eyes—a pain I had never seen before. I tried touching her hand, but she pulled it away. Her expression reminded me that what I'd done was far worse than any horde. I wasn't a bad person. But I'd made a mistake that I desperately wanted to undo. Dammit, I was not a bad person.

"I know you're not," she said.

Shit, had I said that out loud?

"You can stay with me in the bed, but that's as far as it goes."

"Thank you—I mean it." I took off my shoes and lay on the covers to show my good intentions. "See? No funny business."

Maybe I imagined it, but I thought she'd cracked a smile.

. . .

I didn't remember falling asleep. When I opened my eyes, it was night. I was on that lonely forest road again—the one where I had crashed my car. Up ahead, Jim's dog stared at me with fierce, glowing eyes. His head was low and menacing. Behind him, in the middle of the road, was Bob Creasy. He was in front of his van, waving at me, silhouetted by the glaring headlights.

As often happens in dreams, I couldn't run fast. I didn't look back, but I knew Perro was gaining on me. A tremendous force knocked me down. The pavement had the consistency of liquid tar. Viciously, Perro tore at my back through my clothes. It didn't even hurt.

Now, it was daytime in Tres Marias. I stood in the street, gazing at the Beehive. Cars swerved past me, blasting their horns. Inside, Jim and Missy sat in a booth by the window, drinking schooners of beer. They were dead. Gray, bloody flesh slid off their faces and neck and plopped into their glasses. With their eyes betraying no emotion, they made each other laugh.

Moving closer to the bar, I noticed that everyone around me was dead—even the passing drivers. Jim and Missy leaned into each other and tongue-kissed. Black sludge squirted from the edges of their gory mouths, leaving kidney worms writhing on the table. They watched me through the glass. Looking at my reflection, I saw that I was dead, too.

A shadow fell over me. Pivoting, I saw Detective Van Gundy. The flesh on his face oozed downwards like warm cake frosting. His eyes were dark crystals.

"This is your fault," he said. "All of it."

His voice was tinny, like a 1930s radio show. "I know about Jim and Missy and the dead woman in the forest. And I know about Fred and Stacey and Irene. All your fault."

"I'm not a bad person," I said in a milky vacuum that swallowed me up.

I woke up in a cold sweat to the sound of a shriek. For a second, I thought Missy had tracked me down. Each time I tried closing my eyes, I saw her face crawling with maggots.

"This isn't over," she said and licked my cheek with her black tongue.

CHAPTER
FORTY-TWO

I AWOKE from another hellish nightmare to find Holly dressed. Her hair was wet, and she smelled wonderful. I pretended not to care.

"There's coffee," she said and switched on the news.

After a shower, I put on my clothes in the bathroom to avoid any awkwardness. A little while later, our group gathered outside on two adjoining balconies.

Ben kicked things off. "Anybody come up with a plan?"

"Normally, I'd advise getting to safety," Landry said. "But after listening to the news, it sounds like there may be nowhere that's secure."

"What if we stayed here?"

"I suppose we could keep to our rooms, but how would we get food?"

"We could head to San Francisco or even Portland."

The teacher scoffed. "May I remind you that the town is under quarantine? No one gets in or out."

Aaron's dad was adamant. "But we're not infected."

"Tell me, Ben. What does infection look like exactly? How do we know we're not already carrying the virus?"

"Maybe there's a blood test they could do," my wife said.

Landry shook his head. "Afraid not. I think our best bet is to wait it out. We need to find somewhere safer than this motel."

"But is that even possible?" Aaron said. "I mean, what are our chances?"

"Not good. And it's not just a matter of securing a building. Eventually, there might not be any electrical power or fresh water or food."

Something occurred to me. "And what if one of us gets sick and needs a doctor?"

Our collective mood had sunk to a new low, but the teacher kept at it.

"Our weapons will hold out for a while, but we'll need a steady supply of ammo. Besides the infected, we could end up fighting some very dangerous individuals—worse than what we saw at the market."

"The Red Militia," I said.

"And don't forget. There are also others planning what to do next. When it comes down to it, it'll be us versus them."

"But won't most people try to leave?" Holly said.

"If they do, Black Dragon will shoot them on sight."

Though I hated arguing with Landry, I tried another suggestion. "What about the backroads?"

"I don't think so. The authorities can't afford to let the virus spread any further."

"Do you think they can contain it?" Aaron said.

"You saw what happened at the high school. We're pretty much on our own."

Ben turned to my wife. "What are your thoughts?"

She looked at the others in turn, then at me. There didn't seem to be any doubt in her mind, and I braced myself.

"I wanna stay," she said.

What the hell was this? *Stay?* No way I wanted to stick around. Like any rational human, I preferred taking my chances on the road with my axe and my guns.

"Why?" That came out angrier than I intended.

"Because I grew up here," she said. "And I guess I'll die here."

The three of us had retreated to Ben and Aaron's room, which was the farthest away. I didn't want Holly listening through the paper-thin walls. Ben handed out cups of hot tea.

"I need you to talk some sense into her," I said to the teacher.

"Sounds to me like her mind is made up."

"But staying here is suicide. This town is like—"

"The epicenter, I know."

"Then explain it to her. There's got to be a way out."

Landry blew on his tea. "Let's examine the situation from Holly's perspective."

I hated it when he did that. Considering an alternative meant giving it validity. I glanced at Aaron, hoping he felt the same. No such luck—he was enthralled.

"Maybe we could gather enough supplies and look for a way out," he said. "We already know the main exits are blocked. And I assume the fire roads are out of the question."

I set aside my cup. "I got through before."

"You were lucky. Black Dragon hadn't finished securing the area. They're everywhere now."

"What if we hike through the forest?" As the words left my lips, I remembered Ben's hip. Not to be mean, but how far would he get on foot?

The teacher drained his cup in one gulp. "You're forgetting the hordes. And what about the helicopter patrols? Okay, let's say, by some miracle, we managed to get on the freeway. Where do we go? North? South?"

"I was thinking LA."

"Dave, you know as well as I do that there are tons of tourists here in August, many from Los Angeles. All it would take is for one infected person to return and spread the disease. It's likely they already have."

"LA is huge. We'd have more of a chance to survive." I was grasping at straws.

"And what about getting there? We're not the only ones trying to leave. You think there won't be criminals and psychos of every shape, size, and creed on the highway? Did you ever think it won't be the infected who kill us but ordinary people?"

I was beginning to feel like Landry was against me. Desperate for allies, I appealed to Ben and his son. From their expressions, it was clear they were on his side.

"What are we supposed to do?" I said. "Wait around to get bit?"

The teacher sighed the way he used to with a thick-headed student. "We need to find someplace we can defend until this is over."

"So you agree with Holly?"

"I didn't say that." He looked at me with those piercing blue eyes I knew all too well from countless science lectures. "I'm simply weighing the pros and cons."

"Okay, how about this?" Ben said. "Suppose we stay and are unable to find a safe house. What if it's moving from one place to another, fighting hordes every day and the Red Militia on weekends? How long could we survive?"

I wanted badly to hit somebody. "Is everyone crazy? This is what I've been saying. I vote we get the hell out and take our chances."

Landry held up a warning hand. "This is too important to vote on without some serious thought. And you need to calm down. Ben?"

"I'd like to talk it over with Aaron and sleep on it."

"Fine," I said. "But in case you hadn't noticed, hell already put out the welcome mat."

The teacher chuckled. "Let's not overdramatize."

"Over— Shit, I can't believe you guys!"

I flung my cup across the room, where it splashed the wall and bounced onto the carpet. Convinced I was the only sane person on the planet, I stomped out.

Stewing in my own juices, I sat on the floor in our room. By now, it was evening. I had spent most of the afternoon doing laps around the motel. Trying to convince myself there was another solution. Thinking back, it was stupid to have been outside by myself.

"Did you guys come to a decision?" Holly said.

"They want to sleep on it."

"I don't expect you to stay with me. I've already made my decision. You should do what's best for you."

Her eyes were red, and there was a small, bloody cut where she had chewed her lip.

"You'd stay here and go it alone?"

"If I have to."

She was holding a rosary—the kind they gave away at the Children's Mass. It was made of blue plastic with a little white crucifix.

I pointed at it. "You remember how to use that?"

"Want me to show you?"

"Maybe later," I said.

I went outside and, leaning on the balcony railing, gazed at the night sky. Every instinct told me to run. And why not? There was nothing keeping me here. My wife and I were finished. She had absolved me from the need to protect her. I was free to do what was right for me. Selfishly, I wanted to take her up on it. For the first time, I felt like I had no home. I was, like the song says, *free fallin'*.

Landry must have spotted me because now he was on his balcony, looking up. "Pretty, aren't they? Can you show me where Ursa Major is?"

"I think I was sick that day."

He pointed. "It's right over there. And there's Ursa Minor."

"Little Bear."

"You do remember."

"What I remember is a time when I could look up at the sky and not worry whether a murderous freak was sneaking up behind me. And I recall what it was like to be a kid— when my only worry was being late for hockey practice. I don't feel so young anymore."

"We all have to grow up sometime, son."

"Not like this."

"Looking back, do you remember what it was like being at your best?"

"Yeah, I do. On the ice with a stick in my hand."

"And what did that feel like?"

"Like I ruled. Nothing could stop me, not a broken nose or a bigger opponent. It was the one time in my life I wasn't scared of anything—or anyone."

"You need to get that feeling back, and soon."

After he left, I looked at the stars again, trying to find my courage. But I could only contemplate a bleak, lonely future without Holly. Whether I lived or died made no difference now.

"Time to party," I said and grabbed my keys.

CHAPTER
FORTY-THREE

WHEN I OPENED MY EYES, I was lying in a sea of empty beer bottles in Jim's kitchen. From the smell of me, I must have pissed myself. I had a blinding headache and a very real urge to hurl. The sun wasn't yet high, and I could feel the cool of the morning from a breeze blowing in through the open front door.

"Get up."

I tilted my head, and daggers of pain tore at my eyes. Through a drunken fog, I discovered Ben and Aaron staring at me. They hoisted me by the arms and dragged me towards the kitchen table. Before reaching it, I staggered to the sink and brought up more sick than I'd seen in a long time. Reeking, it was everything I had eaten or drunk in the last five years. The stench made me go again. This cycle lasted for minutes till I was left with the dry heaves. Not one of my better days.

"You about done?" Ben said.

"How did you guys..."

"Not important."

Aaron handed me a glass of water. As I drank, I felt the high returning.

"Where's Landry?" I said.

Ben side-eyed his son. "With Holly. We told her you were out checking the roads. You stupid sonofabitch. One of those things could've wandered in here last night and…"

"So?"

He grabbed me by the arms and aimed my ass at a chair. But I missed it and landed on the floor, hitting my head on a cabinet door. I had never seen the guy so angry. In truth, I was a little scared.

"This is how it starts," he said. "And before you know it, the whole group falls apart."

Aaron played good cop. "Come on, Dave. We need you."

"You'll be fine."

Calmer now, Ben righted the chair and helped me into it. "Don't you get it? We have to stick together."

I rubbed the back of my head. "You don't need a drunk slowing you down."

Exasperated, he threw up his hands. Aaron took a seat next to me.

"Remember the cul-de-sac?" he said. "You were a hero to me that day. We never would've made it out if you hadn't been so focused."

"We got lucky, is all."

From the look on his dad's face, it was clear he hadn't shared our little adventure in petunialand.

Ben began rummaging through the cabinets. "Let's see if there's any coffee."

"Top right," I said.

After nuking the sink with bleach, Aaron found some cups and rinsed them. While the coffee brewed, my mind wandered.

Glimpses of the night before flickered in my head like an old movie spliced together with Scotch tape. And it starred me heading straight for Jim's house. You see, that's the thing with alcoholics—all we need is an excuse. We're sad. We're happy. We're upset. We're bored. In my case, I was empty.

Ben poured me a cup of strong black coffee, and I managed to keep it down. After a few minutes, my head began to clear. I yanked open a drawer, revealing an economy-size bottle of ibuprofen. Good ol' Jim. I swallowed four and pocketed the rest for later.

"I suppose you guys made up your minds," I said to Aaron.

"We're staying with Holly."

"Sure."

"It's the best option," Ben said.

I still had a choice to make. Pack my shit, get on the road, and hope I could stay sober long enough to find somewhere safe. Or grow a set and stick with my friends. After two more cups, I agreed to talk it over with the teacher. Ben didn't think I was in any shape to drive. Good call. Aaron took the truck, and I rode with his dad in the motorhome.

As soon as we were on the road, Ben started in like a concerned dad. "Look, I know you and Holly are having problems right now. But seriously, we need to find a way to survive together."

"Once she finds out what I did, she won't want me around. So, there's that."

"Give her a chance," he said. "What have you got to lose?"

At the motel, I spotted a forest ranger shuffling towards our building. Though a foot was missing, it moved with purpose.

"Don't worry, I got this," Ben said.

He pulled over and grabbed his shotgun. When he was clear of the vehicle, he pumped the gun once and took off most of the freak's head in a single blast. Wiping his mouth, he got back in and drove over the remains like it was trash. The guy was starting to impress me.

Holly and Landry watched us from the balcony. I staggered up the stairs, determined to get this over with. When I looked at my wife, I could tell she knew exactly what had happened.

"Glad you're all right," she said.

Miserably, I watched as she covered her nose from the smell and retreated to our room. At first, I thought she was disappointed. But when she yanked the curtains shut, I knew she was angry. But why, though? It wasn't like we were together anymore.

"So what's it going to be?" the teacher said.

"The truth is I'm too scared to do this on my own."

"Good. Get yourself cleaned up. We need to come up with a plan."

I never told the others the real reason I chose to stay. It was because of Holly. Though being there wouldn't change her feelings about me, at least I could make myself useful and protect her. A shower and a change of clothes would be a good start.

"Leave your clothes outside the door," she said and handed me a towel. "I need to burn them."

CHAPTER
FORTY-FOUR

A DEAD MAN wearing a Black Dragon uniform wandered into view. Landry was the first to spot it. Weaponless, its bloody right hand was missing fingers. The front of its shirt was stained black where it had puked. Its head twitching, the freak headed for the motel office. The teacher grabbed a weapon and fired a round.

With its jaw hanging half off, it continued to stagger. The second bullet tore open its temple. This time, it went down. I was glad Holly wasn't there to see the kill. But the gunfire brought her outside. She peered over our balcony and blinked.

"Was it—"

"Not a person," I said.

We waited for others to appear, but none came. Anxious to find a better place to meet, I suggested the motel office. I wanted to check on Ram anyway. After loading up our vehicles, we went inside, carrying our weapons. As usual, the motel manager was behind the desk at his computer.

When he saw my axe, his eyes got huge. "How can I help?"

"We're not here to rob the place," I said.

I expected him to call the police. Instead, he said nothing and went back to work. We assembled near the front door.

"I didn't expect the rest of you to stay," my wife said.

Landry peered through the window. "We talked it over, and it's the right thing to do. Most of us know this area. On the road, we'd be in unfamiliar surroundings. One mistake could cost us our lives."

I smirked at the others. "Way to sugarcoat it."

He ignored me. "The immediate goal is to find somewhere that's big enough and that we can lock down. Also, it has to be practical. When the power and water run out, it's going to be rough going. Something as basic as a working toilet will become precious."

I noticed Ram listening intently to our conversation. "Got something to add?"

"Come to my house," he said. "I have everything you need."

The teacher marched up to him and squinted. "What exactly do you mean?"

"Everything to survive."

"What about this place?"

The motel manager pointed at his laptop. "What do you think I've been doing over here? Playing video games?" He left the front desk and joined us. "For weeks, I am researching websites and watching the news. And I know what I have invested in will save us."

I side-eyed the others. "I don't understand what—"

"Come and see Ram's fortress."

"How far?" Ben said.

"Few miles. We can go now."

With no good options, it didn't take long for us to decide. He went behind his desk and packed up his laptop. When he returned, he was wearing a backpack and carrying a pump-action shotgun.

Holly pointed at the windows. "Look!"

I joined her. More freaks had wandered onto the property, attracted by the gunshots.

"What do we do?" I said.

The teacher cracked the door and peered out. "We need to get to those vehicles. That's our objective right now."

They hadn't yet seen us. As they wandered without purpose, a squirrel made the mistake of crossing their path. With surprising speed, one of them snatched it and ripped the animal's head off with its teeth.

I grabbed my wife's hand. "Are we shooting our way out?"

"We have to be careful," Landry said. "We don't know how many there are. And above all else, we can't get bit."

Ram pushed his way to the door. "This is my motel. I go first."

"Okay. Where's your car?"

"Behind this building."

The teacher looked at the rest of us. "How are we fixed, gun-wise?"

We raised our weapons. Landry had a rifle. Ben gripped his shotgun, and Aaron showed off a handgun and hunting knife. I had my bullpup and axe.

"What about me?" Holly said.

She was right. Training or not, she needed to defend herself. I exchanged Aaron's gun for my bullpup and placed the smaller weapon in my wife's right hand with the barrel pointed at the ground.

"This is a Glock," I said and pointed out the safety trigger. "Keep your index finger on the trigger guard like this. When you shoot, make sure your finger covers the whole trigger, or the gun won't fire. And remember, aim for the head."

"What about you?"

"I'm fine with your mom's axe."

The motel manager stood by the door, his shotgun raised. He looked like he knew what he was doing. We moved in close to cover him.

It all happened fast. As soon as Ram stepped outside, the attackers released a collective death shriek. Careful not to hit our vehicles, he blasted away, all the time marching forward. The rest of us followed. I pulled Holly over and positioned her next to me.

"Remember," the teacher said. "Choose your target like we practiced."

As the others began firing, I went after an out-of-shape scoutmaster who had come around from the side. I hacked off the grasping hands so it couldn't latch on to anyone. When it came at me again, I went for the head.

Landry glanced back at me. "Watch out for blood."

I concentrated on what was in front of me. My wife raised her weapon and fired at a vicious-looking soccer mom. The first round struck it in the chest and the second in the face. The girl kicked ass.

"Yeah!" she said as the juddering freak fell at her feet.

We shot and chopped our way to the vehicles. When it was over, twenty or so bodies lay on the asphalt. There was black blood everywhere. God help me, it was starting to feel routine.

"Let's hope Ram's house is a fortress," I said.

CHAPTER
FORTY-FIVE

OUR CARAVAN HEADED up a deserted private road that rimmed the forest. I kept pace with Ram's black Land Rover, occasionally checking the rearview mirror for the motorhome. Next to me, Holly stared straight ahead, with the handgun lying in her lap.

"You okay?" I said.

She gave me a withering look. What had I done now?

Her lips pressed together, she shook her head. "When I shot that woman..."

"It wasn't human anymore. It was—"

"When I shot her, I..." She put her hand on her mouth. "I feel so ashamed. Because I think I might've enjoyed it."

"It was the adrenaline. And your instinct to survive. You did nothing wrong."

She was quiet for a long time. I decided to leave it.

"How did you know about my mother?" she said.

"I saw her when..."

"When what?"

She had caught me off guard. I'd promised myself never to tell her about that.

"At Shasta Lake. I was looking for you when I found her. She'd already turned. And then Landry caught her." The more I explained, the worse it sounded.

"He said you practiced before. Did all of you take turns shooting the—"

"Holly, don't."

"Was my mother there?"

"I didn't shoot her—I swear. I couldn't."

She gave my hand a squeeze and looked away. I wanted to tell her more—explain what I had felt seeing Irene like that. But I'd already said more than I should have.

"Thank you for telling me the truth," she said.

The compound sat on a hill. We had a magnificent view of the town and the surrounding forest. I didn't know anything about security. But in later conversations with Ram, I learned that the place was protected by an induced-pulse electric fence. It was the same kind that correctional facilities use. A series of retractable steel bollards fronted the property to prevent vehicles from breaching the perimeter.

Inside the fence, there were steel poles with video cameras and lights mounted high. As we got closer, the bollards lowered, and the gates opened. The driveway was massive and easily accommodated our vehicles.

There were several buildings, all made of concrete. Though attractive and modern, they were meant to be practical. The main structure, which I assumed was the house, had narrow, dark windows. I wouldn't have been surprised if they were made of bulletproof glass.

"Glad you decided to stay with us?" my wife said. "Let's hope this guy doesn't have a wet bar."

As we exited our vehicles, six barking German shepherds

came running from the side of the main building. For a sec, I thought we would be torn to pieces, and I yelled at Holly to get in the truck. Calmly, our host spoke to them in German.

"Nein. Bleib. Setz."

They stopped and sat in a straight line, their ears pointed forward. Aaron grinned like a little kid.

Ram stroked a dog's neck. "Trained in Germany."

Landry gazed around him, his hands on his hips. "How long have you been planning this?"

"Five years."

"But you couldn't have known about the outbreak," Ben said.

"I knew something like this would happen eventually. It is the fate of every great civilization. Think of this as another Mongol invasion."

Our host let us in through the front door and turned off the alarm. The one-story house looked comfortable and warm, with Oriental rugs and rooms graced with expensive English furniture.

There were eight bedrooms, each with a bathroom, desk, and laptop computer. Wi-Fi was available everywhere, powered by a satellite dish. There was a game room, a den, and a library containing books and a dozen e-readers.

The basement spanned the entire house—five thousand square feet—and was sealed off by a four-inch-thick steel door. The teacher's eyes grew wide at the racks of nonperishable food and bottled water. It was enough to last months.

A command center was positioned in the middle of the room. Multiple monitors showed video feeds of the property's interior and exterior. Near that, there were two beds, a workout area with weight machines and free weights, and a small kitchen. And there were bathrooms with showers.

A steel door stood at one end of the basement. Using a

keypad on the wall, Ram opened it and showed us a room filled with weapons and ammo, enough to mount an invasion. He informed us that another building housed an indoor shooting range.

Upstairs, the kitchen looked big enough to cook for an army. A large refrigeration unit with clear glass doors stood along one wall. There was a walk-in pantry and a restaurant-quality gas range and hood. And outside, through an archway, a formal dining room.

After the tour, we sat around the kitchen table, drinking soda and munching on chips. Landry chuckled, then looked at our host with a serious expression.

"What about electricity?" he said.

"Liquid-cooled standby generator, one hundred fifty kilowatts. There are also solar panels on the roofs of all the buildings."

"What happens when the bottled water runs out?"

"There is an artesian well on the property, with a water-purification system."

"Gasoline?"

"I buried a five-thousand-gallon tank under the driveway. The gas pump is next to the garage."

Aaron nudged his dad. "Five thousand gallons. Holy shit."

The teacher rubbed the back of his neck. "Amazing. I can't think of anything else. Ram, you are officially my hero."

"I have a question," I said. "Are you saying we can stay here?"

"Of course. As my guests."

Ben squinted at him. "For how long?"

"As long as necessary."

"Not that we're ungrateful," I said. "But why would you do that?"

He looked at each of us in turn. "I see many people at the

motel—all kinds. After a time, I get to know who is good and who is not. There are going to be dark days ahead. Indeed, it will become hell on earth shortly. This place is safe, but I cannot run it by myself. You are good people. And with you, I feel I can survive."

I leaned in and looked at him, dead serious. "How much is all this going to cost?"

My wife belted me in the arm. "For shit's sake."

"We were all thinking it," I said.

Ram laughed good-naturedly. "You believe I love money, right? No, this is not correct. It is a test."

"A test. Sure."

"People argue about money, and I know they are not good for me. You, my friend, never argue. That's the kind of people I know I can survive with."

Red-faced, Ben laughed. "And to think I was mad at you."

I shook the Indian's hand. "Dude, I can't figure you out."

"Plenty of time for that," he said. "Now, who wants lunch?"

CHAPTER
FORTY-SIX

THE ROOM HOLLY and I were assigned was comfortable. For safety, there were no windows. Ram explained that those we saw outside were false. There was a three-foot gap between the outer and inner walls. The glass was added for appearance's sake. We had a security monitor connected to the high-def video cameras outside to provide a view.

"I thought I asked for separate beds," she said.

At the motel, we had worked it out that we would sleep together without intimacy. But it would be too frustrating to lie close to my wife. To smell her scent and hear her breathing. I was better off on the floor.

"I'll ask for a different room."

She brushed my hand. "It's fine. I'm not ready to be alone yet."

"That chair doesn't look too bad. I'll get our stuff."

Taking my wrist, she gave me a smile. "Thanks."

"For what?"

"For coming back."

"About that night, I—"

"It's okay," she said and left to check out the bathroom.

I walked into the kitchen to get a bottle of water. There was a security monitor on the counter. Landry stayed glued to it like a man expecting out-of-town guests.

"You think any freaks will find us way up here?"

"I don't know," he said and walked out.

Dinner was incredible. An excellent cook, Ram made us a full Indian meal. He said that lucky for us, he was from the south. I wasn't so sure how lucky we were. The food was so spicy I thought my teeth would melt. Though I had to drink a lot of water to get through it, everything was delicious.

Ben smiled at his son. "Mom loved this kind of food, remember?"

We looked at him. I had never asked what his story was— why he wasn't in any hurry to return home with his son. I'd assumed he was divorced.

He stared at his hands. "Lynn passed away a few weeks ago. Pancreatic cancer."

"Oh, Ben," Holly said.

"She put up a good fight. But in the end, all she wanted was to go peacefully. We moved her to a hospice nearby. Aaron and I stayed with her until the end. After the funeral, we couldn't bear to be at home. So we decided to do a little camping and fishing."

"Which, normally, would've been a great idea," I said.

"I guess these aren't what you'd call normal times. Lately, I've been wondering if maybe she wasn't luckier than us."

My wife touched his hand. "You and Aaron are together. That's what matters now."

"You're right." He gave his son's shoulder a squeeze.

"What about you?" I said to our host.

"I came to this country as a student. Got my engineering degree from Stanford. I was going to start my doctoral program but decided to take some time off and work."

"But you ran a motel. How can you afford this place?"

"Not to boast at all, but I come from a wealthy family. I convinced them to support me."

"Lucky for us," Aaron said.

Landry was uncharacteristically quiet. When he looked at Ram, something passed between them.

"But it seems there are concerns," our host said. "I think this is a good time to discuss. We mustn't keep any secrets."

The teacher seemed more interested in stirring his coffee than drinking it. "I'm worried. And not just about the infected."

Holly seemed to understand. "The Red Militia."

He began arranging objects on the table—napkin holders, silverware, and glasses. We pushed our plates aside to make room.

"I've taken a close look at all the plans for this place. And I've been watching the monitors. I'm concerned that, if someone wanted to, they could take out the electrical fence, kill the dogs, and break into the house."

He used his hand to plow through a defense made of cutlery. I got to my feet and studied the table. The others did the same.

"The fence wouldn't be that difficult, would it?" I said. "All you'd need is a grenade to punch a hole and knock out the power."

My wife looked at me with concern. "On the news, they're saying these guys are stealing weapons from Black Dragon."

Ram didn't seem concerned. "There are alarms everywhere. If someone were to try that, we would be waiting with guns."

I wasn't convinced. "But wouldn't it depend on how many were attacking us? Someone might get through."

"The point is we need to prepare for the worst." Landry picked up the salt and pepper shakers and positioned them outside the perimeter. "That means a twenty-four-hour watch from now on."

"I don't get it," Aaron said. "When did this become a military operation?"

Grabbing paper and pen, Ben created a schedule. Each of us would take a four-hour shift. The plan was to monitor everything from the command center in the basement. If anything suspicious happened, the person on duty would wake up the designated backup. In an emergency, it was all hands on deck.

We weren't hardcore about bathroom breaks, but the teacher admonished us to remain vigilant. The video cameras and alarms around the property were first class. However, history has taught us that even the best security can be defeated.

Now that we were together, I appreciated Landry more than ever. I had only known him as my science teacher. Soon, I learned that he was a voracious reader. When he put his mind to it, he could master a subject in weeks. Which was why he was more prepared than most when the outbreak happened.

The teacher's biggest worry was with the people who had constructed the compound. They must have been locals and would know how everything worked, including any chinks in the armor. They might have even designed weaknesses, the way a computer programmer can build a backdoor into a software program.

And this was where I came to appreciate Ram, that mad Indian genius. Instead of using local talent to build his fortress, he brought in construction experts from India on H-1B visas. And while he was planning, he studied and obtained his contractor's license so he could handle all the necessary permits himself. Though the blueprints were on file at City Hall, he assured us he'd updated the physical design after submitting them. Which meant the final revisions never made it into the official record.

Unable to sleep, I went to the basement, where I found Aaron at the security console. Ben was in the workout room, bench-pressing a hundred pounds. Aaron's dad was an interesting character. He didn't say much. I had the impression his wife's death had drained away his happiness. For all I knew, he might have been the life of the party back in the day. When he saw me, he set the stainless steel bar on the stand.

"I know," he said. "It's not much weight, but I've got to start somewhere."

"You won't hear me making wisecracks. Look at this flab."

"You might want to consider getting into shape."

I sat on a bench as he wiped the sweat from his neck and face. "What do you think about all this?"

He looked at me with a neutral expression. "My honest opinion? Most of us are going to die."

I laughed coarsely. "Wow. Um, these projects you used to manage—were any of them successful?"

"What can I say? Lynn was the optimist."

"You might be right, the odds aren't good. What does your son think?"

"Aaron has always been a glass-half-full kinda guy—like his mom. He's my world now. And I want him to make it, even if I don't."

"I'm with you there."

"How's it going with you and Holly?"

"Baby steps. I like to think she hates my guts a little less every day."

He let out a high cackle and lay on the bench for another set. "I need to remember that line."

I started to walk away and stopped. "Seriously, how did you guys find me?"

"Your wife. She knew where you'd be."

"Shit."

"I'm pretty sure she's still in love with you. FYI."

I left the basement to work on how to get through another night of being with Holly, together and alone.

"Anything's possible," I said to the walls.

CHAPTER
FORTY-SEVEN

THE ATTACK CAME LATE at night. Motion sensors triggered floodlights as armed men tried to shoot out the vandal-resistant lights and cameras. When that didn't work, they retreated. Aaron activated the alarm, and the noise was high and piercing. Emergency lights pulsed in our rooms and hallways. Outside, the dogs barked.

I awoke with adrenaline coursing through my blood. Holly and I threw on our clothes and, grabbing our weapons, joined everyone else in the basement. Landry and Ram were huddled around the monitors, assessing the situation.

"They must've hiked in," the teacher said. "Look."

There were seven of them, all wearing dark clothing. The surveillance system lacked sound, so we could only imagine what they were saying to each other. I couldn't believe that one was about to test the fence.

Aaron turned to Ram. "Can't they see the warning signs?"

"There is an energizer on that fence. The voltage is very high."

"Did you release the dogs?" I said.

"I was afraid those men would shoot them."

The moron approached the fence and looked up to gauge its height. As soon as his hands made contact, he flew backwards and hit the ground, unconscious. The others fell back, dragging their friend with them.

"What do we do?" Ben said to Landry.

"We wait."

The intruders scattered like rodents. Three stood in front of the house. Cycling through the video feeds, Ram tried to locate the others. Four had broken off, with two on each side of the house.

The teacher's expression was grim. "Even if they can't find a way in, they'll tell others. And if enough of them show up, they could overpower us."

"Are you saying we should shoot them?" my wife said.

"If it comes to it."

She took my arm. "I don't wanna kill anyone without a good reason."

"I agree," Ram said.

These guys may have been dumb, but they were also persistent. Over the next few minutes, they inspected every inch of the fence.

A UPS driver appeared under the glare of the floodlights and attacked one of the intruders watching the front of the house. Before his partners could pull it away, it had torn open the victim's neck. Someone smashed his rifle butt into the freak's skull. It wobbled and fell to the ground, and they shot it repeatedly until it stopped moving.

The victim lay writhing on the ground, blood gushing from his neck. Next to him lay the body of his attacker. The intruder in charge gave a command. Without mercy, they opened fire on their injured friend, ending his life with shots to the head.

Sickened, Holly turned away and pressed her face against

my chest. The survivors dragged their comrade's body away from the fence. But it was too late. Under the bright lights, a horde rushed them. The terrified men fired at them, but the freaks were attacking from all sides.

It was like watching a silent horror movie. In the confusion, several intruders got bit as more hostiles appeared. The others kept shooting till they ran out of ammo. Those who were infected died. Then, reanimating, they rose to join the slaughter.

"They're turning faster," I said.

My wife tugged at my sleeve. "Can't we do something?"

Landry shook his head. "They're the enemy."

The last intruder shot his attacker in the face, but not before it bit him. As the horde moved in, he stared at his savaged arm. Out of ammo, he drew his hunting knife and slashed his own throat, collapsing against the electrified fence.

Smelling blood, the horde closed in. Though a powerful voltage coursed through them like rushing water, it left them unaffected. The electricity made their bodies dance like demented marionettes. Each would fall away and immediately return for more. In any other universe, the scene would've been comical. After reducing the intruders to blood and bone, the horde returned to the darkness of the forest.

None of us could sleep after that, so I made coffee. In one sense, I felt remorse for not helping those men. But I had an even stronger urge to protect our group at all costs. The victims weren't innocent. They were trespassers who wanted to do harm. Sometimes, survival meant making hard choices. Though the argument sounded reasonable, it left an ache in my gut.

We sat around the kitchen table, sickened by what had happened. Holly kept to herself. Each time I tried comforting her, she pulled away as if I had been the one responsible for the carnage. Maybe all of us were guilty. The teacher tried putting a bow on it.

"We did what we had to," he said. "They would've killed us and taken the house."

Ben nodded his agreement. "Otherwise, why would they try shooting out the lights and cameras?"

My wife wasn't on board. "We could've at least given them a chance. Killed the horde so they could get away."

Ram got himself more coffee. "They might have betrayed us after we saved them. We will never know."

Your ability to rationalize your own bad deeds makes you believe that the whole world is as amoral as you are.

Douglas Copeland wrote that. But was it amoral to want to stay alive? Protect the ones you love?

Aaron looked at each of us in turn. "What do we do with the bodies?"

"Leave them," Ben said. "As a warning to others."

PART FOUR

THE COMPANY YOU KEEP

CHAPTER
FORTY-EIGHT

TWO DAYS LATER, Black Dragon showed up in three Humvees. A dozen security guards climbed out, all wearing body armor and helmets and packing AR-15s.

We observed them on the security monitors in the basement. Several talked among themselves and pointed at the buildings. Two guards split off and examined the intruders' remains, which lay wet and bloated in the hot August sun. They were covered in blowflies and—this was just a guess—reeked like Lucifer's butthole.

"Any ideas?" Ben said.

I caught the calculating expression on Landry's face. "Irwin?"

"Better to get ahead of the situation. If they decide to breach the fence, they have the means. Might as well see what they want." He looked at Ram, who nodded his agreement.

Ben and Aaron remained in the basement. The rest of us exited through the front door with our weapons lowered. The guards had terminated two freaks wandering out of the forest.

Our dogs barked their heads off till their master ordered them to stop.

"Hello?" he said to our visitors.

We halted halfway across the yard, waiting for the guards to acknowledge us. I recognized one from the television interview with Evie Champagne. Studying the fence, he reached out his hand.

"It's okay," I said. "We deactivated the fence."

"Are you the property owner?"

Ram pushed past me. "This is my house."

"Chavez, Black Dragon Security supervisor. Why haven't you people evacuated?"

"We are fine here."

"Aren't you concerned about getting sick?"

"We're well aware of what your people are telling civilians," the teacher said. "Like my friend said, we'll take our chances."

The supervisor studied him, his mouth sliding into a lazy grin. "I get it. But we have our orders. Everyone who's healthy needs to report to a shelter."

I'd had enough of this clown. "And if we don't?"

"We're authorized to use force."

Holly broke away from the group and approached the fence. What the hell did she think she was doing? I started after her, but Landry motioned for me to stay put.

"Why don't you come inside?" she said. "We can talk about it like adults."

Chavez looked at my wife like he wanted to rip her clothes off. "Fine."

Another guard stepped forward. He was around thirty and stocky, with short sandy-colored hair. "Are you sure it's safe?"

"Wait here," the supervisor said. Then to Holly, "Is it safe?"

She blushed like a freshman invited to the senior prom, and it made my blood boil. Instead of saying something I'd regret, I sucked it up and waited for the gate to open.

Everyone gathered in the kitchen as Aaron and my wife handed out cold drinks. Chavez looked like he should be on television. His teeth were white enough for a toothpaste commercial. I hated him.

"As you can see, we're fixed up pretty good here," the teacher said. "Plenty of food, water, and ammo. We have a generator for power, and the building is secure."

"I heard dogs."

"Trained German shepherds," Ram said, but the supervisor ignored him.

Landry continued. "The group talked it over, and we feel we'll do better if we stay put. Who knows what kind of hell we'll find out there."

"You got that right," Chavez said. "Can I see the house?"

We followed the supervisor as he poked his nose into different rooms. When we reached the stairs leading to the basement, he addressed the teacher.

"How long do you figure you can hold out?"

"Six months easy. More if we ration our food." Landry pointed downstairs. "We can hole up down there if necessary. Plenty of guns and supplies."

"I hope you aren't Red Militia sympathizers."

"You're dealing with rational people. Like you, we want to make it through this thing."

Chavez started down the stairs. "I don't know..."

In the basement, Holly brushed past me to get to the supervisor. "Can I ask how many people know about this house?"

"All my directs. No idea about the locals, though."

I pointed at a security monitor showing a view of the

forest. "We have it good up here. High enough so we can see everything."

"I noticed. Pretty sweet."

Ben showed Chavez the video feeds. "You guys are on the ground, fighting the infected. And then there's the looters."

"And what about the Red Militia?" my wife said. "That's who we think attacked us."

The supervisor lowered his head. "I've lost sixteen men and women to the nailheads."

"Nailheads?" the teacher said.

"Ormand Ferry's followers."

I couldn't help myself. "And what do you call the undead?"

Chavez smirked like a high school kid who had cheated on his math test. "Draggers."

We had made our case and returned to the kitchen. It was up to the supervisor now. If he decided we were through, we'd have no choice but to evacuate. Though this was Ram's house, we deferred to Landry. Folding his hands, the teacher peered at him.

"What if we were to join forces?" he said.

"I'm listening."

"Assign a few guards to stay with us, and we'll help you with intel."

"Or we could force you to leave and take over the compound."

I gripped my weapon. "Or I could blow your head off right here and leave your body for the draggers."

"Dave, please," Holly said. "Can't you see Mr. Chavez is a reasonable person? He wants what we want—for him and his people to stay alive."

Swallowing my bile, I stood down. The supervisor thought

about the offer for a beat. After draining his Red Bull, he shook everyone's hand and headed to the front door.

"Do we have a deal?" Landry said.

Chavez opened the door a crack and gave my wife a big, toothy grin that made her blush again. I wished I had my axe.

"Okay," he said. "We'll do it on a trial basis."

That night, one Humvee returned carrying four men. Like I figured, Chavez was among them. Fun times ahead. In a show of good faith, he brought us food, water, and ammunition. He and his men agreed to sleep in the basement near the command center.

I wasn't sure whether I trusted these guys. What was to stop them from gaining our confidence, then taking us hostage and turning over the facility to Black Dragon? Landry had the same idea but decided if that was their plan, they could have shown up with reinforcements and overpowered us.

Holly had a different view. She knew how valuable our base was to Black Dragon. Keeping us happy and safe was a small price to pay. Everybody wins. I hated to admit it, but there was an advantage to having the extra men. For starters, it meant fewer guard-duty shifts.

"So you think this was a good idea?" I said as she brushed her teeth.

"I guess. With all this unrest, what choice do we have?"

"Unrest. Interesting way of putting it."

"You know what I mean."

She grinned as toothpaste ran down her chin. Seeing her in that lacy butter-yellow camisole made me long for the old days. As she flossed in front of the bathroom mirror, her breasts pressed against the material. Aching from loneliness, I had to look away.

During our time together at the compound, my wife hadn't outright avoided me or treated me rudely. But she wasn't—how do women like putting it?—emotionally available. On one level, I regretted my choice to stay with the group. On another, I pretty much knew what my chances were alone on the outside. Especially after seeing those Red Militia idiots getting eviscerated.

"I wonder if Enrique is married," she said, rubbing lotion on her hands and elbows.

"Who the hell is Enrique?"

"You know. Chavez."

"How should I know? Why don't you ask him?"

"Maybe I will."

I decided to take a walk outside. As I approached the kennel, the dogs barked and snarled. When they saw who it was, they whined and wagged their tails.

"You guys are pushovers," I said.

A breeze blew in from the north, and the air was cool. Standing in front of the house, I gazed at the night sky. Somewhere, a screech owl hooted. Two nighthawks swooped into view, chirping. A death shriek came from somewhere deep in the forest. The sound reminded me that the world wasn't normal and might never be again. Soon, coyotes joined in, yipping and howling like a demonic Greek chorus.

Though I considered the odds of us surviving low, I had hope. Jim, Missy, and countless others died and came back to murder indiscriminately. Outside the electric fence, death awaited us in the form of draggers and nailheads. But I wanted to believe there were other survivors fighting to hold on to a way of life rapidly slipping away.

Something stirred outside the gate, tripping the floodlights. It was stupid of me to be out there alone. If a nailhead saw me, he might decide to shoot. But it was only a family of raccoons under the bright lights.

Earlier, the security guards had burned the bodies in a freshly dug fire pit. The remains smoldered, the smell dark and sweet. Ignoring the barking dogs, the raccoons scavenged through the ashes, looking for tasty morsels of cooked human flesh. I heard them tearing at it.

It was the sound of mortality.

CHAPTER
FORTY-NINE

THINGS REMAINED tense between Holly and me. She didn't outright flirt with Chavez, but whenever he was around, her temperature went up. He was neutral, though, which helped assuage my jealousy. I might have misjudged him.

Each morning at six, after a breakfast of strong coffee, the supervisor left to join his people in town. The three remaining guards—Warnick, Quigley, and Yang—organized patrols through the surrounding forest. Quigley, who went by "Quigs," and Yang were around my age. They were likable enough and enjoyed telling off-color jokes and playing *Call of Duty*.

Sometimes, their banter became uncomfortable, though they insisted it was all in fun. Yang liked calling Quigs "TT" or "T-Squared," and Quigs referred to Yang as "DWA" or, more often, "DW." "TT" was short for *trailer trash* and DWA stood for *driving while Asian*. Like I said, uncomfortable.

Warnick was the sandy-haired guard who had warned Chavez about us, and he couldn't have been more different from the others. For example, he rarely smiled. Also, he was a big fan of Weezer, especially "Island in the Sun." One day, I found him disassembling his AR-15 as music played on his phone.

"What are you doing?" I said.

"Replacing the stock so I can bump fire. During a civil disturbance, we're permitted to use only semiautomatic weapons."

"I'd say we're way past civil disturbance."

"I'd say you're right."

"So, do you have a family or—"

"I'm not into chitchat," he said, making me feel like an ass.

At first, the idea of hunting draggers seemed insane. But Warnick explained that we needed to eliminate as many as possible to curb the spread of the virus. After the second day, I decided to join the guards on their patrols. Mostly, it was out of boredom. My wife told me I was crazy and declined to join. Ben and Aaron had no interest, and Landry was noncommittal. Ram wanted to come, but I insisted he stay behind to run the compound.

Usually, we would come across one or two and dispatch them with a bullet to the head. I was getting pretty good with the bullpup. As a precaution, I brought my axe, which I wore slung across my back with a rope. It wasn't long before the teacher joined us, wearing his shark suit.

There's something you need to know about draggers. Being dead doesn't mean they can't move fast. I know, it makes no sense. Usually, rigor mortis sets in within a couple hours after death, then dissipates. Next, the body begins to bloat with gases. But not with these little beauties. Many become lean—even athletic. And shit, could they run.

After taking them out, we split up to cover more ground. A groaning straggler surprised me. Before I could get off a single round, it took a swipe at me and knocked the bullpup out of my hand. I grabbed my axe and swung it over my head, slicing into the neck. With its head half-off, it observed me like a curious dog. Maggots bubbled out of the dry, pulpy wound.

Though they were dangerous, they always followed the same pattern. It went like this. First, they grab. They're strong, and it's hard to get away once they've got you. Next, they try sinking their teeth into your face, neck, or arms. After getting that first taste, they go to work. A feeding frenzy ensues, and before you can call dinner, you're the party platter.

I did the logical thing and hacked off its hands. It flailed at me, struggling to pin me with the stumps. Dancing around it, I tried getting to where my gun lay. Hearing the commotion, Quigs came running out of the forest and began laughing at my Kabuki routine.

"Nice moves, Pulaski," he said. "Would you like some music?"

"A little help?"

Spitting, he aimed his rifle and shot the dragger through the eye. The body rocked for a beat and fell over. I retrieved my weapon and leaned against a tree while the guard examined the remains. I wanted to punch him in the mouth for laughing at me.

"He surprised me," I said.

Trying to look serious, I laughed, too, as Warnick and Landry joined us in the clearing. Warnick poked at the remains with his gun barrel.

Quigs looked past him. "Where's DW?"

A scream startled us. Following the sound, we discovered the missing guard on the ground, with a middle-aged female on top of him, ripping open his arm with its teeth. Warnick grabbed its greasy hair and fired two rounds into the skull. Shuddering violently, it collapsed. Warnick pulled away the carcass and checked Yang's wound.

"Thanks, man," the injured guard said. "If you hadn't..."

His eyes widened as we circled him. He must have known what we were thinking. Landry raised his rifle and pointed it at Yang's head. Before the teacher could fire, Warnick pushed him aside. Grabbing my axe, he kicked the guard's arm away from the body and stood on his hand. Yang struggled to get away.

"What're you— No!"

Warnick hacked off the limb above the elbow in one swing. The guard screamed till his voice cut out as blood squirted everywhere. Warnick used my rope as a tourniquet. After several minutes, he got the wounded guard to his feet. Yang was already going into shock and couldn't stand.

"We're not taking him back?" I said.

Landry kicked the severed arm out of the way. "He's infected, dammit."

Warnick helped Yang into a sitting position. "He was bleeding pretty bad. I might've stopped the virus from getting into his bloodstream."

The teacher gawped at him. "That's horseshit."

"There's a chance he might not turn."

"I don't know. Seems risky."

Quigs draped Yang's good arm over his shoulder and got him to his feet. "We have to try. You're not getting PTO that easy, DW."

The two friends headed for the compound. We were about to follow when Warnick pulled Landry and me aside.

"I promise I won't put the group in danger."

The teacher nodded grimly. "And if he turns?"

"I'll do him myself," Warnick said and walked ahead to join the others.

CHAPTER
FIFTY

WE DIDN'T ENCOUNTER any more hostiles on the way back. Using radios, we alerted the command center about the injured guard. By the time we arrived, Holly was waiting for us with medical supplies.

Keeping his promise not to endanger us, Warnick locked Yang in the service building that housed the generator. Then he radioed Chavez, asking him to bring blood for a transfusion. In the meantime, we did our best to make the patient comfortable. After giving him water and painkillers, we met outside.

"I don't like it," Landry said.

My wife was more compassionate. "What if it was one of us? I'd give you the benefit of the doubt."

"I appreciate that, but staying alive means making tough choices. If it was me in there, I'd expect you to do the smart thing."

As good as our intentions were, we had a problem. There was no way for us to know how long it would take before we could consider Yang healthy. All of us had seen people turn.

Was it possible an individual could be immune and still carry the virus?

Soon, the supervisor showed up with blood and more medicine. We learned that before going into the army, he was a paramedic. He cauterized Yang's arm and gave him a transfusion. Two hours later, he set up a drip containing antibiotics and morphine.

"How you feelin', DW?" Quigs said.

"Good enough to kick your ass."

Chavez took Yang's wrist to check his pulse. "Let's put him in my vehicle. I'll drive him down to the hospital."

The teacher was anxious to be rid of the patient and gave the supervisor a thumbs-up.

Warnick took Chavez aside. "With all due respect, that's a bad idea. If he's infected, we won't know how long before he turns. What if he attacks you on the way down?"

The supervisor considered this as he gazed at his surroundings. "Is this building secure?"

"Affirmative. And we can monitor him using the video cameras."

"Okay. Someone give me the keys. I'll finish up in here."

During his shift, Quigs kept his eyes on the security monitor covering the generator building. Some of us went down to the basement to have a look. Others watched from the monitors in the kitchen. So far, Yang was stable. I was beginning to believe Warnick had made the right call. We agreed to convene in the morning and decide what to do next.

I must have dozed off during my shift. When I opened my eyes, I noticed the drip stand lying on the ground. I wished there was a microphone so I could hear what was happening. My gut tightening, I called my backup, Warnick.

Chavez trotted down with him. Together, we watched as Yang staggered back and forth like a drunk. Feverish, he seemed oblivious to his surroundings. Opening his mouth wide, he let go a gusher of black blood.

"Dammit," Warnick said. He kicked a chair and ran a hand through his short hair.

His mouth dripping, Yang stared stupidly into a video camera. I recognized the unmistakable flat eyes devoid of emotion.

"Should I get Quigs?" I said.

The supervisor unholstered his sidearm. "Let him sleep. I'll take care of this."

I laid a hand on Warnick's shoulder. "It was good that you tried, though."

"I would've given you the same chance."

"Take a dog with you," I said to Chavez.

I thought I was being helpful, but I was wrong. Stopping on the stairs, the supervisor glared at me with uncharacteristic hostility. When he was gone, I gave Warnick a WTF look.

We focused our attention on one monitor as Chavez entered the generator building accompanied by a German shepherd. Only moments ago, Yang had swayed rhythmically in front of the camera. Now, he was alert and very interested in getting close to the warm human being standing before him. But he never got the chance.

The supervisor fired twice at Yang's face. The first bullet sheared off his nose, and the second gave him a third eye. Spasming once, the patient fell onto his back. The dog trotted over and sniffed the body while Chavez moved his lips. A prayer? He dragged the body out of view, with the animal following.

Warnick headed for the stairs. "I want to see what's happening."

Ben was just coming down to start his shift. "What's going on?"

"Yang turned," I said, heading past him. "Keep an eye on the generator building."

Outside, we found the supervisor placing a black nylon bag in the back of the Humvee. The dog sat at attention next to him. When he saw us, he slammed the door shut.

"Everything okay?" Warnick said to him.

"Why wouldn't it be?"

"Is Yang's body in there?" I said.

He pointed at the fire pit outside the fence, where a bright blaze was going. "We'd better get inside."

I returned the dog to the kennel. On the way to the house, I glanced at the Humvee. My gut told me Chavez was acting strangely, but I dismissed the feeling. And anyway, what did I expect? He had killed one of his own. Warnick told me the supervisor had gotten shot up pretty bad during a tour in Afghanistan. How could a harrowing experience like that not have an effect?

"You can't get black blood out," he said, showing me his shirt. "I've tried."

CHAPTER
FIFTY-ONE

QUIGS WAS SULLEN ALL the next day, and Chavez relieved him to get some rest. But instead of sleeping, the guard holed up in the game room playing *Call of Duty* offline. Holly tried coaxing him to eat, but it was no use. If Yang's death affected Warnick, he didn't show it. No one spoke of it again.

By the weekend, Quigs had recovered. On Sunday, there was a disturbance outside. Ben was on duty and sounded the alarm. My wife and I watched the security monitor in the kitchen. Two teenagers—a girl and a boy—ran to the fence. Worried they would touch it, I radioed Ben to cut the power.

Warnick and Quigs bolted out the front door, carrying their AR-15s. Holly and I were close behind while the others remained inside. The boy was around twelve and short. His left hand dripped blood, and I worried he had gotten bit. The girl was older—tall and uninjured, with plenty of eyeliner and fingernails painted black.

Clinging to the fence, the kids struggled to get a foothold. Glancing behind them, they begged us to let them in. In the distance, armed men approached. The largest fired a wild shot that missed. We didn't return fire for fear of striking the runaways.

Grabbing his radio, Warnick ordered Ben to open the gate. The kids slipped inside, and as the gate closed, we fired warning shots over their pursuers' heads. The girl and boy cowered behind us as the men fell back. Soon, we found ourselves in a standoff with six leering bozos with guns.

"Yer makin' a mistake," the burly one said. I recognized the voice. It was Travis Golightly, owner of the Beehive and first lieutenant to Ormand Ferry.

My wife enveloped the kids in her arms. "What do you want with them?"

"They're brother and sister. Most likely, both are infected."

"You need to leave."

Taking her cue, Warnick and Quigs marched to the fence, their weapons pointed at Travis's face.

"You know what?" the tool said. Whatever he was thinking, he thought better of it and muttered something to the others. Then to us, "Your funeral."

The nailheads disappeared down the driveway. Still, we remained vigilant in case they changed their minds. When it was safe, Holly brought the kids into the house. Despite his injury, the boy seemed fine. She examined his hand in the kitchen. The wound was a straight line down the middle of the palm and no longer bled.

"Cut's pretty clean," she said. Then to us, "A dragger didn't do this."

The boy sneered. "Got into a knife fight, is all."

Ignoring his surly attitude, she cleaned and bandaged the hand. The girl watched, sharing unspoken messages with her brother. I could tell Landry was already gearing up. And I didn't blame him. We knew nothing about these two.

"We can't take chances," the teacher said. "The boy doesn't stay in the house."

"Hang on a sec." My wife got them cold sodas. "What are your names?"

"I'm Griffin Sparrow," the girl said. "This is my brother Kyle."

"I'm Holly. Kyle, how old are you?"

"Thirteen."

Warnick had been observing the teenagers the whole time. As soon as the girl made eye contact, he approached her.

"What were you doing in the forest?"

"That guy you talked to? He was married to our mom."

"Wait," I said. "Travis Golightly is your stepfather?" Then to the others, "How lucky can you get?"

My wife rolled her eyes. "Why were you guys running away?"

They stared at their shoes.

"I'd like to know how you made it all the way up here," Landry said.

Griffin looked at him. "We were on patrol."

That got Warnick's attention. "What do you mean?"

"You know. Like you guys do. We were looking for the dead people."

"And what about your brother's hand?"

She picked at her chipped nail polish. "They use us as bait."

Holly's mouth fell open. "What?"

"Because we're fast—especially Kyle. The smell of blood attracts them, I guess."

Ben turned to his son. "Dear Lord."

"Where's your mom?" my wife said.

When the girl didn't want to answer, her brother nudged

her. "She got bit and... Now it's just me and Kyle. And Travis."

Holly took Griffin's hand. "I need to examine you to make sure you're okay. There's a bathroom around the corner."

All eyes were on the boy now. Picking at his bandage, he stared at the floor. When the women returned, my wife wore a neutral expression. But I knew better.

"No bites," she said. "But I think they should have tetanus shots."

Warnick injected the girl, and Holly placed a small bandage on her arm. When he was finished with her brother, she did the same for him.

"Kyle, you're prob'ly telling the truth," my wife said. "But we have to be sure." Then to me, "Let's take him to the generator building."

We decided to let Griffin remain with us, and Ram assigned her a room. I wanted to believe their story, crazy as it was. But the teacher was right about the boy. We walked him to the other building and placed him inside with food, water, and a sleeping bag.

"There are cameras up there so we can see you," Holly said, pointing. "You'll be safe in here."

Kyle began walking in circles. When he found the bloodstain on the floor where Chavez shot Yang, he scraped it with the toe of his skater shoe.

"How long do I have to stay here?"

My wife glanced at Warnick and me. "Until we're sure you're not showing any symptoms. Maybe a day or two."

"I don't wanna be in here by myself."

"We can't risk you infecting us."

"Whatever," he said and kicked the sleeping bag across the floor.

. . .

236

When I walked into our room, Holly was on the bed, a million miles away. I reached out my hand, and for the first time in days, she took it.

"There's something those kids aren't telling us," she said.

"I had the same feeling."

"I found bruises on Griffin when I examined her. And some of them looked fresh."

"You think Travis beats her?"

"Worse. The marks weren't only on her arms and legs. Her inner thighs were black and blue."

"You mean that fat guy on top of..." I couldn't even finish the thought. "I should've shot him when I had the chance."

She crossed her arms over her chest as if the room had suddenly turned cold. I sat beside her and put my arm around her. The thought of a grown man hurting that poor girl filled me with a rage that had no name.

"Dave, she's fifteen."

Before I could stop myself, I blurted out what I was thinking. "How are we supposed to manage with two kids?"

"I'm not turning them over to that monster," she said and left the room.

Twenty-four hours had passed, and Kyle hadn't exhibited any signs of infection. Several of us stood around the monitors in the basement, watching the boy pace back and forth. He looked up at the video cameras every so often, repeating the same words.

"Anyone read lips?" I said.

Outside the generator building, Quigs and I heard the kid calling from behind the door.

"Hello? Still not sick."

Laughing, we brought him into the house. Holly cut away

the bandage and found that the wound had closed nicely. With draggers, the body doesn't heal. She cleaned Kyle's wound and put on a fresh dressing. When she took his temperature, there was no fever.

"Let's get you some food," she said.

We gathered in the kitchen, and my wife told us what she thought. Everyone was hopeful as Warnick examined the boy.

"So I'm okay, right?" Kyle said.

Holly gave him a warm hug. Was she falling for this awkward, unkempt little rugrat? The boy turned red from all the attention, making his sister laugh. And when my wife tousled his hair, he gave in. Maybe somewhere inside, he craved a mother's touch.

I wanted to savor this moment. It was a rare bright spot in an unending struggle for survival. But the feeling wouldn't last long. None of us were prepared for what was coming. And it was going to be bad.

Knife-in-the-gut bad.

CHAPTER
FIFTY-TWO

LIKE ANYONE, I was afraid of death. But what I feared more was what came after. Becoming a dragger, for instance, and harming the ones closest to me. Acting out of blind hunger and rage. Let's face it, losing control—kind of like being drunk. Living at the compound, it's all I thought about.

Holly lay in bed, skimming a book. Wanting me in the room but not with her. Remembering my vow to protect her, I settled in the overstuffed chair.

"What are you reading?" I said.

"I'm studying the commands Ram uses with the German shepherds. Did you know dogs can remember up to two hundred and fifty words?"

Passion had deserted us. When I looked at her, I saw a faded photograph of someone I used to know. Now that she and I were volunteer security guards instead of lovers, we directed any residual emotion and caring towards the kids. I became protective of Griffin, and my wife acted the same with Kyle. I didn't know when it happened, but having those two around seemed natural—a way for Holly and me to connect. It took some convincing, but eventually Chavez agreed it was better they stayed with us despite their connection to the Red Militia.

No one knew when the outbreak would end. Only one Black Dragon battalion had deployed to Tres Marias. According to the supervisor, they successfully quarantined the town but at a terrible cost. Many guards had been lost to the draggers. More died at the hands of the nailheads. And I'm not talking about amateurs. Most of these men and women had seen combat. But, like us, they had never encountered anything like this.

We got regular updates on television with news footage of violent clashes as far north as Monterey and as far south as Bakersfield. The images splashed across the screen in living color. And apparently, the government wasn't talking about how they intended to keep the disease from spreading. Their silence only emboldened the rioters.

In Tres Marias, the intrepid Evie Champagne pressed on. There was a rumor going around that some of the infected had managed to escape. She claimed there was hard evidence that, in major cities, hit squads were going after anyone suspected of getting bit.

Meanwhile, government officials did their best to discredit the reporter, calling her allegations baseless. Memes popped up on social media with images from that old movie, *Night of the Living Dead*. An inventive rapper released a song called "5-Minute Head Start," about an infected postal worker being chased by a contract killer across Chicago.

Soon, the stories stopped being funny. Evie and her cameraman got caught up in a bloody melee between nailheads and a horde. In the aftermath, she vanished and, with her, the daily field reports. I imagined the two of them out there somewhere. Evie in her signature blazer and stilettos, the cameraman in his jeans and stretched-out polo shirt. This time, hungering not for the next big story but for warm, living flesh.

Later in our room, my wife and I discussed our uncertain future.

"If I turned, you'd end me, right?" I said.

She rolled over on the bed and faced the wall. "I don't wanna think about that."

"We have to."

"All right, yes. And what about me?"

"I couldn't let you become a dragger. And the kids?"

"They don't deserve that either."

"Okay, we're agreed."

She sat up straight. "We need to train them to survive."

"You mean guns?"

"And also making the right choices, so they don't end up..."

"Okay. I think Warnick might be on board with that."

After breakfast, Warnick and I took Griffin and Kyle to the shooting range. We spent the morning in the armory, selecting the best weapon for each of them. Though the girl was tall, she was rail-thin. And the boy was small. The guns couldn't be too heavy. Kyle settled on a Glock 19 with a fifteen-round magazine, and his sister chose a Ruger LCP. Warnick had to talk her into the Glock because hers held only six rounds and was only good at close range.

Neither kid had handled a weapon before. Warnick took his time with them, showing them what the guns looked like taken apart and teaching them how to reassemble them. After a while, the trainees were enthusiastic. Later in the shooting range, they were surprised by the recoil. Griffin howled the first time she fired her weapon, making me laugh.

They practiced an hour a day. And by the end of the week, they could hit the target every time. We knew they would have to go out on patrol with us for some real-world experience. After watching them shoot, Landry was convinced they'd be fine.

Chavez came around less and less, then not at all. Black Dragon was struggling against the hordes. Not to mention the constant skirmishes with the nailheads. What was worse, security guards were going AWOL out of fear of getting bit. We heard some had even defected to the Red Militia. And who could blame them? Most had seen friends eaten alive. The last time we saw the supervisor was at dinner.

"My people are trained. Many—like Warnick and Quigs— served in Afghanistan. And when you kill an insurgent, he stays dead. But here..."

Holly took the boy's hand. "What are your superiors telling you?"

Chavez gave us an eerie laugh. "We're on our own."

Landry looked pensive. "Strange how they haven't sent in reinforcements. Any way to get to the bottom of it?"

"There is no bottom."

The supervisor didn't seem concerned that there were children at the table. Maybe he figured they needed to know the score.

Aaron side-eyed his dad. "What are we supposed to do?"

"It's about survival," Chavez said, addressing the teenagers. "You worry about yourself."

CHAPTER
FIFTY-THREE

IT WAS LATE AUGUST. Holly and I had been at the compound for six weeks. Since arriving, Chavez and his men replenished our provisions regularly. But now that he was MIA, we never heard from anyone in command. Warnick and Quigs tried contacting the supervisor by radio. After days of this drill, we concluded he was no longer among the living.

Our only connection to the outside world was via satellite TV. After Evie's disappearance, the national and international channels made no mention of Northern California in their daily broadcasts. The local stations had long since switched to recorded programming—reruns of old sitcoms mostly. Like the Roanoke Colony, Tres Marias had fallen off the map.

Warnick and Quigs decided to visit the town to find out what was happening. To appear less conspicuous, they took my truck instead of the Humvee. When they didn't return by sunset, we began to worry. Around eleven, after the kids had gone to bed, my truck pulled up. We assembled in the kitchen for coffee and sandwiches.

"Did you locate Chavez?" Landry said.

Warnick side-eyed Quigs. "Negative."

"What did you find out there?"

Quigs rubbed the back of his neck. "We're not sure who's in charge."

Concerned, Ram confronted him. "What are you saying?"

"It means everyone who isn't dead defected," I said.

Warnick smacked the table with his palm. "Hold on. Not everyone in Black Dragon has gone over. We still have guards in place to—"

"To what, Warnick? Manage the situation?"

My wife stroked my arm. "It's not his fault. We need a new plan, that's all."

"Holly's right," the teacher said. "No use grousing."

Warnick and Quigs decided to remain with our survival family. And we were happy to have them. Each day, we continued our patrols, though we never ventured out after dark. On a moonless night, it would be too easy to get lost. As a precaution, we put markers on trees using luminescent paint. That way, if we were ever separated from the group, we could find our way home.

I had gotten past my fear of letting Holly go out with us, and she always took her turn. I insisted on accompanying her, though. As a result, I went out every time she did, in addition to my regularly assigned days.

One time, my wife and I explored an unfamiliar area. As we made our way to a clearing, a flock of crows cawed shrilly from high in the trees. Up ahead, I noticed something dark and round sitting on top of a wood pole. I didn't like the looks of it.

With weapons up, we slowed our approach. Holly screamed, sending the crows scattering into the air. Warnick and Quigs appeared in the clearing, and we stared at the grisly, familiar object.

It was Yang's head on a pike. The crows had pecked out the eyes, and the skin was ripped everywhere. What was left of the straight black hair fluttered in the wind as bark beetles crawled over the mortified flesh.

"I don't understand," my wife said. "How did..."

I remembered the day Yang died. Chavez had been acting strangely. I pictured the guard's body burning in the fire pit. And the black bag the supervisor had tossed into his Humvee. No one ever thought to check whether the charred corpse was missing a head.

I probed a flap of neck skin with my gun barrel. "Chavez did this."

Quigs turned to me, bug-eyed. "No way."

"I need a shovel," Warnick said and started for the compound.

Holly and I walked behind the guards a short distance away.

"Why would Chavez do that?" she said.

"Maybe this place finally got to him. I'm surprised we haven't all gone crazy."

She lowered her voice. "Warnick and Quigs seem okay. Anyway, I'm glad he's not staying with us. He's dangerous."

When we caught up with the guards, Quigs continued to deny my accusation till Warnick advised him to shut his cake-hole. Later, they returned to bury the head.

Griffin and Kyle hounded us every waking hour to take them on patrol. Both had been training diligently and were anxious to test their newly acquired skills. We would've done it sooner, but Holly was opposed, fearing for their safety. As time passed, it became harder to come up with excuses. Finally, the adults held a meeting in the kitchen while the teenagers hung out in the game room.

"We need to do it sooner or later," Landry said. "What if they get into a situation they can't handle?"

Teaching the kids how to use a gun had been my wife's idea. But it was clear she was terrified of them being in the shit.

She squeezed my hand. "Kyle acts all tough, but I know he'd be scared to shoot a dragger."

"What about Griffin?" I said. "She's getting pretty good."

"Sure, with targets."

"They need field experience," Warnick said.

Quigs nodded. "It's time, Holly."

She walked around the table, stopping in front of Ben and Aaron. Though they hadn't spoken up, I guessed that by the look on their faces, they were on board.

"But what if Travis is out there?"

"I doubt it," Warnick said. "I'm pretty sure he got the message the last time."

Ram raised his hand. "We must vote on it. All in favor?"

Everyone except my wife was in. She leaned against the counter and sighed. "Can I restrain?"

I was the only one who laughed. It had been a long time since Holly had done her word-bending. Finally, she raised her hand.

"I'm agreeing to this," she said. "But I don't like it."

The kids were gun-deep in *Left for Dead* when we walked into the game room. The teacher watched them with admiration.

"I think they're ready," he said.

The plan was to take them out early the next morning. We would cut a straight path down to the stream and head back.

That was a total distance of around five miles—enough to get them used to hunting.

My wife insisted on coming with Quigs and the boy. Warnick and I took charge of the girl. Usually, we wouldn't have taken so many out on patrol, but this was different. We were putting those two in mortal danger and didn't want any screwups.

Before going out, I happened to see Kyle with his phone. Startled, he slipped it into his pocket and gave me a goofy smile. At the time, I didn't think anything of it.

"Can't get a signal for shit," he said and walked off.

CHAPTER
FIFTY-FOUR

WE GOT a late start because Holly had insisted on giving Griffin and Kyle a big breakfast. Along with the bullpup, I had my axe. Warnick and Quigs each carried a knife—a Benchmade 9100 SBT—and their ever-present AR-15s. My wife and the kids preferred their Glocks.

The trip was uneventful. The air was cool, and I could already feel fall approaching. In ordinary times, we might have enjoyed the birds singing and the squirrels chasing each other up and down the tall, fragrant pine trees. But we were constantly on alert. Each of us knew that, at any moment, we could die.

At the stream, we decided to take a rest before heading back. Holly was the first to spot the horde. They were on a ridge making their way down. Dull and unaware, they moved like a chain gang.

"How many?" I said to Warnick.

"Maybe two dozen."

The boy stared at them, his eyes filled with terror. "I can't do this."

My wife took his hand. "Yes, you can, Kyle. You know how to shoot now. The key is not to panic."

I turned to Warnick. "How do you want to do this?"

"Each of us chooses a target. Remember, aim for the head. Quigs, I need you looking this way."

Closing one eye, the girl tried aiming. "They're too far away."

"Don't waste ammo on their bodies," Quigs said. "You'll just make 'em mad."

Holly grabbed my sleeve. "I don't think they've seen us yet. Maybe we can hide until they pass."

Warnick surveyed our surroundings. "Okay, everybody, find a tree."

As we split up, a shot rang out, the bullet striking a dragger. The noise alerted the others, and soon the horde was running down the ridge. They moved as one, like someone had rung the dinner bell.

"Who fired that shot?" my wife said.

I searched the trees but couldn't see where the bullet had come from. Another round whizzed past my head. Scattering, we hid. Unknown assailants fired at us from one side while the horde came at us from the other.

"Any suggestions?" I said to Warnick.

"The hostiles are the priority. Quigs, see if you can get over to the other side."

"Copy."

I turned to our young recruits, who were behind another tree. "Remember, go for the head."

The boy trembled. "I don't know if—"

"Do it, Kyle," his sister said. "It's just us now."

Holly gave him a comforting smile. "It's okay. Pretend it's *Call of Duty*."

But he wasn't listening. Dropping his weapon, he sprinted

into the dense foliage opposite us before Griffin could stop him.

"Kyle, no!"

"Leave him," Warnick said. "Focus on the horde."

The guard was in his element. He took down three with clean shots to the head. My wife and I did our best to keep up. I hit one as it rushed down the incline. The girl aimed, her hands shaking.

"Steady," I said. "Remember to squeeze."

Wetting her lips, she fired, taking down an approaching dragger with a shot through the mouth. It fell, the back of its head blown out.

The others tripped over it as they tried getting to us. Doubling down, we focused on eliminating the rest of the horde. When it was over, Griffin sat on her haunches and wept. Holly wrapped her arms around the trembling girl and held her close.

Quigs had been across the way, out of sight. When he showed up, he was grinning. "Good training, guys."

Suddenly, a bullet tore through his shoulder just above his body armor. Dazed, he staggered back. Another round ripped out a piece of his neck. Then hostiles came at us from out of the foliage—Red Militia. As they advanced, we took cover.

"What do we do?" I said.

Warnick aimed at them. "Shoot the bastards."

My wife looked at him in desperation. "What if Kyle's out there?"

As we opened fire, they scattered. I kept hoping I'd see Travis to kill him for what he did. I hadn't paid attention. A hostile came within arm's length when a shot to the chest brought him down in front of me. I turned to find Holly pointing her weapon.

"You're welcome," she said.

More attackers appeared. We could have handled the situation better if Quigs hadn't been hit. Now it was up to Warnick. I saw his lips moving as he aimed. Was he praying?

The three of us chose our targets. Like us, the hostiles had trees protecting them. But what they didn't have were Warnick's eyes. He seemed to see through the foliage. He would wait, notice movement, and fire. Each time, a man screamed.

The enemy had us pinned down in this position for over an hour. We weren't sure how many we'd taken out, but we knew there were more. The attackers must have gotten impatient because they decided to storm us. There were five in all.

Warnick took out the leader and a second hostile with shots to the head. My wife and I wounded one in the chest, and Griffin hit a man in the legs. Cursing, all of them fell. Warnick crawled on his belly and put a bullet into each man's head. He didn't even bother to see what state they were in. But it was too late for Quigs, who lay in the clearing, bleeding out.

"Let's get him to the compound," Holly said.

Warnick examined the guard and found a bite mark on his left hand. The blood was fresh.

"Did you get bit? Answer me."

His eyes glassy, Quigs looked at his friend and nodded. Warnick did his best to stop the bleeding, but everyone knew it was over. The injured guard became quiet and stopped breathing altogether. Warnick began CPR on him, but it was no use. He got to his feet and, aiming his weapon at the dead man's head, waited.

I thought maybe he was having second thoughts like he did with Yang. He wasn't. When the dead guard opened his gray, viscous eyes, he wasn't Quigs anymore. As he opened his mouth to bite, Warnick shot him in the face. Wiping his nose, he took the weapons and ammo off his comrade.

"We need to get back," he said.

My wife searched the trees. "What about Kyle?"

"Too dangerous."

"We can't leave him. Dave, tell him."

"He's not out there," the girl said, her voice monotone.

"What? How do you know?"

A massive explosion knocked us to our knees and sent birds screeching into the sky. At first, I thought a Black Dragon helicopter had crashed. As we got to our feet, a distant billow of black smoke spread across our field of vision.

"Look," Holly said. "Isn't that the compound?"

CHAPTER
FIFTY-FIVE

A NOXIOUS GRAY cloud of greasy fumes hung like a fog over the property. Nearby, trees burned. A wide crater next to the main building revealed the still-glowing remnants of the fuel tank. Thick smoke poured out of the main building. The front door lay several feet away in the driveway.

The gate was down, and several vehicles I didn't recognize stood outside, also on fire. Men's bodies lay scattered on the ground, bites covering their arms and legs. Our dogs lay dead, all with fresh bullet wounds. My eyes burned from the acrid smoke.

We found Ben and Aaron among the dead. The rest, we assumed, were nailheads. Holly ran to our friends and checked for signs of life. There were none.

"What did this?" I said.

Warnick pointed at an object lying on the ground among the debris. It was a rocket launcher. I joined him as he picked it up and examined the printing on the side.

"One of ours."

"They must not have known about the fuel tank."

The heat coming from the main house was intense. Our

weapons up, we made a thorough search of the property, looking for survivors. For good measure, Warnick and I put a bullet into the head of every corpse we came across.

Most of our vehicles sat low to the ground on tires melted from the blast. A tree had fallen onto the cab of my truck, flattening it. The Humvee was burned out. To keep the driveway clear, Ben had parked the motorhome in the back-yard, away from the buildings. Miraculously, it was intact.

We checked the generator building and found it to be in good shape. Ram had given Warnick an extra set of keys. The guard unlocked the thick metal door. Inside, it was quiet except for the sound of machinery.

It was late afternoon. Each of us had water and a few energy bars. The only weapons and ammo were what we carried. We assumed Ram and Landry were somewhere in the house, dead. It would be hours before we could get inside to confirm.

"We need to leave," I said. "Find someplace safe."

My wife looked at me as if I'd suggested aliens were real. "And where would that be?"

"I don't know."

"That's not a place. Do us all a favor and shut up, okay?"

"Stop yelling at him," Griffin said. "He's trying to help."

Warnick stepped in between us. "Can everyone stop for two seconds? I'd like to get away as much as you, but I'm tired. And I don't feel like driving around all night. We'll stay here and leave at first light."

Holly laid her hand on my arm. "That sounds good."

We tried making the best of our situation. There were no blankets—only the sleeping bag we had given Kyle. Warnick and I insisted the women share it. The cement floor was cold and unforgiving as we huddled close together. Fingering his AR-15, the guard was quiet.

"Griffin?" my wife said. "I want you to tell us what happened."

I stared at her. "Before we left today, I found your brother using his phone. He was texting someone, right?"

She shook her head, trying to make it all go away. But I kept at it.

"He contacted your stepfather."

Holly touched the girl's face. "Is that what happened, honey?"

Griffin stared at the floor, her voice practically inaudible. "It was Kyle. I swear, I didn't want to be a part of it. He made me promise not to tell."

"A part of what?" Warnick said.

"Travis promised he would stop...hurting me if we agreed to the plan."

"That whole story about wanting to go on patrol... You betrayed us."

The girl looked at my wife with desperate eyes. "He told us Ormand needed those weapons to fight. And that Black Dragon was killing innocent people. We believed him. After getting to know you, I told Kyle Travis had lied to us. I thought I convinced him."

"Those other men were already waiting for us by the stream," I said. "And the horde was the icing on the cake."

Contrite, Griffin nodded. "I was supposed to go with him. They told us which way to run so we wouldn't get shot. But I couldn't do it. While we were in the forest, Travis took my brother to the compound."

"He figured the others would kill us while he took out everyone up here," Warnick said.

Holly wasn't buying it. "But that doesn't make any sense. Ram would never have let those guys in."

"He would if they had her brother with them," I said.

Warnick nodded. "He would've assumed the rest of us were dead. Maybe they promised to release the boy in exchange for food and weapons."

"But what about the explosion?" my wife said. "Everyone died. And we never found Kyle's body."

I turned to Warnick. "Or Travis's."

The girl's eyes glistened. "My brother was trying to protect me. Travis promised not to kill anyone. All he wanted was the weapons."

I felt bad for her. Travis had abused her for years. Nevertheless, we could no longer trust her. For a second, it crossed my mind that we should leave her behind. Warnick confiscated her weapon.

"A lot of people died today because of what you and your brother did," Holly said.

Griffin crawled off and sat in a corner, holding herself and whimpering. I hated seeing her this way. From now on, she would have to be watched. There was no telling how strong a hold Travis Golightly had on his stepdaughter.

"I wish I was dead," she said.

CHAPTER
FIFTY-SIX

I AWOKE AFTER MIDNIGHT, sore and cold. Nearby, Holly and Griffin lay curled up under the sleeping bag. Warnick was by the door, weapon in hand. Seeing I was awake, he signaled me to join him. I grabbed my axe.

"On my count," he said. "One...two...three."

He unbolted the door, and we stood ready to kill whatever was outside. But there was only the wind.

As he stepped out, a livid, spiky hand grabbed his arm. It was Kyle. Only not Kyle—not anymore. Most of his body was charred from the explosion. The clothes hung on in tatters. Part of the brain was exposed where the skull had been crushed. Both arms were raw and bit. Reeking of smoke and gasoline, he glowed ghastly white in the sterile moonlight.

As Warnick pulled away, I swung my axe and hacked off the arm. The disembodied hand clung to the guard, who pried it loose. I brought down the weapon, nearly decapitating the dragger. Then Warnick finished the job with a gunshot to the temple. By now, the women were behind us.

"It's not fair," the girl said. "He did it for me."

She bolted past us into the cruel night. My wife tried grabbing her, but it was too late.

"Griffin!" Then to us, "We need to go after her."

Warnick dragged the corpse away from the door. "This might be another trap."

"We can't leave her alone out there." Holly glared at me as if I were the enemy. "You know I'm right."

We gathered our supplies and weapons. There was a good chance we wouldn't be coming back. And worse, we were about to break rule number three—never go into the forest at night. A bank of clouds obscured the moon. We stood in the blackness, waiting for our eyes to adjust.

"Where do you think she went?" I said to Warnick.

"I'm guessing she went to find her stepfather."

"Let's try the stream," my wife said.

Warnick warned us to be careful. This was how people got injured. You could twist an ankle in a ground squirrel hole or trip on a tree root and break a limb. We hesitated to use flashlights for fear of revealing our location. I was grateful we had the luminescent paint on the trees to guide us.

I tried to imagine how the girl could have gotten as far as the stream. Taking a chance, we called out to her. A peal of thunder echoed through the forest. Then, it started raining. Soon, it came down in sheets as we continued towards our destination. Heading downhill, we took care not to slip on the mud and wet pine needles.

"This is a trick," Warnick said.

Like Landry, the guard was a realist. But I had seen the look in Griffin's eyes, and I wanted to believe her remorse over her brother's death was genuine. Besides, she could've run away with him when she had the chance but chose to stay and fight.

Halfway down, Warnick put up his hand. We stopped and

listened. I thought I heard a dog whimpering. We waited a beat.

"Who is it?" someone said.

I recognized the voice. "It's Dave. Where are you?"

Suddenly, an animal charged us. Warnick tried shooting it, but I grabbed his arm. As the German shepherd closed in, she wagged her tail. The fur on her body was singed, and blood dripped from her hind leg. Ram and Landry followed, wearing backpacks and carrying weapons. Everyone embraced.

"What happened?" I said.

Ram was sullen. "We couldn't stop them. Then after the explosion..."

"Those dead men we saw were covered in bite marks."

"The dogs," the teacher said. "The nailheads managed to kill them, all except this one."

Holly examined the animal's injured leg. "How did you guys get out?"

"We had to make our way upstairs from the basement and crawl through the rubble." He pointed at the dog. "That's when we found Greta."

The sky cleared, revealing a bright moon. A scream sent us hurrying through the darkness. When we reached the stream, Griffin was standing in shallow water as moonlight reflected in the ripples. A dragger made its way over the slippery rocks towards her.

"I got this," Warnick said.

Before he could reach her, the dog bolted, her ears flat. She sank her teeth into the dragger's leg, pulling it away from the girl. As Warnick moved in, he put a bullet through the attacker's head. Grabbing the terrified teenager by the wrist, he brought her to safety.

Shaken, she could barely speak. "Stupid, stupid..."

The guard gave my wife a look, and she took over. Though Griffin was taller, Holly held her in her arms and stroked her hair.

"It's okay. Shh. You're safe now."

"I didn't have a gun."

We sat beside the stream, vigilant in case more draggers appeared. A sudden roar destroyed the calm. A Black Dragon helicopter whooshed over us, heading deeper into the forest. My wife jumped like she was going to take off. Warnick grabbed her arm.

"Can't we try and flag them down?" she said.

"They'll assume we're hostiles and shoot us."

Landry gazed at the sky. "Sounds about right."

I gave the dog a pat on the head. "Where to now?"

"We must return to the compound," Ram said. "To see if any of the vehicles are operational."

"I think the motorhome survived the explosion."

Holly pulled the girl to her feet. "I need to do something first. Want to help me, baby girl?"

My wife dug through her backpack till she found a first-aid kit. She walked the teenager through cleaning and bandaging Greta's injured leg.

"Couldn't have done it better myself."

She gave Griffin a kiss. Whining, Greta licked the girl's face, making her laugh. The rain had started again as we got going. It didn't take long for us to reach the compound, with our canine scout leading the way.

"Who's got the keys?" the teacher said, staring at the motorhome.

We took a minute to decide who would retrieve them from Ben's decomposing body. But Warnick was already on his way. Next, we hauled the dead to the fire pit, doused them with gasoline from the generator building, and ignited them.

The rancid corpses went up in a bright orange ball of flame in the pouring rain. We had to cover our noses and mouths against the smell. Watching the flesh turn black, I imagined myself in that hellhole.

It was almost dawn when we boarded the motorhome. There was a full tank of gas, and the vehicle started without a problem.

"What about the dog?" I said.

Holly looked at me impatiently. "What do you mean? She's coming with us."

Ram nodded. "She is good protection."

"Yeah, I know, but... She bit a dragger. Am I the only one here who thinks she might infect us?"

My wife looked at Griffin as the girl held the animal close. "We'll have to chance it."

"Irwin?"

"It's possible she's a carrier. We'll keep an eye on her."

Warnick took the wheel, and the rest of us crowded behind him. After starting the engine, he spoke in a monotone—the opposite of a peppy tour guide.

"The streets aren't safe," he said. "Quigs and I ran into a few platoons who were in control. They told us about others who'd gone to the dark side."

Holly took Griffin's hand. "What about the high school? Maybe the horde moved on."

Landry peered through the windshield. "Out of the question. I say we try to find whatever's left of Black Dragon and travel under their protection."

"Maybe this is a good time to try an escape," I said.

Warnick scoffed. "You saw that helicopter. There's no way out."

With no solid plan, we made our way down the long driveway. On the way, we encountered a dragger pack. Rather than wasting ammo, we ran them over like armadillos on a Texas highway. Some stayed dead, their heads crushed on the wet pavement. Others tried crawling after us, their mangled bodies desperate to feed.

"Anyone know a song?" I said.

CHAPTER
FIFTY-SEVEN

THE RAIN HAD STOPPED as we reached the outskirts of town. Abandoned Black Dragon Humvees and LMTVs lined the wet dawn-lit streets amid scatterings of other wrecked vehicles. Fires raged in the distance, making the air tart. Packs of wild dogs fought over what I thought was garbage. It was a human arm.

"We're a gigantic target in this vehicle," Warnick said.

He pulled behind a line of cars and squinted at the dew-covered street signs. The weather had turned cold. We were hungry and exhausted. As I stretched, Griffin pushed away my arm playfully. She gave Holly a warm hug, and the three of us joined the others while Landry remained in the back, brooding.

"What happened to the security guards?" my wife said.

"Probably holed up somewhere." Warnick grabbed his radio and tried the usual channels. There was only static. "We'd better hide the motorhome."

The empty streets and abandoned vehicles were surreal—a dream we couldn't awaken from. In a few short weeks, Tres Marias had gone from a vibrant, friendly town to a dark wasteland. Even if we managed to locate Black Dragon, how long could we survive? I used to take the future for granted. Now I treasured every precious moment of safety.

We found a warehouse on a side street and pulled behind it. I was frightened for us. We were about to leave the safety of our vehicle and venture into streets filled with menace. Gathering our weapons and extra ammo, we stepped into the stillness of a bleak unknown.

Holly handed the girl her Glock. "Stay close."

Ram helped Greta out of the vehicle. She was favoring her injured leg, and I worried she might become a liability.

"What if she barks?" I said.

Kneeling, he whispered a command and looked up at us. "She won't bark."

Keeping to the side streets, we headed to the center of town. Warnick advised us not to speak. Instead, we communicated using hand signals. We made our way past bullet-scarred buildings and broken glass, the whole time watching for hostiles.

At an intersection, we passed the park my mother used to take me to when I was little. It lay before us, disfigured by dirt pits filled with black, smoldering bodies. Hundreds of dogs had descended on the holes, competing with angry crows for cooked flesh and bones.

We had been walking for some time when Warnick signaled us to stop. Somewhere up ahead, a group of men talked and laughed. I heard a familiar splashing noise. Someone was taking a leak.

The dog was alert, her ears pointed forward. As our friend had promised, she didn't make a sound. Straining to hear, I caught bits of the conversation. It sounded like they were Red Militia. My suspicion was confirmed when someone mentioned Ormand Ferry. The man sounded drunk, and his tone was mocking. Another nailhead cautioned him to shut his yap.

Waving us back, Warnick slipped past us and started in the opposite direction. Hurrying, we followed him into an alley, where we formed a tight circle. Everyone spoke in a whisper.

"It's too dangerous," he said. "Let's return to the motorhome."

My wife scoffed. "And go where?"

"The forest. It's the only safe place right now."

Holly noticed Griffin's nervousness and put a comforting arm around her. "What about the helicopters? You said they're hunting people."

The teacher checked his weapon and started walking. "Anywhere's better than here."

It took us only a few minutes to retrace our steps. On the way, we passed an LMTV that looked intact.

"How about switching vehicles?" I said. "More protection."

Warnick motioned for everyone to get behind him. "Take Ram and check it out."

Scanning the street, we trotted over and peered through the driver's-side window. Nothing inside. Ram jogged around and checked the rear. Also empty. I opened the door and poked around inside. The keys were tucked in the visor. I tried starting the engine, but it wouldn't catch. When I looked at the dash, I saw the gas gauge was on empty. We rejoined the others and continued our retreat.

Silently, we boarded the motorhome as Warnick started the engine. There was a steady rumbling noise that sounded like trucks. And they were getting closer. The first vehicle—a Humvee—turned the corner ahead of us. The bright headlights shone in our eyes. For a second, I thought we were saved.

"Black Dragon!" my wife said.

Warnick's expression told me otherwise. Soon, six vehicles —Humvees and LMTVs—came into view, heading our way. A black flag fluttered out of the lead vehicle's passenger window. I recognized the iconic goat's head. Someone was a fan of the black metal band Bathory.

"Grab on to something," the guard said.

We moved to the rear and held onto whatever we could. Warnick hit the gas and tried turning the motorhome around, but other parked vehicles were in the way. He plowed into them to clear a path. The repeated impacts tossed us from side to side. When there was enough room, he floored it and headed in the opposite direction. Gunshots followed us as we made our escape.

"Everybody down!" Landry said.

We lay on the floor on our stomachs. Holly covered the girl's body with her own as best she could. Ram held onto the dog. We must have been doing sixty as Warnick made every evasive move he could think of to gain distance. Griffin shrieked as a side mirror exploded.

I could see Warnick's grim expression in the rearview mirror. He caught me looking at him and narrowed his eyes. I didn't know what was going on. Why was Black Dragon after us like we were criminals? When the guard spoke again, the reality of the situation became clear. And with it, any hope for a rescue.

"Those aren't the good guys," he said.

CHAPTER
FIFTY-EIGHT

WARNICK street-raced to the next block and rounded the corner sharply, nearly tipping us over. My axe slid off the table, and the handle struck Landry on the head.

"You okay?" I said.

"Been better."

With the hostiles falling behind, the guard made another sharp turn into an alley and hit a dead end. He threw the vehicle into reverse and stopped abruptly. I noticed we were next to a steel door that led into an office building. Grabbing Holly's hand, I pulled her to her feet.

"You and Griffin go inside," I said.

"Why can't we all go?"

"Because then they'll know where we are."

I tried the door handle—locked. Stepping back, I kicked. After two more tries, the door flew open. I turned to find my wife standing beside the girl, her arms folded in defiance.

"I'm not leaving you," she said.

Marching back, I took her hand. She must've sensed my conviction because she relented. The teacher collected weapons and backpacks and handed them to the girl. Then he surprised me by kissing her forehead. Griffin gazed at the German shepherd, and Ram gave Holly the nod.

"Greta, hier," my wife said, and the dog came.

I wanted so much to embrace Holly, but there wasn't time. She seemed to know that, too. They slipped inside and secured the door.

Warnick started the motorhome and floored it in reverse. When we reached the alley entrance, three vehicles blocked our escape. In the remaining side mirror, I saw a group of Black Dragon security guards approaching.

"It's no good," Warnick said. "Time to surrender."

Dammit, but he was right. We came out with our hands raised. Ill-dressed guards packing AR-15s met us. Some wore bandannas around their heads. Others sported cuts down their cheeks, the blood dark and crusty. All had removed any visible identification. A scruffy-looking specimen with a chipped tooth waved us over.

Their leader, a Latina in her late twenties, stepped forward. Short and chunky, she had smooth, dark skin and wore her brown hair in a military bun.

"I'm Estrada," she said, eyeballing Landry. "You okay, old-timer?"

His head bleeding, the teacher ignored her.

"Just you four, huh?" She looked past him. "Warnick? Is that you, man? What are you doing with these COBs?"

"Helping them stay alive."

"Shit, yeah. That's what we're doing. Right, guys?"

She turned to the others, who laughed like hyenas. The guard next to her leered at Ram.

"S'up, Sandeep. Draggers take over the 7-Eleven?"

Estrada belted him in the arm. "Shut up, Neidermeyer."

She ordered two guards to search the motorhome. My breath caught as a third went to check out the alley. Soon, the first two guards exited our vehicle, carrying weapons, ammo, and my blood-stained axe.

"Anybody else in there?" Estrada said.

"Negative."

The blood pounded in my ears as the third guard approached the steel door. *Don't let him try the handle.* He was about to reach for it when...

"All right, let's move out," Estrada said.

I wanted to leap for joy as they shepherded us into the Humvees. Warnick and Landry rode with Estrada, and Ram and I accompanied that racist prick Neidermeyer. As we cruised the streets in the wet, chilly morning, I begged God to keep the women safe. Not since my mother died had I prayed so fervently.

On the way, we passed bullet-scarred buildings and countless abandoned cars, trucks, and motorcycles. A flatbed truck with wood side rails accelerated past us. It carried a dozen or so draggers in chains. Their skin and clothes were as gray as the sky. Our driver blasted his horn and heehawed at his comrade. These dildos were like children who'd stolen their parents' car keys.

In a few minutes, we entered an office park I recognized. Behind it was the ice skating rink where I used to play hockey. Around twenty guards patrolled the perimeter, wearing helmets and plastic ponchos. Any hope for the future evaporated when I realized this was all that was left of Black Dragon Security.

The guards ushered us into a building in the middle of the campus. Inside, cubicles stood in rows surrounded by offices around the perimeter. They directed us to a conference room and ordered us to halt. Confiscating our phones and radios, they made us sit around the table. One guard remained, gripping a modded AR-15.

The walls were covered with framed motivational posters with slogans like THE SKY'S THE LIMIT and NEVER SETTLE FOR SECOND BEST. A whiteboard with a technical drawing hung on a wall. Written in red dry-erase marker was a warning that read SAVE.

"I figured I'd run into you numbnuts again."

Chavez stood in the doorway, giving us his trademark grin. Unlike the other guards, he looked fit in his crisp, clean uniform and polished boots.

"Warnick, you're not dead?" The supervisor shook this hand. "Still keeping the faith?"

My friend wasn't enthusiastic. "How are you?"

"Doing well. You guys look like shit, though."

"We had a rough night."

Chavez glanced around the room. "Where's Quigs?"

"Dead."

"That's too bad."

The supervisor took a seat and signaled the man guarding us. "Get these men some chow." Then to us, "What about the others?"

Warnick's expression didn't change. "All dead."

Chavez turned to me for confirmation. "Your wife, too?"

I gave him a sneer. "What part of *all dead* don't you get?"

Two guards appeared with MREs and bottled water. The others tore into their food. Having lost my appetite, I decided to stick with the water.

"Why did you guys leave the bunker?" the supervisor said.

Ram looked at him sullenly. "Crazy bastards blew it up."

"Sounds like that sonofabitch Ormand Ferry. I warned him, you know."

"Wait," I said. "You met with him?"

"When we first arrived. He tried convincing us to go along with his dumbass agenda. He said it would be better for everyone. Is he dead? I hope he is. And that shit-for-brains sidekick. What's his name? Travis something. Heard he sent a couple of kids to infiltrate your compound. What happened to them?"

Not blinking, I met his gaze. "They're dead."

He studied my face, trying to see the lie. "Too bad. Casualties of war, huh?"

Chavez was quiet while everyone ate. His being there felt creepy. I couldn't figure out why he had let it all go to shit. He was a soldier, for God's sake. Warnick must have read my mind.

"What is all this?" my friend said. "It's not by the book."

"Those days are over. Desperate times, desperate measures. Know what I'm saying?"

The teacher wiped his mouth and pushed aside his meal. "Enlighten us."

"It's like I said before, they left us on our own to deal with this situation. And deal with it, we shall."

"What about the government?"

"The government." He banged his fist on the table. "The government is doing dick. Don't you get it? We've been cut off."

"Is that what they told you?"

Landry didn't seem to appreciate that this guy had lost it. He was a crazy man trying to convince people he was making a straight path using the severed heads of his enemies as paving stones. And here the teacher was, heckling him from the peanut gallery.

Getting to his feet, the supervisor tucked in his shirt. Stopping at the door, he whispered to a guard, who pointed his weapon and signaled us to stand. Expecting the worst, we looked at each other.

"You're under arrest," Chavez said. "But don't worry, it's for your own protection."

CHAPTER
FIFTY-NINE

THE GUARDS ESCORTED us to an employee training room. There were rows of tables with desktop computers and eighties-era keyboards and mice. All the monitors were shattered. When I saw the shell casings, I guessed our captors had used the screens for target practice.

A long whiteboard spanned the front wall. On it were bullet points on sexual harassment in the workplace. In a corner, someone had made a crude sketch of a man hitting golf balls at an oncoming horde.

Taking seats, we studied our surroundings. There was no way out other than through the double doors—the windows were too narrow. Besides, a guard was stationed outside, and more patrolled the parking lot. Trying to escape would incur casualties. There were four of us now, and we couldn't afford to lose anyone.

Without thinking, I mentioned my wife's name but stopped when Warnick pointed at the doors. I had forgotten people were listening. Staring at my calloused hands, I fingered my wedding ring.

"I should've been there for her," I said. "And now she's dead."

Landry picked up a Staples mouse pad and flung it across the room. "It's all our fault. We won't make that mistake again."

"Next guy calls me Sandeep, I'm going to kick his ass," Ram said.

We had been asleep on the floor when gunfire and shouting awakened us. Heavy footsteps pounded past the doors. Then an explosive device detonated, and the concussion shook the room. Warnick signaled us to crawl to the doors as bullets shattered the windows and zinged over our heads. I scanned the room—no weapons or implements of any kind. Outside, more explosions as a fierce gun battle ensued.

"We can't stay here," I said.

Landry pointed at a table. "We can use it as a battering ram."

Someone had started a fire outside, and smoke seeped into the room, choking us. After pushing away the useless computers, we collapsed the table and carried it to the door. Lifting it as high as we could, we awaited Warnick's command.

"One...two...three!" The doors cracked but didn't open. "Again. One...two...three!"

This time, the doors gave. Outside, all the lights were out, and nothing moved. Weaving past rows of cubicles, we made our way to the front entrance and pressed against the walls on either side. By now, the fighting was intense.

Security guards shot into the darkness, but I couldn't see what they were aiming at. A volley of incoming gunfire shattered the front doors, letting in the pungent smell of gunpowder. A swarm of hostiles with AR-15s crossed the parking lot, shooting as they went.

"Red Militia," Warnick said. "We can't go out this way, or we'll get caught in the crossfire."

I peeked outside as a bullet caught a nailhead in the stomach. "What if we split up? Whoever finds a way out can alert the others."

Jogging past a coffee station, I searched for a rear exit. When I saw the green letters glowing in the distance, I kept going. But before I could reach the door, someone blocked my path, and everything went black.

When I awoke, I was on the floor in a different room. The fluorescent lights glowed harshly, revealing a dingy, windowless storage area. The air was warm and stale. Stacks of cardboard storage boxes surrounded me. I sat up and immediately succumbed to a blinding headache. Touching the side of my head, I could feel the stickiness.

"He's awake."

Weak and dizzy, I tried focusing on my friends as they helped me into a wobbly desk chair. I felt like my head was going to explode.

"What happened?" I said.

Warnick examined me. "A guard clocked you."

A low groan pierced the dank air. I turned to see where the sound was coming from. My gaze landed on a stranger wearing camo and lying against the wall. He was maybe nineteen or twenty and in worse shape than me. His face was bloody, and one eye was swollen shut.

"Nailhead. They brought him in here a little while ago."

I tried standing, but I was too woozy. Instead, I stayed put as Warnick crouched in front of the kid, who looked up and scoffed.

"I already told the others what I know. Which is nothing."

"What's your name?"

The teacher walked over and loomed over the injured prisoner. "Steve Pinkerton. Former student of mine."

"Mr. Landry?"

"What the hell, Stevie? Why are you mixed up with Ormand Ferry?"

"He gave me a place to stay after my dad died. He's not what you people think."

Warnick gave him the greasy eye. "What do we think?"

"That, that he's some kind of evil genius. He's the only one trying to save this town."

"By killing the security forces?"

"We had no choice—you attacked us."

The teacher shook his head. "This is hopeless."

They rejoined Ram and me. We waited for the kid to fall asleep before saying anything more.

Glancing at him, Warnick shook his head. "Chavez worked him over pretty good."

"Whatever they have planned for us, it'll be worse for him," Landry said.

Sometime during the night, Steve Pinkerton died. We found him cold and stiff, with a trickle of dried blood on his chin. I worried he would reanimate, but he never moved again. Further proof that if you weren't infected, you didn't turn. The teacher had taken it hard and wiped away his tears.

"Poor bastard. He never could get a break. His mother left him when he was four. Father was a crackhead and a petty thief. And he had no friends to speak of."

"Except Ormand Ferry," I said. "He was a very good friend."

CHAPTER
SIXTY

IF LIFE HAD TAUGHT me anything, it was that people like Ormand Ferry were born evil. He pretended to be your friend while screwing your wife. Over the years, he'd built up a loyal following of the disillusioned, the disenfranchised, and the just plain stupid—guys like Steve Pinkerton.

After the guards carted away the kid's remains, sleep became impossible. Warnick convinced them to give us a first-aid kit for my head. Then he bandaged me up and handed me ibuprofen. It had been hours since I was knocked out. My vision was blurry, and I was unable to stand without help.

"Mr. Chavez sends his apologies," a guard said.

Landry rolled his eyes. "That's pretty generous, considering our friend has a concussion."

"You should've remained in the room."

As compensation, our captors gave us blankets but no pillows. We found a box of plastic garbage bags and filled them with crumpled printer paper. While the rest of us lay on the floor, Warnick remained by the door, chatting with the guard as he was about to leave. Our jailer assured us the nailheads had been dealt with and that all was secure. When my friend rejoined us, we gathered in a circle.

"You think they'll execute us?" I said.

Warnick picked at a hangnail. "Unlikely."

The teacher looked each of us in the eye. "Chavez is up to something—I can feel it."

I gave him the stink eye. "And that reminds me, Irwin. Why the hell do you keep getting up in his grill? Can't you see he's nuts?"

"He's right," Ram said. "We need to show respect and not make them mad."

Contrite, Landry nodded. "What do you say, Warnick?"

The guard took off his boots and lay on the floor with his hands tucked behind his head. "From now on, we need to be super careful."

Good ol' Warnick, master of understatement.

In the early morning, they allowed us upstairs to use the bathroom. After that, they gave us breakfast—if you wanted to call it that. There's nothing worse than industrial coffee. But at least I felt better. A little while later, Estrada strode into the conference room where we were eating. She seemed pleased, and that worried me.

"Time to head out," she said.

Groaning, Landry gathered his trash. "Where are we going?"

"To a happy place."

They put us into Humvees and drove us around to the rear of the complex. There were bullet scars and shattered glass everywhere from the recent attack. Spot fires burned all across the office park. Finally, we pulled up to the ice skating rink.

Happier Times was housed in a low, drab building painted gray and yellow. Graffiti covered one wall. The words SMELLS LIKE TEEN SPIRIT stood out in drippy red paint. The sign hung precariously, the blue-and-yellow neon no longer illuminated. The front windows were boarded up with plywood. In the parking lot, two wild dogs fought over the carcass of another canine.

Estrada grinned as we exited the vehicles. "You guys look like you could use some exercise."

We stood at the entrance, wondering what kind of passion play awaited us. Estrada spoke to a guard. Nodding, he drew his weapon and shot the dogs.

"This will not end well," Warnick said.

I narrowed my eyes at him. "Ya think?"

It was dark inside. Half a dozen guards kept their weapons trained on us as we passed. Beck's "Loser" blasted from ceiling-mounted speakers as colored laser lights reflected off an antique glitter ball onto the rough ice decorated with faded markings. All of it was pretty much as I remembered it except for the plywood-and-barbed-wire doors that blocked the emergency exits.

As a kid growing up without a father, this place was my home away from home. Any problems I might have had at school melted away as I lost myself, stick in hand. Though the building was old, it had always been kept up. But not anymore.

There were bloodstains on the ice and grimy white walls. On one side, rowdy guards played vintage arcade games. They laughed and shouted while racing snowmobiles and killing bad guys. Estrada led us to the player entrance, where Chavez was waiting in a freshly laundered uniform.

"Games now?" the teacher said, apparently forgetting our earlier conversation.

The supervisor glared at him. "Training. I need to toughen you up for what's ahead."

I almost laughed in his face. "And that would be…"

"End times, my friend," he said without humor.

They ordered us to remove our shoes. At the rental counter, I met an old friend, Eddie Greeley. Before the outbreak, he had owned Happier Times and was like a grandfather to all the kids. Now, he was Chavez's slave, handing out skates. His hands were gnarled, and his fingers were yellow from years of smoking filterless cigarettes. Resolute, he scoured the cubby holes for the right-size skates as if this were a middle-school birthday party.

"Eddie?"

"Oh hey, Dave." Cataracts dulled his pale blue eyes. "You're an eleven, right?"

"What're you doing?"

"Staying alive, I guess," he said and handed me my skates.

We stood behind the boards, watching a kid who couldn't have been more than eighteen. He skated fast, swinging a hockey stick like he was cracking heads. I knew he was a hockey player when he executed a perfect V-stop.

"How does this work?" Warnick said to the supervisor.

"Sure. A normal period in hockey is, what, twenty minutes? I'm guessing you pussies are out of shape." He ignored Landry's glare. "Each of you will remain on the ice for ten minutes. If you survive, you're home free."

I watched the kid power skating around the rink. "What do you mean, *if* we survive? Are you planning to use us for target practice?"

Chavez smiled with those damn perfect teeth. "Negative. But you won't be alone out there."

"What kind of bullshit is this?" the teacher said.

Nervous, I looked at the supervisor to see what he would do. He gazed at Landry with cold, lifeless eyes. I expected him to pull out his gun and shoot the teacher on the spot. Instead, he addressed the rest of us.

"See that guy? That's Keller. He passed and is now on our team. So, who's going first?"

We looked at each other. I was pretty sure I was the only hockey player in the group. So it made sense for me to volunteer.

"I'll go," Warnick said before I could speak up.

Pleased, Chavez slapped him on the back. "My man. You always were a team player. When's the last time you skated?"

"When I was eight. I hated it then, too. Do I at least get a weapon?"

"Absolutely. See those equipment bags over there? Take your pick."

The guard teetered on his skates to the black nylon bags lying on the floor. I thought he might fall on his face. This guy wouldn't last two minutes on the ice. He went through everything, pulling out wood and aluminum baseball bats, golf clubs, and a red pipe wrench. At last, he settled for an old hockey stick greasy with blood.

"What about protection?" he said.

The supervisor laughed. "This isn't sex. Don't worry, though. Your opponents won't have any *protection* either."

Warnick made his way to the player entrance and waited for the guards to pull open the dasher board gate. As Keller left the ice with a flourish, my friend skated into the rink and immediately fell hard. Getting up, he glided unsteadily to one end.

I walked up to the acrylic shielding to take a closer look. The ice was rough. More proof that Eddie was no longer in charge. I heard a thud behind me and found Ram on the floor, cursing in his native language. Landry tried helping him and also fell.

"This is going to be fun," Chavez said with a smirk.

Rolling my eyes, I gave each of my friends a hand. "You idiots are going to have to do better than this."

The supervisor stood at the player entrance. "Go ahead and do a couple of practice laps. Take your time, buddy."

The party atmosphere was insane. By now, the other guards had taken their seats in the bleachers. They nudged each other and made side comments, probably betting on how close Warnick would come before crapping out.

He gripped the stick with both hands and skated counterclockwise around the rink. As he became more confident, he picked up speed. Next, he tried swinging it as he glided. I had to give it to him, he was a quick study.

"Okay, that's enough," Chavez said.

The supervisor signaled someone in the announcer's booth. The laser lights stuttered as "Fight for Your Right" by the Beastie Boys blasted. I didn't know what to expect and imagined guards with bats swarming onto the ice. They would make a game of it—a hazing ritual where you'd end up crippled. But I was wrong.

Men with clubs would have been a blessing.

CHAPTER
SIXTY-ONE

THE DOUBLE DOORS leading outside flew open, letting in blinding blue daylight. The crowd erupted in wild cheering and whistling. Over the din, there was another sound I never thought I would hear indoors. It was a death shriek.

All eyes were on those doors as six draggers stumbled in. Each had a wire noose around its neck attached to a catch-pole. Guards wearing body armor, helmets, and gloves pushed the snarling prisoners to the boards. Two more guards held open a long gate the Zamboni driver used to enter the rink.

The draggers snapped and clawed as their captors propelled them onto the ice. As soon as they were free, they searched the room with flat, crafty eyes. As if talking among themselves, they made sharp guttural noises. When they laid eyes on their prey, they bared their teeth and shrieked again. I couldn't begin to fathom how Chavez had dreamt up this shitshow—or why.

A look of terror crossed Warnick's face. This man of faith

was being tested like never before. Tightening his grip on the stick, he began skating in slow, wide circles. Each time he passed, his opponents swiped at him. Six on one. This wasn't a contest—it was a ritual sacrifice to an angry god of destruction.

Their jaws snapping, they came after my friend, falling over themselves onto the ice. It was comical till I remembered that all they needed was to get ahold of their victim. Though I was afraid for Warnick, what scared me more was the thought that soon, I would take his place. The guards in the bleachers went crazy, stomping and screaming. Some yelled at their fellow guard to watch himself. Others—the heartless ones—encouraged the hostiles to get busy.

The first one to reach Warnick was a young woman in an orange tank top. With her mortified breasts spilling out, she came at him with waiting arms that terminated in dangerous, spiky fingers. He shattered her wrists, leaving her hands limp and useless. Furious, she tried latching onto him. As she advanced, he hooked her by a shirt strap and flung her across the ice. Falling, she slid backwards and crashed into the wall.

Eight minutes.

By now, the draggers had learned how to navigate the ice. Drenched in sweat, my friend circled again as other hostiles went after him. I picked up on what he was doing, and it was dead smart. Instead of taking them on one at a time, he administered well-calculated shots at whoever came nearest. As a spectacle, it wasn't as exciting as MMA and led to constant booing.

Three minutes.

Warnick's plan was working—till he slipped on a blood slick and fell hard on his side. When I tried going to him, The supervisor grabbed me by the collar.

"You'll get your chance soon enough."

Before the draggers could reach him, my friend rolled to the side and scrambled to his feet. When the first one came at him again, he hit a line drive to the head, caving it in. A black roux of rotting brains spilled out. That was the good part. But the force of the blow snapped the stick in two.

"Give him another weapon," I said.

None of the guards made a move to help. Disgusted, I pushed past them and rummaged through the equipment bags, looking for the aluminum bat. Chavez pointed his gun at my head.

"If you're going to shoot me, get it over with, you sonofabitch."

He smiled with a coldness that chilled me and put away his weapon. "It'll be a pleasure watching you die on the ice."

I returned to the rink and heaved the bat over the shielding, where it clattered. Avoiding the hungry draggers, Warnick skated around to retrieve the weapon. What happened next was like a black-blood ballet. And the effect caused pandemonium in the bleachers.

"Good Riddance" by Green Day pounded over the speakers as he smashed heads and crushed kneecaps. All around the rink, guards cheered and whistled. This was hockey from hell, and they couldn't get enough. If only my friend could last a little longer, he would be home free.

Ninety seconds.

A fat dragger with Elvis hair latched onto Warnick's foot, making him fall. The bat skittered across the ice, just out of reach. Inching dangerously close to his leg, the creature's mouth snapped at the sweaty flesh. The room fell silent as my friend struggled to recover the bat.

Fifteen seconds.

Warnick drove his skate blade into the dragger's skull. A sickening crunch echoed as its head split open like a coconut. Grunting, it released his leg, and he rolled away to the sound of the buzzer.

On his feet again, he gazed at the carnage spread over the ice as guards made their way across, dispensing headshots to any dragger that moved. Everyone cheered as he skated to the gate, drenched in sweat and black blood. As he walked out, the guards slapped him on the back and cheered again. Others joined in, including our group. Despite what the supervisor thought he engineered, he had made Warnick a hero.

"Impressive," Chavez said. "You cost me five hundred bucks."

"You bet against me?"

"Who knew you'd be a stud on the ice?"

The guard dropped the bloody bat at the supervisor's feet and sat on the bench, where I joined him.

"Thanks for the assist," he said.

After Warnick's heart-stopping session on the ice, we returned to the office building basement. The plan was for us to eat lunch and rest. In the afternoon, another combatant would take on the draggers solo. It was up to us to choose.

"Pure insanity," Landry said. "I haven't skated in forty years. What does this even prove?"

The guard rubbed his sore ribs. "That Chavez is in charge."

I handed him ibuprofen from the first-aid kit. "Dude, you did a lot of damage out there."

"I got lucky."

"Boys, I can't do this," the teacher said, massaging his temples.

Ram crouched in front of him. "You must try. We all must."

"What about you?" I said. "I hope you know how to skate." His expression said no. "Okay, this is ridiculous. I'll go next."

Warnick thought for a second. "Okay, then Irwin."

Ram let out a rueful laugh. "I suppose money and education aren't everything."

My friend strode to the door and banged on it. "Hey, open up."

During the tournament, he had impressed the other guards. Now he used the goodwill to get a meeting with Estrada. Later, when he returned, he gave us a thumbs-up.

"You're up next, Irwin," he said.

I waved at him. "Hello? Former hockey player over here."

"Don't worry, I have a plan."

Landry sighed like the man who'd bet his savings on a horse and lost. "Glad I don't believe in hope."

"And me?" Ram said.

Warnick clapped him on the back. "Estrada agreed to let you practice in the rink tonight. But only one of us is allowed to go with you." Then to me. "That's where Mister Hockey Player comes in."

"Wow, how did you swing that?" I said.

"I appealed to her better angels."

The teacher rubbed his hands together, his determination restored. "Okay, so who's up for giving an old guy some pointers?"

"I can't help you skate better—that's Dave's department," the guard said. "But I can show you some moves that could save you."

He ransacked every cabinet and closet in the room. Stopping, he gazed at the ceiling and climbed onto a desk. He pushed aside the plastic sheeting covering the fluorescent lights and removed a tube.

"This is the bat," Warnick said, handing it to Landry. "Imagine you're a ninja."

CHAPTER
SIXTY-TWO

LANDRY LOOKED pale as we entered Happier Times. I had never seen him so frightened. Warnick and I had given him every pointer we could think of. It was up to him now. Inside, the security guards yawned and shifted in their seats. We hadn't even put on our skates when the double doors opened, and Eddie Greeley came rolling in on his ancient Zamboni.

Watching him chug around the rink, I saw myself at fourteen in my hockey uniform, waiting impatiently with the other boys. In those days, I was skinny but strong, and I was fast.

For a second, I wondered why I'd ever stopped skating. Then, with bitterness, I remembered it was a few years later that Jim and I discovered the magic of beer. And after those first few binges, I never got on the ice again.

As the teacher laced up his skates, Chavez walked over, more serious than he was in the morning. Everyone knew he had it in for my friend. Now, there was a cool detachment about him. And if he wanted Landry dead, he wasn't showing it.

"It'll be the same as before," the supervisor said. "I'll give you a few minutes to warm up."

The teacher stood on his skates, a little unsteady. He studied Chavez with those piercing blue eyes and spoke loudly enough for everyone in the vicinity to hear. I guessed at this point, it no longer mattered what he did.

"I've given this a lot of thought," he said. "You're sick. And somehow, you've convinced these young people to go along with your agenda."

The supervisor was like a statue, his face inscrutable. His cold eyes never left Landry's.

"History is filled with madmen. I think you may have heard of some of them. The point is—and I hope you listen—in the long run, they never succeed."

A squall of hatred crossed Chavez's face, and like a shifting wind, it was gone. He handed the teacher the bloody aluminum bat Warnick had used and closed Landry's fingers around it.

"Time to make history," he said.

Grimly, the teacher nodded. He was going to his death, and there was nothing I could do. Armed guards were positioned at every exit. Even if we could overpower the supervisor, we would never get out alive. A fleeting image of my friend wearing his shark suit crossed my mind, making me smile.

The guards opened the gate, and Landry wobbled onto the ice. Unlike the superhero who chased flesh-eaters in a sunlit field, he looked old and vulnerable. As he skated forward, he lost his balance and fell. Cursing, he tried getting up but couldn't manage it. A minute passed as we watched his pathetic attempts to stand.

Rolling his eyes, Chavez pointed at me. "Help him up."

The guards reopened the gate, and I walked out onto the

ice. There were tears of frustration in the teacher's eyes. I felt sick, wishing I could stop this. I remembered what the supervisor had told us. *End times, my friend.*

"This isn't dignified," Landry said.

I reached out my hand. "I know. But if you don't try, they'll shoot you."

"That might be preferable."

The guards in the bleachers were getting impatient. They booed and cursed at us. Someone hurled a soda can over the plexiglass, striking the teacher in the back. Furious, I picked up the object and glowered at the asshole.

"You're stronger than this, Irwin," I said. "I know you are."

He looked up at me, his jaw set, and broke into a familiar grin. "You're right, I am. Get me the hell up."

I embraced him. "Remember. Keep moving forward, and you won't fall."

"Thanks, Dave."

Landry skated with determination. Several times, he looked like he might topple over again. And each time, he recovered.

"Okay, that's enough practice," Chavez said.

Someone fired up Metallica's "Enter Sandman." The double doors flew open to cheers and catcalls as the guards brought in fresh draggers. They were rowdier than the last bunch and fought their captors every step of the way.

Closing my eyes, I asked God to let my friend survive. When I opened them, he was doing what Warnick had taught him. He skated in wide circles as his opponents stumbled in and fell onto the ice. Methodically, he went after whatever he could, staying out of reach of their deadly, grasping talons.

Four minutes.

By now, the teacher had hit his stride and seemed to have

enough stamina to finish. Though slower than Warnick, he had taken out three opponents with crushing blows to the head. I was beginning to think he might have a shot and cheered him on till my throat was raw.

Taking a bad swing, he fell into the arms of a ravening beast. There was a collective gasp as he rolled over and used the end of the bat to keep the snapping mouth away from his face. As he struggled to hold back the dragger, the other two descended.

"Get out of there!" Warnick said.

Growling with rage, Landry pushed his opponent into the others and rolled sideways. Scrambling to his feet, he gave us a thumbs-up and coasted awhile to catch his breath.

Two minutes.

Focused and alert, the teacher circled again as he sized up the three remaining draggers. One looked like a strung-out rocker that might be easy to take out. Another was a middle-aged woman with varicose veins. But it was the third one that worried me. Massive and ugly, it resembled an angry linebacker.

Landry easily kneecapped the rocker, causing it to fall. When it tried dog-paddling after him, the room erupted in laughter. Next, the teacher whacked the female in its gory, lipstick-smeared mouth, sending it spinning into the wall.

Twenty seconds.

"He's going to make it!" Ram said.

Landry positioned himself to take on the linebacker. Rushing him, it drove the teacher into the wall and bit off his ear. Screaming, he managed to pull away and beat his opponent's head into a black pudding.

The buzzer sounded, and guards walked onto the ice. As before, they shot the surviving draggers in the head. My friend skated towards us, his ear gushing blood. Despite the pain, he smiled with pride.

"I almost made it," he said.

I looked at the supervisor. "Don't make him suffer."

Nodding, Chavez signaled Estrada. Landry knew what was coming and fell to his knees. It was the most magnificent demonstration of strength I had ever witnessed. When he looked up at me, his bright blue eyes were clear, and his voice was steady.

"Don't give up," he said. "History is also filled with heroes."

Standing behind him, Estrada drew her weapon and pointed it in a two-handed hold.

"Sorry, old-timer."

A bullet ripped through the back of the teacher's head, leaving a blood spray on the floor. He fell forward, still on his knees. Using his boot, the supervisor tipped over the body.

"That was one salty sonofabitch," he said and walked off.

CHAPTER
SIXTY-THREE

I SKATED AROUND THE RINK, holding Ram's hand and trying to keep him from falling again. Except for the security guards, we were alone. As much as I appreciated the man who had generously taken us into his home, my mind was on Landry. Chavez had won. The teacher called him out, and now he was dead.

"You need to relax," I said. "Keep moving forward."

"I know, I know."

My friend fell again, and weary of it all, I stopped. It didn't help that his skates were too big.

Two bored guards lay on their backs in the bleachers, their rifles resting on their stomachs. They watched with indifference as we drilled. I thought about trying to talk them into letting us go. But even if we could make it outside, we'd have to deal with all the others. And what about Warnick?

"I lied," Ram said as we continued to circle.

"Oh?"

"I skated once—badly—in New York. I was there at Christmas visiting a girl. She took me to Rockefeller Center, and it was beautiful. Everyone dressed in winter clothes, the shops, the Christmas lights. She did as you are doing. Held me up. It was a wonderful time."

"Did you and she..."

"I'll never forget New York."

"What happened to her?"

"She was in her last year at Columbia. After graduation, we lost touch. I think she's married now."

"Dude, don't look now, but you're skating."

When he realized I was no longer supporting him, he let out a whoop. Startled, the guards sat up. They laughed when they saw him whiz past, waving his arms like a kid.

"Time for hot cocoa!" he said.

None of us slept that night. Instead, we talked about what happened and the people we had lost. I choked up when I thought about Holly and Griffin. Why didn't I go with them as my wife suggested?

"The inmates are running the asylum," Warnick said.

I had to agree. "And they have guns. You okay, Ram?"

"I'm excellent."

Warnick put down his little black Bible. "If we ever make it out of here, I'm going to find other guards who can help us restore order."

I scoffed. "What makes you think there are any left?"

"I know they're out there. It's like Landry said. Most are following orders. I think we can turn this around."

"What are you saying? That we should have faith?"

"How do you think I made it this far?" he said.

Sometime around dawn, I drifted off. I remember the guard reading his Bible as Ram lay beside him, snoring—probably dreaming of New York and hot chocolate.

. . .

Entering the ice rink, I felt groggy. Unlike Warnick and me, Ram seemed rested and at peace. We stayed close as he laced up his skates. He wobbled over to the equipment bags for a weapon. Not giving it much thought, he picked up the pipe wrench. I thought it was an awkward choice, but this wasn't my rodeo.

"Want to warm up?" Chavez said.

"No need. I'm ready."

There wasn't any music. The supervisor signaled for the contestants to be brought in. There were more this time. Previously, it was six against one. Now there were eight. I looked at my friend with concern, but he didn't seem frightened—he was pleased.

The shrieking draggers slipped and fell getting onto the ice. Ram skated in circles at one end, swinging the pipe wrench. If the previous outings had taught us anything, it was that in seconds, the hostiles would figure out how to get around without falling. My friend was patient. He didn't even try taking advantage of the situation. It was almost as if— As if he needed them to walk.

The audience booed and cursed. They wanted a show, and Ram wouldn't cooperate. One by one, the draggers got up. Joyfully, he skated around one last time and performed a wobbly V-stop. As the hostiles closed in, he threw away the pipe wrench and shut his eyes.

I pressed my hands up against the plexiglass. "No!"

It took no time for them to dismember him as the audience watched in horrified fascination. He never made a sound—never opened his eyes. It was like he had already vacated his body for some new destiny as scavengers feasted on his remains.

When it was over, the guards took to the ice. Someone

sent a bullet through my friend's head. But they needn't have bothered. All that was left were pieces and parts.

It was Warnick and me now. As we sat in our dank basement prison, I could feel the hatred coming through the door from the guard outside, as though it were our fault that his fun had been spoiled.

"He might've chosen the best way out," I said.

I pictured Ram smiling with those beautiful white teeth. Skating with his girl in Rockefeller Center at Christmas and having the time of his life.

Warnick showed me his Bible. "There's always hope."

"I left religion behind a long time ago."

The words stung as they left my lips because I knew how deeply Holly believed—enough for both of us. Once again, I wondered if she and Griffin were safe. The thought of them dead drove me into black despair.

"I'm not talking about religion," the guard said. "Faith, remember?"

"Is that how you survived so long?" I was hoping to start a fight.

"Dude, I'm not that old."

That made me laugh. For a moment, all the negative feelings left me like an exhale of stale air. And anyway, it wasn't him I was mad at. It was this place—this cursed rabbit hole we had fallen into. We were trapped in a world of madness. How else could you describe it?

"I don't even know your first name," I said.

"Nathan."

"So, do you they call you Nate?"

"Negative."

As my time neared, I thought about the people I loved, one of them a teenage girl I hardly knew. What if they showed up on the ice to fight me? If that happened, I would take Ram's way out, no question. A deep, longing agony wracked my body, jarring me out of my numbness.

"Hey, can you read to me?" I said. "You know, to help me sleep?"

Warnick seemed to understand and opened his Bible. Clearing his throat, he read aloud from the New Testament. Later, I learned it was from Colossians.

> Mortify therefore your members which
>   are upon the earth; fornication,
>   uncleanness, inordinate affection,
>   evil concupiscence, and covetous-
>   ness, which is idolatry:
> For which things' sake the wrath of God
>   cometh on the children of
>   disobedience:
> In the which ye also walked some time,
>   when ye lived in them.
> But now ye also put off all these; anger,
>   wrath, malice, blasphemy, filthy
>   communication out of your mouth.
> Lie not one to another, seeing that ye
>   have put off the old man with his
>   deeds;
> And have put on the new man, which is
>   renewed in knowledge after the
>   image of him that created him...

Maybe I was getting religion in my old age. I felt a spark

cutting through the pain like a blade. Though the feeling only lasted a moment, it warmed me. Made me think there might be something good waiting for us out there—a glimmer of light resembling hope.

Whatever I felt, those words sounded good to me now.

CHAPTER
SIXTY-FOUR

I COULDN'T EAT the following day. Though I was the most experienced on the ice, I knew in my soul Chavez would find a way to screw me. Last time, it had been eight draggers instead of six. What now—a horde?

Warnick tried giving me a pep talk, but I wasn't listening. In my mind, I searched the equipment bags, examining each weapon in turn. After minutes of mental anguish, I settled on the aluminum bat. Though it was light and good for my balance, I craved something sharp.

On the way over, everyone acted cordial towards me— another clue I was in for a cornholing. My friend sat beside me in the backseat, reading his Bible. He didn't look up till we arrived at Happier Times. Instead of escorting us, the guards let us walk in by ourselves. Stopping, I vomited, and some splashed on Warnick's shoes.

"No Weezer for you," he said.

My friend helped me through the doorway and led me to the counter, where Eddie was already waiting with my skates. The old man had gotten me the best pair he could find— black leather with red trim and white laces. He'd even polished them. I never loved him more than I did now. He couldn't look me in the eye. That's when I knew I was right about the supervisor.

As I walked away, the old man piped up. "Be seeing you, Dave."

While putting on my skates, I noticed that the mood was way more subdued—or maybe it was in my head. Warnick was nearby, chatting with Estrada like they were the best of pals. Weird.

When Chavez walked over, my anger erupted. Like Landry, I had nothing to lose and decided to speak my mind. I could tell my friend was against it, but I no longer gave a shit. When you're going to hell, the least they can do is let you make a farewell speech. And anyway, the supervisor planned to get me killed in there. Might as well say my piece.

"You never meant for us to survive," I said. "Except maybe Warnick. Or are you saving him for later?"

Chavez was silent, his cheerful grin hardening into resentment. "Everyone has the same chance. Only the strongest survive. Way it is."

"Whatever."

I picked through the weapons in the equipment bags, looking for the aluminum bat. When I found it, I didn't take it. If I was going to die, I wanted to go out my way. These gimcrack leftovers were of no use. I needed a real weapon.

"Hey, Enrique," I said. "I want my axe."

With a threatening look, he approached me, but I held my ground.

"Look, I get this is all a big show. Let me give you one."

From his expression, it was easy to see that granting my wish wouldn't make a difference one way or the other. Let this dumb bastard think he's got a snowball's chance. It'll make his death all the sweeter. The supervisor signaled Estrada, and they spoke offline.

"Can I see your Bible?" I said to my friend.

I didn't know what I was searching for. Nevertheless, I turned the pages, looking for a jolt of strength. Part of me felt these were only words, even as they screamed at me to have faith.

Ten minutes later, Estrada was back, carrying my axe. Side-eying Warnick, she handed it to me. By now, those in the bleachers had settled down. For no good reason, I felt happy as I skated in. Eddie—God bless him—had run the Zamboni again, and the ice glistened.

As they closed the gate, I skated fast, swinging my weapon in one hand, then the other. Axes are way heavier than hockey sticks, and I had to work on my balance. But it felt good to be on the ice. I pictured myself as a kid, going up against guys twice my size. Never in my life was I as free as when I played hockey.

Pushing the random thoughts way down deep, I focused on skating. I was rusty. My dirty clothes felt stiff, and my skates were too tight. None of it mattered, though. I thought about the ice, my axe, and whatever shit-storm was about to come through those double doors. Whatever it was, I felt ready.

It was the same as last time—no music or flashing lights. Chavez gave the signal. A second later, the doors banged open, but no one cheered. I couldn't make out the backlit figures—there were only four. This had to be a mistake. Had they run low on combatants?

As my eyes adjusted, I saw three guards pushing a female dragger. Like an enraged animal, she fought the catchpole and tried grabbing it. There was something familiar about her. As she advanced into the light, I stumbled. This was what the supervisor had saved for me. And it was how I would die.

"We thought you'd enjoy mixing it up with Wanda," Chavez said.

Giggling, he explored Estrada's hair bun with his finger. She wasn't into it. As I stood, my eyes went from him to my opponent.

He stood at ease. "This little beauty took out eight of my men before we could bring her down. I won't tell you how many she's killed on the ice. It would only depress you."

I stared at the dragger, knowing all too well the torn, blood-soaked clothes. The skin had mummified to a dark, leathery sheen. Thin strands of dirty brown hair adorned the bald head, which was scarred and dented. The eyes protruded from their sockets, twitchy and searching. The nose had long since fallen off. And the lips had shrunk savagely, revealing dagger-like teeth.

It was Missy.

CHAPTER
SIXTY-FIVE

THEY DRAGGED Missy to the center and, releasing her, ran like hell. A guard fell, and the others carried him out by the arms. Keeping to the outside, I skated counterclockwise, determined to escape the death I knew awaited me just across the ice.

"She's not like the others," Chavez said. "We figured you already had an edge, being a hockey player and all."

Invigorated, the audience chanted like drunken lunatics. "Wan-da! Wan-da!"

Missy's flat eyes scanned the ice, looking for prey. When she caught sight of me, I stopped. It might have been the lights, but I thought there was a glimmer of recognition. Then she made a noise like red-hot bearings in a burned-out motor. But it wasn't a death shriek. It was a word—a name.

"Daaaaaaaaaaaaaaaaaaaaaave!"

"What the hell?" someone said.

"She knows him?"

"Dude, this is awesome!"

On cue, the person in the announcer's booth fired up the

lights and put on Whitney Houston's "I Will Always Love You." Out of their minds, the guards screamed with approval.

My blood turning cold, I nearly crashed headlong into a wall and scrambled to regain my balance. Even dead, Missy would never stop. She was my sin calling to me—shouting every wrong I had ever committed. The bad grades, the abuse I'd hurled at my mother, the drinking. Betraying Holly. I wanted to accept my punishment and die like Ram. But it was Warnick's voice that spoke to me.

> But now ye also put off all these; anger,
> wrath, malice, blasphemy, filthy
> communication out of your mouth.

They were words that made me believe I might have something worthwhile to do in this life. Something precious to protect.

> Lie not one to another, seeing that ye
> have put off the old man with his
> deeds;

Maybe it was better to stay alive asking for forgiveness than dying without it. Holly and Griffin were out there somewhere—I could feel it. And if Landry was right, I could help them.

> And have put on the new man, which is
> renewed in knowledge after the
> image of him that created him.

I needed to stay alive to become this new man, washed

clean of his sins. As the voice in my head faded, a red band of blood pressed against my eyes, almost blinding me. Praying for strength, I skated away from the demon that wanted to destroy me.

Missy stopped cold as I went around her faster and faster. After guessing where I would be, she leaped through the air. The crowd lost it. This was what they had come to see—life and death. As I shot past, my friend gripped his Bible in front of him with both hands.

I couldn't run out the clock—Chavez wouldn't permit it. I performed a V-stop, sending a shower of ice at the wall. Missy hurtled towards me as if running on asphalt. I raised my weapon and waited those impossible few seconds as she threw herself at me. At the last moment, I shifted sideways and swung the axe, taking off most of her left arm. The blow threw her off balance and spun her into a crushing fall. As she hit the wall, I skated away.

"Keep her in front of you!" Warnick said.

Good advice. As she came at me again, I skated backwards. Everyone in the stands was on their feet now, mesmerized. Soon, I'd have to turn around or risk crashing into a wall. Sucking in air, I stopped cold. But I had miscalculated.

Missy was way closer than I realized, and I didn't have time to swing my axe. Instead, I whacked her in the face with the handle, making a crunching noise. Her jaw hung open, revealing deadly black teeth. Growling, she tried taking my weapon away. The strength of her grip was unreal.

Gripping both ends, I dropped to my knees and flung her over my head in an insane game of leapfrog. The audience screamed themselves raw. As she hit the ice, I got to my feet and skated backwards in the opposite direction.

I desperately needed to rest, but there wasn't time. Missy was already on her feet and coming at me fast. My only hope was to take off the other arm, or her head if I was lucky. Chavez was right—she wasn't like the others. She was cunning. It didn't matter whether I feinted left or right. She always matched me, always anticipated. She was like a heat-seeking missile that never lost its target. Impatient for blood, the crowd booed. Suddenly, I remembered something.

When I was little, I didn't start out playing hockey—I took figure skating. Maybe I could... No, I was wearing the wrong kind of skates. But I had to try. As Missy came at me, I began spinning. Confused, she kept coming. I went faster and faster. When she lunged at me, I sliced off the other arm like a butcher cutting a pig.

Dizzy, I stopped and watched her spinning away from me, armless and shrieking. Still, she came at me. It was time for this to be over. When she was in range, I crushed her kneecap. As she fell forward, I brought down the axe and skated backwards, the head tumbling after me. It rolled to a stop near the wall, the hate-filled eyes glaring.

It's not true what they say about draggers, that they retain nothing of their former selves. Though they're no longer capable of rational thought, some of the old personality remains—like Missy. In their decayed, unfeeling state, they remind us they were once people with hopes and dreams and memories.

My lungs burning, I swung the axe once more, splitting the skull in two, and skated to the dasher board gate well before the time was up. Everyone stared, unable to believe I had survived Wanda. Sweat poured down my face, and at first, I didn't see the supervisor pointing his weapon at me.

"I was right," I said. "I was never supposed to make it."

Shrugging, he aimed at my head. "What are you gonna do?"

I didn't close my eyes. I wanted to see the bullet coming—

to know the exact moment of my death. Before Chavez could pull the trigger, Estrada swung the pipe wrench, connecting with the back of his head. The crunching blow sent him forward in a spray of blood. She stared at the sociopath as he struggled to comprehend what had happened.

"Dude," he said.

His voice sounded thick as blood ran from his nostrils. Others swarmed around from all sides. I forced my way next to my friend, where I found the supervisor convulsing and gurgling. The back of his head had been crushed, exposing a pink, pulsating brain. Amazingly, he tried to stand, but no one helped. Instead, they watched as the life bled out of him. Estrada was still holding the pipe wrench and let it slip from her blood-soaked fingers.

Alone and scared, Chavez seemed younger. He reminded me of a frightened child. Something had gone horribly wrong after Black Dragon arrived. A sickness had taken over. And it manifested in the bloodthirsty leader of a band of violence-prone acolytes. Searching the faces of these young guards, I could tell they didn't have the stomach for it anymore.

The supervisor's eyes fluttered, then closed for good as blood pooled like oil from a shallow well. It set him apart from the rest. Made him unwanted—a pariah. Estrada unholstered her weapon and sent a bullet into her supervisor's broken head, silencing the evil internal voices forever. Warnick climbed onto a bench and addressed the other guards.

"Listen up," he said. "We're putting this house in order." Then to the Latina, "You okay?"

Looking stunned, she didn't answer.

I felt old, like I had lived through a hundred years of war in only a few weeks. Somewhere out there, Holly and Griffin were fighting for their lives. And I needed them alive—especially Holly. I needed her forgiveness.

Eddie handed me my boots as the guards scraped Missy's remains off the ice. "Who was she?"

"Someone who didn't deserve this," I said.

PART FIVE

ZOMBIE WEATHER

CHAPTER
SIXTY-SIX

NO ONE KNEW how many security guards there were in Tres Marias. Our group consisted of fewer than a hundred. We spent the next few days cleaning up. This was the last place I wanted to be—I needed to find Holly and Griffin. Warnick reminded me that I would likely die without Black Dragon's protection. Point taken.

My friend assigned crews to assess every building in the office park. He and I stuck together, taking a few guards with us. Estrada took charge of the rest, assigning team captains. Though she had saved my life, I didn't trust her. She'd gone along with everything that maniac Chavez had cooked up, and now she felt remorse? Too easy. Warnick looked at it differently. He saw in her a person who had made a wrong choice to stay alive. Potato potahto.

While cleaning up, I spotted Keller—that cocky kid from the ice rink. I learned he wasn't a civilian but a Black Dragon intern. In truth, no one except Warnick and me had survived the games. The rest had been processed into meat for the draggers.

Black Dragon had set up many buildings as housing for

313

the guards. One had been designated as a storage unit for those who had fought and died in the tournaments. When I saw them stacked up, I wondered how long the supervisor had been at this.

The decaying bodies stank, and many vomited from the smell. After retreating, we put on particle masks and returned to make sure nothing was alive. We thought about burning the corpses in the parking lot, but that would take too long. In the end, we decided to leave them.

By lunchtime, there was one building left to check in the back near Happier Times. Some of the other guards warned us about going in there. My friend had left to supervise another crew, and the rest of us were too exhausted to listen. Stupidly, we walked in through the front entrance, unprepared for what came next.

When the lights came on, we found hungry draggers wandering from one end of the open floor to the other. This must have been where Chavez kept them for the tournaments. They came at us, shrieking and clawing. Fortunately, the guards had their handguns, but I was weaponless.

The others created a line of fire as we backed out. Near the doors, a skinny FedEx driver attacked the guy next to me. I recognized him as the one who had thrown a soda can at Landry. Screaming, he shot his attacker through the head.

Once we were outside, we locked the doors. The injured guard stared at the festering bite mark on his arm. Everyone backed away as he tried to explain himself with gibbering excuses. His comrades side-eyed each other, and another guard—Neidermeyer—drew his weapon. Contritely, the condemned man nodded. Then, he bolted.

Neidermeyer fired, striking the runner in the back. Screaming, he stumbled and fell on his face. Like a machine, the shooter marched up to the whimpering guard and shot him in the head. Pivoting, he holstered his gun and spat.

"We need to report this," he said.

In the late afternoon, I attended a meeting in a conference room with Warnick, Estrada, and the team captains. My friend decided it was too risky to eliminate the remaining hostiles. There were too many places they could hide. And we couldn't afford to lose any more people. I suggested we set the building on fire. At first, everyone except Warnick laughed— he liked the idea.

Working quickly, we rolled in drums filled with gasoline. We placed them around the building and rigged them to explode. The plan was dangerous, and there was no going back. Once the building caught fire, the flames would likely spread to the other structures. My friend made the call. We would proceed as planned. If the other buildings went up, we'd let them burn. I looked around the table. These were the same people who had cheered us on in a frenzy of blood lust at the ice rink. Now they resembled lost sheep.

I turned to Warnick. "After this, where do we go?"

"We need to find a building we can secure."

In his zeal to control the situation, Chavez had ordered all computers to be destroyed. Estrada grabbed a pile of satellite maps of the town and laid them across the table.

"What about the high school?" my friend said to her.

"It's no good. We checked it out a few weeks ago. The place is overrun."

Thinking of my neighbor Mrs. Hough, I appealed to him. "But there might be survivors."

"Too risky," he said. "We'll avoid it."

After reviewing the maps, we settled on a location off the

main highway. I recognized it as the old Arkon Insurance building. It seemed large enough. With luck, the doors would be locked and the structure dragger free.

As night fell, Warnick directed crews to gather all working vehicles. Each would be stocked with weapons and whatever food and water we could find. Before evacuating, we set off the fuel drums.

A series of ear-splitting explosions created a brilliant ring of fire. Flames shot inward, consuming everything inside. A giant fireball blew out the front doors and windows. Another blast rocked the adjacent buildings. Thankfully, there was no wind.

We stood next to our vehicles, waiting for the draggers to emerge. The front entrance was now a gaping hole with angry flames that licked the sides. Soon, they came—and they were on fire. Burning like torches, some made it to within a hundred feet of our vehicles. One by one, they fell, blazing on the ground like toxic trash. The smoke was unbearable—sweet and greasy. Others followed, marching relentlessly forward till the fire reduced them to ash.

After the last of the draggers fell, we piled into our vehicles and departed for a new unknown.

CHAPTER
SIXTY-SEVEN

I HAD a plan of my own. After getting everyone settled in the Arkon building, I'd search for Holly and Griffin. Thanks to Warnick, I had my phone, but the battery was long dead. Even if I could charge it, who knew if there would be any cell service?

Two guards—Springer and Popp—rode with us. They looked fresh out of high school. Both were blond, buff, and from opposite ends of the state—Santa Rosa and San Diego. And both surfed. I wasn't sure how much use they would be in a firefight, though.

As the convoy made its way to the new location, I was tempted to ask them why they had gone along with Chavez's demented plan. Earlier, my friend had advised me to avoid these kinds of conversations. He was in the process of building trust and didn't want anyone derailing his efforts. So I pretended it was all good.

I pointed at a Walmart up ahead. "Can we stop here for a sec?"

Warnick pulled into the parking lot, and the other vehicles followed. The outdoor lights were on. They buzzed like angry wasps and bathed the store in an otherworldly orange glow. Scanning the area, I didn't notice any movement. Still, it was creepy, and I was glad my friend had given me a gun.

Shopping carts lay scattered everywhere next to dead shoppers. The corpses had been eaten away. But it was the dead children that did me in. All around, mothers' bodies lay on top, trying to protect their precious offspring.

Every inch of glass at the front entrance was shattered, and the looters were long gone. Inside, the fluorescent lights shone bright. I planned to run in and get a charger for my phone. Warnick stayed close, clearing the aisles as we made our way to the rear of the store.

"Hang on," he said, raising his AR-15.

Something moved in the distance, big like a bear. I recognized Detective Van Gundy. His face was pasty, and fresh blood ran from his torn lips. One hand was missing. Aiming his rifle, my friend fired a short burst. The bullets tore off half the cop's face, and the lumbering giant fell backwards into a circular rack of clearance summer wear. We continued to the electronics department. I pored over the glass cases while Springer and Popp gathered supplies.

"See if there's a charger for my phone," Warnick said.

Outside, all was quiet, which only served to heighten my unease. The guards brought out nonperishable food, water, clothing, batteries, and first-aid supplies. Across the parking lot, dead shoppers wandered among the cars like they had forgotten where they parked. They hadn't yet spotted us.

Instead of messing with them, we decided to get out of there. Never fight if you don't have to, I remembered my friend telling me once. As we pulled out, a car horn blasted, and he hit the brakes.

"What?" I said.

"Someone might be alive."

"Or it could be draggers trying to trick us. Hey, I know. Let's check it out."

"That's the spirit," he said.

The other guards waited in their vehicles as Warnick and I crossed the parking lot. I carried my axe for extra protection. A silver Volvo Cross Country was parked way off in a corner under a tree. Its emergency lights were flashing, and I thought I detected movement inside. A dragger pack milled around the vehicle. We waited a beat, and the horn went off again.

My friend radioed Springer and Popp. As the four of us moved in, he signaled us to spread out. Inside, a terrified woman pleaded with us through the windshield. Behind her was a rear-facing car seat.

I side-eyed Warnick. "I hate it when you're right."

The draggers surrounding the Volvo used to be teenagers. All were dressed in ripped jeans or shorts and T-shirts. The thought of shooting them sickened me. I hadn't gotten over the little girl at the lake and had to remind myself what they were. We chose our targets. It was easy to pick off the ones farthest away from the vehicle. Soon my friend ordered us to stop.

"We can't risk shooting the civilian," he said. "Any ideas?"

The others exchanged a look. Springer pointed at my axe.

I turned to Warnick. "You've got to be shitting me."

"It's the only way to keep her and the baby safe."

"What about my safety? Fine. But you guys owe me."

My friend tried calling for backup but couldn't get through. While he kept at it, I holstered my gun and took a couple practice swings. I marched towards the hostiles and stopped just out of reach. The others moved into position, their weapons trained on the dragger pack. Unaware of my presence, they pawed at the windshield.

"Hey, dipshits," I said.

A teenager with cystic acne spun around and growled with pleasure. When it was within range, I swung the axe in a wide arc and took off its head. Hoping for a free meal, the others came at me. As they moved away from the vehicle, the guards put them down with precision gun bursts.

Popp's rifle jammed as a kid with green hair descended on him. I used the axe handle to cave in its head. Pushing the guard out of the way, I finished it with the blade.

"Thanks, man," he said, getting to his feet.

"Don't mention it."

I thought we were done. But when I turned around, a horde was crossing the parking lot. Frantically, I looked for backup, but there was none.

Warnick signaled the woman. "Unlock the doors!"

"Hey, guys?" I said. "Any time."

Springer, Popp, and I faced the approaching hostiles. I glanced back to find my friend helping the terrified woman out of the car. Once she was free, he flung open the rear passenger door and tried unbuckling the car seat as the baby squalled.

"How's this thing work?" he said.

Shoving him aside, she unfastened the harness and removed the car seat.

Warnick checked his weapon. "Okay, let's go."

The hostiles decided we were sitting ducks and tried rushing us. Springer, Popp, and I created a line of fire as my friend escorted the woman to our vehicle. As soon as we had the chance, we ran. He tried getting the woman inside our Humvee, but she wouldn't budge.

"I forgot the diaper bag," she said.

"No time."

"Please, there's baby formula in there."

Rolling his eyes, Warnick looked at me. "Get the bag."

Springer and Popp accompanied me. Halfway there, the horde engaged us. Fortunately, more guards had arrived to assist. As they fired on the hostiles, I ran to the Volvo. *Get the bag, Dave. Sure, no problemo.* I snagged it and sprinted to our vehicles. Most of the mewling draggers had been put down, but more were emerging from the darkness. One grabbed Popp's arm. Before it could bite him, he filled its mouth with lead.

After securing the area, my friend ordered a squad to return to the store to gather formula and diapers. Everyone else piled into the vehicles and waited. Before long, we were out of there. Springer and Popp sat in the backseat with the woman and baby.

"How long were you out there?" I said.

"Since this morning. My car wouldn't start. I didn't know what else to do."

Warnick glanced at her in the rearview mirror. "You're safe now."

"I can't thank you guys enough."

I thought the baby might have smiled at me. "What's his name?"

"She's a girl, and her name is Evan. I'm Nina Zimmer."

"Dave Pulaski."

She was around thirty. Attractive, with chestnut hair and violet eyes that were filled with determination. To me, she looked like a born survivor.

Nina kissed her daughter. "I prayed someone would find us. Do you believe in God?"

"Funny you should ask," I said.

CHAPTER
SIXTY-EIGHT

IT WAS LATE when we arrived at the Arkon building, and Nina and her daughter were asleep in the backseat. I joined the other guards to await instructions.

"After we clear the building, we'll bring in the civilians," Warnick said. "Dave, stay with Nina."

"But I'm coming with you."

"Fine. Popp?"

"Copy.

Under the streetlights, the front doors looked secure. Another squad circled the building to make sure no other entrances had been breached. Springer and I followed my friend to the rear. A bobtail truck was backed up to the loading dock. Inside was a man with his chest carved out like a Halloween pumpkin. His skeletal hands clung to the steering wheel.

"I remember this building," Estrada said, unfazed. "We secured it weeks ago."

Warnick spoke over his radio, requesting a locksmith. Soon, another guard joined us, carrying a leather pouch. Using the tools, he got to work. Once inside, squads proceeded to clear every floor. Fortunately, there was power, which meant the elevators were operational.

I was desperate to charge my phone, but our priority was to confirm that the building was safe. Checking out the restrooms, we discovered that the plumbing worked as well. The only place left to clear was the basement. Our weapons at our sides, we rode the elevator down.

Unsure what to expect, my nerves were jangly. And when the doors opened, I almost fired on a group of gaunt, hollow-eyed civilians.

"Is it over?" someone said.

Around thirty men and women looked at us hopefully. The hallway was filled with trash and several dead bodies. The smell was sickening. We brought them in groups up to the first floor and gave them food and water. Some were so weak they had to be carried. One man gulped down his water gratefully.

"Why did you stay down there?" my friend said.

"Your people ordered us."

"How long ago?"

"Hard to remember. Five weeks?"

Annoyed, Warnick turned to Estrada, who could only shrug.

The civilians stayed alive by drinking water. The supplies Black Dragon had left for them were gone. Not long after, the vending machine food ran out. Ragged and frail, they had bleeding gums and dry skin. We administered basic medical care and set them up in conference rooms and cubicles to sleep, promising they were safe now.

It was morning when we finished. After making Nina and the baby comfortable, I got out the chargers and grabbed my friend's phone. Discovering an outlet, I plugged in both. When mine turned on, I saw that I had one bar. I heard a chime as a voicemail came through. It was from Holly. My heart aching, I listened to her voice.

Griffin and I are okay. Two Black Dragon guards found us. We're hiding from the Red Militia. Later, we'll search for food and water. Hope you're safe.

That was it—short and to the point. Not knowing whether my wife had found a phone charger, I decided to text her anyway.

Tell me ur alive.

I gave her our building's address. With luck, she and the girl would find their way there. When our phones were fully charged, I tracked down Warnick.

"Holly's alive," I said. "I need to go."

"Wait until tonight. Besides, you need rest."

Maybe he was right. Besides, riding around in the daylight might be dangerous. I found an empty room and tried sleeping. After lying awake for an hour, I gave up. There was plenty to do, and I decided to make myself useful.

The time passed quickly. In the afternoon, I thought I might try sleeping again. But first, I wanted to look in on Nina. I found her in the first-floor lunchroom, changing Evan's diaper. The baby was calm and happy as she gazed into her mother's eyes. I took a seat at a round table. She dressed the baby and washed her hands in the sink. Sitting across from me, she stroked her daughter's cheek and gave me a sly smile.

"You want to know what I was doing out there," she said.

"The thought had crossed my mind."

"It was stupid, I know. But I needed formula and diapers.

I should've left with my neighbors—they begged me to. But I was so scared for Evan. I didn't know what we'd find out there, so I barricaded us in our condo."

"Which was fine till you ran out of food."

"I was sure Walmart would be deserted."

"Why didn't you park closer to the entrance?"

"I did think about it. But the parking lot looked so deserted. I figured it would be safer. Like I said, I was stupid." She laughed. "Before I knew it, I was surrounded. When my car wouldn't start, I thought…"

"I'm glad we stopped." I gave the baby a goofy smile. "She's beautiful."

"Thanks." Nina looked at me intently. "We're not going to make it, are we?"

I didn't know what to say. I could have been a man and given her the big speech. But it was a question that had been nagging at me, too.

"I honestly don't know. Can I ask, are you married?"

"We're not together right now. He's living in San Francisco."

"Does he care about you?"

"I think so. He tried coming back, but all the roads were blocked." She glanced at my wedding ring. "What about you?"

After telling her my story, I thought she would judge me. But she was kind.

"She's lucky to have you," she said. "Thank you for saving us."

She kissed my cheek and left the room. Surprisingly, sleep came immediately. The last thing I remembered was staring at my phone. Praying that a message from my wife would reach me across this never-ending nightmare.

. . .

When I awoke, Warnick was making coffee. I rubbed my stiff neck and checked my phone. No more messages. We stood by the large windows in the reception area, gazing at the full moon. Outside, guards patrolled the perimeter.

"I can't go with you," my friend said. "I need to make sure everyone stays on task."

"You don't trust your second-in-command?"

"She's on probation. I'll assign you two guards. That's all I can spare."

"I don't even know where to look."

"I'd start with where Estrada picked us up."

"Sounds good. What if we run into any nailheads?"

"Don't," he said.

After saying goodbye, I stood on the loading dock, grateful that Warnick had assigned me Springer and Popp. In truth, those two were starting to grow on me. Another guard accompanied us, waiting to lock the door once we were on our way. My friend had provided a Humvee. Springer took the wheel, with Popp riding shotgun.

As we entered the street, I looked back at the building, wondering if I would ever return. That was the worst part about living like this—the uncertainty of every moment. No one ever thinks that when they leave their loved ones, it might be for the last time. I'll admit, it can be liberating not being tied down. It's how Jim and I saw life in the thick of our drinking days. But it was a lonely existence, too.

I didn't know what we would discover out there. Part of me wanted to stay at Arkon and look after Nina and the others. But the desire to find Holly and Griffin was way stronger. Springer glanced at me in the rearview mirror as if reading my mind.

"We'll find them," he said.

CHAPTER
SIXTY-NINE

WE COUNTED on the darkness to keep us safe. As we neared our destination, we ditched the Humvee. Then we headed out with our weapons and ammo. The night was humid, and I was drenched in sweat after only a few blocks.

As we pressed on, we encountered draggers in various states of decomposition. The fresher ones—if a dead, stinking body could ever be considered fresh—hunted in packs, and we dispatched them.

The long-timers, those near total collapse, wandered alone. Some lay by the side of the road, staring at the moon with unseeing eyes—waiting for what? These pathetic wraiths seemed to exist in a perpetual twilight of death longing. We let them be.

"Pretty sure it's this way," I said.

We entered a familiar alley, where we found Ben's motorhome. Someone had set fire to it for no reason other than to watch it burn. It stood there charred and empty, a rotting testament to a dream gone wrong.

Beyond the wreck, I recognized the side entrance Holly and Griffin had used to escape. It seemed like a million years ago when I watched them disappear inside. I prayed we would find them alive. Why hadn't I insisted on more guards? It was stupid to think the three of us could keep everyone safe, especially if my wife or the girl were sick or injured.

The guards mounted flashlights on the rails of their AR-15s. Springer pushed the door open and poked his weapon through. When he gave us the signal, Popp and I followed him inside. The interior was inky as they played their flashlight beams from one side of the trash-filled room to the other.

A noise startled me. As we advanced, a dragger with filmy eyes gaped at us, a hand hanging from its mouth. Springer didn't fire for fear of attracting others. Instead, he drew his knife and ran the blade through the skull before the creature could strike. It fell with a groan.

We found the emergency stairs and began our ascent. I wasn't sure how I ended up in front. Right away, I noticed that the metal railing was wet and sticky. I signaled Popp, who shone his flashlight on my hands. They were stained with blood.

Farther up, there was a noise. Popp directed his beam upstairs. Nothing but shadows. On the second floor, a shuffling sound, followed by soft mewling. Something scratched at the door. Thinking it was Greta, I grabbed the door handle. Springer shook his head and pointed at Popp, who slid in front of me. Waiting a beat, he flung open the door, revealing an empty floor with offices and a reception area. We decided to investigate.

Rounding a corner, Springer found the light switches. When he flicked them on, we discovered we had walked into a nest of slavering draggers. The one closest to me hissed. Disoriented, I fell backwards into the guards. Regaining their footing, they shot those in front through the head. As the others came at us, we retreated.

I took a position next to the wall and began firing. The hostiles pushed forward, ignoring the bullets that riddled their bodies. An intense volley took them down, one after the next, and the noise was deafening. One of them moved in on Springer. I didn't fire my handgun for fear of hitting the guard.

"Push it away," I said.

Springer obeyed. I aimed at the dragger's head and squeezed the trigger. *Click.* I was out of ammo. A burst of bullets went through its temple, and it went down. When I turned to see, Popp lowered his weapon. I gave him a thumbs-up and reloaded.

Two more appeared. As I raised my gun to fire, a decaying hand grabbed me. I let myself go limp. The bewildered creature came at me again, and I shot it in the mouth. The slug shredded its slithering tongue into black confetti. When it was over, we sat on the floor, exhausted.

"Whole damn building's infested," Springer said.

I got to my feet. "I have to find Holly and Griffin."

Popp nodded at his friend. "Break's over."

It took us an hour to clear the building. Eventually, we arrived at the top floor. Halfway up the stairs, we found the body that the disembodied hand belonged to—a guard around the same age as my comrades. He had been shot in the head. Springer opened the stairwell door and peered into the hallway. As Popp and I entered, a voice droned. Thinking it might be my wife or the girl, I started to follow it. Annoyed, Springer grabbed my arm and signaled me to get behind the other guard.

We entered the office suite through walnut doors. Inside, there were rows of fabric-covered cubicles on either side of us. Each was filled with personal items—family photos, stuffed animals, and children's drawings taped to miniature whiteboards. Near the windows, there was an executive conference room. The stranger's voice grew louder as we approached. My guts twisted as I imagined Holly and Griffin hurt. Springer grabbed the handle and cracked the door.

Inside, a guard lay in a corner by the windows, muttering and rocking. When Springer shone his flashlight on him, the stranger pointed his handgun at us. He looked so young lying there, alone and scared. I remembered my wife's voicemail. He and his partner had been protecting the women. I wanted to question him.

"Easy," Springer said as his partner closed the curtains and switched on the lights. "I'm Springer. What's your name?"

Feverish, the guard tried speaking. His speech sounded suspicious, like he might be turning. Springer moved in slowly, his hands visible in front of him. The injured guard raised his gun higher.

"Put down the weapon, son."

Confused, the guard blinked, then dropped his arm. Most of his right foot was missing. He had made himself a tourniquet using his rifle strap. A brown blood trail led from the door to where he lay. Popp raised his weapon, but I grabbed his hand before he could fire. Crouching close to the injured guard, I looked him in the eyes. The name on his uniform read BARNES.

"Barnes, listen to me," I said. "There were two women in here earlier. One of them is a teenage girl. They had a dog. You and your friend were protecting them, right?"

He stared at me, mesmerized by the sound of my voice. I glanced at Springer and Popp, who seemed impatient.

"This is important. I need you to tell me where they went."

"Thirsty."

Springer pulled out a water bottle from his backpack and handed it over. I helped Barnes sit up and let him drink.

"Do you know where they are?"

"Ran away. When the draggers came...from the alley. Covered them as best we could. Too many. My friend, he— Are they safe?"

Barnes was near death, and it wouldn't be long before he turned. We didn't know where he was from or whether he had a family. I wanted to help him, but it was too late. He was handed a death sentence the moment he got bit. Sad and frustrated, I looked at Springer.

"Better wait outside," he said.

CHAPTER
SEVENTY

I FOUND a cubicle and sat in the darkness, fighting my tears. Moonlight streamed through the windows, casting light on photos of a man and woman with their two small children. One looked around three and the other eighteen months. They were inside the Monterey Bay Aquarium. I recalled going there with Holly once when we were dating.

"Please, God," I said. "I'm so tired."

I waited for a gunshot that never came. In a little while, the door opened, and Springer and Popp walked out. Without a word, they waited for me to pull myself together. Fresh blood shone on Springer's knife, along with strands of hair. I handed him a tissue box, and he wiped off his blade.

Popp laid a hand on my shoulder. "There's still a chance we'll find them."

"It's fine."

When we reached the ground floor, I heard the far-off barking of a dog. Thinking it might be Greta, I bolted to the alley door.

"Wait, dammit," Springer said.

They caught up to me as I reached for the handle. Holding

it shut, Springer gave me a disapproving look that made his buddy grin.

"You can't keep doing that—you'll get us all killed."

Cracking the door, he checked the alley, which was deep in shadow. When he was satisfied, he signaled us to follow single file. A death shriek pealed through the streets, followed by more barking. We checked our weapons and left behind the safety of the alley. I almost called out my wife's name when a bullet whizzed past me.

Teetering, Springer went down. Bright blood leaked through his fingers as he clutched his throat. While Popp covered me, I knelt to examine the fallen guard.

Another round struck Popp in the forehead, and he collapsed. When I looked around me, I realized too late we had run into a group of nailheads. Now, tricked-out vehicles with bright headlights surrounded me. A dozen hostiles got out and pointed their weapons. One of them held a vicious-looking pit bull on a chain.

"Well, lookee here."

Travis Golightly limped out of the darkness. He was badly burned. The skin on his face looked like it had melted, the morbid tissue obscuring one eye. His hair was singed down to the roots, and his arms were covered in black, crusty skin. The fingers of his right hand were seared to the bone, and his weapon was duct-taped to his hand. A skeletal digit rested against the trigger guard.

The others grabbed me as I tried to escape. Travis hit me across the face with his rifle barrel, making my ears ring. I could feel warm blood trickling from my nose.

"Where's my daughter?" he said.

I could barely stand. "Dead."

"Wrong answer."

He came at me again, jamming the barrel under my

shoulder blade. As searing, hot pain shot through me, my arm went numb, and I fell to my knees. Growling, the dog lunged and bit my hand. I didn't even feel it.

Travis patted the animal's head. "That wasn't very nice, Sally." Then to me, "Where's Griffin?"

"Dead."

"Hey, Travis?" his friend said. "He don't look so good."

Bone cold, I awoke in a room surrounded by giant beer tanks. An imposing metal door stood across from me. My vision was blurry, and I could barely read the labels on the containers. I was inside the Lucky Moon microbrewery at the edge of town.

Outside, voices chattered. I reached into my pocket for my phone. It wasn't there. I spotted it across the room and crawled to the opposite wall. The screen was smashed, but I put it in my pocket anyway.

I knew they were going to kill me. But not before Travis beat the truth out of me about his stepdaughter. The world had unraveled, and all this dumb bastard could think about was carrying on the abuse.

Someone unlocked the door. I tried crawling back to where they had left me and made it about halfway. A Red Militia crazy walked in, swilling beer from a bottle while holding a second one in his other hand. A Latino boy around ten or eleven followed him in.

"Thought you might be thirsty."

He tried handing me the beer, but I didn't take it. Shrugging, he twisted off the cap and set it on the floor beside me.

"Mebbe later," he said.

He signaled the boy, who set down a cloth bag and removed a square of cardboard and a Ball Mason jar. Something inside was moving. I tensed as he handed the container to the man, who let out a moose belch. Kneeling, he grabbed my arm and rolled up my sleeve. The jar contained live bees.

"What're you doing?" I said.

"Testing you."

The cap had holes punched in it for air. After several drunken attempts, he managed to unscrew it. He replaced the top with the cardboard and flipped the jar onto my arm. After sliding out the square, the bees came in contact with my skin. Grimacing, I waited for the inevitable stinging to begin. Instead, the insects crawled on me benignly.

"Sweat bees don't lie," he said.

Satisfied, he separated the insects from my arm and screwed the cover on the jar. The boy put everything in the bag.

I squinted at the soak. "I don't get it."

"Whenever anyone gets bit, the bees won't come near 'em. You're fine."

"What are you going to do with me?"

"Up to Travis. If I was you, I'd tell 'im what he wants to hear."

"That his daughter's alive?"

"Whadda you think?"

"But she's dead."

"Tell 'im anyway."

"Then will he let me go?"

"No. But he might go easier on you before he kills your sorry ass."

I turned to the kid, who wouldn't make eye contact. "What's your story?"

The man pulled him aside. "Vete."

When the boy was gone, I gave the man an accusing look.

He shrugged sheepishly. "Makes himself useful, if you know what I mean."

"Glad to see you boys setting a good example for the youngsters."

"Some are into it. Not me, though."

"Does Ormand approve?"

Instead of responding, he unzipped his fly and peed on the wall. I got to my feet to jump him, but a second nailhead walked in and pointed his weapon at my head.

"Ulie, what did I tell you about not paying attention?" he said.

"He ain't goin' nowhere. Too broken up 'bout Griffin, I expect. He's clean, by the way."

I couldn't believe the absurdity. "Do you two even believe in what you're doing?"

"That ain't the point," the one with the gun said. "It's like this town is one big, happenin' club. And it don't matter who you came in with, it's who takes you home. Him and me are with Ormand."

Ulie finished his beer. "You got that right."

The comedians walked out and locked the door. I focused on the beer bottle. There was frost on the brown glass and little beads of condensation. What did it matter? Soon, I would be dead. Why shouldn't I enjoy a last beer? I brought it up to my nose. The smell was familiar and inviting. Maybe a sip. Where was the harm? One bottle. No way to get wasted. I could handle myself. Yeah, there I was, lying to myself again.

As I contemplated swallowing the contents, something strange happened. It might have been the blow to my head. Or maybe God was speaking to me. But I saw Holly standing across the way. She was wearing a pretty pale-green summer dress, the one I had seen her in on our last anniversary. I reached out to touch her. She looked at the beer, her head cocked to one side.

I had promised myself I wouldn't go back. More importantly, I promised her. Chances were excellent this wouldn't end well for me. I would be dead, and these jerk-offs would go on terrorizing others in what was left of the town—as if draggers weren't enough. Without giving it another thought, I flung the bottle against the wall, where it shattered into dust.

They would find me dead, but I'd be sober.

CHAPTER
SEVENTY-ONE

MOST PEOPLE HAVE no idea of the suffering the human body can endure. It defies reason. Ormand Ferry called it *cleansing* and appointed that paragon of patriotism Travis Golightly to administer it. They were always careful not to go too far. They did just enough to make me scream till my throat went raw.

After the first few times, I could barely feel anything. Enraged, Travis looked for new ways to hurt me. His anger came from wanting his stepdaughter, which I knew. But no matter how close to the edge those sessions brought me, I never changed my story. Griffin was dead.

Random thoughts flitted into my head like confused bats during those cruel, pain-filled hours and days. Most centered on Warnick and the other guards. Why hadn't they come for me? Springer and Popp were dead. I was near death. Was everyone else gone, too? That last thought drifted in and out of consciousness like a kid on a swing.

The nailheads liked staying drunk. There was enough beer to keep them in that state for weeks, maybe even months. When I wasn't blind from pain, I watched Travis struggle to control his people. Seeing me in agony was a boring waste of time for them. All they wanted was to drink. What started out as an audience of a dozen foot soldiers dwindled to a lone, faithful acolyte—Ulie.

Mostly, I saw men in this place. Occasionally, one or two women would make an appearance. I guessed that, like the Latino boy, it was their job to entertain. They were young and scared, and they had chosen to stay rather than face what was outside. Some couldn't have been much older than Griffin.

After the last cleansing, Travis realized I would need to eat if he wanted to keep up his sick game. They had stolen a cache of MREs and threw one in with me in the cold room. Ulie remained behind to prepare my meal. When the food was hot, he removed the package from the flameless heater and handed it over with a plastic spoon.

"Might be your last meal," he said. "Pretty sure Travis is gonna do you tomorrow."

"Maybe killing me will bring back his daughter."

"Yeah." He looked ashamed. "Lemme know if you change your mind about the beer. I grabbed these from the first-aid kit."

He retrieved two crumpled foil packets from his shirt pocket and placed them in my hand. I tore them open and swallowed the ibuprofen.

"Thanks," I said. "Why do they call you Ulie?"

"Dunno. Guess it's because I like to talk a lot. Passes the time, you know?"

After my sympathetic jailer left, I stared at the pouch. I was too sick to eat. My body ached, especially my leg. A few of my teeth were loose, and my lip was swollen. I thought a few ribs might be cracked, and I was almost blind in one eye.

Although I didn't want to prolong this black hell, I remembered what Warnick had said about faith. Then I drank some water and forced myself to eat.

Outside, men cursed and sang while women screamed. I couldn't tell if the noise was from pain or drunken glee. But they were on a real bender out there. Maybe they knew they were doomed and decided to go out partying. In another universe, I might have joined them. The constant cold made me drowsy. Even though my head hurt, I couldn't keep my eyes open. Soon, the voices floated away like snowflakes.

Falling, I drifted into a dreamless sleep while imaginary sweat bees tickled my arm.

Ulie leaned in close, his breath ripe with stale beer and jerky. "It's time."

A second nailhead had accompanied him. Both looked grim as they got me to my feet. Intense pain shot through my left leg—I couldn't walk on it. Taking my arms, they half-carried me.

The main area was empty and silent. The floor was swept, and there was no sign of the debauchery that had taken place the night before. When we reached the manager's office, I expected Travis to be waiting for me with his rifle attached to his bony hand. But as I entered, I found only Ormand Ferry. He sat behind the desk in a plush leather chair. The light from the desk lamp glinted off his wire-rimmed glasses. He wore his trademark brown suit with the red pocket square. It occurred to me I had never seen him up close. He was smaller —older—than I remembered.

The nailheads eased me into a chair opposite the desk and left us alone. My head felt thick. For a few silent moments, the leader of the Red Militia observed me, his manicured hands folded in front of him. Sighing, he examined my injuries and poured me a glass of water. As I set down the glass, streamers of blood lay suspended in the water. This small detail did not go unnoticed and seemed to trouble him.

"I want to apologize," he said.

"For what?"

"Travis. He shouldn't have gone so hard on you. Usually, our methods are less destructive. The fact is he's devastated over the loss of his stepdaughter." He paused for effect. "He seems to think you're lying about her. I've assured him there's no reason you would do that. Is there, Dave?"

"Is there what?"

He shifted in his chair, apparently unused to disrespect. I stared at the blood in the glass comingling with the water.

"Is there a reason you would lie about Griffin?"

"No reason."

The bruises on my face made it impossible for him to read me. Keeping my voice flat, I made sure to maintain eye contact.

"I didn't think so. Besides, it's unlikely you could've stuck to a lie after what Travis did to you. To be honest, I've overlooked a lot where Travis is concerned."

"Been a bad boy, has he?"

"He can be unpredictable. And with everything going on... It's difficult for me to stay on top of all facets of this operation. I'm sure you can appreciate that."

"What is going on?"

"We're gaining ground in our campaign to bring order to Tres Marias."

"I thought that was Black Dragon's job."

"Their mission was to put down civil unrest."

"Was?"

"Surely, you don't believe they care about you and me? They want to stop any activity they see as disruptive, then be on their way."

He was on his feet again. I expected the nailheads to haul in a soapbox.

"They're mercenaries. Are you aware they're shooting civilians at will and burning the bodies?"

"I thought they were killing draggers to rid the town of this scourge."

He chuckled artificially. "Once you label someone, you can do as you please, is that it?"

"Wait. Are you suggesting these are sick people who can be treated?"

"Not for me to say, I'm not a doctor."

"They're dead, okay? And they're eating people."

He seemed uncomfortable. "The, uh, the point is our organization is more interested in preserving this town than those paramilitary thugs. And I would hope you do, too."

"Are you asking me to join you?"

"You say that like it's a bad thing. We're helping people. Not like those overpaid contractors. We feed and shelter our citizens. And we'll continue doing so even after this scourge, as you call it, is over."

"How noble."

"I can see you're headstrong. You've stood up to this—"

"Torture?"

"Cleansing. And you've come through it like a man. You seem to want to live. I'm giving you a chance to do that."

He came around the desk and sat on the edge. His brown shoes had been freshly polished. "They tell me you don't drink."

"Used to."

"You see? We need people like you. Folks who can control their dark urges and work for the good of the community."

"Where are all these people you're talking about? The ones you say you're protecting?"

"Somewhere safe. The troops who were sent to save them have failed. They're in our care now."

"You're killing security guards."

"We always offer them a choice, as I'm doing with you. Some have seen the wisdom of what we're offering and have come over to our way of thinking. The ones who don't, well... Which reminds me. I want to thank you for removing Chavez from the equation."

"How did you know?"

"Give me some credit."

"Why haven't more guards been deployed?"

"I don't have that information. All we know is that the area is completely sealed off. No one gets in or out. So it's up to us."

I stared at the ceiling. "I need to think about it."

"Of course. You have until tomorrow morning. I won't be here, but you can tell Travis your decision."

"How do you know he won't kill me anyway?"

"I see what you mean—I don't."

He looked past me. Ulie and his friend were in the room now, and they helped me to stand.

The leader of the Red Militia made a face. "Leg bothering you?"

"I'm fine. Do you think you'll win?"

"It's not about winning—it's about doing what's right. And yes, we will always do what's right."

I stopped at the door and faced him. "What if there's no way out?"

He walked up to me, his cold eyes obscured by the reflection on his glasses. Taking my hand, he pulled me in. His breath smelled like hard candy.

"I'll tell you a secret," he said. "There's always a way out."

CHAPTER
SEVENTY-TWO

I THOUGHT I was immune to fear. But that brown-shoed devil scared the shit out of me. Without realizing it, though, he had given me insight into the limitations of his operation. He had no more idea what was happening in Tres Marias than I did. Maybe he'd assumed I had inside information about Black Dragon that I would share in exchange for my life. In that case, it might make sense for me to join his mad circus. Then I could go in search of Holly and Griffin.

What they said about Ormand Ferry was true. He was charming and charismatic—a psychopath. And what he said almost made sense. Almost. Though they may have been words of peace, they implied a genuine threat. But what was the endgame? Right now, he was hard at work being the town's savior. And after that? Get elected mayor?

Thanks to the medication Ulie gave me, my headache subsided. My leg was another story. Swelling and tenderness burned around the tibia. That was where they'd beaten me mercilessly with a length of iron rebar. I thought the bone might be fractured. I tried putting weight on it again—too painful. Despite my condition, I looked forward to a meal.

When the door opened, I expected Ulie to walk in with my MRE and some water. But it was Travis.

Looking worse than the last time I saw him, he emitted a foul odor—gangrene. He remained by the door, staring at me, his rifle appendage pointed downwards. In our drinking days, Jim and I used to be able to carry on a civil conversation with him. Did he even remember back that far? I hated him for the pain he had inflicted, but I remained calm.

"That arm looks bad," I said.

"Already been to the hospital. They wanted to amputate it. That's not happening."

"Is the Beehive still standing?"

"Don't think about it much anymore. There's more important work."

"Like saving Tres Marias."

"Ormand believes your story. About Griffin, I mean."

"I wish it wasn't true."

"How'd she die?"

"Are you sure you want to hear this?"

There are three things you have to remember when telling a lie. First, relax and try not to sweat. Second, provide a sufficient amount of detail, but not too much. Otherwise, it'll sound made up. Third—and most important—mix the lie with the truth. That way, there are always parts of the story others can confirm.

"Okay," I said. "After your men destroyed the compound, there were bodies everywhere. Kyle was among them. We had to shoot them all, including the ones who weren't dead yet, to keep them from turning. When Griffin saw what happened to her brother, she went crazy."

"Never could control her emotions. Like her mom."

"We chased her down to the stream, but it was too late.

346

The horde... Travis, you have to believe me, we tried to save her."

He stared at his skeletal arm. "I sent some men to search for her and her brother. They never found the bodies."

"Did they check the fire pit?"

He shook his head. "I loved that girl. You might not believe it, but I did. I hope you die in here."

As he walked out, Ulie brushed past him, carrying my food. Instead of leaving, he sat and offered me a beer. I declined.

"What happens when all this is over?" I said.

He glanced at the door to make sure we were alone. "Ormand has some big ol' dreams. Wouldn't be surprised if he's lookin' to run for governor."

"But he murdered Black Dragon personnel. They'll send him to prison."

"Way he sees it, a lot of them guys went batshit crazy. Like Chavez. Ormand was doin' what he could to protect civilians. So, you gonna join us?"

I gave him a weak laugh. "What did your friend say? This is the happening club. And I want to live."

"I believe you made the right choice."

"Travis won't like it."

"Don't you worry about him. Ormand's got 'im on a short leash."

"Thanks, Ulie."

He drained the beer and headed out. At the door, he gave me a little salute. I had made my decision. And it made total sense. Nothing else mattered except surviving for my wife and the girl.

Now, all I needed was a weapon.

CHAPTER
SEVENTY-THREE

FRANTIC BANGING and death shrieks awakened me. Outside, gunfire echoed in deadly bursts. Men shouted and women screamed, but it wasn't a party. Rapid footsteps pounded in every direction. As I tried focusing, a gunshot exploded outside the door. Resigned, I prepared myself to die.

"Maybe he's in here." It was my wife's voice.

"Holly!"

"Dave, hang on!"

I used every ounce of strength to stand, but my damn leg wouldn't support me. After more gunfire, the door burst open. For a second, she and Griffin stared at me. I couldn't believe it. They were like a mirage—a beautiful vision—both wearing body armor and packing handguns. Greta bounded in, barking and whimpering. She landed on top of me, knocking me back and covering my face with dog slobber till the girl pulled her back. With tears streaming, Holly triaged my injuries.

"You look like shit," she said.

"You have no idea the week I've had."

"Seriously, though. A brewery?"

"You can smell my breath."

Leaning in, she took a sniff. "Hmm." Then, she kissed me.

With each one grabbing an arm, they helped me to my feet. As we made our way to the door, I couldn't get my bad leg to do any more than drag uselessly behind me.

Outside, it was pandemonium. Nailheads and Black Dragon guards shot it out while a sea of draggers poured in. Ulie's body hung lifelessly between the blades of a forklift. As the draggers devoured him, they ignored Travis's pit bull tearing at their legs. When the animal saw Greta, it lowered its head. But before it could attack, Griffin shot it dead.

"Move your ass," my wife said, grunting.

"How did you find me?"

"Tell you later."

Soon, we were joined by Warnick and two other guards, Vincent and Fyffe. Watching for crossfire, we entered the main area. Everywhere, guards and nailheads battled it out. Though I wanted to help, I was too weak.

A couple half-drunk nailheads aimed their weapons at us. Baring her teeth, Greta charged. As they struggled to escape, Holly and the girl killed them. Halfway to the exit, we ran into a dragger pack. My friend signaled Vincent and Fyffe.

"Hold them off."

Unafraid, Griffin took the lead as Warnick and my wife guided me to a side exit. I could see the green sign—we were almost there. As we passed an equipment rack, a bullet caught my friend in the shoulder, making him stumble. The slug ripped through his uniform and left a hole in a cardboard box behind him. Holly let go of me, and I slid to the floor.

Travis appeared from out of the shadows. His small eyes were glassy, and his face was red from fever. The smell coming off his arm made me want to puke. He glared at his stepdaughter.

"You look damn good for a dead girl," he said. "Get yer ass over here—*now*."

Pointing the rifle at her head, he sneered as my wife raised her weapon. "Pull that trigger, and I'll kill her."

The women laid down their weapons as another nailhead joined Griffin's stepfather. Woozy, Warnick could barely stand. Another hostile hit him on the forehead with his handgun, forcing him onto the floor.

Griffin shook with fear. Despite her newfound strength, I saw the effect her stepfather had on her. Even the dog was scared. Grinning through yellow teeth, the miscreant stroked her face with his good hand.

A gunfire burst erupted behind us, and a bullet struck the other nailhead in the throat. He tried screaming, but all that came out was blood. Grabbing his stepdaughter by the hair, Travis dragged her out the door as she fought him.

Grabbing her weapon, Holly started to follow. The last nailhead fired at her wildly, missing her small torso. Furious, she pivoted and sent a round through his face. None of us could stop what was happening. When Vincent and Fyffe appeared, she pointed at the exit.

"They took Griffin!"

While the guards went after them, my wife knelt next to my friend and tore open his shirt. Fortunately, the slug had missed the artery.

Frantically, she looked around. "I need to stop the bleeding. Warnick, keep your hand pressed to the wound."

"Leave me. Go find Griffin."

"Vincent and Fyffe are on it. You need a doctor."

Two guards took charge of my friend, who was going into shock. We managed to make it outside into the blackness of another violent night. The gun battle had attracted a horde.

As they moved in, Greta let out a low growl. Holly squeezed my hand.

"I'll stand by you," she said.

A dead guard lay on the asphalt before us, his AR-15 at his side. My wife picked it up and, checking the mag, propped me against a light pole. Then she rapid-fired at the front line, striking all of them in the head.

"Who are you?" I said.

As the rest of them scattered, more guards joined us, picking off the hostiles till there weren't any left. Laying down the rifle, Holly did her best to help me to the Humvee, with Greta at her side. I was determined to walk and endured burning agony as I limped beside her.

"How bad's your leg?" she said.

"It might be broken."

Eventually, we reached our vehicle, where we found Vincent and Fyffe. They were alone. She peered inside the Humvee.

"Where's Griffin?"

Vincent side-eyed his partner. "We never saw them."

My wife's voice echoed as she drifted through the parking lot, calling the girl's name. Running after her, Vincent took her by the wrist and guided her to our vehicle.

"Let me go—we can't leave her!"

"She's gone. We have to get out of here."

The other guards brought Warnick over. Someone had treated his wound with a QuikClot bandage. Holly appraised him, semiconscious and bleeding. She looked at me, her broken husband. Nodding, she got into the backseat with my friend and me.

Vincent drove us to the hospital with the dog next to him. Two more vehicles trailed us in case we ran into trouble.

"How'd it go back there?" Warnick said to Vincent.

"Nailheads are taken care of. The other guards are mopping up."

"We lose anybody?"

"Two that I know of. Everyone else is accounted for."

I turned to Vincent. "Are you sure they'll be okay back there?"

Incredulous, my friend narrowed his eyes at me. "Have you forgotten these are trained security guards?"

"Sorry you got shot, Warnick."

"Sorry you got your ass kicked in a brewery," he said.

CHAPTER
SEVENTY-FOUR

I MUST HAVE DRIFTED OFF. When I opened my eyes, I saw the hospital across the street. The lights were on in the emergency room. The parking lot was crawling with draggers wandering among the abandoned cars and ambulances. Vincent grabbed a pair of field glasses from the seat.

"I don't see anyone inside," he said.

Sitting between Holly and me, Warnick leaned forward. "Are the doors secure?"

"Looks like it."

"Any ideas?" I said. "Warnick and I are a mess."

My friend shifted uncomfortably. "Speak for yourself."

Vincent opened his door. "I'll check it out."

Without being asked, my wife joined the other guards. Greta watched them from the vehicle, whining softly. I waved at Fyffe to get his attention. "Can you leave us a weapon?"

He gave me his handgun. In the rearview mirror, I watched a dozen people gathered in the darkness, including Holly, who seemed so at ease with the others. Warnick caught me watching her.

"When did she become a badass?" I said.

"A lot's happened while you were gone."

My friend shifted his position to ease the pain. There was a blood smear on the seat back. I didn't know when he lost consciousness, but soon, I was alone.

I thought I heard the scream of a mountain lion—or was it a dragger? Greta's ears pointed forward, but she didn't move. While the guards worked on a plan, I gazed at the sky. The stars were out. It was a beautiful, dangerous night. I forgot the pain racking my body for a second and enjoyed being alive.

"Thank you, God," I said.

I had changed after meeting with Ormand. Maybe it had to do with the inevitability of it all. For the first time, I saw things with clarity. We are born. We die. Somewhere in between, we live. And how we live is up to us. It doesn't matter if it's an earthquake or a flood or people returning from the dead. It has always been up to us.

Vincent opened the back door, and he and my wife helped us out. I was in bad shape, but Warnick was way worse.

"We get one shot at this," Vincent said.

Holly took my arm and held on tight. "Still not crazy about this plan."

My leg throbbed, making me nauseous. But I was determined to make it across the street. Vincent gave the signal, and a decoy squad ran across the parking lot, whooping and hollering. As the hostiles gawped at them, a guard shot one in the chest. That did it. The horde went after them, with the guards capering down the street like Mardi Gras revelers.

We waited a bit and moved out. Vincent and Fyffe assisted my friend while my wife helped me, with Greta following. My leg had stiffened badly from all the sitting. It took us minutes to get across. As gunfire echoed in the distance, Vincent tried the doors. Locked.

"I don't want to break the glass," he said. "Maybe there's another way in."

As he jogged around the side, a nursing assistant in blue scrubs and carrying a handgun crossed the lobby.

Holly hopped and waved. "Hey, let us in!"

Cautiously, he approached the doors but didn't unlock them. "Who are you?"

"Black Dragon Security," Fyffe said. "We have a medical emergency."

He must not have believed us. Behind us, more draggers appeared in the street. When they spotted us, they moved in.

"Please," my wife said, glancing back.

Holly and Fyffe started firing at them. But as they went down, more appeared. Vincent rejoined us, and when he saw what was happening, he pointed his rifle at the assistant's head. The automatic doors opened, and we hurried inside.

"We were ordered not to let anyone in," the assistant said to my wife.

"Never mind. Is there a doctor available?"

He found a wheelchair for Warnick. As we made our way to the elevators, hungry draggers gathered at the doors, lowing and scraping at the glass.

After letting us out on the second floor, the assistant disappeared. The floor was deserted. I thought I heard music coming from the nurses' station. We found an Asian man in a medical lab coat sitting at a computer. A small radio sat on the desk next to him. When he saw us, he picked up a handgun.

"Easy," Vincent said, lowering his weapon.

"Are you guys legit?"

"Black Dragon Security."

"You're a doctor, right?" Holly said. "This man has lost a lot of blood. And I think my husband's leg might be broken."

The doctor sized us up. Laying down the gun, he came around and examined my friend. "We'll treat the gunshot wound first. There's a surgeon on staff."

He made a call. Soon, another nursing assistant showed up. She and the doctor transferred Warnick to a gurney and wheeled him into an operating room. The other guards went with them, leaving my wife and me alone with the dog. She leaned against the wall and clutched my hand.

"We should have never let her come with us," she said. "He's going to kill her."

"You both managed to survive out there on your own. You're strong, and so is Griffin. This is not your fault."

"We have to get her back."

"We will. But right now, Warnick is the priority."

She pressed her head against my chest. "And you."

The doctor returned, carrying a chart. "Your friend is being prepped for surgery." Then to me, "I can examine you now. We'll need X-rays and blood work. I'm Dr. Vinh Tran, by the way."

"Are there other doctors and nurses?" Holly said in the examination room.

"We have people scattered throughout the building."

"Any patients?" I said.

"Only a few. We tried saving the critical ones, but it was too late for them. When all this started, your guys secured the building. But we haven't seen Black Dragon since."

My wife side-eyed me. "You have no protection?"

"Used to. The Red Militia would check in on us from time to time. In exchange, we agreed to treat their wounded."

"What about the infected?" I said.

"They never brought us those. What's it like out there?"

356

Holly sighed. "War zone."

Ignoring the searing pain, I stripped to my underwear while my wife waited outside with Greta. Vinh made a thorough examination, making notes on my injuries.

"Looks like somebody worked you over pretty good," he said. "This eye looks bad. Can you see out of it?"

"It's kind of blurry."

"Okay, lie down so I can look at your leg."

"Do you have family here?"

"In LA. I have a girlfriend, but..."

The swelling was worse than I thought, and the skin was discolored. I worried about infection. As Vinh palpated me, I bit down on the shooting pain.

"Am I going to lose the leg?" I said.

"Don't think so—you might have a stress fracture. The X-rays will tell us more." He hurried to the nurses' station and returned a minute later. "I found us a radiologist."

Vinh and another doctor wheeled me on a gurney to Radiology. On the way, I got the story on the Red Militia.

Until recently, a stream of sick and injured came through each night, with plenty of food and water for the hospital staff. Then a few nailheads broke into the pharmacy and stole opioids. When Ormand found out, he had them executed. Later, he returned the drugs, along with an apology.

No one had come around for days, which meant no more supplies. The doctors, nurses, and other medical personnel survived by eating what they could find in the cafeteria. They were down to rice, pasta, and some canned goods. With no protection, they spent their nights in fear of the hospital being breached.

The radiologist was an African American woman in her forties. She took a series of X-rays, including some of my rib cage. Afterwards, we viewed the images on the computer screen. No broken ribs. She moved on to my leg.

"I'm seeing calcification. Were you beaten?"

"Repeatedly."

"I want to do an MRI," she said.

The white machine took up most of the scan room, with a hole in the middle big enough to fit a human body. Holly and the radiologist helped me lie on the patient table. The woman handed me a set of earplugs.

"I don't know where our headphones went," she said. Then to my wife, "You might want to wait outside. It can get pretty loud in here."

"How long will it take?"

"We're only doing the leg, so ten minutes?"

Holly clasped my hand. "Going to check on Warnick. Greta, hier." The dog accompanied her at once.

After they had gone, the doctor said something.

I took out an earplug. "What?"

"Be sure not to move, or we'll have to start over."

The clicking noise was loud, even with the earplugs. The radiologist set the machine to perform an automated scan. After ten minutes, the sound stopped. I'd gone in feet-first and had to crane my neck to see behind me. When the doctor returned, a stranger with a gun was behind her.

The man wore jeans and a bright shirt. I assumed a nail-head had gotten in. He waved his weapon threateningly. The radiologist freed me, and as I rose, Greta appeared in the doorway. Growling, she lunged at the man, tearing at his gun hand. Screaming, he fired. The bullet ricocheted off the machine and into a ceiling tile.

Running footsteps now. Holly appeared with the other

guards. Fyffe pulled Greta off the hostile as Vincent disarmed him. Shoving him against the wall, he pressed his gun barrel to the man's forehead.

"Don't kill me," the stranger said. "It's my daughter—she's sick."

CHAPTER
SEVENTY-FIVE

THE MRI IMAGES on the computer screen confirmed myositis ossificans, which meant that bone had begun forming in my leg's large muscles. Though the condition wasn't life threatening, it was damn painful. The only cure was rest.

"You're lucky," Vinh said. "I thought you might've gotten an invasive GAS infection. But the blood tests came back negative."

"Thanks, Doc. Anything else?"

"You could use a Vitamin D supplement."

"I promise to get some when the undead are no longer walking the earth."

Laughing, he handed me a crutch and advised me to stay off my leg—not something I was likely to do. After shaking his hand, I limped out of the exam room and found Holly sitting alone with Greta near the nurses' station.

"No broken bones," I said. "Where is everyone?"

"That guy's daughter is infected."

"Where are they?"

I followed her to a patient room. Vincent stood in the doorway, gripping his weapon, as Vinh examined a little girl lying in bed. She couldn't have been more than three or four. One arm was bandaged. Standing on the other side, her father held her tiny hand. The stranger's name was Perry, and apparently, he had acted out of desperation.

He told us about a horde that had attacked their neighborhood. He and his daughter barely escaped. The other neighbors had long since fled, but Perry's wife was bedridden, and he decided to stay.

The child didn't like being examined and whined. Stroking her hair, her father made soft shushing noises and asked her to be brave.

"My wife begged me to leave with Kylie," he said. "I just couldn't. When things got worse, she convinced me, for our daughter's sake. I barricaded the bedroom door and said goodbye. It was the hardest thing I've ever done."

No Black Dragon guards came to help them. While making their way to their car, Kylie got bit. By the time they reached the hospital, Perry was half out of his mind.

Vinh finished his examination and motioned for everyone to step into the hallway. He took Perry aside.

"I can try to make her comfortable. But I'm afraid that's all I can do."

"Is she going to die?" Perry could barely get the words out.

"She's infected. I'm not sure how to put this..."

Holly took the man's hand. "She won't stay dead."

Lost, he turned to each of us, hoping someone had a better answer. Or a miracle. My wife teared up, and I was on the verge myself. There was no way anyone could save this man's child. Finally, he looked at Vinh, his face grim.

"She's in pain," he said.

The doctor seemed to understand and nodded. "I'll be right back."

Vinh spent the next few minutes setting up a morphine drip. Soon, Kylie's pupils contracted, and her breathing became slow and regular. Her father went to her side. Taking her smooth little hand, he sat beside her.

"Daddy," she said.

"Hi, kitten."

"I have to check on another patient," Vinh said.

"Thank you, Doctor."

The radiologist walked in carrying a stuffed animal. It was a blue bear wearing a T-shirt with the words *I can't bear it when you're sick.*

"Hey," Perry said to her. "I didn't mean to—"

"Forget it."

Gently, she placed the toy in the little girl's arms, and the child hugged it. The radiologist excused herself. Soon, Kylie was asleep. We decided to leave them alone. On the way out, Perry grabbed Vincent's sleeve.

"I need my gun," he said.

The guard gazed at the dying girl. When he turned to me, I knew we were thinking the same thing. What if, in his grief, this guy lost it and started shooting up the place?

"Please. I don't want her to suffer."

After a beat, the guard handed him the weapon.

The distraught dad held the gun without looking at it. "I never grew up around guns."

Vincent left, and Holly and I returned to the nurses' station to wait for Warnick to come out of surgery. I didn't know why, but my wife seemed nervous around me. Not knowing what else to do, I took her hand and gave it a gentle squeeze. There was so much I wanted to say—how proud I was of her. And Griffin. But I was afraid she would get emotional over the teenager's disappearance. Then I reminded myself that she was stronger than me.

"How did you find me?" I said.

"It was Springer."

"But I watched him die."

"You saw him get shot. The bullet only grazed him. He played dead until the nailheads left. He was able to get to the Humvee and return to base."

"That's amazing. How did he know where I was?"

"Before they left, those idiots tossed a bunch of empty Lucky Moon beer bottles into a dumpster. Springer put two-and-two together. After a little recon, Warnick planned the assault."

"How did you get inside?"

"That was easy. Everyone inside was drunk."

"Except me."

"Except you." She kissed my cheek. "There was a horde outside. We caught a break when a nailhead came out to take a leak. He never made it back in. We left his body in the doorway to attract the draggers. While the nailheads were fighting them, we entered through another door."

"Thanks for saving me. How did you and Griffin make it to the Arkon building?"

"Long story. If I hadn't gotten your text... What are we going to do about Griffin? We don't even know where Travis took her."

"I promise you we'll find her," I said.

As I leaned over to kiss her, a gunshot rang out from the direction of the little girl's patient room. Holly ran to see, with me limping after her. She was about to enter when another blast stopped her. I thought she'd gotten shot. When I caught up to her, she buried her face in my chest.

Perry lay sprawled across the bed like he was protecting

Kylie. The back of his head was blown out. Bits of brain, bone, and blood slithered down the white plastic curtain.

He was still holding his dead daughter's hand.

CHAPTER
SEVENTY-SIX

GRIFFIN HAD BEEN MISSING A WEEK. During those last days when I was a prisoner, Warnick and Estrada had located more guards in other buildings around Tres Marias. Though I felt less hostile towards the Latina, I wasn't sure where her loyalty lay. After all, she was a follower. And at present, she was happy to go along with the program. But what about tomorrow?

When I looked in the mirror, I hardly recognized myself. The beard hid most of the cuts and bruises. But there was a weariness belonging to someone else—especially the eyes. They belonged to a person who had crawled out of the mouth of hell with a message.

Unlike me, Holly was lean and ripped. She had always been responsible. But now, there was a new maturity about her. It made me believe she could lead her own troops into the Valley of Death. And they would happily follow.

Thanks to my friend, the Arkon building was secure, and with my wife's help, I made a good recovery. The other survivors were doing better, too. They were eating regularly and putting on weight which, in turn, lifted their spirits. The guards kept them busy, training them to defend themselves.

I checked in on Nina Zimmer and her daughter often. Both were fine. Warnick's men had managed to obtain more baby formula, diapers, and a few books for Evan's mother to read to her. Under Black Dragon's protection, a pediatrician from the hospital visited the mother and daughter. Other medical personnel, including Dr. Tran, stopped by to check on the survivors.

My friend kept his people focused and motivated. Finding Griffin was a priority, but there were others, too. High on the list was Ormand Ferry. Tres Marias wouldn't be safe till we stopped him by any means necessary.

We had no idea where he was, and the nailheads had refused to reveal his whereabouts. After the fighting at the brewery had ceased, the guards locked the survivors in the cold room, intending to interrogate them later. What they didn't know—and I'd never guessed—was that they had hidden weapons behind the tanks. The guards burst in at the first sounds of gunfire, only to find the prisoners—men, women, and the Latino boy—dead from bullet wounds to the head. They entered just as the last nailhead put a gun to his mouth and squeezed the trigger.

Warnick was confident that his people had significantly weakened the Red Militia. It was time to finish what the guards had started. Patrols went in search of Ormand's command center. And as the days went by, they met less and less resistance. Soon, the only vehicles cruising the streets belonged to Black Dragon.

There were few signs of the Red Militia now. My friend surmised that those the patrols spotted were doing reconnaissance. One time, I heard a skirmish outside that set me on edge. Later, I learned it was the hordes that continued to plague us. Every day, Holly was in the shit with the other guards. I wasn't permitted to help till my leg got better, which didn't do much for my confidence. One night, we sat in a conference room by ourselves, eating a dinner of MRE chicken chunks. The food tasted even worse than it sounded.

"We cleaned out a dragger nest," she said. "Two nailheads tried ambushing us."

"What happened?"

"They refused to surrender, so."

I didn't like that my wife had volunteered to defend our base. Not because she wasn't capable—she rocked at it. But I worried. I mean, what else did I have to do?

"I fired a rocket launcher today. Under Warnick's supervision, of course."

I felt useless. "Wish I could've been there."

"You need to rest, babe."

I couldn't remember the last time she had called me that. She scooted her chair over, and I slipped my arm around her.

"Hey," I said. "You promised to tell me how you and Griffin got here."

After leaving us behind, they made their way through the building, relying on Greta to protect them. Upstairs, they found two security guards—Barnes and Logan. The men had managed to locate a small amount of food and water. They planned to wait till it was safe, then search for other Black Dragon guards who weren't loyal to Chavez.

Holly had forgotten about the busted lock on the alley door. On the third night, draggers found their way inside and infested the building. Barnes and Logan did their best to provide an escape route for the women while they stayed behind and fought. My wife hadn't known what happened to the guards till I told her.

The women were almost spotted when they discovered a

neighborhood grocery store that looked safe. The building sat in the middle of town, dangerously close to the daily patrols conducted by rogue guards. Hiding upstairs in a small apartment, they never turned on the lights and were careful about water usage. No one on the outside had any clue they were there.

One night, something startled Greta, and she barked. The women thought they'd had it, but no one heard. Draggers tried getting into the building from time to time. Thankfully, the owner had fortified all the doors and windows.

During that period, they had enough food, water, and medicine to survive for weeks. Eventually, Holly located a phone charger. When she saw my text with Arkon's address, they planned how to make their way there safely in the dead of night. On the way, the women were seen near the Arkon building. But before the Red Militia could take them prisoner, our guards showed up, and a vicious firefight broke out. Our people killed the nailheads and rescued my wife and the girl.

After all my desperate prayers, God had listened.

CHAPTER
SEVENTY-SEVEN

DR. TRAN HAD SHOWN Holly how to perform physical therapy on my ailing leg. The exercises were agonizing. But anxious to rejoin the fight, I gritted my way through the program. One day as I performed stretches, my wife burst into the office we had converted into our sleeping quarters.

"They found Griffin!" she said. "She's at the high school."

"I thought that place was overrun with draggers."

"That's what everyone thought. Vincent and Fyffe were out patrolling this morning. They found a nailhead in an alley, barely alive. He got bit, and his so-called friends left him to die."

"Why didn't they just shoot him?"

"Anyway, when the guards found him, he was half-dead. He told them Ormand was holed up at the high school with civilians. Vincent asked about Griffin, and he confirmed that she was alive."

I was ecstatic to learn about the girl, but I was worried, too. Ormand's methods had always been calculated. He was determined to win, and he was willing to sacrifice everything —and everyone. I asked Warnick to call a meeting.

. . .

"Ormand doesn't care about those civilians," I said. "He's using them as human shields."

Estrada scoffed. "How would you know that?"

"Because I met with him. It's all he's got. His plan was to show that while you and your pals lost it— You know what I'm saying."

"No, I get it."

"He wants to demonstrate that, in all the craziness, he and his people are the sane ones, the only ones who care about the town. He'll argue that the deaths of a few security guards were necessary to save Tres Marias."

Warnick considered what I had said. Over these past weeks, I felt I had gotten to know him. He was smart, if a little cautious. But there was no way he wouldn't come to the same conclusion.

"Okay," he said after a beat. "If you're right, he's keeping the civilians—and Griffin—very close. If we attack and innocent people are killed, he could always say it was our fault."

Holly addressed the room. "Wait, so we're not going in?"

My friend turned to the Latina. "What else did Vincent and Fyffe have to say?"

"We know there aren't more than a hundred nailheads defending the high school."

"Interesting. And we haven't seen them on the streets for days."

"Which means they might be expecting us."

Warnick looked around the conference table. "Let's not keep them waiting. Dave, how's the leg?"

"I'm ready to do this," I said.

After taking a break, we got to work. There was no other

choice—we'd have to use force. Ormand would never show himself out in the open. And worse, the civilians were as good as dead if we waited. Our only hope was to storm the place.

The plan was to leave a squad behind at Arkon while everyone else deployed to the high school. We had more weapons and vehicles now and would make an impressive showing. It would be threatening enough that the nailheads might choose to surrender instead of fight.

My wife wanted badly to join me, but Warnick and Estrada forbade it. She had become a valuable asset, and they didn't want to lose her. My friend put her in charge of the building. She would see to it that the civilians remained safe. And she wouldn't be alone. Many were now strong enough to defend against an attack.

Since my rescue, Holly had given me strong signals that she wanted to get intimate. The night before we deployed, she sent Greta out, locked the door to our room, and drew the blinds. I could think of more romantic settings than an insurance office. But we were so hot for each other, nothing else mattered. And we almost got away with it, too, till the dog started whining and scratching at the door.

"Greta," my wife said.

The animal persisted. Groaning, Holly let her in. Once Greta was satisfied that we were fine, she curled up in a corner as my wife and I held each other close.

"What am I gonna do with you?" Holly said, stroking my hair and beard.

"Stay with me."

"I'll think about it."

I tried kissing her, but she pressed her fingers to my lips. "Do you ever think about her?"

Caught off guard, I turned away, deeply ashamed. "What I think of most is what I lost. Especially your love."

"You have it," she said. "Always and always."

CHAPTER
SEVENTY-EIGHT

MORNING CAME TOO SOON. Holly and I had slept in each other's arms, our love never stronger. I had won her back and vowed to die rather than hurt her again. It wasn't yet light when Estrada began rapping on the door.

"R&R is over, Pulaski," she said.

"Be right there."

I sat up and began my leg exercises. When my wife tried pulling me towards her, I took her hands and kissed them.

"I'll be back soon," I said.

She giggled as the dog nibbled her fingers. "Are you taking Greta?"

"Better if she stays with you."

I didn't want to prolong our goodbye, so I helped her to her feet and kissed her. She reached for the crucifix I was wearing. It was hers—the one she had given me in Mt. Shasta. Smiling, she straightened the gold chain.

"You're a pretty awesome guy. Come back to me, okay?"

More knocking. When I opened the door, Warnick and the Latina were waiting. Holly stuck out her tongue at them.

"What?" I said. "Can't a guy say goodbye to his wife?"

. . .

It was dark when we moved out. Heavily armed, we were two hundred strong. We split up into four convoys, each coming at the high school from a different direction. I rode with Warnick, Estrada, and Springer, whose neck was bandaged.

I gave his shoulder a squeeze. "So glad you made it."

"Appreciate it, man."

My friend glanced at me in the rearview mirror and gave me a rare smile.

"Looks like you and Holly are back on track," he said.

The sun came up as we neared the high school. The parking lot was deserted except for a few draggers wandering along the fence. I wondered where all the vehicles had gone. Most likely, the nailheads had hidden them. Using field glasses, Warnick checked out the administration building's second-story windows. At first, there wasn't any movement. Then all of a sudden, the shooting began.

"It's showtime," he said.

Scrambling, we took their positions. We didn't know if civilians were upstairs and didn't want to risk firing rocket launchers. Instead, we used riot guns to clear the floors. The CS gas would force anyone inside to surrender.

As more guards arrived, we moved in. Our squad headed for the gymnasium. As we approached the building, I recalled the slaughter I had witnessed the last time I was there with Landry and the others.

Vincent and Fyffe forced open the heavy double doors with crowbars. It was dark inside, and the stench was revolting. A sea of dark shapes floated towards us, but they weren't survivors. The gym was infested. Amid death shrieks, we fired bursts from our AR-15s. Those in front went down while more followed.

"There's too many of them," I said.

We shut the doors and pressed our weight against the steel, even as draggers tried to escape. The frame was damaged, and we couldn't seal off the entrance. Meanwhile, another guard arrived with a heavy chain and looped it through the door handles. As I backed away, gray, grasping hands reached for me through the opening.

My friend took Springer and me aside. "These guys can finish up here. Let's find Griffin."

By now, guards had breached all the buildings and disarmed the nailheads, who seemed resigned to defeat. Women came out with them, raising their arms joyfully at seeing us. One held a small boy's hand. Sadly, Griffin wasn't among them. I was surprised it had taken less than an hour to secure the high school. Instead of being hardy freedom fighters, these people were sick, hungry, and scared.

Squads searched every building, hoping to find the girl. While we stood on the steps of the administration building, someone cried out. Warnick signaled us to respond while he took off in the opposite direction.

Rounding a corner, we found Travis dragging his stepdaughter towards the auto shop. When she fell, he began kicking her. Shrinking into a ball, she refused to stand. Springer and I moved into the open, training our weapons on the angry hostile.

"Travis!" I said.

Griffin looked back. "Dave, help me!"

The nailhead pointed his rifle at the girl's head. "How many times we gotta go through this?"

A rapid stutter of gunfire blew apart his diseased forearm. The rifle tumbled to the ground, his skeletal hand still gripping it. Wailing in pain, he dropped to his knees. Griffin scrambled away and held onto me as another squad joined us.

My friend walked into view, pointing his rifle at the back of the hostile's head. "Where's Ormand?"

Snorting, he clutched what was left of his putrid arm. "Guess you're gonna hafta kill me."

Before I could stop her, the girl grabbed my handgun and marched up to her stepfather. She pointed the weapon at his face, her eyes filled with tears of hatred. Warnick tried to intervene, but she warned him away.

"Don't do it," my friend said. "You're better than this."

"No, I'm not."

Travis looked up at her in terror. "Griffin? Sweetie? Y-you wouldn't shoot your daddy?"

"You're not my father," she said. "You're not anything."

Then, she mag-dumped him. His face opened up like a blood flower, and he fell onto his side. Dropping the gun, she kicked his lifeless body till I took her arm.

"It's okay," I said. "He's dead."

She fell into my arms, shivering. Warnick let Springer and me stay with her while he and the other guards went to look for Ormand.

When the girl had recovered, Springer and I took her to the football field, where Black Dragon had assembled the prisoners on the grass. There were fifty or sixty men, a dozen women, and the boy. How could this be all that was left of the Red Militia? My friend paced, his face screwed into a scowl.

"Where is Ormand Ferry?" he said. "People, it's over. We want to help you. But I need you to tell me where he's hiding."

Estrada marched up to the woman holding the boy. "I think maybe she knows."

The frightened prisoner shook her head violently. The man beside her took her hand. As the guards trained their weapons on him, he addressed Warnick in a voice devoid of emotion.

"That lyin' bastard left us here to die," he said. "Only Travis knows where he was headed."

The Latina scoffed. "You expect us to believe that shit?" She aimed her handgun at his head. "Tell us where he is."

Furious, the woman stood between them. "Can't you understand? He doesn't know. No one does."

My friend ordered Estrada to stand down. Frustrated, she holstered her weapon and rejoined the other guards. Taking a breath, he addressed the crowd.

"We're going to evacuate you," he said. "You'll have access to food and medicine. But you'll remain under arrest." Then to the Latina, "Prepare to move out."

I grabbed Warnick's arm. "What about Ormand?"

"Tomorrow's another day. We need to get these people to safety."

Some of the civilians were in bad shape and needed assistance. Griffin and I took charge of the woman and her boy. As we made our way to the parking lot, the kid screamed.

A horde was heading our way—hundreds of them. My friend ordered the guards to spread out. Despite taking out dozens, more hostiles made it onto the field and attacked the prisoners, who were too weak to fight. Each time a civilian or a guard died, they reanimated, increasing the threat. I signaled the woman to get behind me.

"I'm getting you out of here," I said.

Carrying the boy, I told the others to follow me to the exit. I couldn't see where Warnick and Springer had gone. As we reached the gate, I found Estrada trying to protect a group of women as the draggers descended. Screaming with fury, she fired at them till they tore out her throat and fed on the warm blood.

I found our Humvee and got the woman and boy inside. When I told them I needed to return to the field, she pleaded with me not to leave. In the distance, gunfire and insane screaming raged as more prisoners and guards were eviscerated. When I saw the terror in her eyes, I was back where I started—a coward who had let someone die when I could have helped.

"What's your name?" I said.

"Nanette. This is Jonathan."

"Listen to me. I have to help my squad." She shook her head. "You'll be fine here."

"No, please."

I handed Griffin my rifle. "Stay with them. Lock all the doors after I leave."

The girl seemed to understand and nodded. When they were safely inside the vehicle, I hurried to the rear to retrieve my axe. Standing on the driver's side, I admired how Griffin gripped the AR-15 like a seasoned soldier. I started to walk away when she got out and came after me.

"What happens if—"

"Protect Nanette and Jonathan," I said. "That's your mission now."

CHAPTER
SEVENTY-NINE

I DIDN'T KNOW whether I was destined to live or die. But, like Warnick, I had faith. In myself and God that somehow I would survive so I could return to Holly. I saw her face as I tore into the shrieking pit of vipers attacking our people. Each time a dragger came at me, I sent it back to hell.

Ignoring my throbbing leg, I focused on swinging my arms in a deadly rhythm. With each thrust of the axe, I took off a head or a hand. As I did, other guards followed and finished off the hostiles with kill shots. I no longer thought about getting bit. I went where needed, separating limbs from torsos and splitting skulls.

I don't remember how long we were at it—it seemed like hours. My back and arms ached, and I worried I wouldn't have the strength to raise my weapon again. As we cleared a path to the gate, I found Warnick and Springer out of ammo and skewering draggers with bayonets to the head.

"Fall back!" my friend said.

We barely had enough time to secure the gate before the hostiles regrouped. The field was covered in bodies. Despite our efforts, the civilians had perished. And Black Dragon lost over half its guards. Every victim was now among the ranks of the undead.

The surviving guards returned to the Arkon building. Vincent and Fyffe weren't among them. Warnick, Springer, and I stayed behind. Heading to our vehicle, I expected to find everyone safe inside. Instead, a guard in a crisp uniform had flung open the Humvee doors and dragged out the occupants. Nanette screamed as he tore the AR-15 from Griffin's hands and pushed her to the ground. When the woman tried to resist, he hit her.

The guard fired at us, and everyone took cover. Exhausted, I hid behind a vehicle. My arm hurt bad—it was bleeding. An intense wave of pain and nausea overcame me. Then I heard the Humvee starting up. The rogue guard was behind the wheel.

The others were across from me. Though my vision was blurry, I could make out my friend holding up three fingers. Two... One... We opened fire on the Humvee as it lurched forward. But we had forgotten that the windshield was bullet-proof. As a result, the rounds zinged off in all directions, only pitting the glass. Looking around in desperation, I spotted the grenades hanging off Springer's tactical vest.

"Springer!" I said, pointing.

Dropping his weapon, he grabbed a grenade and pulled the pin as the driver accelerated away from us. He tossed it at the oncoming vehicle. It bounced off the roof and exploded, making the Humvee swerve. He got another grenade and underhanded it like a bowling ball. As it rolled under the rear axle, it went off, lifting the vehicle up and sideways. The gas tank went up in a ball of flame and sent the Humvee careening into a maintenance shed.

We crept forward as the driver emerged from the burning vehicle. Though his face was covered in blood, I knew it was

Ormand Ferry. Firing at us wildly, he staggered towards the gym. Using the other buildings as cover, we followed as he mag-dumped us. Out of ammo, he switched to a handgun.

I stared at the entrance to the gym—the chain was gone. Now I knew where the horde had come from. Standing erect, the leader of the Red Militia faced us, defiant and still confident.

"No way out," Warnick said.

Ormand wiped the blood from his eyes. "There's always a way out."

Giving me a vicious smile, he jammed the gun barrel under his chin. But when he squeezed the trigger, the only sound was a click. Frantic, he tried reloading. But before he could finish, three draggers emerged and surrounded him, grabbing his arms and legs. They carried him into the darkness of their lair to the sound of his fading, ululating cries. By now, Griffin and the others had joined us. Nanette covered her son's ears as Ormand's screams turned to whimpering and, eventually, silence.

No one spoke as we piled into a Humvee. As we drove away from the high school, the draggers on the field broke through the gate and swarmed the campus. While the boy sat in his mother's arms, the girl laid her head on my shoulder. Against all odds, we had rescued her. Ormand and Travis were dead, and with them, the Red Militia. But the scourge was far from over.

Nursing my bandaged arm, I wondered if we would ever rid the town of the plague. I remembered a particularly brutal hockey game. All throughout, I had made unforgivable mistakes that nearly cost us the regional title. Afterwards, the coach said something that stuck with me as I sat on the bench, sulking.

Sometimes, you need to take the win.

CHAPTER
EIGHTY

MY INJURY WASN'T life threatening. With Vinh's help, I recovered quickly, resuming my duties as a volunteer security guard. At Warnick's suggestion, Springer improvised a training program for Griffin, who was a quick study. After only a few days, she was as good as anyone working for Black Dragon.

Over the next few weeks, we concentrated on eliminating the remaining hordes and rescuing civilians. Though draggers lurked in the woods, we were confident that at least part of Tres Marias was secure.

I wasn't sure exactly when it happened, but Holly, Griffin, and I had become a family. We even had a pet. Never mind that Greta was trained to kill. We avoided talking about Travis. Sometimes, though, the girl would reminisce about her mother and Kyle.

On a morning patrol, we stopped at an intersection near City Hall. Half a dragger pulled itself along the street in pursuit of wild dogs who had stolen its legs. If I had seen this a year ago, I would've checked myself into a mental hospital. Instead, I rolled my eyes. Warnick pulled over, and my wife put the creature out of its misery.

Up ahead, a black Escalade stopped in front of City Hall. The rear door opened, and two people got out. The first was a man I didn't recognize—mid-fifties and fat, with thinning gray hair. With him was an attractive woman with reddish-brown hair and carrying a laptop bag. The mayor greeted them as they climbed the steps to the entrance. I asked my friend if this meant we were getting more people.

"Pretty sure that guy isn't with Black Dragon," he said.

"Guys, you've got to see this," Springer said as we walked into the Arkon building.

We rode the elevator to the top floor, where we found an executive conference room. We hadn't paid any attention to it after securing the building. Trying to be dramatic, Springer posed outside the closed walnut doors.

"Are you ready?" he said.

Warnick gave him the stink eye. "Enough."

Undeterred, the guard ceremoniously swung open the doors. When we walked in, some IT guy with a pained expression fiddled with the video-conferencing system. Finally, after tweaking the controls on an iPad, the screen came on, and we saw a familiar face—the reporter Evie Champagne.

She and her cameraman, Jeff, sat in a conference room similar to ours. Both looked haggard. At least they were alive. But we couldn't hear what she was saying. Wearing a scowl, the IT guy began troubleshooting the sound.

"How did you find them?" I said.

"They're over in our satellite building. Every day, I'd come up here and try all the IP addresses, hoping to reach someone. They must've done the same."

Holly walked up to the camera and waved. "What happened to the sound?"

"No idea. Maybe if I had more time..."

Griffin and my wife began going through the cabinets, where they found blank copier paper and dry-erase markers. Warnick wrote *Any other survivors?* and held the sheet up to the camera. Catching on, Jeff slid out of frame and returned with a flip chart. He wrote something and showed it to us.

All dead.

My friend let them know the Red Militia had been neutralized. Then he asked whether they were safe.

Not safe. Heading out soon.

"What about the draggers?" Holly said. "Ask them if they can hold out until we get there."

Don't think so. They're everywhere.

Impatient, Warnick snapped his fingers at the IT guy. "How far away is that building?"

"Clear across town on the other side of the railroad tracks."

Borrowing a marker, he drew a rudimentary map showing our building and theirs. He wrote down a couple street names to orient us. Springer pointed to an area in the center.

"The quickest way is through no man's land," he said.

A nasty horde made up of dead nailheads had taken over a section of town that sat directly between the two buildings. We had avoided it for fear of losing more guards.

My friend studied the map. "Too risky." He wrote that we couldn't come to them and to tell us where we could meet.

Evie spoke to Jeff, who began writing. They stopped and faced the doors. For several agonizing seconds, they moved in and out of frame, gathering supplies. Before abandoning the room, Evie scribbled a quick note and held it up.

Robbin-Sear Industries, Old Orchard Road.

These were the same words written on the side of Bob Creasy's van. I remembered them from when he picked me up after my car accident. Could that be where they were headed? She wrote more, and what I read chilled me to the bone.

We know what happened.

Then, they were gone.

At sunset, I joined Holly, Griffin, and Warnick on the roof. We gazed at the wrecked, empty streets surrounding our building. Life was better, but the nightmare wasn't over. I remembered something Ram Chakravarthy had said. *There are going to be dark days ahead.*

To keep up our spirits, my friend told us he had a plan to rescue Evie and Jeff. While a squad headed into the forest, the remaining guards would look after the civilians at Arkon. And they'd continue clearing the streets. With luck, Black Dragon would send in reinforcements.

Someone in the building had dug up a music player. Faintly, The Pretenders' "I'll Stand by You" echoed up the stairwell. It sounded right. I recognized Jim's dog, Perro, in the distance. Massive and bloody, he bared his teeth. I felt like he was challenging me to discover the truth about what had gone wrong in Tres Marias.

My wife must have seen him, too, because she took my hand. We watched the animal disappear into a landscape of charred buildings and smoke-filled skies. The constant death shrieks reminded us of our mortality. Yet despite the danger, I felt calm—I had my family beside me.

The faces of those we lost along the way paraded before me like prisoners in a death camp newsreel. I missed them all terribly. But the only way now was forward. No one could predict when the end would come—or how. All that mattered was that we were strong and of a single mind. We would live and die for each other, no matter the cost.

And that gave me hope.

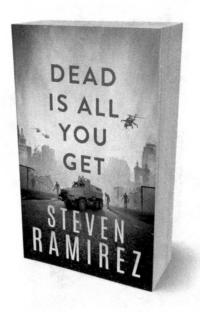

UP NEXT...

When science alters your world, trust no one...

Dave Pulaski discovers that the bizarre virus turning its victims into flesh-eaters is the result of a government-funded bioscience experiment. And the mayor may be in on it.

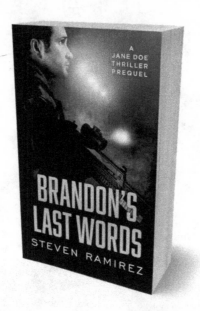

ABOUT THE AUTHOR

Steven Ramirez is the award-winning author of thriller, supernatural, and horror fiction. A former screenwriter, he's written about zombie plagues and places infested with ghosts and demons. Steven lives in Los Angeles.

AUTHOR WEBSITE
stevenramirez.com

instagram.com/byStevenRamirez
goodreads.com/byStevenRamirez
bookbub.com/authors/steven-ramirez

Printed in the USA
CPSIA information can be obtained
at www.ICGtesting.com
LVHW041251151023
761121LV00001BB/66